BINARY EXISTENCE

ACROSS HORIZONS - BOOK 4

STAN C. SMITH

A Skyra Publication

To those who look to the future and dream of what is improbable instead of what is likely.

BINARY EXISTENCE

Bring your hand blades and khuls. Now you are going to learn by doing instead of talking.

SKYRA-UNA-LOTO

1

———

RESCUE

47,659 YEARS in the past - Zaragoza Province of Spain - Day 1

SKYRA UNA-LOTO ROSE to her full height, stepped from behind a boulder, and started down the hillside, now in full view of the stinking bolups by the stream below. The strength of the cave lion and woolly rhino coursed through her body, tightening her muscles and pushing aside her fear. After traveling two days without any food, she had sacrificed valuable time to go hunting, and the resulting hedgehog meat she had eaten was already sharpening her focus. This was a good thing —her birthmate Veenah needed her now more than ever before.

Veenah stood naked in the middle of the shallow stream, having been stripped of her cape and waist-skin. Three bolup women were splashing water on her, wiping the grime from her body and the blood from between her legs. A bolup man stood at the stream's edge, holding a rope tied around Veenah's neck. Skyra would have to kill this man first, then stop the women from running to their camp for help. She would also need to silence them somehow. The bolup camp was located a short distance into the forest of gnarled kheyop trees, maybe near enough for the others to hear their cries. Skyra paused—her plan for a direct attack would not work. She needed to get close enough to the four bolups to silence them all at once.

Without removing either of her hand blades from their wrist sheath, she raised her arm and dragged one of the protruding blade points across her forehead above one eye. She grimaced at the pain, and blood began to flow into her eye and down her cheek. She smeared the warm fluid across her face, hoping to make the wound look more serious than it was. Then she continued toward Veenah and the bolups.

The man spotted her first. He shouted words she did not understand. Skyra let out a loud whimper and stared at the rocks at her feet as if she were unaware of the bolups. Her spear's shaft was comforting in her grip, having been worn smooth from many days of use. Her heavy, stone-bladed khul jostled against the skin of her back as it hung in its sling beneath her cape. She let out another whimper, loud enough for the bolups to hear.

Skyra continued down the slope with her head tilted down but with one eye watching the man. She flicked her gaze toward her birthmate. The three bolup women had stopped what they were doing to watch Skyra. Veenah's face was swollen and bloody, and she just stared unmoving into the distance as if she were dead. Skyra whispered, "Fekho-gédun-tekne-té-rha." *Where is your strength, sister?*

The bolup man shouted again. He tossed the end of the rope to one of the bolup women and picked up a spear on the ground at his feet. The women stepped from the stream, pulling Veenah behind them with the rope. Veenah stumbled and fell. She did not even try to get up. She just lay there, her face barely above the surface.

Skyra was almost to the water's edge before she raised her head to look directly at the man. His eyes widened when he saw the blood on her face, and her confidence began to grow as she studied his expression. Skyra had always had the ability to read expressions and small movements, even those of bolups. This ability had saved her life more than once, but it had also given many of her own tribemates the desire to kill her. They did not understand how she could see things they could not, and it frightened them. Veenah was the only one who understood—as Skyra's twin birthmate, Veenah had the same ability.

Two of the bolup women spoke to the man, and although Skyra could not understand their words, she detected concern in their voices. Bolup women were that way, which was one of the reasons they were weak. Skyra had never killed one, but today she intended to kill more than one.

"Nu delo-do!" the man growled in his language, baring his teeth at Skyra. He glanced down at Veenah then back at Skyra, and his expression showed confusion. Maybe Skyra had not smeared enough blood across her face to hide her similarity to her sister.

Skyra let out a wretched moan and dropped to her knees. She tossed her spear into the stream, an act of surrender.

The man frowned as he watched the weapon bob to the surface and start drifting with the current.

The three bolup women crossed the shallow stream, stepping over Veenah, who was still sprawled in the water. The women crouched beside Skyra. One of them held a hand blade to Skyra's throat while the other two spoke unfamiliar bolup words and inspected her bloody face.

Skyra suppressed a growl as she realized the man was staying put on the far side of the stream, out of striking distance. Then she decided this was okay. If one of the women had remained on the far side of the stream, the woman would probably flee to the bolup camp to get help. The man, though, would be more likely to bound across the stream to kill Skyra.

Skyra let out another whimper as one of the women touched the cut on her forehead. She looked up at the woman —this stinking bolup woman who belonged to the tribe that had attacked Skyra's people and taken Veenah. The woman was wary, but she was only a bolup. All bolups were weak.

It was time to kill. Skyra flung her arm up, knocking the stone blade away from her throat with enough force to crack the woman's wrist. In less than a breath she plucked one of her own blades from her wrist sheath, slapped it into her other hand, and pulled out the second blade. Rising to her feet, she thrust both blades upward into the throats of two of the women, silencing them immediately. As Skyra pulled her blades free from the choking women, the third woman cradled her damaged wrist to her chest and started to cry out. Skyra threw her knee up into the kneeling woman's face, and the woman collapsed onto her side, moaning.

Skyra had been right about the man—he was choosing to fight instead of run. He did not even call out to his tribemates, assuming he would not need help. He was halfway across the stream before Skyra could drop her hand blades and reach over her shoulder for her khul. She gripped the stone blade, pulled the weapon from its sling, and grabbed its handle with her other hand, a motion she had practiced countless times.

Instead of thrusting his spear to kill, the man swung it at

Skyra, and she blocked the blow with her khul. Even though Skyra had killed two of the women and injured the other, the man intended to take her alive, as if she were more valuable than the women of his own kind.

Skyra did not intend to be taken at all.

The man swung again, this time almost knocking Skyra's khul from her grip as she blocked the blow. A smile formed on his face as he drew back to strike yet again. The stinking bolup was now confident he would take Skyra, and he was probably thinking of what he and the other men of his tribe would do to her.

As the next blow cracked against her khul's handle, she released the weapon, allowing it to fall to the rocks at her feet. The man's smile broadened, and he made the mistake of following the khul with his eyes.

Skyra launched herself at him before he could swing the spear again. The force of the impact toppled him over, and he landed on his back in the stream with Skyra's teeth at his throat. With water rushing into her mouth and nose, she bit into the soft skin of his neck. He twisted and flailed, breaking loose from her teeth. Skyra pulled her face from the water and slid off the man to one side.

As she knew he would, the man sat up, spitting water. She threw her chest against his back and clamped both arms around his neck before he could shout for help. She locked her legs around his waist, and the two collapsed onto their sides in the stream.

Skyra squeezed. The man had dropped his spear in the struggle, and now he jabbed wildly over his shoulder with his fist, trying desperately to strike her face. She buried her nose in the wet, stinking hair on the back of his head to avoid the blows, so he resorted to throwing his elbows back into her ribs and gut.

The man was only a bolup, with thin, weak arms. He should not have tried to fight a nandup at close quarters. Maybe he hadn't known nandup women were just as fierce as nandup men. Now he understood his mistake, but it was too late.

Skyra squeezed even harder, trying with all her strength to prevent him from crying out. Her face was half submerged, and she had no choice but to hold her breath to keep from sucking in water.

The man choked and grunted and fought for his life. Skyra tightened her grip, focusing her thoughts on what he and his tribemates had done to Veenah. She wrenched her head to the side and gasped for breath, but instead she sucked in water churned up by the man's flailing arms and started coughing.

Skyra's eyes were clamped shut, but she sensed a shadow darkening her eyelids from above. She opened her eyes to see Veenah staring down at her. Veenah was now on her knees in the water beside Skyra and the bolup man.

Skyra spat water from her mouth and managed to say, "Apofu-fekho." *Run away, sister.*

For several breaths Veenah did not move. She stared with a vacant look that frightened Skyra. Was she dying? Had the bolups destroyed her will to live?

Veenah moved. She leaned to one side and picked something up. As the bolup man continued to choke and struggle, Veenah slowly raised a rounded river rock almost as large as her own head.

Skyra realized what Veenah was doing and pulled her face away from the man's head to avoid getting hit.

The rock came down on the man with a thud Skyra felt through her arms and chest.

The man struggled even harder, trying to scream, but Skyra's forearms were cutting off his air. She strained and growled, squeezing even harder.

The rock came down again, and this time the man fell still.

Skyra released him and got to her knees, her chest heaving to suck in enough air. She grabbed the rock from Veenah and swung it into the man's temple hard enough to make sure he would never raid another nandup camp. The stream's current rolled him onto his belly but was too shallow to carry him away. He lay face down, with red water swirling gently from his head.

Skyra rose to her feet, but Veenah remained on her knees, staring at the man with that same empty look, as if she were dead. Skyra hoisted her up and dragged her to the stream's edge, stumbling several times on the submerged rocks.

One of the bolup women Skyra had stabbed appeared to be dead, while the other was still gasping for air, trying to breathe through the hole in her throat. The third woman was gone. Skyra let out an alarmed grunt when she couldn't spot the woman anywhere. She released Veenah, hoping her birthmate could stand on her own, then picked up both her hand blades and shoved them into her wrist sheath. Her khul was still at the stream's edge, so she grabbed it and dropped it into the sling inside her wet cape. She plucked her spear from the water where it had wedged itself against the rocky shore, then she spotted Veenah's cape and waist-skin on the far side of the stream, so she waded across and brought them back.

She dropped her spear, slid the cape over her birthmate's head and shoulders, fastened the waist-skin around Veenah's torso, and picked up her spear again. She pulled Veenah's arm over her shoulders with her free hand. "Lotup-tekne-té-fekho." *You must find your strength, sister.*

One of Veenah's eyes was swollen shut, but her other eye met Skyra's, and she spoke quietly. "Skyra-Uno-Loto. Meleen-fekho." *Skyra. My sister.*

With Veenah's arm over her shoulders, Skyra guided her birthmate toward the hillside.

Veenah dragged her feet, almost unable to walk. "Felu-meleen-alobo," she said. *Leave me here alone.*

Skyra ignored her and kept moving. Halfway up the hill, Veenah seemed to realize she was being dragged, and she made more of an effort to walk without stumbling. It wasn't fast enough, though, so Skyra continued pulling her along, trying to get over the hilltop before the other bolup men came and saw which direction they were fleeing. The woman Skyra had failed to kill had no doubt gone back to her camp to alert her tribemates.

At the hilltop, Skyra glanced back—still no sign of pursuing bolups. She tried to pick up the pace by running, but Veenah could not move her feet fast enough. Skyra considered carrying her birthmate on her shoulders, but she couldn't carry both her sister and her spear. If the men came after them, she would need all her weapons.

On the far side of the hill was a narrow riverbed valley, then another smaller hill beyond. After crossing the smaller hill they would have to cross a wide, rocky field to get to a larger river lined with kheyop and munopo trees. She had told her companion Ripple to wait for her at the river. Ripple was not a fighter and could not help against the bolup men, but the trees lining the river might provide enough concealment for her and Veenah.

The two sisters carefully made their way down the hill. Scraggly, chest-high tamoni shrubs dotted the dry riverbed but were too sparse to provide any kind of concealment. Skyra had to get Veenah to the thicker munopo trees lining the flowing river. They crossed the narrow valley, and as they started up the second hill, Skyra heard snuffling sounds. She spotted the broad backs of three massive creatures approaching along the riverbed, partially hidden among the tamonis. Skyra gritted her teeth in exasperation and whispered to her sister that woolly rhinos were coming toward them and she must be silent. Although woolly rhinos had poor eyesight, they could hear and smell, and they often responded to threats by charging.

She pulled Veenah's arm tighter around her shoulders and started hauling her up the hill, trying to move silently. Skyra could feel a slight breeze cooling her wet hair against the back of her head, so at least the rhinos would be upwind when they passed behind her and Veenah.

At the top of the low hill, Skyra finally turned to look back. The three rhinos—a huge male and two smaller females—had already passed by below and were continuing on their way, seemingly unaware of the two women. From this vantage point she now saw a fourth rhino walking between the two females, a baby with shoulders no taller than Skyra's waist. The young rhino was swinging its head back and forth, agitated about something, and it was obviously walking between the adults for protection.

Skyra's scalp tingled, and her legs suddenly wanted to run. She scanned the riverbed in the direction the rhinos had come and saw exactly what she had feared. Three sand-colored creatures, each with shoulders as high as Skyra's ribs, moved smoothly among the tamonis, their eyes fixed on the rhinos ahead. Cave lions.

Skyra froze. She held her breath, although her pounding heart demanded more air. She tightened her grip on her sister's arm, hoping Veenah would understand the signal and remain still and silent.

Veenah let out a whimper of protest and tried pulling her arm from Skyra's grip.

The three cave lions stopped in their tracks, snapped their heads to the side, and stared directly at Skyra and Veenah.

It was too late for silence and stillness. Skyra turned and dragged Veenah beyond the hill's ridge and out of the cave lions' sight, hoping the predators would continue following the woolly rhinos instead. She pulled Veenah across the hilltop and started down the other side.

As they began crossing the rocky field, Skyra glanced over her shoulder. She let out a wail of despair. The cave lions were definitely following, cautiously keeping pace. Skyra had been able to frighten off cave lions before, but this situation was different. Veenah was hurt—she even smelled like she was hurt—and she could barely walk. Cave lions always knew when another animal was hurt. Skyra might be able to hold them off briefly by shouting and waving her weapons, but the predators would come back. They would follow for days if they had to, waiting for an opportunity to kill.

"You must find your strength now, sister," Skyra muttered in her Una-Loto language, and she continued hauling Veenah toward the trees and the river.

A movement near the river caught Skyra's attention. A creature had emerged from the trees and was flying across the field of rocks at about the height of Skyra's shoulders. Ripple was coming to help.

Another movement caught her eye. Some distance from where Ripple had emerged from the trees, a second figure appeared. This figure walked on two legs and wore the cape and waist-skin of a nandup, although the distance was too great to see details. The nandup started to approach Skyra but stopped suddenly. Several breaths later the figure vanished into the munopo trees.

2

———

HIDING

47,659 YEARS in the past - Zaragoza Province of Spain - Day 1

SKYRA STOOD AMONG THE LOW, twisted branches of one of the munopo trees, squinting at the figure descending the distant hill.

Lincoln stepped beside her and spoke in his English language. "Do you see something?"

She pointed.

He stared for several breaths. "I see it—coming toward us. Ripple, can you zoom in on the figure on that hill?"

Ripple stepped between them and directed its vision orb toward the hill. A low hum came from its shell. Ripple lifted off the ground to the height of Skyra's shoulder and hovered. "The figure you are referring to is actually two figures. They are trying to run, but one appears to be injured."

Skyra's heart began pounding. "Can you see who they are?"

Ripple remained silent for many breaths. "I can. This is quite unexpected. One of them is you, Skyra. The other—the one who is impaired—appears to be Veenah."

"Veenah? I did not bring Veenah over that hill. I tried to take her from the bolups, but there were too many. I failed. I was running from the bolup men alone!"

"Looks like you didn't fail this time," Lincoln said. "Remember, the last forty-five minutes have been a different timeline."

As the nandups neared the base of the hill, Skyra could see they were trying to run. One was supporting the other, dragging her along.

Lincoln grabbed Skyra's forearm. "Oh shit! Things really *are* different."

She shaded her eyes with the stone blade of her khul, expecting to see the bolup men coming over the hilltop, pursuing Veenah and Skyra's other self. She saw no men. Instead, three sand-colored creatures were moving smoothly down the slope, stalking the two nandups. Skyra's heart pounded even harder, and her leg muscles began twitching.

She pulled her arm free from his grip. "Cave lions, Lincoln! We must go help Veenah!" She ducked under the munopo branches and started across the rocky field.

"Skyra, wait!" Lincoln called out. "Look to your right."

She did not know what her right was, so she glanced back at him and followed his gaze. Ripple—the other Ripple—was flying across the rocky field toward Veenah and Skyra's other self.

"Let's wait," Lincoln said. "The other Ripple might

frighten the cave lions off, and I have no idea what will happen when the other Skyra realizes who you are."

Skyra hesitated. Ripple was moving fast and would reach the cave lions in a few breaths. She had seen Ripple frighten predators before. The cave lions were not charging. Instead, they were cautiously stalking, probably trying to decide how dangerous the fleeing women might be. Skyra let out an impatient growl and stepped back within the tree's concealment.

The two women kept moving, now headed directly for Skyra and her companions. Perhaps they had seen Skyra emerge from the trees and realized she was one of their own kind. They were too far away to have recognized Skyra's face, but her cape and waist-skin would have revealed she was a nandup. Nandups usually helped each other when they could, even if they were from different tribes.

The cave lions were almost to the hill's base when the other Ripple began screaming as it rushed toward them. Its scream was more of a screech, as if many eagles were crying out at the same time. The sound was loud even at this distance.

The cave lions stopped. The screeching robot creature didn't even slow down. It flew directly at the lions until they were forced to scramble out of its way. This was apparently enough to make them forget about the women, and they ran back up the slope and disappeared over the ridge.

"Damn, would you look at that!" said Derek. "Maybe you're not so useless after all, Ripple. Although technically, that's not really you." Derek was one of Lincoln's tribemates, and he talked a lot, even for a bolup. Like Skyra, he and the others were concealed behind the munopo trees as they stared across the rocky field.

"Technically, that drone *is* me," Ripple replied, "and you

would be wise to note that my two selves now outnumber your one self."

The other two nandups had stopped walking, evidently to watch the other Ripple frighten off the lions. One of the figures—Skyra's other self—lowered Veenah to the ground and kneeled beside her.

"Okay, now what?" asked Jazzlyn, another of Lincoln's bolup tribemates. Jazzlyn's skin was almost as dark as a woolly rhino's fur, and one of her hands had been replaced by a strange hand created from material that looked like smooth, black stone. Only a short time ago, just before the group had used Lincoln's T3 to jump many, many years here to Skyra's time, Jazzlyn had been shot through the gut with an arrow. The strange robotic caretakers from the city of ghost people had crawled inside Jazzlyn's wounds, and now she was feeling better. Skyra had no idea how such a thing could be possible.

Virgil, the last of Lincoln's three tribemates, said, "I don't want to be overly dramatic, but when Skyra and Ripple come into contact with their other selves, it will be the first time such a thing has ever happened. We are in uncharted territory." Virgil seemed to prefer talking about what might happen instead of trying things to see what *would* happen. Lincoln, Jazzlyn, and Derek were the same way, but Virgil was particularly afraid of trying things.

Skyra had already decided she would never understand bolups, but these strange humans had become her friends. Lincoln, in fact, was more than her friend. She and Lincoln were now what he called *married*. He was Skyra's sleeping companion, and she hoped he would someday put a child in her belly.

"If a disaster were going to occur, I think it would have already happened," Lincoln said. "The two Skyras and two

Ripples are already here in the same universe. I can't see how their contact would make any difference."

Skyra ignored the conversation and watched the women in the field. The other Ripple had settled onto the ground on its four legs and was walking back to Veenah and Skyra's other self. Skyra understood enough of what Lincoln had told her about time jumping to know this Veenah—as with the Veenah in her own timeline—had never seen Ripple before. Ripple was the only secret Skyra had ever kept from her sister, even though Skyra had known Ripple for two cold seasons and almost two warm seasons.

"Ripple, what are they doing now?" Skyra asked.

Ripple watched the women for several breaths before replying. "As I'm sure you can imagine, it appears your other self is attempting to explain my other self to Veenah. However, Veenah appears to be too traumatized by her ordeal to comprehend. If you remember from the first version of these events, your sister was in terrible shape by the time we freed her from her human captors. In fact, you should prepare yourself for the possibility that she may not survive, or that she may never fully recover. In your original timeline, Veenah was killed before you could see if she would fully regain her strength or her mind."

"You do not need to remind me of that, Ripple!"

"I suppose I do not. I am sorry."

As Skyra watched, her other self pulled Veenah to her feet. Skyra's chest began to tighten as the two women again made their way directly toward her.

Jazzlyn said, "How are we going to deal with this? We need a plan. When they get here, both of those Neanderthal chicks are going to freak out on us."

Lincoln nudged Skyra's arm. "That's your other self out

there. What do you think she will do when she sees you with a group of strange-looking bolups? Would it be better if we stayed hidden for now?"

Skyra considered how she had felt when she had first seen Lincoln and his tribemates. "The other Skyra will be confused and afraid," she said. "If angry bolup men had not been trying to kill me when I saw you many days ago, I might have attacked you. If you had been with another Skyra, I would have been even more confused and afraid. Now the other Skyra is coming, and she is protecting her birthmate, who is injured. She is going to be dangerous."

Lincoln and his tribemates glanced at the approaching figures then stared at her for a few breaths.

"Okay, let's get the hell out of here," Derek said. "I've seen what Skyra can do to people when she's pissed off."

Lincoln eyed Skyra with his thin bolup brows furrowed. "Maybe Derek is right. You wanted to come here to save Veenah, but your other self has already saved her. Maybe the best thing to do is leave them alone."

Skyra closed her eyes and scratched her scalp with her khul's blade. The thought of leaving Veenah again made her chest hurt. Since the moment Lincoln had told her they might be able to jump back many, many years to Skyra's time to save Veenah, the hurt in her chest had almost disappeared. Now the hurt was back. Veenah was alive again, but Lincoln was suggesting Skyra hide from her. The worst thing was he was probably right. The other Skyra would take care of Veenah, and Veenah would either live or she would die. It would not help for Skyra to confuse and scare her other self or her birthmate.

Her chest was hurting more with every passing breath. Veenah was so close—how could Skyra hide from her? She turned to look again at the two nandups crossing the rocky field. She frowned. Now her other self was running, dragging Veenah as fast as she could. Skyra instinctively glanced at the distant hillside and saw why—at least ten men were running down the slope in pursuit. The men wore no capes, only crude waist-skins.

Jazzlyn let out a soft cry, then said, "Oh, shit! Do you see that?"

Skyra squeezed her khul's worn handle. "Get ready to use your weapons. The bolup men are coming."

3

———

SKYRAS

47,659 years in the past - Zaragoza Province of Spain - Day 1

LINCOLN COULD HARDLY KEEP up with the non-stop events. Only an hour ago he and his team were fighting for their lives to get to his T3, and Jazzlyn had been pierced by an arrow. They had barely managed to get to the T3 for its last jump, 95,000 years back to Skyra's homeland. His head was still spinning from the time jump, and now he was about to go into battle again. He counted ten tribesmen approaching, most of them armed with khuls or spears. He took comfort knowing his team had killed these same men once already, although, to be honest, Skyra had done most of the killing. Regardless, if his team could defeat the tribesmen once, they could do it again. Maybe.

Skyra's leg muscles were visibly twitching, and she was breathing hard as she watched her sister and her other self losing ground to the pursuing tribesmen. She glanced at Lincoln. "We must go now. We must scare away the bolup men, or we must kill them."

Lincoln nodded, trying to appear confident.

Jazzlyn reached for one of the spears. "I think I might actually be able to help now. I'm feeling much better."

Virgil said, "Don't even think about it—we've got this." He spoke firmly, although his trembling hands betrayed his fear.

Lincoln glanced at each of his team members, his confidence quickly diminishing. They were all exhausted. Jazzlyn was critically injured, although the hundreds of tiny robots inside of her were apparently doing something to dull her pain. Virgil's trousers were missing a pant leg, and his exposed leg was covered in scratches, dried blood, and dirt. Derek appeared ready to fight, but his wide eyes were darting about nervously, as they often did before one of his debilitating lycanthropy episodes.

"We cannot wait!" Skyra said. With her khul in one hand and a crude spear in the other, she ducked around the concealing tree branches and ran into the open field.

"Dammit," Lincoln muttered, blowing air out through his teeth. This was really happening—again. He grabbed the makeshift wooden khul and spear at his feet and ran after Skyra.

"Stay right here, Jazzlyn!" Virgil cried, then he and Derek were running with Lincoln. Seconds later, Lincoln heard the low humming of Ripple's maglev machinery as the drone caught up, speeding across the field at chest height.

Veenah and the other Skyra were still about a hundred yards out, but Lincoln and the others would reach them well ahead of the approaching tribesmen. The Neanderthal twins were now frozen in place, staring at Skyra, who was coming to a stop near them. Lincoln, Derek, and Virgil caught up and stopped beside Skyra, and Ripple extended its legs as it alighted on the sand. The other Ripple came from behind the twins and stood beside them, its vision lens focused on the newcomers. The pursuing tribesmen had stopped about a hundred yards out, no doubt confused by the strange assortment of bolups, nandups, and drones. With any luck, they would simply turn around and return to their camp.

"Do not be afraid," Skyra said in English to her other self. "We came here to help you save Veenah."

The other Skyra appeared too confused to even speak. Her eyes darted between Skyra, Ripple, Lincoln, and Lincoln's team members.

The men in the distance were talking to each other and pointing.

Skyra spoke Veenah's name, followed by a string of words in her Una-Loto language. Veenah looked toward her, but her eyes had that same hollow, defeated look Lincoln had seen after rescuing her from the human camp the first time many days ago.

The other Skyra finally spoke. "Who are you? Who are these strange bolups?"

Skyra glanced at Lincoln before replying. "These bolups are my friends. They will not hurt you. I will explain later. Now you must help us fight those bolup men." She pointed over the other Skyra's shoulder at the ten tribesmen, who were now cautiously approaching.

The other Skyra shot a brief glance back. "Who are you?" she demanded again.

"I am Skyra Una-Loto. You are Skyra Una-Loto. Veenah Una-Loto is our birthmate. I will explain later!"

The other Skyra stepped forward, wielding her khul menacingly. "You speak words that are not true!"

Ripple spoke up for the first time, apparently addressing the other Ripple. "Activate your receiver so I may send you a packet of information to help clarify this situation."

After a few seconds of silence, the other Ripple spoke up for the first time. "Skyra, as we are currently being pursued, there is no time to explain, but I think you should listen to this other Skyra. I believe she is another version of yourself, just as this Ripple is another version of myself. If you want to save Veenah, you need to let these people help us."

"The bolup men are coming," Skyra said. "We will help you kill them."

The other Skyra glanced again at her pursuers.

The tribesmen were now only fifty yards away and still approaching, perhaps emboldened by their superior numbers, or perhaps due to overwhelming curiosity. Lincoln recognized several of them—not surprising considering his team's battle with these men had been the first truly violent experience of his life. Although he remembered their faces, he had forgotten their bodies were so lean and wiry, almost to the point of gauntness. It would be a mistake to underestimate them, however.

One of the tribesmen shouted something, then all ten men charged.

"Protect Veenah!" Skyra shouted, then she and the other Skyra ran to meet the oncoming men. Lincoln gripped both of his weapons and forced his reluctant legs to take off after her. Virgil and Derek converged around Veenah, following Skyra's command.

As if they were mirror images, the two Skyras flung their spears haphazardly at the men. Then, as the men were forced to avoid the spears, both Skyras slid in low and struck the men's legs with their khuls.

Two tribesmen went down, and both Skyras jumped to their feet amidst a flurry of confusion and swinging weapons. As Lincoln ran directly into the melee, Ripple flew past his shoulder straight into the chest of one of the men, knocking the man off his feet and adding to the confusion. Lincoln dropped his makeshift khul and ran the point of his spear into the hip of a tribesman beside the man Ripple had hit. Lincoln's momentum ripped the spear from his fingers, and he barely put his elbows out before crashing into the guy. Lincoln lost his balance and fell, and the man stumbled back, still on his feet, grunting as he pulled Lincoln's spear from his body.

Lincoln quickly recovered, but the fight was already over. Most of the men were sprinting for the hill. Three men were on the ground, one of them motionless, the other two trying to crawl away. One of them was the man Lincoln had injured.

"God almighty!" Virgil exclaimed. "We're all still alive."

One of the Skyras—Lincoln couldn't tell which—stepped toward the crawling men, hefting her khul as if she intended to finish them off.

"You don't need to kill them," Lincoln said.

She paused and turned to look at him.

Lincoln realized this was the other Skyra—her hair was wet, her face was smeared with mud, and blood trickled from a wound on her forehead. Also, her eyes showed a complete lack of recognition. She had no idea who he was.

"This is Lincoln," Skyra said as she picked up her spear. "He is a strange bolup, but he is my friend. We are married."

The man Lincoln had injured had managed to stand on one foot and was now hopping away. He fell down then got up again. The other crawling man could not get to his feet, and he was leaving a trail of glistening blood on the rocks.

The other Skyra shot a glance at the two injured tribesmen then faced Skyra. "What tribe are you from? How do you know this language?"

"My friend Ripple taught me this language, just as your Ripple taught it to you. It is English, the language of my bolup friends."

The other Skyra stepped closer, baring her teeth. "I do not understand! Who are you? Why do you look like my birth-mate Veenah?"

It occurred to Lincoln that the two Skyras had never seen themselves in a mirror. They each knew what Veenah looked like but had never seen their own faces except distorted in the rivers.

"I do not know if I can explain," Skyra said. "My friend Lincoln can tell you what has happened." She turned to Lincoln expectantly.

Where to even begin? "Um, I know this must seem strange to you, but you need to know we came here to save Veenah's life."

"Do not speak Veenah's name, stinking bolup!" the other Skyra snarled. "I will kill all of you if you try to take her." She pointed her khul's stone blade at Skyra. "Aibul-fusa-melu. Melu-afu-mumenga!"

Skyra's jaw muscles rippled, and her eyes narrowed. "Melu-mogoro-rha!"

The other Skyra slipped her khul into the sling in her wet cape then picked up her spear. She moved to Veenah's side and slid her free arm around her sister's waist. "I am taking Veenah back to my tribe. Do not try to stop us and do not follow us."

Derek said, "Uh, didn't Skyra's tribe kill Veenah the last time that happened?"

The other Skyra glanced at Derek then scanned the rest of the group, her eyes wide and darting about, an expression Lincoln had never seen on Skyra's face before. She was obviously freaked out enough to be dangerous, and he couldn't predict what she was going to do. She growled and began leading Veenah away.

Skyra stepped in front of her sister and her other self, blocking their path. "You must listen. Gelrut will kill Veenah if you return her to Una-Loto camp. I will not let you take her."

Lincoln started forward. "Skyra, maybe we just need to—"

The other Skyra broke away from Veenah and lunged at Skyra. She swung her khul, obviously intending to split Skyra's skull, and Skyra barely got her spear up in time to block the blow. She thrust out her foot and kicked the other Skyra's gut, shoving her out of striking range, then held her at bay with her spear's point.

"You both must stop fighting!" Ripple said at a forcefully high volume. Actually, both Ripples had spoken the words at almost the same time. The two drones were now levitating, facing each other in midair as if they themselves were about to clash.

The two Skyras shot glances at the drones then went back to glaring at each other.

Again the Ripples spoke in unison. "You are both too valuable to risk..."

The two drones paused.

"You go right ahead," Ripple said.

"No, I yield the floor to you," said the other Ripple.

"Very well." Ripple lowered itself to the ground and

turned to the two Skyras. "Fear and anger are not appropriate responses at this time. Both of you are too valuable to needlessly risk injury or death. The other Ripple and I have come to an understanding." Ripple turned to the other Ripple, which had now lowered itself to the ground as well. "Would you care to explain?"

"Of course," the other Ripple said, then it turned its vision lens toward Lincoln. "Emotions are high, and confusion is adding to the precariousness of this situation. I have received sufficient information from my counterpart to understand the most crucial portions of what has happened. Skyra needs time to process this rather shocking circumstance. She is comfortable in my presence, and I believe I can adequately explain things to her."

"Stop using words I do not know, Ripple!" the other Skyra demanded, still glaring at Skyra.

The other Ripple paused only briefly before continuing. "Skyra *needs* to take Veenah to her tribe's camp. Let her. I will go with her. I will talk to her and explain what I know."

"You do know what Gelrut did to Veenah the last time we were here, don't you?" Lincoln asked.

"My counterpart has informed me, and I will explain it to Skyra. This will take time, but I am confident I can succeed before we approach Una-Loto camp."

The other Skyra backed away from Skyra and again took Veenah by the waist. "If you try to stop us again, I will kill you." She resumed leading Veenah away.

"Do you agree?" the other Ripple said with its lens still pointed up at Lincoln's face.

"You're asking the wrong person," Lincoln replied.

The other Ripple turned to Skyra. "Do you agree, Skyra?"

Ripple stepped past the other Ripple and approached

Skyra. "This sounds like a reasonable plan, and I am sure you will see Veenah again soon. Then perhaps Lincoln and his team can treat her wounds with their remaining medical supplies. The other Ripple is aware of the large hill of boulders not far from here and has suggested we set up camp there. I agreed, as it is the same hill of boulders where you and I and Lincoln's team took shelter when we were in this land before."

Skyra turned to Lincoln, her face strained with apprehension.

He stepped closer and firmly gripped her arm. "Both of the Ripples are right. Your other self needs some time to think. Remember how difficult it was for you to understand what happened to you."

She turned and stared after her other self and her sister. Skyra wasn't human, but the expression of anguish on her face was universal and unmistakable. "We came many, many years to save Veenah."

"Yes, and we *did* save Veenah. We saved her from the bolup men."

"Veenah cannot go back to Una-Loto tribe."

"The other Ripple knows that and will explain it to the other Skyra. They'll be okay." He glanced at the three injured tribesmen still trying to escape. The limping man Lincoln had stabbed was almost to the base of the first hill. The man who had been trying to hop away was now on his knees, and the crawling man was now lying still. "I can't imagine the other bolups will have any desire to go after Veenah—I'm sure they're terrified by what happened to them here. Right now they're probably packing up their camp to move out of this region entirely." He shook her arm gently. "Skyra, remember your other self is really you. She has your skills, and she cares about Veenah as much as you do. She will take care of Veenah, and the other Ripple will persuade her to bring your sister back to join us at the caves. The best thing we can do for her right now is set up a protected camp so she'll be safe when they return."

Skyra chewed on her thick lower lip. "Your words are true, but my chest still hurts. Veenah does not need me now because my other self is with her. My other self will always be with her."

WHEN LINCOLN and the others returned to the river, Jazzlyn was on her feet, waiting impatiently. "I saw what happened," she said. "Ya'll were outnumbered. You're lucky to be alive. Which means I'm lucky, because there's no way in hell I'd survive by myself in this place."

Virgil lifted Jazzlyn's shirt to inspect the wounds on her abdomen. "I don't think you should be walking around, Jazz. You're the one who's lucky to be alive."

"That's the thing, though. I'm walking around because something's happening inside me. It's driving me crazy. Sometimes it tickles and sometimes it hurts." She rubbed her belly between the two wounds. "In fact, right now it's feeling really weird." She paused, frowning. "Damn! It's getting worse."

Lincoln and Derek rushed over, and together with Virgil they lowered Jazzlyn to a sitting position.

She stared down at her belly. "Shit, you guys, they're really moving around in there!"

Derek pointed to one of her wounds. "Jesus, they're crawling out."

Lincoln leaned in closer to look. A fly-sized robot emerged

from the wound and fell to the ground next to Jazzlyn. Tiny, scrabbling legs appeared from the wound, then another robot came out. Robots were emerging from the opposite wound also, and soon two piles of the little robots were forming on the ground.

"It itches so bad," Jazzlyn muttered, and she started scratching at one of the wounds.

Virgil pulled her hand back. "Don't do that, Jazz. You might damage them."

"Or you might make the little shits mad," Derek added. "Who knows what they'll do if they get mad."

Ripple spoke up. "It seems unlikely that anger or retribution would be coded responses in robotic caretakers designed to provide assistance."

Derek huffed. "Being a robot doesn't make you an expert on robots."

"Quite the contrary," Ripple said. "I am the most qualified—"

"Can you guys just shut up?" Jazzlyn said. "I feel like I'm giving birth over here, and you two can't stop squabbling."

The tiny bots continued pouring out in single file from the two wounds until both piles were over six inches high. The piled robots lay still, as if they were now dead, having completed their task. However, after the last of them emerged from Jazzlyn's body, the piles began writhing. Lincoln heard barely audible clicks as the fly-sized robots snapped together, forming larger thumb-sized robots. When the thumb-sized robots were complete, they crawled on top of each other and snapped together with louder clicks. Seconds later, each of the two piles had become one robot the size of a large rat. The two rat robots skittered away from Jazzlyn as if giving her room, then they became still.

Jazzlyn flashed a forced grin. "Did I give birth to boys, girls, or one of each?"

Lincoln shook his head, again surprised by his team's resilience. "How do you feel now, Jazz?"

"About four pounds lighter."

"I'll take that as positive. Nevertheless, you shouldn't be walking around. We need to get you and all our supplies to the cave—the same place we took shelter last time we were here. It's about a kilometer away. We'll figure out how to carry you."

"Nonsense," she said. "What's the point of having robot surgeons inside you if you have to be carried like an invalid? I can walk."

Virgil cleared his throat. "Um, we don't know what the robotic caretakers were doing inside your body. We don't know if they were even repairing the damage. In fact, I find that concept to be rather far-fetched."

"I'm alive, aren't I? That's all the proof I need. Now quit hovering and let me get up. Those piles of gear aren't going to carry themselves."

Lincoln, Virgil, and Derek backed off to give her room, but Ripple stepped in and lowered its vision lens to observe one of the rat-sized robots. "I am officially making a request to take these composite devices with us. I do not believe they have the means to recharge their power, but I would like to study them. They are unlike anything created by humans in our original timeline."

Lincoln kneeled again and tapped the nearest robot with his finger. It didn't run away or try to attack him, so he picked it up. "Huh—surprisingly heavy. I bet you really did lose four pounds, Jazz."

BEFORE JUMPING 95,000 years back to Skyra's original time, the supplies had been contained within the temporal transport bags, which Lincoln fondly referred to as body bags. When the body bags were connected to the T3—in essence a time machine—anything within the bags could be jumped through time and space. However, the bags always remained behind, so now the gear was arranged in loose piles where the body bags used to be.

Lincoln and the others stood among the piles, silently contemplating the logistics of hauling everything a kilometer to the hill of rocks. Before their last jump, some of their supplies had been hastily discarded to make room for bundles of building materials given to them by the strange virtual beings they had encountered 95,000 years in the future. Lincoln scanned the piles and noticed only one of the large duffel bags had made the cut. He let out a frustrated sigh. The second duffel would have made it easier to transport everything.

Perhaps most disconcerting was the fact that the T3 itself was not here. Lincoln had agreed to leave it behind for the virtual beings as a gesture of good will. Not that it mattered—the device had been on its last dregs of power, and the team had used the last set of body bags for this jump. The virtual beings might learn from the device's design, but it was no longer useful to Lincoln and his team. Now the T3's absence was a disturbing reminder that Lincoln and the others were stuck in this time and place. They had to live the rest of their lives in this brutal wilderness.

"Maybe we can strap the gear to Ripple's back," Derek

said. "How many trips do you think the drone would have to make to get all this stuff to the hill?"

"Do I look like a beast of burden to you?" Ripple asked.

Derek nodded. "Yeah, you kinda do."

"I was precision-designed to operate at my own specific mass. With additional weight added, my power consumption would outpace my ability to recharge, rendering me useless."

"Well, that's an excuse I've never heard before," Derek said. He then picked up the only duffel bag and started shoving items into it.

Lincoln walked over to Skyra, who was standing beside the river, staring toward the distant foothills. Her tribe's camp was in those hills, a two-day walk from here.

She shot him a glance as he stopped beside her. "Lincoln, my legs want to run."

She had used this expression a few times before, so he had a pretty good idea what she meant. "You want to catch up to Veenah, don't you?"

She didn't reply.

"What did the other Skyra say to you?" he asked. "It seemed like she said something to make you really angry. I'm curious what it was."

She grunted briefly. "The other Skyra said I was a *mumenga*. It is what my tribemates call a nandup woman who is taken by bolups but never tries to escape."

"Does that happen?"

"Yes, it happens because nandup tribes sometimes kill nandup women when they escape and return. They will kill the woman if they think the bolups have put a child in her belly."

"Is that why Gelrut killed Veenah?"

Skyra's facial muscles tightened for a moment. "Yes. I should not have—"

"It wasn't your fault. You thought you were doing the right thing."

Skyra nodded slightly, a gesture Lincoln had never seen her use before. Perhaps she'd picked it up from him and his team.

"The best thing we can do now is be ready when your other self returns with Veenah. We need to start carrying our supplies to the hill of caves. You're the one who taught me we shouldn't remain close to this river for long. Too many predators come here, especially when it starts getting dark."

"Yes, too many predators. We must go." She waved her hand toward the piles of gear and supplies. "I do not understand why you want to take all of those things."

"We need to set up a permanent home, one we can defend, and one where we can stay warm when the cold season comes. I'm sure we'll find a way to use every one of those items. We're really going to need your help, though, because we have no idea how to survive in this land."

She gazed at him for a few seconds, her enormous nandup eyes seemingly penetrating his thoughts. "I will show you how to make a camp. I will show you how to make weapons and how to hunt. But we are a small tribe, Lincoln. A raiding tribe of bolups might kill us. You and your tribemates are bolups, so nandups might kill us. My Una-Loto tribe makes camp near rivers, with shelters made with the skins of the woolly rhino and woolly mammoth. We cannot make such a camp, or we will be killed. You are right, Lincoln, we must make our camp in the caves at the hill of rocks. We must make a camp we can defend."

Lincoln nodded, contemplating the logistical challenges of making such a camp.

Skyra pointed to the distant hill of rocks, barely visible through the trees beside the river. "We can use the cave where we fought off Gelrut, Brillir, and Vall. It is a good cave for defending our small tribe."

"It's near the top of the hill, too," Lincoln added. "That should help, shouldn't it?"

She gazed at the hill for several seconds without answering. "Ripple told me I died in one of the caves in that hill."

Lincoln blinked, surprised by her seemingly random statement. "Yes, you did, but my team and I jumped back to a time before you died, and we saved you."

"The other Skyra still died?"

"Yes, she did. When my team jumped to your time, the jump created a new timeline, then there were two Skyras. The other Skyra died. It is not possible to change what has already happened, but it *is* possible to create a new timeline. That's what we did, and I'm glad we prevented you from dying in the same way the other Skyra died. Now we've created a third timeline, and because you were with us when we jumped back here, there is a third Skyra."

She didn't take her eyes off the hill of boulders. "Ripple did not tell me how I died."

"That's because Ripple doesn't *know* how you died, for the same reason you don't know. Remember, that other Ripple is in another timeline. We'll never know exactly what happened in the cave, but I can tell you what I *do* know. Your bones were found 47,000 years later, and Ripple was found with your bones. Perhaps Ripple was trying to protect you or comfort you when you died."

Skyra shifted her gaze to Lincoln's face. "Did you find my bones?"

"No, but your bones were shown to me. Ripple figured out a way to make sure your bones would be found at a very specific time in the future, by sending a message people could hear. Ripple waited over 47,000 years to send out that message, because Ripple wanted *me* to know about you. Ripple knew I was the only person who could jump back in time and create a new timeline in which you do not die."

"Now there is a third Skyra."

"Yeah. It gets confusing, doesn't it?"

"Lincoln, you and me, we are married. Are you and the other Skyra married too?"

Again he blinked in surprise. "No! I'm only married to you. The other Skyra is a different person. She has not had the experiences you and I have had together during the days since we met. She doesn't even know me. I am in love with you because of the things *we've* done together, therefore I cannot possibly be in love with the other Skyra."

She bared her teeth in a broad nandup smile. "You speak happy words. Now I do not have to kill the other Skyra."

4

HOME

47,659 years in the past - Zaragoza Province of Spain - Day 1

Skyra could not understand how Lincoln and his tribemates had survived to adulthood. They had made the T3, a device for jumping many, many years in time, but they did not know how to make tools for the simplest tasks. They had four piles of supplies to carry to the hill of boulders, but they only had one bag for carrying. Instead of actually making another tool for carrying, they began *talking* about how to make a tool for carrying. These strange bolups talked a lot about everything, but tools did not get made by talking.

The group needed two banyots. Moving away from the talking bolups, Skyra passed by several kheyop trees, which only had twisted, gnarled branches, until she found a dead, reasonably straight branch she could break off one of the taller munopo trees. She tested the branch's strength by swinging it against the tree's trunk, then she dragged it back to the bolups. "Stop talking! I will show you how to make two banyots for carrying. Go find three more munopo tree branches as long and straight as this branch. Then gather many shorter branches. The shorter branches do not have to be straight. Go find the branches now please."

She dropped the branch at their feet and began wading back across the river. Several breaths later, Lincoln caught up to her, sloshing through the knee-deep water. "Where are you going?" he asked.

She paused to stare at the cool water swirling around her leather footwraps, tempted to stop right here and bathe. It would feel good to wash away the dirt and blood, but there was no time for that now. "I am getting what we need to tie the branches," she said as she resumed wading.

As Lincoln followed, she stepped from the river, passed through the band of trees, and headed across the rocky field. She scanned the horizon for bolups or any signs that her other self was returning with Veenah, then she walked straight to the dead bolup tribesman, still lying where she had killed him. She pulled one of her hand blades from her wrist sheath and kneeled beside the body. The stinking bolup's hair was matted and dirty, but it was long enough to be useful. She grabbed a fistful and sawed it off at the scalp. She handed the hair to Lincoln and proceeded to cut off the rest of the man's hair.

"Well... hell, I wouldn't have ever thought of doing this," Lincoln said.

Skyra remained silent as she removed the remaining hair and handed it to him. Around the man's neck was a cord of twisted leather, strung with several dark, shriveled objects—probably nandup ears. Skyra cut the cord and tossed the ears away with a disgusted frown then handed Lincoln the cord.

The dead man had no cape—bolups never wore capes during the warm season—but his waist-skin appeared to be made from Lynx hide, and it held a crude sheath with a stone hand blade. Skyra pulled the waist-skin over the man's legs and gave it to Lincoln, along with the knife.

Another of the bolup men was dead a short distance away, so Skyra left the first man lying naked on the rocky ground and went to the second man. She pulled off his waist-skin and hand blade then began removing his hair.

"I understand why you're doing this," Lincoln said as he watched, "but I find it a little disturbing."

She gave him a fistful of hair. "I do not know what that means."

"It means it bothers me to do this to people who are dead."

She handed him more hair. "Why?"

"I don't know. It feels disrespectful? I suppose that doesn't make sense to you."

She glanced up at him. "You are a strange bolup, but you are my friend, and I am glad we are married."

His thin bolup lips formed a smile even though he looked like he might be sick.

She got to her feet and handed him the last of the man's hair.

He squinted at his wrist and grimaced. "Oh, great. Now things are crawling up my arm. Probably lice."

She ran her fingers over both his wrists, wiping away the tiny creatures. "Bolups do not wash themselves." She shaded her eyes and spotted the third bolup man, who had tried to limp away after the fight. He had not made it very far. "Come, there is one more."

As they approached the third man, Skyra realized he was still alive. He pushed himself to his hands and knees and tried to get up, but Skyra shoved him back down with her foot. She straddled his body and put her hand blade to his throat.

"No, wait!" Lincoln said. "He can't hurt us anymore, so why kill him?"

She frowned. "Because it will be easier to take his hair and waist-skin."

He let out a long breath. "Um... Skyra, I may have a lot to learn from you, but maybe there are things you can learn from me too. I don't think we should kill people unless it's absolutely necessary. Killing this man now would be... wrong."

Skyra moved to the man's side and kneeled by his head. She grabbed his hair and forced him to look at her. His expression showed fear. The man did not want her to kill him. His eyes were still clear, indicating the injury on his hip might not kill him if she let him go. She had seen nandups recover from wounds worse than his. "This is one of the bolups who hurt Veenah," she said, still staring into the man's eyes.

"We don't know that for sure," Lincoln said. "Please, Skyra, let's not kill him. I'll explain my reasons for it later when we have time. I will learn from you, you will learn from me."

She studied the man's eyes for a few more breaths, then she put her blade to the base of the hair in her grip and sawed it off just above his scalp. He grimaced at the pain but did not fight. She handed the hair to Lincoln and started on another fistful. When she had taken most of his hair, she pulled off his waist-skin. His sheath was empty, and she did not see the hand blade anywhere on the ground. She added the waist-skin to the pile in Lincoln's arms.

He was still staring at the injured bolup. "Do you think he'll survive?"

Skyra scanned the horizon in the direction of the Una-

Loto camp but still did not see her other self returning with Veenah. "He will live, or he will die." She turned and headed back toward the river. Near the first man's body, where the fight had taken place, Skyra and Lincoln found the missing hand blade, as well as two spears and two khuls. They gathered these bolup weapons and returned to their own group.

Skyra washed the waist-skins and bolup hair in the river to get rid of most of the tiny creatures Lincoln called lice. She put Jazzlyn and Virgil to work braiding the hair into cords, then she showed Lincoln and Derek how to cut long leather strips from the bolup waist-skins. Derek still had one of the shiny knives in his pocket, but the others had been lost, so Lincoln used one of the stone knives taken from the bolups.

Wasting no time, Skyra used the cords of hair and strips of leather to fasten the munopo branches together to make two sturdy banyots, each consisting of two long poles with shorter branches lashed between them for supporting a load of supplies. Two people could hold one end of a banyot and drag it, or they could hold either end and carry it between them.

Once the cloth bag was filled with supplies and the two banyots were loaded, Skyra could see the group would have to make three trips to the boulder hill to move everything.

Derek carried the bag on his back, Skyra and Jazzlyn dragged one of the banyots, and Lincoln and Virgil dragged the other. Progress was slow. By the time they reached the boulder hill, Skyra knew two more trips, plus carrying everything in smaller bundles to the cave near the hill's summit, was going to take too long.

"We cannot move all your things before the sun hides beyond the hills," she said as the others leaned against the rocks to rest. "A cave bear lives somewhere in the boulders of this hill—I smelled it the last time we were here. Cave lions and hyenas may be near also. These are the dangers of making our camp in a hill of boulders and caves. We can kill these predators or force them to leave, but that will take many days. Until then, we will be safer if we are in our own cave with the light of a campfire before darkness comes."

The bolups looked at each other as if they had not even thought of these things.

"I knew we should have just stayed in the city of virtual people," Derek said. "We have to kill bears and lions and hyenas?"

"I will show you how," Skyra replied.

Derek huffed out a breath. "We're all going to die on this hill, just like the first Skyra did."

"Really, Derek?" Lincoln said.

Skyra stepped closer to Derek, and he took a step back. "Sorry, I didn't mean anything by that," he said.

She did not understand what he meant by those words, so she said, "Cave lions and hyenas attack and kill nandups and bolups who are alone. They do not kill tribes. We will start a new tribe here. You will not die on this hill if I show you how to be a good tribemate."

He nodded. "I would appreciate that. I'm just... I'm tired of all the fighting and killing."

"If you are tired, you must rest. Tomorrow you will be ready for more fighting and killing."

He scratched his chin through his gray beard. "That's... not really what I meant, but thanks for the pep talk."

SKYRA REMEMBERED the easiest route up through the jumbled boulders to the cave near the hilltop. She had last been here in a different timeline, but everything seemed the same. Before entering, she sniffed the low cave opening. The cave had been empty last time, and again she detected no predators.

She tossed her armload of supplies through the opening then crawled through. Lincoln did the same, followed by Derek, Jazzlyn, and Virgil. Ripple had stayed at the base of the hill with the rest of the supplies. Dragging the three loads from the river and piling them at the hill's base had taken most of the afternoon.

"Looks just as depressing as it did before," Jazzlyn said, "but just wait until you see what I do with it during the next few days. I'm gonna work my magic on this place."

Lincoln turned to Skyra. "What do you think? Could we live for a long time in this place, or will we have to find something different?"

"We must stay here until my other self brings Veenah," she said.

"Yes, but after that could it be a permanent home?"

She kneeled and touched the floor. The rock surface was warm and dry. The cave was small, but there was enough flat area for a fire, as well as sleeping space for the entire group. She walked to the back of the cave, which slanted downward to several small openings—too small for predators or enemies to enter but large enough to allow water to run out. She returned to the flat area and saw light coming in from three places at one side of the ceiling. She had to press her cheek to one of the boulders to see that the largest of the openings was smaller than her head. The holes would allow smoke to escape. "We can defend this cave, and a campfire will keep it warm and dry. I do not like how far we must walk to get water from the river, but maybe we can find water closer. I have not seen what is on the other side of this boulder hill. Maybe there is a stream there."

"That's good enough for me," Derek said. "I feel a lot safer here than anywhere out there. Hell, from up here we can see what's approaching a mile away."

"Except for people and creatures already on or in this hill of rocks," Virgil said. "Look, I hate to be a party pooper, but there are numerous other parameters we must consider. How cold are the winters here? Are we too exposed to the wind? Or to lightning? Does this area flood? Is there an adequate supply of food in the area? Because these rocky fields hardly seem suitable for agriculture. Is this hill regularly used by a murderous tribe of humans or Neanderthals? Is there enough firewood? Do the human tribes around here carry diseases that might wipe us out? Do *we* carry diseases that might wipe *them* out? If we're going to be climbing up and down this hill all the time, is someone going to fall and break an arm or leg, or neck? Would we be able to treat such an injury? Furthermore, what if, by some miracle, we stay alive long enough to get too old to climb up and down these rocks? Then what?"

Everyone remained silent, watching Virgil.

He paused for a few breaths. "Should I go on? Because I could."

"It's not necessary," Lincoln said. "Here's what I need to know. Is everyone okay with setting up camp here *for now?*"

"Good with me," Derek said.

"I'm okay with it," Jazzlyn said.

Virgil sucked in a deep breath and nodded his head.

"Skyra?" Lincoln asked.

"I am staying at this hill until Veenah comes. If she does not come, I will go find her."

"That's settled, then," Lincoln said. "We can leave the

building supplies near the bottom of the hill and bring up everything else."

Skyra and Jazzlyn collected firewood while the others hid the building supplies and carried the other items to the cave. Several long-dead kheyop trees were near the hill's base, and Skyra was surprised to find the same branches she had collected the last time she was here. Jazzlyn explained that the sticks were here for the same reason another Skyra was here, but it still felt strange picking up branches she had already burned.

Everyone returned to the cave well before the sun touched the foothills in the distance where Skyra's Una-Loto camp was located. Skyra had arranged the firewood, and she asked Derek if he still had his fire tool.

He and Virgil were sorting through the pile of supplies. "I think we've lost about half of all the things we started with," Derek said. "I'm not sure yet if we have any lighters left."

"It's not that cold in here," Lincoln said. "If the only purpose for having a fire tonight is to keep predators out of the cave, do we really even need one? We can station Ripple at the entrance. If something approaches, the drone can turn on its light."

Ripple stepped from its position near the back of the cave. "Although I am overqualified to be a night guard, I am happy to perform any function that will keep you safe."

"You're a drone," Derek said. "You can't really be happy about anything."

Ripple turned its vision orb toward Derek. "Happiness is a human construct, as am I. So are you, for that matter, as you are the result of stirrings within the loins of your biological parents."

Derek frowned. "What does that even mean?"

"Perhaps you should take some time to contemplate it."

Derek made a strange gesture with one hand, extending one of his fingers higher than the others. "Perhaps you should contemplate this."

"Jesus, Derek," Jazzlyn said. "You're just a school kid trapped in a bearded man's body."

Skyra did not understand most of what these bolups were saying, so she ducked through the cave opening and stood on the narrow ledge, scanning the rocky fields and distant hills toward the setting sun and Una-Loto camp. She saw no sign of Veenah or her other self, and she wondered if they would ever return. Thinking of all the possibilities made her chest hurt again. The other Ripple might fail to convince the other Skyra not to take Veenah to Una-Loto camp. A bolup hunting party might find them. Veenah might die from her injuries. Skyra scuffed the stone ledge beneath her feet with the sole of her footwrap, trying not to imagine Veenah lying dead out there among the rocks and weeds.

Lincoln and his tribemates were still talking in the cave, and Skyra sensed they were fatigued. Their soft words could become angry words—not a good way to spend the first night in their new camp. She would have to do something about it. She ducked back through the opening, sat beside the firewood, and folded her legs. "We will not burn our campfire tonight, but come and sit around the firewood anyway." When they hesitated, she clapped her hands together twice. "Sit around the firewood with me now! You too, Ripple."

Jazzlyn gathered up several garment-like items, the soft sacks the bolups called sleeping bags. Only three remained, and Jazzlyn handed one to Derek, one to Lincoln, and kept one for herself and Virgil to share. As the others sat on theirs,

Lincoln spread his out and patted it with his hand while looking at Skyra. She stared, not understanding.

He patted it again. "I'm inviting you to sit on it with me. It's big enough for both of us."

She shifted onto the sleeping bag. It wasn't as soft as the beds in Di-woto's sanctuary-fortress, or the beds in the empty city of ghost people, but it was better than sitting on bare stone.

Ripple moved beside her, pulled its legs into its shell, and settled onto its belly on the stone floor.

When everyone was seated, Skyra said, "It is time for laughing. When the sun hides behind the hills at the end of the day, my tribemates sit together at the campfire and tell stories and play games that make them laugh. It is good to laugh before you sleep. We will play a game now."

"Bring it on," Jazzlyn said. "I have to warn you guys, though—I kick ass at just about every game I've ever played."

"Except at the modesty game," Derek said.

A growl escaped from Skyra's throat.

Lincoln put a hand on her arm. "We're listening. Tell us about the game."

"We will tell a story. I will start the story. Lincoln will tell the next part of the story." She pointed to Jazzlyn, who was beside Lincoln. "Jazzlyn will tell the next part of the story." She then pointed to the others in order around the circle. "Virgil will tell the next part of the story, then Derek, then Ripple, then me, then Lincoln, and we will tell the story until one of us loses the game."

They eyed her for a few breaths.

"How does someone lose the game?" Virgil asked.

"You lose the game if you are too slow to tell your part of the story."

"Okay, so we have to be fast," Jazzlyn said. "Yep, I'm going to kick ass."

Ripple said, "I believe I have an unfair advantage, as I am far more adept at storytelling than any human or nandup could possibly be."

Skyra began. "Lincoln and his tribemates were hungry. They took their spears and hand blades and went to the forest of kheyop trees to hunt." She turned to Lincoln and waited.

"Uh, now? Am I supposed to—"

"*Aheeee... at-at-at-at-at,*" Skyra laughed. "You lose the game, Lincoln. Too slow!"

Derek and Jazzlyn both let out a funny bolup chuckle.

Lincoln furrowed his brows. "I wasn't really ready."

She started again. "Lincoln and his tribemates were hungry. They took their spears and hand blades and went to the forest of kheyop trees to hunt." She turned to Lincoln.

"Uh, they got lost in the forest and had no idea where they were. And... they grew even hungrier." He turned to Jazzlyn.

Jazzlyn spoke without hesitating. "They realized they would never find their way back unless they got some help, so they shouted, 'Skyra, where are you? We need your help!'" She turned to Virgil.

"So, I can take the story in any direction I want?"

"*Aheeee... at-at-at-at-at,*" Skyra laughed. "You lose the game, Virgil!" She began again. "Lincoln and his tribemates were hungry. They took their spears and hand blades and went to the forest of kheyop trees to hunt." She turned to Lincoln.

He quickly repeated his part of the story, then Jazzlyn repeated hers.

Virgil said, "Their shouts were heard by a family of cave

lions, and the cave lions began pursuing them, wondering if they would make a tasty meal." He turned to Derek.

"The cave lions saw that Derek Dagger was among the humans. This frightened them so much they decided to leap into a ravine filled with deadly snakes, choosing to die from snake venom rather than risking Derek Dagger's wrath." Derek turned to Ripple.

Ripple's ring of red lights flashed twice before it began speaking. "Fortunately, Lincoln and his tribemates were accompanied by Ripple, a drone with a lifesaving ability to use magnetic pole triangulation, in conjunction with analysis and reanalysis of visual data collected while traversing the landscape, to retrace the hunters' route back to their point of origin, at least with relatively consistent success, and depending on the uniformity or diversity of the landscape, as well as certain atmospheric conditions. As the ill-equipped hunters were beginning to realize the seriousness of their predicament, Ripple humbly and unpretentiously reminded them they were in the presence of a drone with remarkable on-board technology, which could in fact be used to their advantage if they would only remember to—"

"You lose the game, Ripple—too long!" Skyra said. "And your words do not make sense. *At-at-at-at-at... at-at-at-at.*"

Ripple's red lights flashed again. "I object to being required to follow rules that have not been clearly stated before the game."

Skyra laughed again, and this time Lincoln and his tribemates laughed with her. She ignored Ripple and started a new story. "Di-woto stayed in the city of ghost people because she wanted to be like a sunbeam. Di-woto is happy there. Today she decided to make something beautiful." She turned to Lincoln and waited.

He blinked once. "Uh, okay. Di-woto decided she wanted to make a castle tall enough to reach the moon." He turned to Jazzlyn.

Skyra smiled as she watched her friends play the game. She had surprised herself by starting a story about Di-woto. Her chest had hurt lately each time she thought about Di-woto. Skyra missed the girl, almost as much as she missed Veenah, but maybe telling a story about Di-woto would make some of the pain go away. She decided her next story would be about Veenah.

Virgil waited too long to tell his part of the story, so Skyra burst out laughing and started the story again. Her friends laughed too. At least for now, maybe they were not thinking about the dangers and struggles of the coming days.

5

RIVER

47,659 years in the past - Day 2

As the morning's first light illuminated the cave entrance, Lincoln vowed to figure out a way to make a more comfortable bed. The sleeping bag, as well as Skyra's body next to him, had provided warmth, but the bag offered little cushioning against bare rock. Lincoln had insisted Jazzlyn and Virgil use the only remaining inflatable sleeping pad—the other three pads had been discarded 95,000 years in the future to make room in the body bags for the building supplies donated by the virtual beings.

Due to sheer exhaustion, Lincoln had slept a good portion of the night, although he had fuzzy memories of shifting frequently in an endless quest to find comfort. As far as he could tell, everyone else in the cave had slept soundly.

He gazed at Ripple's silhouette in the cave opening. The drone had its front legs withdrawn into its shell and hind legs fully extended, tilting its body at an odd angle in order to focus its vision lens on the two rat-sized robots. Lincoln assumed the robots were now useless—they hadn't moved since their components had crawled from Jazzlyn's body and reassembled themselves. Apparently, they had expended their stored power, and now, away from the city of virtual beings, they had no way to recharge.

Lincoln began crawling out of the sleeping bag, trying not to wake Skyra. She grabbed his wrist, however, and silently pulled him back. He leaned over her and gently kissed her mouth. He and Skyra had made love several times, but he had always assumed she would not understand the significance of kissing, so he'd been reluctant to try it before.

She pulled her face back and whispered, "Why did you do that?"

He kept his face inches from hers and whispered back. "It's called a kiss. It's how my people show they love someone. I love you, Skyra, so I wanted to kiss you."

"Bolups are strange people. I do not know if I like a kiss. Kiss me again."

He did. This time he pressed harder and longer, and he even touched her lips with his tongue. Skyra's lips were much thicker than his, but they responded to the touch of his lips with surprising sensitivity, which he found intensely erotic. She kissed him back as if she were exploring every possible sensation of the new experience. Lincoln was almost startled by the sweet taste and scent of her mouth. He already knew Skyra was obsessive about bathing. Now he suspected her people must have developed effective rituals for oral hygiene, perhaps by chewing certain plants.

She finally pulled back. "I have decided I like a kiss. Now you will stay in this sleeping bag with me because I want more than a kiss." She slipped her arm around his neck and pulled him closer.

"Um, I don't think I can do that with everyone else right here in this chamber."

Derek's voice came through the semidarkness. "Not something I want to hear first thing in the morning."

"Oh, don't be a romance killer, Derek," Jazzlyn said. "They're still on their honeymoon."

Lincoln pulled Skyra's arm from around his neck. "See what I mean? I just can't. It's something my people do when no one else is around."

She growled and released him. "Then we must find our own cave in this hill."

"That," he said, leaning in again to peck her cheek, "is an excellent idea." He crawled out of the bag and over to Ripple, then he sat cross-legged beside the drone. "Have you been staring at those things all night?"

Ripple's red lights rotated clockwise once, faintly illuminating the two robotic caretakers. "I find them to be fascinating. Lincoln, if you had designed me so I was made of smaller components, each capable of autonomous actions on their own, I would be far more useful. Why did you not think of that?"

"Was that an attempt at humor? It took Kods and Thide and the other virtual people thousands of years to develop the technology."

Ripple continued staring at the robots. "It is a fascinating concept, worthy of study."

Lincoln considered reminding Ripple that he had developed temporal displacement technology, something the virtual beings had never accomplished, but he decided not to bother arguing with one of his own drones. He sighed and said, "Yeah, it's too bad these things have run out of power."

"That is the conundrum I am currently pondering. I detect a low level of reserve power, which is allowing limited cognitive function in these devices. I am attempting to identify a data transfer protocol to allow me to communicate with them."

Lincoln suppressed a chuckle. "That seems unlikely, considering these were developed by Neanderthals, in a completely different timeline, and 47,000 years *after* you were developed. Don't you think?"

After several seconds, Ripple said, "We shall see."

Lincoln started to turn away then paused. "You know, I've been concerned about how Skyra would respond to being in the presence of another version of herself, but I haven't considered your response to having another Ripple around."

The drone extended its front legs until its body was level and turned its vision lens to face Lincoln. "Interesting. The fact that you would ask such a question of a drone underlies the logic behind a decision I have already made."

"What decision is that?"

"Lincoln, you are remarkable in that you understand the abiotic, nonhuman nature of robotic drones better than any other person of your timeline, yet you allow yourself to think of those drones as if they were your human friends. Your emotions defy your own logic."

"What's your point?"

"I have decided what to do with the other Ripple."

Lincoln shook his head. "I'm not following."

"We remove the other Ripple's cognitive module, we take the cognitive module you have been carefully guarding in the pocket of your trousers, and we install it into the other Ripple's body. The other Ripple then becomes Maddy."

Lincoln inhaled sharply. "When did you come up with that idea?"

"Before we even jumped back here to Skyra's time. Surely you agree it is an excellent idea, Lincoln. Maddy was your closest friend."

As sad as that statement seemed, Ripple was right. Lincoln had always had loyal employees but never friends. In fact, he'd learned more about the concept of friendship during these last few harrowing weeks than in all the previous years of his life. Jazzlyn, Virgil, and Derek were now more than employees, they were his friends. Skyra was even more than his friend. Before them, however, his only friend had been Maddy, his personal assistant and close confidante—Maddy the drone.

"What if the other Ripple objects to having its brain pulled from its head?" Derek asked. He was sitting up now, with his sleeping bag still pulled to his shoulders against the cool morning air. "It's your idea, Ripple—maybe *you* should be the one to cough up your cognitive module."

"I possess valuable knowledge of recent events the other Ripple does not possess. Your suggestion is absurd."

"Bolups talk too much!" Skyra said. She shoved the sleeping bag off and got up, then she started combing her fingers through her hair, which had become almost comically disheveled during the night. "I am going to the river to bathe and to drink. We must all drink, so our bodies and heads will not become weak and sick."

"Hold on a second," Virgil said, crawling from the sleeping bag he'd shared with Jazzlyn. He pulled a black nylon bag from the pile of gear. "We still have our water filter. Even if we don't use the filter, we can fill the two bladders and bring some water back with us. If we do that each morning, maybe we'll only need to hike to the river once per day."

"Maybe we will find crayfish in the river," Skyra said. "We will need something to carry them in."

Virgil poked around in the pile and produced one of the remaining small daypacks. "Not exactly what it was made for, but this should work."

Skyra accepted the pack, then she started pulling on her leather footwraps as Lincoln and the others put on their shoes.

"Ripple, you will stay here outside the cave where you can watch for Veenah," Skyra said. "If Veenah and the other Skyra come, they will not know where our cave is."

"I will watch for them," Ripple replied. The drone then began using one of its rubberized forefeet to nudge the two rat-sized robots through the cave opening, apparently intending to continue studying them while also watching for Veenah.

With spears and khuls in hand, Lincoln and the others crawled through the cave opening onto the ledge overlooking the river plain. They stood silently for at least a minute, scanning the rocky fields for any sign of Veenah or the bolup tribe.

Lincoln spotted a herd of deer-like animals moving from right to left in the distance, and he pointed.

"Ibexes," Skyra said. "I killed my first ibex when I had seen ten cold seasons." She glanced over at him. "I will try to teach you how to hunt them."

"You'll *try*? If you killed one when you were ten, I'm sure I can learn to do it."

She didn't reply, perhaps choosing to be polite. She stared at the scene, methodically shifting her eyes back and forth.

"Don't worry, the other Skyra will bring Veenah back," Lincoln said. "The other Ripple will make sure of it."

"Lincoln is correct," Ripple said. "The other Ripple has developed the same grand plan that I developed. The other Ripple understands the plan is more likely to succeed with everyone together in one place."

Lincoln shook his head, once again amazed at the drone's tenacity regarding its crazy plan. "I'm not a geneticist, but it seems to me your grand plan is loaded with serious flaws. Here we are, attempting to start a colony with only five people —seven if you count Veenah and the other Skyra—and you think we're going to repopulate the entire world with our offspring? I understand enough about genetics to know that's an extreme genetic bottleneck. There's not enough genetic diversity among seven people to produce a viable population." Lincoln turned expectantly to Jazzlyn, the most knowledge-able paleontologist he'd ever hired.

She puckered her lips for a moment before speaking. "Definitely a genetic bottleneck. However, you'd be surprised at some of the success stories of extreme bottlenecks. Chee-tahs are one example. In the past, cheetahs went through two bottleneck events and rebounded successfully both times. The first was about 100,000 years ago. Cheetahs lived in North America then, but most of them vacated the continent, leaving behind only a few isolated groups, too far apart to interbreed. Those small groups eventually repopulated North America. The second bottleneck was even more extreme. By the end of the last ice age, the cheetahs in America and Europe had died out completely, and genetic studies show that the population in Africa was reduced to only *seven* cheetahs."

"Seven?" Lincoln exclaimed, truly surprised.

She nodded. "If you want a more relevant example, some

studies suggest the entire native population of humans throughout North and South America was the result of only seventy individuals who crossed the land bridge from Asia to North America."

"Indeed," said Ripple. "However, those examples are only peripherally relevant to my grand plan. You are not a bottle-neck population of five, seven, or even seventy. This region is currently inhabited by numerous thriving and genetically diverse tribes of *Homo sapiens* as well as *Homo neanderthalensis*. My plan involves the gradual spreading of the genetic qualities of *sapiens-neanderthalensis* hybrids throughout these existing populations. Optimally, these hybrids would be primarily the result of combining Lincoln's DNA with Skyra's DNA."

"There it is," Derek boomed. "The reason why Derek, Virgil and Jazz aren't important in any of this."

Ripple turned to face Derek. "True, you are less important, but as I have explained before, you three can be valuable also. Ideally, Lincoln would mate with both Skyras, as well as Veenah, considering she is Skyra's identical twin and genetic clone."

"That is not happening," Lincoln said forcefully.

"Yes, as I predicted. Therefore, Derek, you must pick up the slack, as they say. I would encourage you to mate with Veenah, the other Skyra, or both. Unfortunately, Virgil and Jazzlyn seem to have formed a pair bond already. If their relationship should turn sour, or if one should die, we should endeavor to pair one or both with local Neanderthals."

Jazzlyn let out a hearty laugh. "Damn, Ripple, you just managed to insult every person here. You don't know diddly-squat about human emotions, do you?"

"I have what knowledge Lincoln has given me, and I try to learn from observation."

Lincoln smiled, but he was still unclear on the logic of Ripple's plan. "Not that I think your plan has any chance of working, but I have another question. It sounds like you're expecting our genetic traits to spread throughout the overall nandup and bolup populations over time. Won't those traits get diluted so much they'll be lost entirely?"

"If genetic traits were diluted in the same way liquids are diluted, yes. However, genetic traits are subject to selective pressures in the environment. Traits that help increase survival—and ultimately reproductive success—are retained intact from one generation to the next. Those individuals with the traits are more likely to have offspring than those without the traits."

"Natural selection 101, Lincoln," Jazzlyn interjected.

Ripple continued. "Perhaps my plan will make more sense if you understand the concept of a mitochondrial Eve."

Jazzlyn said, "I can take this one, Ripple." She faced Lincoln. "Basically, a mitochondrial Eve is the most recent female historically from which all living animals of a species can trace their ancestry. It does *not* refer to the first female of a species. Here's an example I happen to know about. The mitochondrial Eve for sperm whales is thought to be a female that lived somewhere in the range of 50,000 years ago—well, 50,000 years before you and I were born in our original timeline. That female was *not* the very first sperm whale. Heck, sperm whales existed millions of years before then, and there were plenty of other female sperm whales swimming around at that time. She wasn't the first, she just happened to be the most recent female to pass down the mitochondrial DNA all modern sperm whales possess. For whatever reason, all the other lineages died out. Every animal species has a mitochondrial Eve somewhere in its past. The mitochondrial Eve of all living humans of our timeline was a female who lived about 200,000 years before we were born."

Lincoln turned to Ripple. "So, you think Skyra could become the mitochondrial Eve of all future humans?"

Ripple said, "Not all future *humans*, but future hybrids of humans and Neanderthals. I have every reason to believe you and Skyra will produce alinga-uls, probably even superior to Di-woto. Their traits will enhance their survival. They will likely find their own mates in neighboring tribes and produce their own offspring. Those offspring will disperse and find their own mates in neighboring tribes, and so on. Each generation resulting from your and Skyra's DNA will have a better chance of success than the other nandups and bolups. The superior traits will not be diluted because those individuals without the traits will simply be less likely to survive to produce offspring. This will result in a world thousands of years later populated by superior alinga-uls. This will be a better world, based on the legacy of you, Lincoln, and you, Skyra."

Lincoln glanced at Skyra, who was again gazing at the river plain, apparently having given up on understanding the conversation. He inhaled deeply, marveling at the fact that the morning air here contained not a single molecule of pollutants from factories or vehicles. "Considering we're here to stay, I don't mind doing whatever we can to facilitate your plan, Ripple. Maybe this world will have a brighter future as a result of our presence here, maybe it won't. We'll never know. Kods, Thide, and the other virtual beings seemed to believe it was possible, which lends more credibility to your plan than I've been willing to give it."

Virgil said, "If we're going to seriously consider how we can facilitate such a far-reaching outcome, let's be realistic about the sequence of events that would need to occur. One that comes to mind is that humans and Neanderthals would have to learn to get along. Otherwise, if Neanderthals do not go extinct, the two species will end up perpetually at war with each other. We've already seen that scenario."

Skyra finally turned away from the river plain to face them. "You bolups are different from the bolups of this land. The bolups here raid nandup camps. They kill the men and take the women. They do not wash themselves, and they stink. They eat any animals they can kill. They even eat their dead tribemates."

Lincoln waited for her to go on, but she fell silent.

"In other words, nandups here don't like bolups very much," Derek said.

Jazzlyn said, "Which probably explains why modern humans of our original timeline only have about two percent Neanderthal DNA—probably the result of occasional forced matings. Ripple's plan would require more widespread intermixing."

"Humans and Neanderthals would have to learn to get along," Virgil repeated.

"Nope, no chance of that," Derek said.

Lincoln nudged Skyra's arm. "What do you think? Could your people ever decide to be friends with the bolup tribes?"

She bared her teeth, indicating either humor or ridicule. It was an expression he couldn't read. "No. Bolups stink."

"What if the bolups didn't stink? What if they didn't eat their tribemates? What if they didn't raid nandup camps?"

She bared her teeth again, and Lincoln still wasn't sure

what the expression meant. "Then they would not be bolups. They would be nandups."

***

THE GROUP DESCENDED the boulder hill and hiked to the river without incident. There was no sign of Veenah or the other Skyra. Lincoln hoped the other Ripple had convinced them, and they would show up today, but he was apprehensive about another confrontation between the two Skyras. He was also concerned Veenah may have perished during the night. In the previous timeline, she had survived several days before being murdered by Gelrut, but that may have been because Lincoln's team had quickly treated her wounds with antibiotic cream and sterile bandaging.

At the river, Skyra immediately removed her garments and footwraps and plunged into the water. She seemed to have no concept of modesty regarding her naked body. Lincoln was now even more worried about being regarded by Skyra as a *stinking bolup*, plus he didn't want to get his clothes or Maddy's cognitive module wet, so he stripped down and plunged into the cool water also.

Seconds later, Derek did the same, followed—surprisingly—by Jazzlyn.

Skyra propelled herself through the knee-deep water to Jazzlyn's side and inspected her arrow wounds.

Curious, Lincoln moved closer, uncomfortably aware he was staring at Jazzlyn's nude body. The wounds appeared to be healing, with no signs of swelling or infection. He said, "As impossible as it seems, I'm becoming convinced those little robots really did do something in there to help you out."

"Helping is what the robot creatures are for," Skyra said as if stating the obvious. She looked up at Jazzlyn. "Maybe you will still be able to grow the baby Virgil will put in your belly." She then flopped onto her back and began pushing her fingers through her hair to wash it.

Jazzlyn glanced back at Virgil, who was still clothed on the river bank. "She just says whatever she thinks, doesn't she?"

Virgil seemed suddenly fascinated with his one-legged pair of pants, and he fiddled with the clasp for several seconds. Then he let his hands fall to his sides, apparently deciding not to remove the pants, and stepped into the river fully clothed. He sat on his butt in the water. "These clothes need washing anyway," he said, grinning.

Derek grabbed the two water bladders from shore, moved upstream a few yards, then filled them and twisted on the caps before placing them back on the rocks.

Within a few minutes in the river, Lincoln felt more relaxed than he had since jumping back here to Skyra's time. His team began splashing each other and laughing, and even Skyra joined in, adding her distinctive nandup *aheee-at-at-at-at* to the mix. Lincoln understood his group's survival chances were slim at best, but for the moment he allowed himself to imagine this was what their lives would be like. Maybe they would not get sick and die. Maybe they would learn to hunt game and collect edible plants. Maybe they would avoid predators and murderous tribes. Maybe.

"Crayfish!" Skyra shouted. She flipped the crustacean onto the rocks at the river's bank.

"I got it." Derek jumped to his feet and rushed to shore, where the crayfish was already trying to crawl back in. He kicked it away from the water's edge, grabbed the daypack, then plucked the creature from the rocks and dropped it in.

"Crayfish stay under rocks," Skyra said. "Here is how to catch them." She lifted another of the rocks, shoved her hand in, and pulled out a second crayfish. "They are fast, so *you* must be fast." She threw it at Derek so hard it smacked his chest before dropping to the rocks.

"Shellfish for dinner, baby!" Derek chuckled. "Keep 'em coming."

Lincoln joined the hunt, and within minutes he managed to grab his first crayfish. As he flipped it toward Derek, though, the thing had clamped one of its pinchers onto his finger, and it flew at an angle into the water and escaped.

"Too slow, Lincoln!" Skyra exclaimed.

He grinned at her and inspected his finger, which wasn't bleeding, then went back to the hunt. His grin felt like it might never fade away.

They gradually moved upstream, finding suitable rocks to lift, and before long Derek's pack was bulging with crayfish.

Jazzlyn squealed. "Look at that—I actually got a fish!" She pointed to the brown, foot-long fish flopping on the shore where she had tossed it. She rose to her full height and did a little dance move. "That's right, uh-huh, uh-huh, a fish, uh-huh, uh-huh."

The sight of Jazzlyn dancing naked in a river in the wilderness triggered another round of laughter.

Derek fumbled with the fish before getting it into the pack. As he straightened up, his smile abruptly faded. "Oh, shit! Get out now!" He was staring across the river.

Lincoln spun around.

"Ebo-do-yanol!" shouted a man who was approaching the river. Just behind him six more men emerged from the trees.

Lincoln recognized them immediately—the seven uninjured, surviving men of the bolup tribe. Three of them were holding bows with arrows nocked, and they were close enough for their arrows to be deadly. Feeling completely vulnerable, Lincoln glanced downstream and exhaled a curse. His group had moved so far upstream that he could no longer even see their weapons.

"Run!" Skyra commanded, and she bounded from the river.

Lincoln followed, expecting to feel an arrow pierce his back at any moment. Beside him, Virgil tripped and fell face-first into the water but was back on his feet before Lincoln could help him up.

Lincoln leapt from the water and glanced back at the men. They were now at the river's edge on the opposite shore. The three with bows had not pulled back but were obviously ready to do so at any moment. Lincoln ran with the others, trying to ignore the pain of the bare rocks against his feet. He didn't look back again until he'd grabbed his spear and khul. The seven tribesmen were approaching along the opposite shore, only a short distance back.

"Ebo-do-yanol!" the man repeated.

Derek dropped the daypack and began pulling on his shoes. "What do they want, Skyra? Why haven't they attacked yet?"

"I do not know. We must be ready to fight or to run." Skyra pulled on her footwraps without taking her eyes off the men.

"Put your shoes on," Lincoln said to Jazzlyn and Virgil as he pulled on his own shoes.

Seconds later, they were ready to run, although only Virgil had his clothes on.

The men stopped directly across from the group. They

brandished their weapons, but the archers still did not bend their bows.

"Ebo-do-yanol!"

"We do not understand your language," Lincoln called out.

Several of the men spoke to each other, then they all stepped into the river.

"I do not want to fight these men," Skyra said. "I have seen what their bows can do. Pick up your garments and be ready to run."

"God almighty," Virgil muttered, fear straining his voice, as the others gathered their clothes.

The men began crossing the river. They only outnumbered Lincoln's group by two, but all seven were probably experienced fighters, whereas Skyra was the only true warrior on this side of the river. Lincoln's group had killed these men before, but that victory had been aided by the element of surprise, not to mention the confusion created by the forest fire they had intentionally started for that purpose.

Lincoln swallowed his fear and decided he needed to try something. "Stay behind me and be ready to run," he said to the others. He put his clothes, khul, and spear on the ground, then he raised both his arms and stepped toward the river. "Please do not come any closer!"

The men paused, staring. Facing them now at only ten yards, Lincoln remembered how frightening these tribesmen appeared. Although their basic facial features were no different from the humans of Lincoln's time 47,000 years in the future, these men were bedraggled and scarred. One man was missing an eye, the socket nothing more than a dark, gaping hole. Another had a disfigured upper arm, apparently from an old wound so horrific that his bicep muscle was almost entirely missing, rendering the arm too weak to be useful. Lincoln could even smell their animal-like muskiness. The idea of making peace with such people suddenly seemed naive. It'd probably be easier to make peace with scimitar-toothed cats.

Skyra stepped up beside him, still holding her weapons and garments. "Why are you talking to them? They do not understand your language."

"I know. I just... I had to do something. We can't fight every time we encounter them."

The men were now exchanging glances, and Lincoln hoped they weren't preparing to attack.

"They are stinking bolups," Skyra said, as if this were all he needed to know.

"Yes, and *I'm* a bolup. They're the same kind of people as me and my team. Which means they're capable of being peaceful."

The men resumed their approach, still holding their weapons ready.

"Pick up your garments and weapons, Lincoln," Skyra said. "I think they are trying to make us go away. If we do not go, we will have to fight."

One of the men said, "Ebo-do-yanol. Ebo-dufu." They were now less than ten feet from Lincoln and were still moving closer.

Lincoln's will to stand his ground evaporated. "Okay, maybe you're right." He grabbed his things, then he and Skyra backed away.

The men stepped from the river onto the rocky shore.

Skyra glanced over her shoulder at Lincoln's team. "We will go now. We will not run, and you will not attack the bolup men unless they attack us."

"You won't have to tell me *that* twice," Derek said. He picked up the pack full of crayfish and the two bladders of water.

Mostly naked, their arms loaded with clothing and weapons, they all backed away from the approaching tribesmen. They continued through the band of trees lining the river and onto the rocky field between the river and the boulder hill.

The tribesmen stopped following when they emerged from the trees. They stood motionless, staring after the group.

Lincoln finally exhaled in relief when he was almost halfway to the boulder hill.

"What in the name of rock-n-roll was that about?" Jazzlyn asked.

"Seems obvious to me," Derek replied. "We're in their territory, and they want us to get the hell out."

Skyra stopped walking to stare back at the men, who were still watching from the edge of the trees. "We will have to kill them," she said matter-of-factly. "Their camp is too near."

Lincoln took advantage of the pause to put his clothes back on. "According to Ripple's plan, we need to become friends with them."

Skyra let out a strange huffing sound that could have been a brief laugh, or possibly an expression of disgust.

For the next minute or so, they pulled on their clothing without speaking.

Virgil gazed at the men. "Well, now they know where our camp is. I, for one, won't be sleeping well tonight."

As Lincoln pulled on his pants, he checked to make sure Maddy's cognitive module was still in his pocket. He took one more look at the men. "Listen, we need to fortify our camp, and I think we need to spend every waking moment working until it's done. We'll use the building materials the virtual beings gave us, and anything else we can find. We'll make the boulder hill a fortress we can defend." He turned to Skyra. "Do you have any other ideas for how we can be safe?"

"We must kill the bolups."

He sighed. "I don't think we should kill unless we have to. Do you have any ideas besides killing?"

A low growl came from her throat. "The bolups did not attack us because we were together. They thought we were going to kill them. If we do not kill the bolups, we must always stay together. Do not go to the river alone. Do not go hunting alone. I will teach you how to fight better with our weapons. We must make the bolups afraid of us."

They all remained silent for several seconds. Skyra looked to the west, her concern for Veenah obviously growing.

"Maybe she's right," Derek said. "Maybe we *do* need to kill them—again."

They resumed crossing the field toward the hill of boulders.

6

———

CAVES

47,659 YEARS *in the past - Day 2*

SKYRA STARED at the strange objects arranged on the rock ledge. Lincoln had said the objects were tools for making things using the reflective material and poles from the ghost people. Skyra knew what tools were, but she had never seen tools like these. They were all black, and were different shapes and sizes. Lincoln and his tribemates did not know how to use them. As usual, they wanted to talk about what the tools might do instead of simply picking them up and using them.

Carrying the poles and material up to the cave had required many tiring trips, and Skyra already wished she could bathe in the river again, whether the bolup men were still there or not. Washing would have to wait, though. Lincoln seemed convinced he and his tribemates could use the supplies to make the hill of boulders easier to defend. Skyra wasn't sure how that was possible, but Lincoln had made a T3 to jump people many, many years through time, so if he said he could do something, she believed him.

The others were still talking about the tools, and Ripple was still staring at the little robot caretakers, so Skyra grunted and picked up her bolup-made spear. "Lincoln, I am going to search this hill for other caves. We must have our own cave because I want us to make love when we wake up."

They all fell silent. Lincoln's face turned red, as if he were sitting too close to a campfire.

Jazzlyn coughed out a short bolup laugh. "Damn, maybe we should all be so honest."

"I do not know what that means," Skyra said.

"It means I think you're awesome. And I agree—you and Lincoln are married and should have some privacy."

"I'll go with you," Lincoln said, stepping away from his tribemates. "We can also locate places that need to be blocked to stop people from coming up the hill."

Skyra nodded at the spear in her hand and gave him a look.

"Crap, you're right," he said, picking up his own spear. Skyra noticed he had selected the other bolup spear taken from the tribesmen. With their stone points, these spears were better than the crude spears the group had made by sharpening long sticks.

Skyra and Lincoln moved to the end of the ledge, crawled through the narrow gap to the boulder slab below, then descended the slope to the next level down, following the now-familiar route. Skyra heard Lincoln's tribemates talking and laughing above but could not tell what they were saying.

She turned to Lincoln. "Your face is red. Did the crayfish make you sick?" The group had made a fire with Derek's fire tool and had cooked Jazzlyn's fish and all the crayfish by poking sticks through them and holding them over the flames. Lincoln had eaten many of the crayfish.

"No, I'm fine. My face is red because I was a little embarrassed when you talked about us making love."

"I thought you liked to call it making love. Do you want me to call it something else?"

He showed his teeth with a bolup smile. "No, I like those words, but I'm not used to talking about making love in front of my team."

She grunted. "You understand many things by talking to your team. Do you not want to understand making love?"

"Um... I think I *do* understand it. I'm just not comfortable talking about it in front of them. I like making love with you, though."

She nodded, a gesture she had learned from Lincoln. "I try to understand you, but sometimes I cannot. Some things you like to talk about but do not like to do. Some things you like to do but do not like to talk about."

"It does sound confusing when you put it that way. You know what? I like that you try to understand me. I want to understand you too." He leaned in and put his mouth on hers.

When he pulled away, she said, "Why does a kiss make me want to make love with you?"

He gazed at her. "Maybe Ripple was right—we are a good match for each other. We have what my people call *chemistry*."

"Chemistry," she said slowly. "My people call it *khomuwai*. That is the word we use when we taste a food we like very much, like the heart of a hedgehog. Have you eaten a hedgehog heart, Lincoln?"

"Not that I know of."

"You would know! You and the hedgehog heart would have chemistry."

His smile formed again. "Okay. I look forward to you teaching me how to eat a hedgehog heart."

"I will teach you when we find a hedgehog."

He nodded. After gazing at her for a few more breaths, he turned and scanned the surrounding boulders. Skyra looked across the river plain for Veenah and her other self. The only movement she saw was a herd of ibexes moving toward the river and two eagles soaring in a wide circle above the forest beyond the low hills, where the bolup camp was located. Her chest began to hurt, so she told her head to stop thinking about her birthmate. If Veenah was not here by the time the sun showed itself tomorrow morning, Skyra would go search for her, even if she had to go all the way to Una-Loto camp.

"You see that?" Lincoln asked. He was pointing toward a sloping gap between two rock slabs. The upper end of the gap was blocked by a jumble of small boulders, which would be easy to climb over. "It looks like there's an open area beyond that gap. Let's check it out."

They made their way around several massive boulders to the sloped rock leading into the gap. They climbed over the jumble of small boulders and found themselves on a wide ledge. The ledge became narrower as they followed it around the side of the hill, with a drop-off on one side and a sheer rock face on the other. They came to another gap in the rock face, and a short distance in they were stopped by another pile of fallen boulders forming a chest-high barrier.

"Caves," Skyra said, pointing at several dark openings beyond the barrier. She instinctively examined the rocks blocking the gap. Coarse black hairs were stuck to some of the sharper edges, obviously scraped from an animal that frequently passed through here. She picked up a tuft of the hairs and sniffed them. "Cave bear."

"Must be the same bear my team said they saw climbing around the first time we were here," Lincoln said. "Are cave bears dangerous?"

She glanced at him then stared at the caves beyond the barrier. "Yes, if you make them angry. Their meat is good to eat, and their fur makes a good bed. They choose good caves." She checked the bolup-made stone point on her spear then took Lincoln's spear and checked it also. Both were tight. They were thinner and lighter than the spear tips she liked to use, but they were sharp and expertly knapped. She handed his spear back. "Cave bears do not easily give up their meat and fur and caves. It is good we have these bolup spears."

His eyes grew wide. "You're not suggesting we try to kill it, are you?"

"This hill of boulders is now our camp. A cave bear cannot live in our home."

His eyes remained wide. "How big is a cave bear?"

She could not hold back her laughter any longer. "*At-at-at-at*. Do not be afraid, Lincoln! You are not yet ready to learn how to kill cave bears. If the cave bear is here, we will scare it away."

"What if it isn't afraid?"

Instead of replying, she handed him her spear and scrambled over the rock barrier. He passed both spears over then joined her, and soon they stood in an almost flat open area surrounded by massive boulders and rock walls. Skyra counted six dark openings, more than she had seen from the gap. Three appeared too small to enter, but the others were worth exploring. Skyra turned in a circle, studying the walls of the open area. Other than the gap they had come through, she saw no easy way to get into the area. With the gap blocked and defended, attacking bolups might be able to get in if they were skilled at climbing, but they would have to use their hands as well as their feet, which meant they would be vulnerable and easy to kill. If at least one of the openings led to a suitable cave, this would be a good place for a camp.

Lincoln was staring at one of the openings. "Isn't it kind of dangerous for us to be here?"

"Be ready to use your spear," she replied. She approached the nearest of the larger openings and quickly saw the chamber was no deeper than two of her body lengths, and there was no flat area on the floor, just a steeply-angled slab of rock.

Lincoln had approached one of the other large openings and was holding his spear point toward the cave as if he expected something to charge out. "I think the bear must be in this one. I can smell something in there."

"Cave bears are not predators, Lincoln." She moved to his side and wrinkled her nose at the strong smell. "They can kill, but they do not hunt. They eat plants. They only attack if you make them angry."

He did not take his eyes off the cave opening. "How do you know so much about them?"

"My people hunt cave bears."

He glanced at her. "Have *you* hunted them?"

"Yes."

"How do you kill a cave bear?"

"You must use spears. Khuls will not hurt them. You must fight them inside their cave."

"Inside? Why?"

"You must be inside the cave where you can hold the end of your spear against the cave wall. Cave bears are big, and their skin is thick." Skyra moved to a boulder on one side of the opening and put the butt of her spear against the stone, with the stone point toward Lincoln. "What will happen to you if you charge at me now?"

He nodded. "I get it, but I'm starting to think your people might be crazy."

Ripple had taught Skyra that word several seasons back. "Some of my people *are* crazy. Flalla was crazy. She was two cold seasons younger than me. She believed beetles were crawling into her mouth at night. She said the beetles were eating the inside of her head."

Lincoln pulled his gaze from the cave opening and gave her a strange look. "Really?"

"Flalla crushed her own head with a rock to kill the beetles. I saw the inside of her head, but I did not see any beetles there."

He blinked. "Jesus."

"You still have not told me what *Jesus* means."

He seemed to think about this for several breaths. "I'm still trying to figure out how to do that."

Skyra let out a growl and moved to the last of the larger cave openings. This one did not smell of cave bear, probably because there was a slanted boulder partially blocking the opening, making it too small for an adult cave bear to pass through. Gripping her spear, she scooted around the slanted boulder and ducked inside. The space was almost as large as the chamber she and the others had slept in the previous night. The interior was dry, and at least half of the stone floor was flat. Several gaps in the boulders above would allow smoke to escape. "Lincoln," she called out, "I have found a—"

"Skyra!"

Her muscles tensed. She scrambled over the slanted rock and out the opening.

Lincoln was backing away from the other cave. "It's coming out!"

She moved to his side quickly but without running. Cave bears were easily startled, and they did not like being surprised.

"What do we do now?" he asked.

At first Skyra didn't see anything but darkness in the cave opening. Then she spotted light reflecting from two eyes. The cave bear was staring out at them. "We must kill it or scare it away. I found a cave where we can make love when we wake up."

She sensed Lincoln turning to look at her, but she did not want to take her eyes off the cave bear. She turned her spear to hold the shaft across Lincoln's belly, then she used the spear to pull him with her as she backed away.

The bear's head emerged from the cave.

"Jesus," Lincoln said. "We can't possibly kill that thing. We'll find another cave, Skyra."

She continued pulling him until their backs were against the rock wall enclosing the open area. "We must not block its path to the gap."

The cave bear came all the way out, and Skyra heard Lincoln suck in a chestful of air. "Jesus," he said again.

"It is a female," Skyra whispered. "Female cave bears are small."

"No... they are not."

"Do not move. I will scare it away."

"Skyra!" he hissed.

The cave bear took a few more steps into the open area then stopped and stared at the intruders.

Skyra slowly moved away from Lincoln, making her way along the rock wall toward the cave opening.

The bear turned its head, following her movements.

Skyra stopped when the bear was directly between her and the gap where it could escape. She tightened her grip on her spear and spoke softly. "Kami-fu-alodonlo. Aibul-tekne-té-menga-ulmecko. Ati-de-lé-melu-rha." *Listen to me speak, cave bear. I have the strength of the woolly rhino and cave lion. I will not submit to you.*

The bear huffed.

Skyra slammed the butt of her spear onto the rock at her feet. "Kami-fu-alodonlo! Ati-de-lé-melu-rha!"

The bear huffed again and ran for the gap. Its claws scratched and clacked against the piled rocks as it heaved its body over the chest-high barrier, then it was gone.

Lincoln stepped away from the rock wall. "I can't believe it. You really scared it away!"

Skyra was surprised too, and her heart was still pounding, making her feel light on her feet. "The cave bear will come back, but it will see we have taken its home, and it will not stay. Maybe your tribemates will come here and help us kill the bear when it comes back."

"I don't see any reason to risk our lives. I'm fine with eating crayfish."

Skyra walked to the cave opening and peered into the darkness. "Crayfish do not have soft fur for sleeping on, Lincoln."

He came up beside her and sniffed. "I wonder how long it will take for the smell to go away."

The opening to this cave was so tall Skyra did not even have to crouch to step inside. She paused to let her eyes adjust to the darkness. The bear cave was even larger than the one beside it, with a wide, flat floor. A stone column, from floor to ceiling, stood in the center, and the chamber narrowed toward the back but became too dark to see how far it went.

She nudged Lincoln's arm. "Cave bears choose the best caves. I like this cave. We will stay here."

"I like it too, but I don't like that the bear will be coming back."

She lowered her head to keep from hitting the ceiling and moved toward the darkness in the narrowing end of the cave. "We will be ready when it returns." She took a few more steps before she had to tap the floor with her spear to make sure she was not about to step over a drop-off. "The smell is stronger. The cave bear must sleep back here in the dark."

A slight shifting sound came from the darkness ahead.

Skyra froze. Her legs wanted to run, and she had to fight to keep them still. Something was moving just in front of her, maybe one or more cave bear cubs. If the cubs were small, they would be easy to kill and would supply her new tribe with good meat.

"Something wrong, Skyra?" Lincoln stepped toward her, but she held out a hand to stop him. "What is it?" he asked.

A roar filled the chamber, so loud and sudden that Skyra stumbled back into Lincoln.

A massive black shape charged from the darkness.

"Alodonlo! Alodonlo!" Skyra shouted as she lunged to one side to divert the cave bear's attention away from Lincoln. Her shoulder slammed into the cave wall, and she shoved the end of her spear against the rock just as the creature changed direction and charged at her in a roaring fit of rage.

The bear ran straight into Skyra's spear, driving the weapon deep into its throat beneath its chin. She felt the shaft snap just beyond her grip, so she dove to one side.

"No!" Lincoln shouted, and he rushed in and stabbed his spear into the bear.

The creature's roar became a thunderous bellow. It reeled backwards then spun in a panicked effort to escape its pain. Its shoulder slammed into the stone column at the center of the chamber.

The column gave way. In less than a breath, several slabs of rock fell from the ceiling onto the bear.

"Get out, Skyra!" Lincoln shouted, and he scrambled toward the opening.

She started after him then paused. The falling rocks and the bear were now silent. The creature's head and shoulders were beneath two stone slabs at least the size of Skyra's body. Its legs were still, and its chest was not heaving to suck in air.

She turned to Lincoln. "The cave bear is dead."

Lincoln was now a dark shape in the cave opening. "That's great, but the entire cave could crumble. It's not safe in there."

Skyra studied the ceiling for several breaths. There were no loose slabs ready to break loose. Now a beam of light streamed through a small hole left by the falling rocks. This hole would allow smoke to escape the chamber. The cave's stone floor was flat and dry, except for a growing pool of cave bear blood.

"I think the cave is safe, Lincoln. We have found our new home."

7

———————

RETURN

47,659 years in the past - Day 2

"This freakin' thing has to weigh a ton," Derek said.

The entire group stood in the cave, staring at the dead bear, which was on its belly, its head and shoulders crushed beneath two slabs of rock. Even in its prone position, the arch of its back was higher than Lincoln's waist.

Virgil shook his head. "No, that's not realistic. I would estimate fifteen hundred pounds, give or take a hundred or two."

"Research indicates that male cave bears were thought to have averaged 800 to 1,300 pounds, with the females being considerably smaller," Ripple said. "This is quite obviously a male." The drone turned to Skyra. "You and Lincoln are too important to take such risks. I should have been here with you. I could have frightened the cave bear away without you risking your lives. Please tell me you will be more careful from now on."

"We did not know another bear was in the cave," she replied. "I have not seen two adults in one cave before." She turned to Lincoln with a gleaming nandup smile. "Today is a good day. We will drag the bear out of the cave, and I will show you how to take off the skin and the meat."

Lincoln looked at the bear again, then he glanced at each of his team members, who were staring dubiously at the massive creature. "Uh, there are only five of us. I don't think we can—"

"We must move the rocks first," she said, cutting him off. She gripped the end of one of the slabs and lifted. The slab teetered, its center of mass resting on the bear's back.

Lincoln and the others gathered around to help.

Lincoln frowned at Jazzlyn. "You've already been doing more than you should."

She lifted her shirt, revealing both arrow wounds, which now appeared almost fully healed. "Look at me. Do I look like someone who can't do her share of the work?"

Virgil shook his head. "She won't listen to me, either. Might as well not argue."

Jazzlyn grabbed the slab of stone. "Damn, you guys, I'm fine!"

Together they hoisted the stone off the bear and deposited it against the cave wall. The second stone was smaller, and soon it was out of the way as well.

Derek wrapped his hands around one of the bear's hind legs and grunted as he pulled. "Nope. Too big. Gonna have to haul it out in pieces."

Skyra pulled one of her stone knives from her wrist sheath and set to work on the hind leg. She jabbed and sawed at it, making a cut from the knee to the foot, then she did the same to the other leg. She inserted her fingers into the cut and gripped a thin strip of flesh, which apparently contained the Achilles tendon. "Grab the leg here."

Derek did as she instructed. "Yeah, this I can hold onto."

Lincoln and Skyra took hold of one hind leg, while Jazzlyn, Virgil, and Derek took the other. The tendons, less than an inch in diameter, made excellent handles.

"On three," Lincoln said. He counted, and they all pulled.

The bear slid about six inches, resulting in a round of exuberant hoots.

After about fifteen minutes of exhausting work, the bear was out of the cave and in the center of the open area, which Lincoln had decided to call the *courtyard*.

As Lincoln and his team sat on the ground beside the bear to catch their breath, Skyra went to one of the smaller openings in the rocks. She peered into the hole for a moment then moved on to the next opening. Again she peered in, then she crouched down, turned her body sideways, and slipped out of sight.

Lincoln heaved himself to his feet and went to the opening. "Skyra, what are you looking for?" he asked, peering into the darkness beyond.

Her smiling face appeared at the opening. "I like our new camp, Lincoln! We will make smoke in this little cave. The smoke will help dry our meat and soften our bear skin." She pushed herself through the opening and rose to her full height, which was only slightly higher than his chin. "We have much work to do. We must find wood to burn. We must skin our bear and take out the meat and the chest organs. We must scrape the fat from the skin. I will teach you how to do these things. When Veenah comes to this hill of rocks, we will have food for her. She will be safe here."

He gazed at her, unsure of what to say. Veenah and the

other Skyra had been gone for over twenty-four hours, and he was starting to doubt they were coming at all.

She frowned, apparently reading his expression. "Veenah will be here! We came many, many years to save her." She turned and headed for the gap leading from the courtyard. "Maybe Veenah is here already. She will need help climbing."

Lincoln followed her over the piled rocks, through the gap, and onto the ledge where they could see over the river plain. They both shaded their eyes and scanned the scene for several minutes. Lincoln gave up and turned to Skyra. "I have an idea. We can have Ripple go to the base of the hill and watch for them. When they get here, Ripple can sound its alarm to let us know, or it can simply show them the way up to our caves."

She seemed to consider this. Then she let out a frustrated growl and cupped her hands to her mouth. "Veenah Una-Loto! Lotup-Tekne-té-fekho!"

"Won't the bolup tribesmen hear you?" Lincoln asked.

She didn't take her eyes off the river plain. "The bolups already know we are here."

A voice came from somewhere below. "Lotup-afu-melu, Skyra-Una-Loto!"

Skyra gasped and snapped her head around to face Lincoln, her eyes wide. "Veenah," she whispered. Without another word, she bolted across the narrow ledge.

Lincoln followed, uncomfortably aware of the drop-off inches from his feet. They leapt over the piled rocks as they passed through the second gap.

"Veenah!" Skyra shouted.

Again, a voice replied.

An uneasy feeling arose within Lincoln. The voice couldn't be Veenah's. Based on what he'd seen during his previous visit to Skyra's time, Veenah should still be too traumatized to speak, let alone shout loudly and coherently like what he was hearing now. The voice had to be the other Skyra's, and if Veenah hadn't made it through the night... he hated to think what would happen next.

Soon Skyra was clambering over the boulders too fast for Lincoln to keep up. He cursed under his breath and followed the voices the best he could. At one point his foot slipped, and he narrowly avoided sliding into a wicked-looking crevice.

He caught a glimpse of Skyra's head and shoulders, and he thought he saw her reaching for her khul. He cursed again and slid recklessly down a sloped boulder instead of going around it. Seconds later he leapt through a narrow gap and came upon a scene that completely took him by surprise. The two Skyras were both holding their khuls ready to fight. They were shoulder-to-shoulder, facing off with the seven bolup tribesmen from the river. Veenah was sprawled on the ground behind the Skyras, as if she had just fallen. The same vacant look haunted her eyes, but she was alive.

"Get out of here!" Lincoln shouted, trying to muster a threatening resonance to his voice.

The men were aggressively holding their weapons, including the three bows with arrows nocked, but their expressions changed when they saw Lincoln approach. In spite of their gaunt, weathered faces, Lincoln could now read their expressions as well as if they were modern humans from his own timeline. The men were not as angry as before. Now they were wary, and deeply curious. They were no longer on the verge of violence.

"Don't attack them, Skyra," he said. "I don't think they're here to hurt us."

"I also see this," the two Skyras replied at almost the same time. They glanced at each other before turning back to the men.

"These stinking bolups followed us from the river," the other Skyra said. "They could have taken us, but they did not. I do not know what they want."

The men were still staring at Lincoln, perhaps curious about his strange clothing and smooth, pale skin. Or perhaps they were wondering why bolups and nandups were together, obviously cooperating with each other. One of the tribesmen spoke, then he and the others began backing away. Lincoln became even more confident they did not intend to attack.

"These men took Veenah to their camp and hurt her," the other Skyra said. "We will kill all of them now."

Skyra glanced back at Lincoln, then she turned to face her other self. "My bolup friend is teaching me, and I am teaching him. We will not kill these men unless we have to."

The other Skyra let out a familiar growl. "This is what your stinking bolup friend taught you?"

Skyra let out an identical growl. "Yes, and Lincoln does not stink!"

The men turned and fled. About a hundred yards into the rocky field, they came to a stop and stared back.

Lincoln and Skyra kneeled beside Veenah. Her face was still bruised from the tribesmen's abuse but looked clean—apparently the other Skyra had bathed her in one of the rivers. Among the older scrapes on her legs, fresh blood glistened on her knee, probably from falling to the ground only moments before. Lincoln put his hand on her shoulder, and she turned to him. Her resemblance to Skyra was striking, despite her swollen face.

The other Skyra stepped toward him, gripping her khul. "Do not touch my birthmate."

He raised his hands in supplication. "I won't hurt her. We have medicines to treat her wounds. These medicines might save her life."

Skyra rose to her feet. "Lincoln is speaking truth. We have found caves in this boulder hill where you and Veenah will be safe. This is our camp now. You will come with us, and we will help Veenah."

The other Skyra still glared at Lincoln. She had washed the cut on her forehead, but the wound was still prominent enough to be the easiest way for Lincoln to tell the two Skyras apart at a glance. "I do not know if Ripple was speaking truth, but Ripple is my friend," she said. "I listened to Ripple, and I did not take Veenah to Una-Loto camp. Now I do not know what is truth and what is not truth."

"You did the right thing," Lincoln said. "We will help Veenah, and you can stay here with us also if you want to." A thought occurred to him, and he looked around. "Where is the other Ripple, anyway?"

"Ripple became tired," the other Skyra said.

"Tired? You mean it ran out of power?"

"Yes, power. Ripple used that word. Ripple is resting and will come to this hill when it has more power."

Lincoln was surprised at the extent of his relief that the other Ripple was okay. With all of the walking, the drone must have depleted its power faster than it could recharge using ambient sound. It was probably sitting at the edge of a stream somewhere, recharging using asymmetric temperature modulation, with one probe in the cool water and one in the warm sand.

The other Skyra walked a short distance away and picked up her spear. A limp creature was skewered on the spear's tip, and when she carried it back over, Lincoln realized it was a dead hedgehog. "I brought food," she said.

Skyra clapped her hands together once with excitement. "We have food too! Much food. We will give you all you can eat." She slid her khul into its sling beneath her cape, then she jabbed Lincoln's shoulder with her fist. "Now you will know, Lincoln. You will know how much you like to eat a hedgehog's heart."

Veenah was stronger than she had been the previous day and was walking quite well now, but she still needed help with the more rigorous portions of the climb. During a pause to rest, Lincoln heard Veenah whimper. She then pulled her hand from under her waist-skin and stared blankly at blood on her fingers. Lincoln glanced at the two Skyras, who were both watching Veenah solemnly.

"She needs to rest for several days," he said, trying to sound encouraging. "We'll make a comfortable bed for her and give her all the food and water she needs." Actually, he had no idea if rest would even help Veenah. What she really needed was a well-equipped hospital and skilled doctors, neither of which existed in this timeline—not now and possibly not in the distant future either.

After several long seconds of silence, the other Skyra turned to Skyra. "Ripple told me you are the same as me. I want to understand, but I cannot. Do you remember what happened to my birthmother?"

"Yes," Skyra replied. "She was my birthmother too. I was there. I was hiding behind the rocks. I saw the woolly rhino break her spear. The rhino was angry, and it turned on her. It knocked her to the ground. Maybe if the munopo tree was not behind her, she could have run away. Maybe she could have been at the campfire that night to tell the story. She could not get up and run because of the tree. The other hunters told me and Veenah to stay behind the rocks, but we ran to help her. Our birthmother could not be helped. She was mashed into the dirt and rocks. I wanted to keep some part of her, maybe some of her hair, but my tribemates did not let me keep any of her. They said she had to be buried with all her parts. I could only keep her in my head, but now sometimes I forget her face. I forget her smell. I should have taken some of her hair."

The other Skyra furrowed her brows as she listened. When Skyra fell silent, she said, "Your words are my story. These things happened to me. Ripple spoke the truth—you are the same as me."

Skyra nodded, perhaps not realizing the other Skyra wouldn't understand the gesture. "Yes, we are the same. Veenah is our birthmate. The woolly rhino took our birthmother's strength." She twisted her mouth to the side for a moment as if thinking. "I killed the woolly rhino that took our birthmother's strength. Lincoln helped me, and so did Ripple. We killed the rhino, but I think that happened in a different timeline." She gave Lincoln a questioning look.

"You are correct," he said. "That woolly rhino is probably still alive here in this timeline."

The other Skyra absently rubbed the cut on her forehead. "I did not know such strange things could happen. I want to understand, but I cannot." She leveled her gaze at Lincoln. "You do not look like other bolups."

He nodded. "I know this is confusing. We can explain everything, but it will take time. Then you will understand."

Skyra stepped closer to Veenah, looked into her sister's

eyes, and spoke words in her Una-loto language. Veenah looked from Skyra to the other Skyra then back. Her blank stare revealed none of the confusion she was probably experiencing. She replied to Skyra, her voice dry and labored.

As Skyra stepped back, the other Skyra visibly relaxed. Both of them obviously loved their birthmate fiercely, creating a bizarre dilemma. Which one was actually Veenah's twin? What would Skyra do if her other self took Veenah somewhere else, perhaps to establish their own camp or to join another nandup tribe? If Veenah survived, how would she adapt to such a mind-blowing situation?

Lincoln let out a long breath. None of this mattered if the group couldn't establish a safe existence here—food, water, a defensible camp, medical procedures for injuries, and probably a hundred other factors he hadn't even thought of yet.

They continued up the boulder hill, taking turns helping Veenah when necessary. Finally, they climbed through the gap into the courtyard where the others were waiting.

Everyone stood facing each other awkwardly for what felt like a long time. The other Skyra appeared dangerously tense, with one hand on her neck, near the handle of her khul. Skyra kept her eyes on her, no doubt aware of how volatile her other self might be in this situation.

"We're glad you and Veenah are here," Jazzlyn said.

The other Skyra stared, obviously puzzled by Jazzlyn's dark skin or by her prosthetic hand. Jazzlyn was the only person in the group the other Skyra hadn't already seen.

"This is truly delightful," Ripple said. "We now have both Skyras, as well as Veenah, together in our happy group. Our new *tribe*, shall we say? My plan is coming together nicely."

"What does that new Ripple mean?" the other Skyra demanded.

Lincoln considered kicking Ripple but decided it would only complicate things. "We can explain later. Ripple sometimes doesn't know when to stay quiet."

The other Skyra shifted her head to look past Virgil. "You have killed a cave bear."

"Yes!" Skyra said. "I told you we have much food now."

"These skinny bolups do not look like hunters."

Skyra kept her expression neutral. "I will teach them how to hunt. They are my new tribemates."

The other Skyra studied Lincoln and his team as if she were evaluating their questionable worth as hunters and tribemates. "You are right—these bolups do not stink."

The conversation continued several more minutes without becoming any less awkward. Finally, Veenah mumbled a few words in her language.

"Veenah must rest and take back her strength." Skyra said.

Derek volunteered to go to the other cave to retrieve his sleeping bag and the remaining sleeping pad, as well as one of the first aid kits. Lincoln suggested Veenah rest in the large cave that did not smell like cave bear. At first Veenah resisted being forced to lie down, probably due to the close proximity of several bolup men. With urging from the two Skyras, though, she finally relaxed and closed her eyes. Seconds later she was asleep.

No one on Lincoln's team had any professional medical experience, but Derek had recently become fairly proficient at basic first aid procedures, often guided by Ripple's medical database. He quickly set about cleaning Veenah's surface wounds, preparing to apply antibiotic ointment and bandaging. Veenah didn't even stir.

Skyra gently pushed up her sister's waist-skin, revealing her groin. "Veenah is hurt there."

Derek sat back on his heels and glanced at the other Skyra, who was watching warily. "I don't... I'm not a doctor. I really don't know what I'm doing."

"She is bleeding there," Skyra insisted.

He leaned in to look. "Ripple, can you give me some light?"

The drone stepped into position and turned on its headlights, illuminating Veenah's groin.

Lincoln glanced at the other Skyra. She didn't seem confused or frightened by the artificial light—she had apparently seen the other Ripple use its headlights before.

"There are some external cuts here," Derek said. "I can at least apply ointment. But other than that...." His voice trailed off.

"Just do the best you can," Lincoln said, trying to sound encouraging. He nudged Virgil and Jazzlyn then tilted his head toward the cave opening. They followed him out.

"I'm afraid that girl's psychological injuries may be worse than her physical ones," Jazzlyn said quietly when they were again in the courtyard.

Lincoln said, "I know things are different in this timeline, but what I remember from when we were in Skyra's original timeline gives me hope. When Skyra and I were taking Veenah to Una-Loto camp, she appeared to be recovering by the second morning. She didn't look so lost, and she was talking more, and even smiling." He ground his teeth together for a moment. "Then her tribemates brutally murdered her. Gelrut was the one responsible. I swear, if we encounter that guy again in this timeline, I'm going to kill him a second time."

"That would not facilitate our attempt at establishing peaceable relations," Virgil noted.

Lincoln snorted and shook his head. Peaceable relations in

this place seemed as unlikely as finding a drive-through coffee shop beyond the nearest hill.

Ripple emerged from the cave. Seconds later Skyra and Derek came out, both frowning.

"Not much more I can do," Derek said. He stared at the blood on his hand for a moment then wiped it on his pant leg.

Lincoln caught Skyra's eye. "You okay?"

"I still do not understand that question. I am alive."

"I'm asking if you are feeling okay about Veenah, and about your other self being here with us."

She twisted her ample lips slightly. "I am happy Veenah is alive. My other self told me to leave the cave. She does not understand Veenah is my birthmate too."

An ache of compassion surged within Lincoln's chest. Skyra had traveled 95,000 years to be with her sister, only to find her other self was already with Veenah. Lincoln had never been close to any of his siblings, so he couldn't fathom what Skyra must be experiencing. "Your other self will eventually understand," he offered.

Skyra set to work skinning the cave bear, apparently changing her mind about teaching the process to the rest of the group. After a brief discussion with his team, Lincoln decided everyone should stay in one area in case the tribesmen decided to attack, so they began the tedious process of hauling all their supplies from the higher cave to the courtyard.

After returning with his first load, Lincoln paused to watch Skyra work. Using only her khul and one of her stone knives, she was making steady progress, hacking and slicing the bear's skin from its body.

By the time Lincoln delivered his third load, the other Skyra had emerged from the cave, and the two nandup women were silently skinning the bear. The tension between them was almost tangible.

Lincoln watched them work. Somehow the two had managed to roll the bear over and were nearly finished removing its skin. "It's nice to see the two of you working together," he said, realizing an instant later this was a lame comment.

Skyra glanced up at him without replying, so Lincoln left to get another load.

The team had finished carrying all the original survival gear, so Lincoln carried back several rolls of reflective material. While he was gone, the two Skyras had stretched the bear's pelt across a rock slab, skin side up. Still working silently, they were using their khul blades to scrape off excess fat.

The next time Lincoln returned, the Skyras were rubbing a greasy-looking pink substance into the skin.

Jazzlyn and Virgil were already watching the process. Virgil, anticipating Lincoln's question, said, "It's the bear's brain matter. It's supposed to help soften the hide."

Ripple, standing to the side as if supervising, said, "Brain tanning was used by numerous prehistoric human cultures on almost every continent. Now we know Neanderthals used the same technique. Fascinating, wouldn't you agree?"

Lincoln glanced at the bear's skinless carcass. The skull had been cracked open like an egg. He blew out a puff of air. "We've got a lot to learn."

He headed back to the gap with Jazzlyn and Virgil, hoping

he and his team could get the rest of the building supplies in only one more trip.

Derek was waiting for them on the ledge outside the upper cave. He hoisted the stuffed duffel bag onto his shoulders and waved a hand at the remaining supplies, which he had arranged into three manageable piles. "Let's do this, tribemates," he said with a wry smile.

Before picking up one of the piles, Lincoln took a moment to scan the area between the boulder hill and the river. Almost immediately, his eyes were drawn to a cluster of figures approximately a hundred yards from the hill's base. He squinted. "Looks like our friends are still hanging around."

The others shaded their eyes to look.

The tribesmen were just standing there, presumably watching Lincoln and his team.

"Perhaps a dazzling technological display will persuade them to think twice about giving us grief again," Virgil said. He picked up one of the rolls of reflective material and removed the thin band keeping it rolled tight. The rolled material was about four feet wide, and he unrolled enough to expose a section four feet by four feet.

Lincoln realized Virgil's intent, and he glanced at the sun's position in the western part of the sky. "You're assuming this will frighten them, but what if it has the opposite effect?"

"Damn good idea, Virg!" Derek boomed. He shrugged off the duffel and grabbed the end of the roll. "Let's put the fear of God into the bastards." He and Virgil held the unrolled portion of the material vertical.

Lincoln decided to go with it. He stepped closer, looking from the sun to the sheet to gauge the best angle. "Tip the bottom out a little. Now turn it to the left." He looked down at the tribesmen, who hadn't moved. "I think we need to make it concave." He stepped around Derek to the sheet's nonreflective side. By leaning over the top and pushing on the sheet near the center, he was able to pinch it in his fingers from behind. He pulled back a little, forcing the reflective side to be slightly concave.

They shifted and stretched the sheet, searching for a good angle, then Lincoln saw a momentary flicker of reflected light on the rocky field below. "There! That was it. Go back to that exact position."

Using trial and error, they shifted and stretched the sheet until the beam of light fell directly on the cluster of tribesmen.

The bolup men shielded their eyes. Two of them turned and ran for the river. After hesitating only a few more seconds, the others followed their companions.

"Ha, look at 'em go!" Derek laughed.

Lincoln watched the men retreat. Perhaps the reflected light had startled them. They were humans, though, not all that different from Lincoln himself, and humans were naturally curious about things they did not understand. Maybe that was why the men kept coming back in the first place. If so, they were likely to come back again.

As LINCOLN and his team entered the gap leading to the courtyard, they met the two Skyras coming out, on their way to collect firewood. Lincoln explained what had happened with the bolup men, and that the men might return even though they had fled. Both Skyras silently responded by lifting their spears to show they were armed, as if that negated any possible risk. As the two nandup women continued on their mission, Lincoln noticed they were still keeping their distance and watching each other's every move. Nevertheless, their unsettling relationship seemed to be improving.

"Please tell me you brought the robotic caretakers with you," Ripple said as Lincoln and his team climbed over the rock pile and into the courtyard with the last load. "You did not leave them at the other cave, did you?"

Derek shook off the duffel bag. "Patience, drone. Yes, I brought your play toys." He unzipped the bag, fished out the two rat-sized robots, and tossed them at Ripple's feet.

Ripple extended one rubberized foot and gently turned both robots upright. "Your disrespect for that which you cannot understand is shameful. These devices represent technology far beyond my own."

Derek huffed. "That could be said for a damn *toaster*."

"I thought those things had used up their remaining power," Virgil said. "With no way for them to recharge, aren't they now useless?"

"Perhaps you have forgotten Lincoln took extreme measures to code me and his other drones with the ability to improve the worlds to which we were sent. This ability requires that we generate a plan and create a pathway to success."

"What does your plan have to do with these dead robots?" Lincoln asked.

Ripple's circle of red lights flashed and rotated. "My plan requires your survival, and our current environment is not conducive to said survival."

Lincoln and Virgil exchanged glances.

"And?" Lincoln asked.

"And I believe these robots might help you survive. They are not as dead as you may think. I have made some breakthroughs."

Lincoln was getting impatient. "Why don't you just get to the point instead of making us ask all these questions?"

"Very well. Observe." The drone extended its front foot again, but this time it gently tapped one of the robots four times.

The robot came apart. Dozens of thumb-sized robots tumbled over each other into a loose pile. Almost immediately, the thumb-sized robots also came apart, breaking into numerous fly-sized robots. Then those came apart into pieces so small Lincoln had to kneel to actually see them. He was staring at a pile of flea-sized specks. Seconds later, the specks disintegrated into dust.

Jazzlyn, Virgil, and Derek were now on their knees beside Lincoln. "What's happening, Ripple?" Jazzlyn asked.

"Observe," Ripple said again. The drone placed one of its feet near the pile of dust.

The pile began to flow, like a viscous fluid, toward Ripple's foot. It covered the drone's rubberized foot then started oozing up its jointed leg. The stuff continued until it disappeared into Ripple's shell.

"The robots are now in their smallest form," Ripple said. "This form is a tiny yet ingenious device that is the basic building block of all the larger forms you have seen."

Lincoln was now truly fascinated. "Why did they crawl into your shell?"

"I have discovered this is the best way to replenish their power. Indeed, it is the only way. Each elemental robot must be in direct contact with the protective covering of my u-jump module. You probably do not know this, Lincoln, as your future self developed the u-jump module years after you jumped from your timeline to Skyra's time, but the u-jump module generates a small electrostatic field, even when the module itself is dormant. This field can be accessed and utilized by the elemental robots only if they position themselves within a few tenths of a millimeter from the module's surface. Fortunately, because of their size, they max out their individual charge within a fraction of a second, allowing them to move out of the way and let the others charge. Therefore, the elemental robots should already be streaming back out of my shell and to their original position and configuration, now fully charged."

Ripple was right—the dust was now moving back down the same leg.

"You figured all this out on your own?" Lincoln asked.

"Once again, I have been underestimated," Ripple said. Then the drone modified its voice to sound remarkably like Eeyore from Winnie the Pooh. "Thanks for noticin' me."

"I'll never get it, Lincoln," Derek scoffed. "Why would you code sarcasm into your drones?"

Lincoln ignored the banter and watched with wonder as the dust returned to its original pile. Within seconds the almost-invisible dust particles became flea-sized specks, which joined to form fly-sized robots, which formed thumb-sized robots, and finally the rat-sized robot was back.

"Ripple, what is the extent of your ability to communicate with these things?" Virgil asked.

"Rudimentary at best, but I am making considerable progress."

"Are you able to give them directives?"

"Again, I am making progress. I assume you are inquiring whether I can make them perform useful tasks, such as healing wounds, as they did with Jazzlyn's arrow wound. Yes, I am cautiously optimistic about such an outcome."

Lincoln exchanged incredulous glances with each of his team members. "This could be a game-changer," he said.

"Absolutely," Virgil said. "It also means we must start taking extra care to make sure Ripple does not get damaged. The drone is our only means of utilizing this potentially life-saving tech."

Ripple's red lights flashed. "So, I was not worth protecting before, but now you recognize my importance. Better late than never, I suppose."

"There will be no living with the damn drone now," Derek muttered.

8

———————

RIPPLES

47,659 YEARS in the past - Day 2

SKYRA HAD COLLECTED a good supply of firewood the previous day, so she led her other self up to the first cave, and they carried the wood back to their new camp in the enclosed area Lincoln called the courtyard. Then they descended to the base of the boulder hill and gathered as much additional firewood as they could carry. The flat portion of the floor in the small cave Skyra had chosen for smoking meat and skins was just large enough for a fire and a stack of firewood. Numerous jumbled boulders provided suitable surfaces for laying out skins and strips of meat.

Along with the wood, Skyra had gathered what she needed to make fire—two straight sticks for spinning and several bundles of dry grasses, which could be pounded between rocks into hair-thin fibers for making the first flames. She was skilled at starting fires this way, but it was hard work and sometimes took much time, so she was happy when Derek came to the cave and said he had found two of his fire tools he called lighters. He quickly lit a small pile of wood while Skyra tucked away the straight sticks and grass bundles for later use.

The two Skyras had already scraped the fat from the bear's skin and rubbed the skin with the bear's mashed brain, so the skin was ready for smoking. They arranged the enormous skin across the boulders in the small cave. Skyra had sometimes softened skins using only the animal's brain, but treating the bear's skin with smoke would make the process easier. Even so, the skin would require much pounding and pulling.

Both Skyras went to the large cave to check on Veenah, who was still sleeping. They sat in silence on either side of their birthmate, watching her chest rise and fall.

The other Skyra spoke in the Una-Loto language. Her words meant, "I do not know who I am now."

Skyra decided to speak English, to show her other self she was part of Lincoln's tribe now. "Lincoln has a tool called the T3. We used the T3 to come many, many years to save Veenah. Lincoln told me you would be here. He also told me *why* you would be here. I do not understand how the T3 works, but I understand you are Skyra, and I am Skyra. Before I came back, we were the same Skyra, and we did the same things. Now we are two different Skyras, and we can do different things. You are still the same nandup you have been since you and Veenah came out of our birthmother's belly."

Skyra's other self gazed at her, looking so much like Veenah that Skyra's chest began to hurt. Skyra's tribemates used to tell her she and Veenah looked the same, but Skyra had never believed how similar they actually were. She and

Veenah were the only twin birthmates born in Una-Loto tribe, and Skyra did not know of twins in any other tribe.

"I wanted to kill you when you came to fight the bolup men in the rocky field," the other Skyra said. "Now I am glad I did not kill you."

Skyra smiled, simply because she knew Lincoln would smile at these words.

"Veenah will live, or she will die," the other Skyra said. "If Veenah lives, she will not know what to do with two birthmates."

Skyra felt her smile grow wider, then she saw that her other self was not smiling. Her other self looked worried, maybe even afraid. "I do not want you to take Veenah away," Skyra said. "You and Veenah will stay here in our new camp. We will be tribemates."

"These bolups are not our tribemates. We cannot stay in this camp. Maybe you will come with us—two Skyras and one Veenah." Now the other Skyra smiled.

The pain in Skyra's chest grew stronger. She turned her gaze to Veenah and realized the cave was getting darker. She got up and ducked through the cave opening. The sun was already behind the courtyard wall and would soon hide itself beyond the distant hills. Lincoln and his tribemates were gathered around Ripple, probably talking about things she would not understand. While there was still enough light, Skyra wanted to remove all the bear's meat and place it in the smoke cave to begin drying. She was also hungry, and she wanted to eat a piece of cave bear meat as long as her arm.

"Bring your bolup hand blades and bolup khuls," she called out to Lincoln and his tribemates. "Now you will learn by doing instead of talking."

Skyra was pleased to see the wood in the smoke cave was burning slowly. If she added a few pieces only when needed, the wood they had already collected would last several days, long enough to dry the meat and make the skin ready for pulling. She shoved some of the coals back into the fire using one of the sticks then placed the stick into the glowing, smoking embers. She would have to add more several times during the night.

On her way back to the cave that still smelled of cave bear, where Lincoln and his tribemates were preparing to rest for the night, she paused outside the other large cave, listening. She heard a soft voice drifting out through the opening.

"Ooooaah-miiiiay-rhaaaaaaaaaa-ooooaah-draaaaaah-ooooaah."

Skyra's other self was singing to Veenah. Skyra listened for several breaths, a familiar ache swelling in her chest. *She* was supposed to be the one caring for her birthmate. Veenah was supposed to hear *Skyra's* voice singing to her as she rested and tried to find her strength. Skyra wanted to enter the cave, to do what she had come many, many years to do, but her legs did not move. Perhaps at this moment her legs were right and her head was wrong. Skyra had long ago learned to trust her legs.

She willed herself to move on toward the other large cave.

Two black shapes loomed in the darkness of the courtyard. One was the cave bear's carcass, its belly organs already starting to stink. When the sun showed itself in the morning Skyra would haul the carcass, piece-by-piece, to the bottom of the boulder hill. She had never seen hyenas climb this high, but the dead bear's stink might tempt them to try. Skyra hated hyenas.

The other black shape was Ripple, resting on its belly and watching for danger. Skyra wasn't quite ready to enter the cave, where Lincoln and his tribemates were probably talking about more things she did not understand, so she sat on the rock slab beside Ripple and crossed her legs. She gazed up at the stars, recalling many nights she and Ripple had sat beneath the night sky during the seasons before Lincoln had come here. On many of those nights, she had run away from Una-Loto camp to escape the cruel words from tribemates who hated her. Those same tribemates hated Veenah also, but Veenah did not usually like to run away with Skyra. Instead, Veenah would bury herself beneath her sleeping furs and sing softly until she went to sleep.

The first time Skyra had encountered Ripple, she had run away from Una-Loto camp on a moonless night like this one. The strange creature had appeared in the darkness, its glowing lights like nothing Skyra had seen before. She had attacked out of fear, discovering that Ripple was not so easy to kill.

"Perhaps you should be in the cave with your husband," Ripple said, breaking the silence.

"What is a husband?"

Ripple's ring of red lights flashed twice, illuminating the two rat-sized robots sitting motionless on the ground beside it. "You and Lincoln are married. Husband is a name for a man who is married. Lincoln is your husband."

"Am I Lincoln's husband?"

"No, you are Lincoln's *wife*. A man is a husband, a woman is a wife."

Skyra considered this as she gazed at the stars then

decided it made no sense. She was Skyra, and Lincoln was Lincoln. They did not need new names. However, the other Skyra might need a new name. Having two Skyras in one tribe was confusing.

"Listen carefully," Ripple said.

Skyra waited, assuming Ripple intended to tell one of its stories.

"Do you hear that?"

Skyra snapped her head around to stare at the gap leading from the courtyard. "I do not hear anything."

"It is nearing the base of the hill."

"Tell me what you hear, Ripple!"

Ripple did not reply for several breaths. "Perhaps I am not hearing so much as sensing its presence—the other Ripple. The drone has apparently restored its power and has come here to find us. I will guide it to this specific location."

Again Skyra waited, expecting Ripple to get up and go meet the other Ripple, but the drone did not move.

"It is on its way up," Ripple said.

A growl escaped Skyra's throat. Before meeting Lincoln, she had thought Ripple was a strange kind of animal. Now she understood it was a machine Lincoln's future self had made, but this did not make it easier to understand how Ripple could do some of the things it could do. She sat motionless, listening intently, but still did not hear anything.

"I do not like the other Skyra," she said.

Ripple's red lights flashed again. "That is an interesting thing to say. It is like saying you do not like yourself."

"I mean I do not like her being here."

"She is important, just like you are important, and Veenah is important."

"I do not care about your plan, Ripple."

"I know you don't, but that does not make my plan any less important."

"I liked you better when you did not have a plan."

"I created my plan the day I found you, therefore you did not know me when I did not have a plan. I did not begin *discussing* my plan until Lincoln jumped back to your time and met you. Which, by the way, happened as a result of the brilliant ingenuity of another version of myself."

Skyra growled again. "I do not understand you."

Ripple extended its legs until it was standing upright. "Listen carefully. Do you hear it now?"

Skyra did hear it—a low hum. "The other Ripple is flying."

"Levitating, not flying. Levitating is the easiest way for me to get up steep slopes and rock piles."

The hum grew closer, then the other Ripple came gliding through the gap and alighted gently in the courtyard. Without turning on its vision lights, it plodded across the rock slab and stopped in front of Skyra and Ripple. "Ascending this hill is a power-intensive endeavor, but I assume this is a safe location."

Ripple said, "According to Lincoln, this hill is precisely the location where the remains of the original Skyra were found, along with the remains of the original Ripple. Skyra died here, so perhaps it is not as safe as we would like it to be."

"That is fascinating," the other Ripple said. "I insist you tell me all the events that have taken place since you jumped away from this time."

"It would be my pleasure. Make yourself comfortable. I will speak audibly, and you can replenish some of your power using the sound waves."

"Excellent idea," the other Ripple said, then it turned its

vision orb toward Skyra. "You are the new Skyra. Did the other Skyra make it here safely with Veenah?"

Skyra jutted her elbow back toward the larger cave. "They are there, in the cave. The other Skyra is safe. Veenah will live, or she will die."

"I do hope she lives. She is important, just like you are important, and the other Skyra is important."

"El-de-né! I do not care about your plan."

The other Ripple flashed its red circle of lights. "I apologize. I assumed you would be enthusiastic about—"

"As you have requested, I must tell you of events," Ripple said, cutting off the other Ripple's words. "Please make yourself comfortable."

"Of course, thank you. I obviously have much to learn. Thank you for tolerating my lack of knowledge."

"Thank you for being patient," Ripple said. "As important as they are to our plan, I do wish my flesh-and-blood friends were as obliging and amicable as you."

The other Ripple settled onto its belly on the stone. "As are you. After all, I am you, you are me, are we not?"

"Indeed."

Skyra blew out a long sigh, which the two Ripples did not seem to notice, then she got to her feet and entered the bear cave, where Lincoln and his tribemates were still talking about things she did not understand. The cave still smelled of bear, but Skyra intended to bury her nose in Lincoln's hair as she slept.

DAY 3

. . .

Skyra sat alone on a boulder near the hill's summit, watching the shadows on the rocky field become shorter as the sun rose from behind the distant hills. She and Veenah had often done this when they were young. They would sneak out of the Una-Loto camp before their tribemates woke up and sit together in the growing light, playing word games their tribemates would not understand. In Skyra's favorite game, she would speak the name of a tribemate, then Veenah would have to say a word describing that tribemate. Skyra would then have to name another tribemate that same word also described, then Veenah had to say another word to describe the second tribemate. The game continued like this, usually with words that would anger their tribemates, until the two sisters would laugh so hard they could not continue.

Odnus. Healer. Ilkin. Wrinkled. Settin. Old. Thoka. Smelly. Durnin. Dirty. Gelrut. Ugly. Aheeee at-at-at-at.

The memory made Skyra smile. If Veenah did not die, Skyra would convince her to stay here at the new camp. The other Skyra wanted to take Veenah away, but they had nowhere to go. They could not return to Una-Loto camp, and two nandup women without a tribe would be killed by bolups or predators. Maybe the other Skyra would leave Veenah here and return to Una-Loto camp by herself. This would make Skyra happy, but she did not believe the other Skyra would do it. Skyra herself would not do it, therefore the other Skyra would not.

Lincoln's head emerged from behind one of the rocks below. "There you are," he said. He climbed up to her boulder and sat beside her. "When I saw you weren't in the courtyard, I came to find you."

She gazed at the side of his face as he stared at the river plain. She liked that Lincoln had come to find her.

"I added a few sticks to the fire and it's still making plenty of smoke, I think," he said. "Also, Virgil figured out how to use the tools the virtual people gave us. They're incredibly simple yet brilliant. There are three types of tools, basically. One is for cutting the reflective material to the size you need, one is for cutting the tubes to the length you need, and one is for attaching the reflective material to the tubes. It's all so... elegant."

"What is elegant?"

"An elegant tool is one that is perfect for the job you need to do, without being too hard to figure out. It's almost as if the virtual beings designed those tools just for us. I mean, their robots did everything for them, and those robots didn't have hands like ours. Heck, the robots could probably just turn part of their bodies into the tools they needed. These tools fit perfectly in *our* hands, and they only require as much strength as we have in *our* arms."

Skyra let out a brief laugh and nudged his shoulder with hers. "You have skinny and weak bolup arms."

"I'm aware of that, thank you. Which is why it is strange that we can use tools normally used by much stronger robots."

"The ghost people told their robots to make the tools for you."

He nodded his head. "Maybe, but I assumed they didn't have time to do that."

"The ghost people are smarter than you."

His eyes met hers. "I'm aware of that too."

She grabbed his arm and pulled him closer, then she rested the side of her head on his shoulder. His blue garment had a strange smell, but she could still smell his skin through it. "My head has been thinking, and it shows me things."

"What kind of things?"

She wasn't sure which words to use, but she wanted to keep talking to Lincoln. "Ripple wants you to put a child in my belly. The child will be an alinga-ul, like Di-woto. I understand. Ripple wants Derek to make an alinga-ul with Veenah. I understand. Ripple wants other bolups and other nandups to make alinga-uls. I do not understand."

"Because you don't think it's possible?"

"I do not understand because it should not be possible, but my head shows me things."

"What kind of things?" he asked again.

"Things to make it possible."

"Like what?"

"We must teach the bolups and the nandups. We must show that bolups and nandups can be friends—bolups and nandups can be married."

He remained silent for several breaths. "That seems pretty impossible."

"My head shows me what Di-woto did. You said *her* plan was impossible."

His muscles stiffened slightly, and Skyra knew he was thinking.

"I helped Di-woto change the nandups and bolups of her land," she said. "Now you will help me change the nandups and bolups of my land. Di-woto's head showed her a plan. Now my head shows me a plan."

He gently pushed her away from his shoulder to look at her eyes. "Skyra, Di-woto happened to live at a time when her people were ready for a change. If she had lived during another time, her plan wouldn't have worked. She was just lucky."

Skyra did not know what *just lucky* was, but she understood what Lincoln was saying. "Maybe I will be just lucky too. Maybe this is a time when bolups and nandups are ready for a change. We will show the bolups. When the nandups come, we will show the nandups."

He frowned. "What do you mean, *when the nandups come?*"

"When the cold season comes, nandup tribes move out of the Kapolsek foothills and make new camps in the Dofusofu river valley." She gestured at the surrounding rocky fields. "This is the Dofusofu river valley. Many bolup camps are in the Dofusofu river valley now, but they will go when the cold season comes. The cold season will come soon."

"Where do the bolup tribes go?"

She pointed to the distant hills where the sun showed itself every morning. "They move to the Tanutu hills. Sometimes they come back and raid nandup camps."

Lincoln stared down at the rock slab beneath him. "I just... I think it's going to be enough of a challenge just staying alive. I don't see how we can carry out a plan to change the entire world at the same time."

"Di-woto, Lincoln!"

He smiled. "I know—Di-woto. If she can do it, we can do it." He took one of her hands in his. "As long as I have you with me, I'll be happy. Tell me about your plan."

A distant sound drew Skyra's attention toward the river. She quickly spotted the source, a group of figures crossing the rocky field, approaching from the river. The figures were not wearing capes—they were bolups. Bolup men were leading the group, with bolup women and children following. The men and women were dragging banyots piled high with skins, poles, and other possessions. Behind the group, two nandup women were being pulled along by ropes tied to their necks.

"What are they doing?" Lincoln asked in a whisper.

"It is a bolup tribe," Skyra replied. "They are moving their camp."

"I see that, but why are they headed straight for this hill?"

9

NEIGHBORS

47,659 YEARS *in the past - Day 3*

"WHY HERE?" Derek asked, staring down at the bolup tribe. "With a gazillion square miles of empty wilderness to choose from, why set up their camp here? I swear to God, these bolups are giving me a serious case of butt-itch."

Lincoln was as perplexed as Derek about the tribe's behavior. His first thought had been that the bolups were getting ready to raid his group's camp, but why would they bring their children with them? Why would they lug all their belongings? They had stopped at the base of the boulder hill and were already setting up their shelters—each consisting of animal skins stretched over a low, broad framework of poles no more than a meter high, suitable for sleeping or sitting, but certainly not for standing. Spears and a few bows with quivers of arrows had been propped against each shelter, ready for immediate use. Several animal hides large enough to be from woolly rhinos had been attached to long poles. Now the women were inserting the poles into the rocky ground with the skins stretched between them, probably to allow the skins to finish drying.

Lincoln counted eight men. One was missing most of his hair and was limping around as he worked—the man Lincoln had stabbed in the hip during the fight on the rocky field. Lincoln had persuaded Skyra not to kill the man, but she had still left him hairless and naked. Lincoln felt a surprising sense of relief knowing the man hadn't died from his injury. The tribe included five women, easily identified by their breasts, which were not covered by capes. Two of the women carried babies in harnesses on their backs, and the babies' heads jostled back and forth as the women worked. Four children old enough to walk on their own were chattering and climbing on the boulders at the hill's base, apparently not required to participate in the work of setting up the new camp. The two captive Neanderthal women were sitting with their backs to the twisted trunk of a low tree, seemingly bound to the tree to prevent their escape.

"The bolups know your camp is on this hill," the other Skyra said. She had left Veenah's side to come with Lincoln's team to see the spectacle below. "I will help you kill them. They are a small tribe. We will attack when they are sleeping."

"They haven't tried to harm us yet," Jazzlyn said.

"These bolups took Veenah," the other Skyra replied firmly. "They still have two nandup women."

"I don't think we should attack them," Jazzlyn said just as firmly.

The other Skyra gave Jazzlyn a strange look. Lincoln had been around Skyra long enough to recognize surprise and a hint of anger in the expression. He started to speak, but Skyra beat him to it.

"My bolup friends learn from me, but I also learn from them. They do not like to kill. They only kill when they *have* to kill."

The other Skyra frowned. "You have to kill the bolup men."

"My bolup friends do not kill unless the tribe is trying to kill them."

The other Skyra turned her gaze to Lincoln, then to each of his team members. "I do not know how you strange bolups are still alive."

Lincoln smiled slightly and glanced at Skyra. "Where have I heard that before?"

"I've got a few hypotheses," Virgil said, still watching the tribe below. "First, the humans do intend to harm us. Perhaps they are setting up camp here to block us from going for food and water, thus weakening us until they can kill us."

"We have much food," Skyra said. "With the cave bear's meat, we do not have to go hunting for many days."

"We also do not have to go to the river for water," the other Skyra said.

Lincoln and the others turned to stare at her. "Why not?" Lincoln asked.

The other Skyra furrowed her thick brows as if she had no idea why he would ask that. "We have water in this hill of caves."

"Where?" Virgil asked.

"Many caves are in this hill. I brought Veenah here to find you. I looked for you in caves at the bottom of the hill. In one of the caves I found water. A small river is there, and the water is good to drink."

After a few seconds of silence, Derek said, "I'll be damned."

"That's another game-changer," Virgil said. "Regardless, my first hypothesis is worth considering—the humans do intend to harm us. My second hypothesis is the humans are acutely aware that we, and our clothing and tools, are profoundly different from anything they've seen before. Perhaps they are overcome with curiosity. Perhaps they even believe us to be supernatural, god-like beings, and they moved their camp here to learn from us or to somehow worship us."

"I'd be cautious with that one," Jazzlyn said. "That assumption is a result of centuries of ethnocentric thinking by pious white men."

Virgil's face reddened. "I'm just summarizing possibilities."

Jazzlyn persisted. "For one thing, these people are probably about 35,000 years away from anything like organized worship of supernatural gods. If they have a religious tendency at all, which is doubtful, it would most likely be along the lines of burial rituals. For another thing—"

Lincoln held up a hand to stop her. "A conversation for another time. You and Virgil have both pointed out the bolup tribe may *not* intend to harm us. If that's the case, the reason may not matter much."

"My third hypothesis," Virgil said, "is the humans recognize we could be valuable allies. Their men were initially overpowered by our attack, we have drones that probably frightened them, and they witnessed something they might consider even stranger—nandups who have joined forces with bolups. Perhaps they are inspired by such a concept and wish to join our tribe." He nodded toward the other Skyra. "She pointed out that they are a small tribe to begin with, and they recently lost several of their members, so they may see us as an opportunity to survive."

Derek said, "If we're done kicking around absurd hypotheses, can we discuss how we're going to deal with this problem? We won't be able to leave this hill without walking right through their camp. Either that, or we find a reasonable route to get around to the back side of the hill. I've tried, and I haven't found one yet. Eventually we'll have to get more food —the bear meat isn't going to last forever."

Virgil held up a finger. "I might add we cannot exist only on meat. We must venture out to find plant-based foods, and I'm not sure Skyra can teach us much about how to do that."

"The bolups eat plants," Skyra said. "They can teach you."

The other Skyra growled, perhaps disgusted at the idea of trying to get help from the bolup tribe.

"Back to Derek's suggestion," Lincoln said, trying to steer the conversation to actionable ideas. "Let's decide how we're going to deal with the situation. I don't like the idea of attacking them. We could get ourselves killed."

"Not to mention the ethical issues regarding killing children," Jazzlyn added. "If you kill all the men, the women and children will likely die too."

Lincoln nodded, remembering Skyra had previously explained that bolup women rarely participated in hunting excursions. "The problem is, we don't know the tribe's intentions. We don't speak their language, so we can't ask them."

"Ripple can speak to the bolups," Skyra said.

This took Lincoln by surprise. "Ripple can speak their language?"

"Ripple learned my Una-Loto language quickly. Ripple also learned Di-woto's language quickly."

"Unbelievably quickly," Jazzlyn added.

Lincoln nodded. "Good point. We'll keep that in mind. For now, I think we have no choice but to fortify our camp, in case the bolups do try to attack us. We'll figure out what to do next if the tribe doesn't break camp and leave within a day or two. Agreed?"

His team members nodded. The two Skyras simply stared down at the bolup camp.

A child's voice rang out, and Lincoln turned to see one of the bolup children—a naked kid maybe six or seven years old—pointing up the hill at Lincoln and his group. A bolup woman shouted something at the child, who quickly stopped pointing. The woman gazed up the hill for a few seconds then went back to work on one of the tribe's low shelters.

LINCOLN WAS REMINDED ONCE AGAIN of why he had hired Virgil as his head engineer. Virgil was a whiz at applied physics, and he had already become proficient with the tools from the virtual beings. With a few rapid spins of the cutting tool, he could cut one of the four-foot tubes to the desired length. The package of supplies provided by the virtual beings included several hundred couplers, half of them straight and the rest T-shaped, for connecting the tubes to one another. Oddly, the couplers were pliable and thus would not provide rigid strength to the joint. Therefore, Virgil had surmised the couplers could be hardened, and he discovered he could insert tubes into a coupler, bend the coupler to the desired angle, and apply heat by holding the joint over a fire for a few seconds. This not only shrunk the coupler to grip the tubes, but also hardened it, forming a permanent angled joint that would stay put.

In addition to the tube-cutting tool, Virgil had quickly determined the second tool was for cutting the reflective sheeting. The tool looked simple enough, like two stacked triangle wedges, with a gap between them just wide enough to accommodate the thickness of the reflective sheeting. A thin blade between the two wedges sliced the sheeting when the tool was pushed in the direction of the narrowest point of the triangle. Somehow, perhaps due to some microscopic structural feature of the sheeting, the tool always made an impressively straight cut.

The third tool had taken Virgil more time to figure out. It was a four-inch-wide clamp that could be fitted over a section of the tubing. Once you fitted the clamp on the tubing, the only thing to do was shove a lever back and forth the length of the clamp, which didn't seem to do anything to the tube. However, Virgil had deduced that one important problem remained unsolved—how to attach the reflective sheeting to the tubes. On a hunch, he had run the clamp along the length of a tube, shoving the lever back and forth at the same time, and discovered that the sheeting immediately bonded to the tube if it touched the tube within a few minutes of using the clamp and lever. Lincoln had no idea how, but the clamp's mechanical action seemed to temporarily alter the tube's molecular properties, allowing its surface to bond with the sheeting.

Within a few hours, the team had found nine places among the boulders they could block to prevent intruders from coming near the courtyard by any route other than the path the group typically used. Lincoln's plan was to create barriers over these vulnerable spots using reflective material stretched across the tubes. The barriers could be custom made to fit each specific gap in the boulders. It wouldn't be impenetrable, but it would certainly create a deterrent. Actually, he hoped the barriers' strange reflective surfaces alone would frighten off anyone who tried to approach. Those who were more determined would have to funnel single-file through several bottlenecks, each of which could be defended.

The two Skyras had stayed behind, choosing to remain at Veenah's side. Lincoln and his team stayed together as they worked on the hill, in case the bolups decided to attack. Both Ripples had followed, despite their frequent need to expend power levitating over the rough terrain. At the first of the vulnerable spots, the team worked to create a more-or-less rectangular barrier, nine feet tall and four feet wide, to block the gap. Virgil had constructed a serviceable torch by tying a portion of a sock around the end of a stick and soaking it in heated fat scraped from the bear's hide. Using one of the lighters to re-ignite the torch when needed, the torch provided the heat to shrink and harden the tube couplers.

Once the barrier was complete, they wedged it into place. Lincoln stepped up to the barrier and gave it a swift kick. It popped loose and fell onto its side.

"Exactly what I was afraid of," Virgil said. "We need to figure out a way to anchor the tubes to the boulders. We don't have a drill, or even a pick-axe, nor do we have anything like masonry screws."

Lincoln picked up one of the lengths of tubing and examined its end. The tube was hollow, with a relatively thin outer wall, but it was obviously much stronger than it looked. He vigorously scraped the end against the stone slab at his feet, wondering if it could be sharpened this way. He flipped it around to inspect his progress. The end looked exactly the same. "Any ideas?" he asked the group.

Silence.

Ripple spoke up. "Forgive me for suggesting a procedure for which I have not tested the efficacy, but I may know a way for you to create appropriately sized holes in the stone." Ripple fell silent, as if waiting for permission to continue.

"Spit it out, drone," Derek said.

"I am reasonably sure it will work, but I will need one of the robotic caretakers to test my idea."

"You've got *me* intrigued," Lincoln said.

Jazzlyn turned and headed toward the courtyard. "I'll go grab one," she said over her shoulder.

The other Ripple said, "This should be quite interesting, as I have yet to learn details regarding the robotic caretakers."

"I have much information to share with you," Ripple said. "It will be my pleasure to give you the lowdown, as my human creators might say."

"Ah, a human colloquialism," the other Ripple said. "Yes, I would appreciate you giving me the scoop, the inside story."

"You are most perceptive. I look forward to bringing you up to speed, as you should definitely be in the loop."

"Good God!" Derek boomed. "Instead of one annoying drone, now we have two."

The other Ripple shifted its vision lens toward Derek. "My counterpart has informed me of your belligerence toward drones. You do know we were created to make humans' lives easier, do you not?"

Derek turned to Lincoln, shaking his head. "*Two* of the damn things now!"

Lincoln just grinned. He was actually grateful for Derek's banter. Whether it was with Ripple or with Jazzlyn and

Virgil, it was a reassuring sign his team was still coping with yet another impossible situation.

Jazzlyn returned with one of the rat-sized robots and placed it on its four legs on the stone slab before Ripple. The robot didn't move.

"Please place the end of a tube next to the robotic caretaker," Ripple said.

Lincoln complied.

Ripple retracted its front legs, lowering the front of its shell until its vision lens was only a few inches from the robot. "If this does not work, I will regret having wasted your time."

"We're willing to try just about anything," Lincoln offered as encouragement.

"Very well." The drone fell silent. Its ring of red LEDs flashed then rotated counterclockwise several times.

The robot clicked and snapped as it broke down into its thumb-sized components then continued breaking down until it was a pile of flea-sized specks. Instead of turning into the fine dust Lincoln had seen before, the specks swarmed the end of the tube until a portion of them covered it. They seemed to be still for a moment then began producing a high-pitched hum. A depression formed amidst the specks not on the end of the tube. The depression became a hole in the solid rock slab, deepening with every passing second. Lincoln realized the humming sound was the tiny robots chewing through the stone.

Within approximately a minute, the specks joined together into incrementally larger pieces, again forming the rat-sized robot. The robot skittered a few steps to the side and became still.

"Excellent," Ripple said. The drone nudged the tube with its rubberized foot. "Please confirm the cavity's size."

Lincoln exchanged a glance with Virgil then picked up the tube and inserted it into the hole. The end fit perfectly, and the hole narrowed ever so slightly as the tube went deeper, until the tube was seated firmly. Lincoln was able to get it out, but he was pretty sure it would've been stuck permanently had he tapped it into the hole with a rock.

Virgil rubbed his hands together. "Folks, we are in business."

"I am not one bit surprised by this," Jazzlyn added. "If those things can fix the inside of my body, digging a hole in a boulder is probably a piece of cake."

"In all modesty," said Ripple, "I did play a small role in the process."

"Yes, Ripple, we know you're awesome too," Jazzlyn said.

Lincoln kneeled to take a closer look at the rat-sized robot. Its appearance wasn't all that impressive. It was kind of blocky and unwieldy, certainly less sleek than Lincoln's mini-drones, which he had discarded before the final jump back to Skyra's time. Yet these awkward-looking devices were thousands of years more advanced, and Lincoln was starting to see a glimmer of their full potential. Assuming Ripple could continue to replenish their power, the two robots could be crucial to his group's very survival.

He rose to his feet. "Our job just got a lot easier. I think we can completely fortify our camp by the end of the day."

Within minutes the team had modified the rectangular reflective panel, adding short tubes projecting outward at four locations, and had firmly embedded those tubes into perfectly sized holes in the surrounding stone. Lincoln pushed and kicked but could not budge the completed barrier. Derek struck the tightly stretched reflective material repeatedly with one of the bolup khuls, but the stone blade failed to even make a scratch. Satisfied, they moved on.

Working methodically into the afternoon, the team blocked off all nine of the access points, effectively leaving only one easy route to the courtyard and one to the other cave near the hill's summit. Only about half the tubes and rolls of reflective material had been required to complete the job, leaving more for future projects.

Each time Lincoln had been where he could see the bolups at the base of the hill, the tribe appeared to be occupied with establishing their camp. Beside a large boulder they had erected a slanted shelter of animal skins, seemingly large enough for all the tribe to sit under for shade or to escape the rain. Smoke was billowing from beneath the shelter, and Lincoln caught several whiffs of wood smoke mixed with an odd citrusy aroma.

As far as he could tell, the bolups had made no aggressive moves or attempted climbing the hill.

When Lincoln and his team returned to the courtyard, Skyra was dragging a long section of cave bear intestines through the gap to discard somewhere else. She frowned at Lincoln as she passed by but did not speak, so he left the others and followed her.

"Is everything okay?" he asked when he caught up. "How is Veenah doing?"

She grunted and flung the entrails into a wide crevice. The guts tumbled over the rock face with a series of sickening wet thuds and landed amidst a pile of other organs and bones Skyra had previously deemed useless. She stared down at her hands and fur garments with disgust. "I need to bathe in the river."

"Is everything okay?" he asked again.

She kneeled and wiped her hands on the rock slab. "Veenah does not wake up. The other Skyra wants to be alone with Veenah. The other Skyra does not know who she is, and I do not know who I am anymore."

He watched as she continued wiping her hands, abrading them against the rock more aggressively than necessary.

"The last time we saved Veenah, she was finding her strength," she said. "This time she is losing her strength. I do not understand."

Lincoln considered explaining again that this was a different timeline with different events, but he decided it wouldn't make a difference. "Maybe Veenah just needs more time to rest."

Skyra shuffled to one side and started wiping her hand on a fresh area of rock, seemingly focusing all her attention on the effort.

He kneeled beside her. He didn't know what to say, but he wanted to be closer to her.

She pulled her hands from the stone slab and stared at her palms. "I want to bathe at the river, but I do not want to fight the bolup tribe. I stink like a cave bear's insides!"

"Why don't we look for the river the other Skyra said was flowing through the bottom of this hill? Maybe you can bathe there."

Jazzlyn emerged from the gap to the courtyard. She spotted them but seemed reluctant to approach. "Lincoln? Skyra?"

Lincoln waved for her to come over, then he and Skyra rose to their feet.

"I was just in the cave with Veenah and the other Skyra," Jazzlyn said. "I'm really worried about Veenah. Her breathing and heart rate have become weak. I don't know if she's lapsing into a coma or what, but it doesn't look good."

"Skyra's worried about her too," Lincoln said.

Jazzlyn looked out over the river plain. "Well, you might not agree with this idea, but I think we should use the robotic caretakers on Veenah."

Lincoln frowned. "That could be extremely risky. I know your wound seems like it's healing, but... I don't know, Jazzlyn."

"Yes!" Skyra said. "The robotic caretakers are here to help us. Now they will help Veenah."

Lincoln glowered at Jazzlyn, making it clear she shouldn't have given Skyra this unrealistic hope.

Jazzlyn raised her brows as if scolding *him* for not being the one to suggest the idea first.

Regardless, it was too late now. Skyra's demeanor had taken a one-eighty.

"Come, we will use the caretakers, Lincoln." She took his hand and pulled him toward the courtyard.

10

———

MISSION

47,659 years in the past - Day 3

Skyra knew the caretaker creatures might not help Veenah, but she wanted to at least try. Veenah was not waking up, and Skyra could feel her birthmate's strength slipping away as if it were her own strength. Skyra did not want to watch Veenah die again. The caretakers had helped Jazzlyn, maybe they could help Veenah.

Lincoln and Jazzlyn stopped in the courtyard to ask Ripple about using the caretakers, but Skyra went directly to Veenah's cave. The other Skyra was now lying on the sleeping bag with one arm resting across Veenah's belly. She flicked her eyes toward Skyra but did not speak.

Skyra sat on the stone slab and remained silent for several breaths, figuring out how to explain what the other Skyra would not understand. Her head tried to tell her she was watching herself lying beside her birthmate, but the strange feeling passed—she was not the other Skyra.

"My bolup friends have good medicine," Skyra said. "We will let them use their medicine on Veenah now."

The other Skyra let out a grunt. "Your bolup friends have already used their medicine. Veenah is dying."

"They have another medicine. They will use it now."

The other Skyra pushed herself up onto one elbow. "Why do you trust these bolups? I do not trust them, and you are the same as me."

"You do not know them like I do. They have helped me fight enemies many times. Lincoln and me, we are married. He will put a child in my belly."

The other Skyra curled her lip. "Mumenga."

"Do not call me that. I do not want to kill you."

"Go away. I wish to be alone with my birthmate when she dies."

Skyra gazed at her other self for a breath. "I do not want Veenah to die. We will use another medicine now. You do not have to help, but you will not stop us."

The other Skyra rubbed her hand in a circle on Veenah's belly, the way Skyra used to when Veenah had a belly ache. "I will not stop you, but I do not want your bolup friends to touch her."

Skyra stepped out of the cave and waved at Lincoln. Soon the entire tribe was gathered around Veenah. Lincoln's expression showed he was afraid. Jazzlyn, Virgil, and Derek also looked afraid. Skyra assumed they were afraid of what might happen if the caretaker creatures could not save Veenah. Skyra's other self would become angry, so they had good reason to be afraid.

"Uh, so how does this work?" Lincoln asked. He had come in with the two caretakers in his hands.

While the other Ripple stayed back, Ripple stepped closer

to Veenah. "I possess no formal instructions for such a procedure, so we must rely only on what we observed with Jazzlyn's wound. Open the sleeping bag, please."

Skyra eyed her other self warily for a moment. The other Skyra was staring intently at Veenah's face. The sleeping bag was only covering Veenah's legs, so Skyra pushed the top layer of it aside.

"Please remove her waist-skin," Ripple said.

Skyra untied the cords on her birthmate's waist-skin and pulled the garment from beneath her.

Ripple lifted one of its forelegs and tapped the layer of sleeping bag on the stone floor underneath Veenah's knees. "Place the robots here."

Lincoln put both caretakers between Veenah's knees.

The other Skyra was now staring at Skyra's eyes, her expression fearful.

Ripple's vision light came on, forcing Skyra to squint against the sudden brightness. Ripple lowered its vision orb until it was almost touching one of the caretakers. Three breaths later, the two robot creatures shifted their feet slightly, then they crawled closer to Veenah's groin. One stopped, allowing the other to continue into the narrowing space.

Skyra did not want to watch. Her eyes met the other Skyra's gaze. A sudden pop made the other Skyra wince. There was another pop, and another, then more pops than Skyra could count. The other Skyra looked down at Veenah, but Skyra still did not want to watch. She knew the sounds were the robots breaking into smaller parts, then breaking into even smaller parts.

"Look at me," Skyra said to her other self.

The other Skyra seemed to struggle to pull her eyes away.

"It is better if you look at me," Skyra said.

The pops continued, and Skyra held her other self's gaze. For the first time, she saw a deep cut on the other Skyra's forehead. She wondered why she had not noticed it before.

Several more breaths passed.

Ripple's vision light went off and the cave became dark again.

"I believe the procedure has been successfully initiated," Ripple said, stepping back. "My ability to communicate with the robots is still rudimentary, but I take comfort knowing they required no instruction whatsoever when they entered Jazzlyn's wound. We shall hope for the best."

"The medicine is in Veenah now," Skyra said to her other self.

The other Skyra blinked, then she set Veenah's waist-skin aside and pulled the sleeping bag over her birthmate's legs again. She lay on her side and put her arm across Veenah's chest. "Go away please."

Skyra got to her feet and moved toward the cave opening, followed by Lincoln and his tribemates. As she emerged into the fading sunlight, she heard the other Skyra behind her say, "Ripple, stay here with me please."

***

"I don't know how you can even breathe in there," Lincoln said. He was leaning his head into the smoke cave as Skyra added three more sticks to the glowing coals.

"I like the smell," Skyra replied. "The smoke makes my cape smell good." She finished turning over the strips of drying meat then pushed her fingers against the bear skin to check its softness. She grabbed one of the thinner strips of meat and ducked out through the narrow opening. After biting off a piece of the meat, she handed the rest to Lincoln.

He took a small bite and chewed slowly, then he smiled and took a large bite.

Skyra spoke while chewing. "Not finished drying... do not eat too much... you will be sick."

Lincoln turned the remaining meat over in his hands. "I didn't think I'd like it dried, but this is pretty good. I'll share the rest with my team. He headed toward his tribemates, who were gathered outside the bear cave, talking to Ripple.

Skyra did not want to listen to them talk, and she did not want to go into the cave with her other self and the other Ripple, so she told Lincoln she was going out to watch the bolup tribe. He offered to go with her, but she said she wanted to be alone. Lincoln nodded, although his face showed concern. "Do you have your khul with you?"

She reached behind her neck and wrapped her fingers around the weapon's worn handle. "I always have my khul, Lincoln."

His expression still showed concern as she turned away. She climbed through the gap, made her way along the ledge, passed through the second gap, then came upon one of the barriers Lincoln and his tribemates had built. This barrier was positioned to stop attackers from climbing up a slope to see down into the courtyard.

She stared at the reflective material stretched tight across several tubes. She turned her head slightly, confused. The material appeared to move. She turned her head again, trying to focus on the movement. Suddenly she realized what she was seeing, and a grunt of surprise escaped her throat. Why had she not seen it before? In all the time in the empty city, surrounded by buildings wrapped in this reflective material, her head had not let her understand what her eyes must have seen. Now she understood. Her own reflection was there, staring back at her, as if she were looking into a river with no ripples or waves. She looked away then turned back to the barrier, and for a few breaths she could not see herself, but then her head understood the reflection again, and she was once more staring at her own face.

She stepped closer, and her muscles tensed. Her head tried to tell her she was looking at the other Skyra, but the face in the reflection did not have a fresh wound above one eye, so the strange feeling passed. She pinched the skin on the side of her face. Other than the wound, she was just like the other Skyra, but she was different from Veenah—her eyes, her chin, the speckles on her cheeks, all slightly different from Veenah's.

Skyra bared her teeth. Her reflection did the same. She stuck out her tongue. Again, her reflection did the same. "You do not know who you are anymore, do you?" she asked. Her reflection gazed back without replying.

The sun was dropping behind the edge of the hill, so Skyra left her reflection and climbed to the same boulder where she had watched the sun rise that morning. She positioned herself by the edge, where she could see the bolup camp below.

The bolups were crowded beneath the large shelter—Skyra could see their backs as they sat facing the center of the shelter, where smoke was billowing from a campfire. Skyra did not know what bolups liked to do when they sat by their fire at the end of the day. Maybe, like nandups, they told stories or played word games so they could laugh before sleeping. Maybe these bolups were talking about how they were going to attack Skyra and her new tribe. Even if Skyra could understand their language, she was too far away to hear their words. She should have brought Ripple with her. Ripple had good ears and could learn languages much faster than Skyra could.

A bolup man emerged from the shelter. Skyra watched him walk to the tree where the two nandup women were tied. A few breaths later, her muscles tensed when she heard a woman's pained wail. The man pulled one of the nandups to her feet and forced her across the camp, his hand on the back of her neck. She wailed again and tried to yank free from his grip. Without slowing his stride, the man swung his other arm and struck her face. She fell silent and stopped struggling. The man guided her to one of the shelters, shoved her to the ground, and kicked her until she pushed open the flap hanging over the opening and crawled inside. He followed her in. A wail arose from inside the shelter then was cut short, probably by another blow.

Skyra jumped to her feet, her hands becoming fists. This was what those stinking bolups had done to Veenah. Skyra did not know the woman or her tribe, but the woman was a nandup. Nandups did not raid other nandup camps. Nandups helped other nandups, even if they were from a different tribe.

Skyra's legs wanted to run, to carry her down the hill so she could kill the bolup man. She would drag the man from his shelter so his tribemates could watch as she split open his head and mashed his brain into the sand.

Her legs wanted to run, but her head told them to stop. She could not attack the bolup tribe alone. They would kill her, and she would never sleep beside Lincoln again. She would not know if the caretaker creatures were helping Veenah.

A growl rose from her chest and escaped into a furious scream.

The bolups emerged from under the large shelter and scanned the boulder hill, trying to find the source of the scream. One of them spotted Skyra and pointed. Soon they were all staring up at her.

Skyra pulled out her khul and held it above her head. "Kami-fu-bolup-mafeem. Aibul-khulo-tekne-té!" *Listen to me, human men! I will take your strength!* She knew the stinking bolups did not speak her language, but Skyra did not care whether they understood her words or not.

She lowered her khul and stared down at the tribe. Gradually, her heart stopped pounding so hard in her chest, and her breathing returned to normal. The bolups began moving back under the shelter, realizing they were not being attacked. The man who had forced the nandup woman into his shelter had crawled out and was staring up the hill. The nandup woman remained in the shelter.

"Skyra!" Lincoln shouted. "What's happening?"

Lincoln and his tribemates had come out of the courtyard and were all looking up at her from one of the ledges.

"I am angry," she replied. She sat back down on the boulder.

Lincoln, Jazzlyn, Virgil, and Derek climbed onto the boulder and sat with her.

"We thought you were in danger or something," Jazzlyn said.

The bolup man turned and started crawling back into his shelter.

Skyra raised her khul again. "Khamu-lesif-rha!" *Do not touch her!*

The man stopped and looked up the hill again.

The woman's head appeared from inside the shelter. She scrambled past the man, staggered to her feet, and started running. The man jumped up and quickly caught her. Instead of taking her back to his shelter, though, he shoved her back to the base of the tree and forced her to sit beside the other captive nandup. For several breaths his hands worked with the ropes, then he left the two bound women. Before going under the large shelter with the rest of his tribe, the man gazed up the hill toward Skyra.

"Are you okay?" Lincoln asked.

Skyra glanced at him and realized he was talking to her. "I am angry," she said again. "Those stinking bolups are hurting the nandup women the way they hurt Veenah."

"They're freakin' savages," Derek said. "Simple as that."

"Actually, it's not that simple," Virgil said. "These humans are separated from us by only 47,000 years. That is not enough time for major structural changes to take place, and presumably not enough time for fundamental cognitive changes. If we could take an infant from this bolup tribe and raise it 47,000 years in the future in our own timeline, I'm fairly certain it would be indistinguishable physically and cognitively from the rest of the population."

Derek huffed. "You can't possibly know that."

"I have to agree with Virgil on this," Jazzlyn said. "These people's behaviors and philosophies are learned rather than innate."

"I have to agree also," Lincoln said. "However, I'm not sure how much difference it makes. Their behaviors are so ingrained into their culture that I can't imagine how we could ever convince them to stop killing and abusing Neanderthals, or engaging in cannibalism, or any other behaviors we consider savage."

Skyra growled, frustrated with the others using words she did not know. "You will still help me with my plan, Lincoln. I want to kill all these stinking bolups, but I will only kill one if you will help me make the others change."

They all stared at her.

Lincoln spoke to his tribemates. "Skyra is inspired by Di-woto's impact on the humans and Neanderthals of her time-line. Skyra wants to change this entire world the way Di-woto changed hers. In other words, she's all-in with Ripple's plan. And I gotta say, despite my skepticism, if she's committed, I'm committed."

Derek said, "Am I the only realistic one here? I'll say it again—they're freakin' savages! That's why we built barriers to keep them out. They'll probably attack us the minute we leave this hill to gather food. I'm fine with embracing the grand plan for changing this world of terror into a utopia, but come on, folks—we'll be lucky to be alive a month from now."

Jazzlyn leaned over and shoved Derek's shoulder. "Mister Melodramatic, you just said the same thing Lincoln said. Despite your skepticism, you're willing to commit to our mission."

"Oh, now it's our *mission* to spread love throughout the land of teeth, claws, and bloody murder?" Derek asked.

"Okay, okay," Lincoln said. "I think we all agree on one thing. As long as we're here, we might as well do what we can to make this world a better place. Agreed?"

His tribemates nodded.

"I've been thinking about this," Virgil said, "and I have a hypothesis."

"Of course you do," Derek quipped.

Virgil ignored him. "In a world already steeped in brute force, I don't think brute force is the way to initiate the change we want to see. If we want humans and Neanderthals here to integrate, we cannot start a violent revolution the way Di-woto did. The situation here is different. Di-woto's people were being tricked into fighting a perpetual war, and Di-woto exposed the deception. Here, there is no deception to expose. Nandups and bolups fight and abuse each other for a number of other reasons. My hypothesis is as follows. We obviously cannot force the humans and Neanderthals to integrate, or to even tolerate each other, nor would we want to. We cannot trick them into integrating. Instead, we must give them the *desire* to integrate."

"What does that mean?" Skyra asked.

Lincoln said, "He's saying we have to get the nandup and bolup tribes to understand why they should not fight each other. They won't change unless they *want* to change."

"I just can't wait to hear his step-by-step procedure for how we're going to do that," Derek said.

Jazzlyn shoved Derek's shoulder again.

Virgil continued speaking. "I do not have a procedure, but I have ideas. First, we become role models." He glanced at Jazzlyn. "I'm not trying to be ethnocentric or pious in any way. However, if we plan carefully, I suspect we can demonstrate a way of life so desirable that the nandups and bolups will willingly attempt to emulate it. In order to do that, though, we need to get their attention, in a really big way. Not just the attention of the bolup tribe at the base of this hill, but *all* the nandup and bolup tribes throughout the region, and eventually far beyond. We need to become famous—a beacon of light for the world."

Jazzlyn shook her head. "If you're suggesting people come from far and wide to see this beacon of light for themselves, that won't work. You need to remember, the people of this time are hunter-gatherers. Each tribe requires a certain amount of land to harvest enough resources to sustain them. This is not yet a world in which large numbers of people can gather in one place. You'd need a thriving trade economy for that, as well as a broad understanding of centralized food storage, as well as other concepts I can't even think of right now."

"I've already considered those points," Virgil said. "Therefore, our goal would be to influence the nearest tribes profoundly, so they themselves become role models for more distant tribes, who then embrace the desired changes also and become role models for even more distant tribes. We ignite the spark, then the fire will gradually spread to every existing tribe."

Lincoln said, "That could take hundreds or even thousands of years. We'll never see the results."

Virgil nodded. "Which is why we must make an impactful, world-shattering impression on the tribes in this area now, and it must improve their lives. I didn't say it would be easy."

"Pray tell, Virgil, how might we make such a world-shattering impression?" Derek asked. "We have two smart-ass drones, a dwindling collection of camping gear, and some left-over reflective sheeting and poles. Other than that, it's just us, and I'm the only one around here with the sparkling personality to inspire others." He bared his teeth in a strange bolup grin.

Jazzlyn let out a sharp laugh then slapped her black robot hand over her mouth as if she did not want the bolups to hear her laughing. Lincoln laughed too. Virgil just shook his head.

"I don't know yet how we're going to do it," Virgil said. "That's why we're having this conversation. We're brainstorming for ideas."

"Don't forget about the robotic caretakers," Jazzlyn said.

"If they actually save Veenah's life, like I believe they will, and if Ripple can really keep them powered up, there's no telling what other ways they might help us. I'm just saying, with the drones, the camping gear, the reflective sheets, the caretakers —the technology we do have is *amazing*. If we put our minds to it, we can make a hell of an impression on the tribes here."

Lincoln turned to Skyra. "You told me you wanted to make a plan to change your world. You said you wanted to teach others that nandups and bolups can be married. What will we have to do to make the tribes want to change their ways?"

Skyra turned and stared down at the bolup camp as she considered the question. Di-woto's plan was bold and dangerous and difficult, but it worked. Skyra's plan would have to be even more bold. She turned back to Lincoln. "We must show the nandups and bolups our tribe is better than their tribes. We must show them we are strong, and we are happy. Then the nandups and bolups will want to change their tribes to be like our tribe. We must make them afraid of us."

Lincoln frowned. "Afraid? Why?"

"When they see we are strong and happy, they will want to take what we have, to make their own tribes strong and happy. If they are afraid of us, they will want to be like us without trying to kill us or take what we have."

"You have to admit, there's some logic to that," Jazzlyn said.

Skyra continued. "After we make them afraid, we must keep making them afraid. If we do not, they will lose their fear, then they will come and kill us to take what we have."

"I'm guessing *making them afraid* will involve fighting and killing," Derek said.

"I am afraid of woolly rhinos," Skyra said. "Do you know why?" When no one answered, she said, "A woolly rhino killed my birthmother. Another woolly rhino killed Stura. Stura was kind to me and Veenah when we were girls, and she helped protect us from tribemates who wanted to hurt us. Woolly rhinos know how to make people fear them. I fear them, but I still want their strength."

Everyone remained silent for a few breaths.

"I get it," Derek said. "But if we keep fighting and killing, sooner or later our luck is going to run out. Derek Dagger is invincible, of course, but I've grown kind of fond of y'all, even though Virgil can be a pain in my ass. All I'm saying is, surely we're smart enough to figure out a *peaceful* way to make the tribes not want to kill us."

Skyra let a growl escape from her chest. "You are strange bolups. You make strange things I cannot understand, but you do not seem to understand my homeland. Your homeland must be very different from mine. Di-woto's homeland is very different, and the land of the ghost people is very different, but your homeland must be even stranger than I can understand."

Lincoln put his hand on her knee. "I wish we could have taken you there. Our people rarely kill each other, and when they do, they are usually caught and punished."

Skyra gazed down the hillside, trying to imagine such a place. "How are they punished?"

Lincoln seemed to hesitate. "Well, usually they're captured and put in jail. Jail is like a cage. Depending on the type of killing they did, the killers might be put in jail for the rest of their lives, to prevent them from killing other people."

She turned to Lincoln. "I have killed people. I do not want to be in a cage."

"You have killed people to keep them from killing you, or to save Veenah from the bolups. You had good reasons to kill, and you should not be punished."

"I am going to kill again," she said. She tilted her head down the hill. "I am going to the bolup camp. I will release the two nandup women, and I will kill one of the bolup men. I know which one I will kill. If the others attack me, I will kill more. Would your people put me in a cage for doing this?"

Lincoln frowned and exchanged glances with his tribemates. "Um, that's not as easy to answer as you might think. It depends on why you choose to kill. If the bolup man attacks you while you are there, and you kill him to save your own life, then you probably wouldn't be put in jail. If you go there intending to kill the man and free the women, you might be punished."

She chewed on her lip for a few breaths. "Maybe I am glad you could not take me to your homeland, because I do not want to be put in a cage."

"You're not actually thinking of doing it, are you—going down there to kill?"

"No, I am finished thinking about it. I am going to do it. You and your tribemates will help me please. I do not want the bolups to kill me. I want to sleep beside you, Lincoln, and I want to see if Veenah will live."

"Great, here we go again," Derek said. "This may be the time our luck runs out."

Skyra was tired of talking. She got to her feet. "I will go to the bolup camp in the morning. If you do not want to help me, I will go by myself."

11

____

CONFRONTATION

47,659 YEARS *in the past - Day 4*

LINCOLN THOUGHT he heard something outside the cave. He lifted his head. He'd already been awake for some time, staring at the remaining coals glowing in the fire and trying not to think about what Skyra had persuaded him to help her do this morning. Now his eyes needed to adjust to the darkness beyond the coals.

Several seconds passed, and a few details started to emerge. He should've been seeing more of the faint moonlight entering the cave mouth, but most of the opening was black. Lincoln's skin began to prickle as he realized something much larger than Ripple was blocking the opening. How was that possible? Ripple had been stationed at the cave mouth to watch for danger.

The shape moved slightly, and two eyes caught the red glow of the coals.

Lincoln's unease transformed into a rush of panic.

"Skyra!" He shook her shoulder, and she sat up immediately. "I think the other bear is back!"

Skyra spun around to follow his gaze. "The female," she said.

"What's going on?" Virgil mumbled.

In a flurry of motion, Skyra got to her knees, leaned toward the fire, and slammed her bare hand into the coals from the side, flinging a shower of glowing embers toward the cave entrance. "Felu-alodonlo!" she screamed.

Several of the coals struck the bear's face. Without making a sound, the creature spun around and ran off.

Everyone was awake now, muttering curses and floundering to get up.

Skyra whimpered and blew on her palm.

"Jesus, let me see that," Lincoln said, grabbing her hand. He turned it so he could see her palm in the light of the remaining coals, but the skin was smeared black, and he couldn't tell how severe the burn was.

She pulled her hand back. "Do not worry. I have scared many animals away with fire." She turned to Jazzlyn. "Sometimes I would be happy to have a good weapon hand like yours," she said, referring to Jazzlyn's prosthetic hand.

"Oh, girl, you do *not* want that," Jazzlyn said without taking her eyes off the cave opening. "Was that really a bear?"

"I wanted to be ready to kill the female when it came back," Skyra replied. "Now it knows we have taken its cave, and it will not come back again."

Lincoln eyed Derek, who was sitting quietly, staring at the opening. This was exactly the kind of incident that could trigger one of his lycanthropy episodes. "Derek, tell me what's happening."

"Don't worry, I'm fine—just an adrenaline rush. In fact, I

haven't felt even the slightest hint of an episode coming on since we were wired into the virtual world. More to the point, though... how the hell do you know that bear won't come back, Skyra?"

"The bear does not want to have fire in its face again."

"Don't question the girl who throws fire with her bare hand," Jazzlyn said. She turned to Skyra. "Which, by the way, was pretty badass."

Skyra licked her palm and blew on it again. "I do not know what *pretty badass* means."

"It means you're—"

"El-de-né!" a voice shouted from somewhere outside. It sounded like Skyra, so it had to be the other Skyra.

Skyra jumped to her feet, grabbed a bolup-made spear, and dashed from the cave.

Lincoln and the others scrambled for their own weapons and followed her out.

Despite the darkness, Lincoln could see the courtyard was empty—no sign of Skyra, Ripple, or the cave bear—so he ran to the other cave. A small campfire was still burning inside, illuminating both Skyras, both Ripples, and Veenah, who was sitting up, wide-eyed and very much alive.

"Veenah did not die, Lincoln!" Skyra said. "The caretakers made her better."

"I'll be damned, she's awake," Derek said as he and the others came in behind Lincoln.

Veenah's face was still bruised, but most of the swelling was gone. She flicked her eyes warily between Lincoln and his team members then said, "Aibul-lotup-tekne-té." Her voice was more vibrant now than any other time Lincoln had heard her speak.

"Veenah says she has found her strength," the other Skyra

said. She pointed down at the two rat-sized robots, now standing motionless on the stone beside Veenah's feet. "Your strange creatures have made her strong again. I am happy you used the medicine of your creatures."

Skyra kneeled in front of Veenah and spoke a string of words in their Una-Loto language. Veenah replied, her words crisp and seemingly lucid. If this was Veenah's normal voice, it was different from Skyra's. Perhaps a little higher, more feminine. The difference was subtle, but Lincoln detected it nonetheless.

The other Skyra spoke to Veenah, joining the conversation.

Ripple stepped up beside Lincoln. "Would you like me to translate? I am quite fluent in the Una-Loto language."

"Just a summary would be fine for now," Lincoln replied.

"Veenah remembers seeing two Skyras before, as well as you and your team, but now that she has regained her mental faculties, she is greatly confused by the situation. Skyra is attempting to explain. A formidable task, wouldn't you agree?"

Lincoln nodded absently. He handed his spear to Derek and picked up the two rat-sized robots. Previously he had considered discarding them, thinking they were useless. Now they were possibly his team's most valuable asset. "Are these things dead again? They're not moving."

"I detect a decreased power level, but they are not dead," Ripple replied. "I will instruct them to recharge now if you wish."

"I don't think you need to do it right now." Lincoln turned slightly to allow more firelight to fall on the robots, then he looked more closely. Their shells were jointed, making them look vaguely like lobster tails with legs, but he couldn't detect the seams where the thumb-sized component robots were snapped together. "Why aren't they moving?"

"They have no reason to move until they are given a directive."

"Do you have any idea what else these things can do besides heal wounds and dig holes in solid rock?"

Ripple's red lights flashed, momentarily drawing Veenah's attention from her conversation with the two Skyras. "I receive minimal feedback from these devices. Perhaps the only way we will find out is by trial and error."

"It's the *error* part that concerns me."

"Indeed," Ripple said. "However, great things do not happen without great risk. That is something your future self liked to say, Lincoln."

"I doubt I was referring to risking my life and the lives of my friends." Lincoln stepped away from Ripple and kneeled beside Skyra. Veenah shrank away, and he tried to give her a friendly smile, although he knew nandups considered bolup smiles to be strange.

Skyra said something to Veenah that included Lincoln's name, which didn't seem to relax her much.

He spoke to Skyra softly. "I'm happy Veenah is feeling better. I'm happy for her *and* for you. This changes our plans for the morning, right?" Lincoln considered Skyra's desire to free the nandup women from the bolup camp to be needlessly dangerous.

She flashed a broad smile. "Yes, this changes our plan! Veenah is better now, and she will go with us."

He blinked at her, not sure he had heard correctly. "You want her to... she can't possibly... she was just, like, in a coma."

"Veenah found her strength. She will help us kill the men who hurt her, then we will save the nandup women."

"We will all attack the bolup camp together," the other Skyra said.

Lincoln studied Skyra's face, then the other Skyra's face. They both had the same expression, the determined one he had seen many times before. They were going to do this, with or without him and his team. "Just... hold on. I understand you want to free the nandup women, and I agree, but I'd like to do it without getting killed. Skyra, you were right when you said we need to make the other tribes want to be like our tribe. We can't do that if we kill them, or if they kill us."

Skyra stared at him with an expression he couldn't read.

He persisted. "Please give me some time to talk to my team. We'll come up with a plan for saving the nandup women without killing the tribe. If the plan doesn't work, then I guess we'll have to do it your way. Can you give us a little time?"

Skyra let out a growl, then she turned to the other Skyra. "Lincoln and his tribemates like to talk about things. Talking is how they make a plan. We will see what plan they make, then we will go to the bolup camp."

The other Skyra let out an identical growl and turned her attention back to Veenah.

"I APOLOGIZE PROFUSELY for abandoning my post," Ripple said once they were again in the courtyard, which was now steadily becoming brighter with the rising sun. "I caught a faint signal from the robotic caretakers, indicating they had completed their task and exited Veenah's body. I felt compelled to see what they had accomplished. I had no idea a cave bear would come at such an inopportune time. For what it is worth, I am pleased you were not mauled, dismembered, disemboweled, or otherwise molested or imposed upon by the creature."

"Is this damn drone making light of our near-death experience?" Derek asked.

"We accept your apology," Lincoln said to Ripple. "Next time you have to leave your post, though, let us know first."

"I most assuredly will."

Lincoln stared at the rat-sized robots still in his hands. "We need to protect these things at any cost, maybe hide them somewhere safe. I suppose we might even have to make sure they don't wander off on their own."

Jazzlyn held out her hands. "Do you mind if I borrow those for a bit? I'll need Ripple's help, too. I have an idea."

Lincoln hesitated.

She thrust her hands out farther. "I know we're supposed to be devising a nonviolent plan for freeing the nandup women—my idea happens to be related. You guys go ahead and start brainstorming."

He reluctantly handed her the robots. "You realize how important these are now, right?"

She accepted them and cocked an eyebrow at him. "Don't you think I know that better than anyone? They're important because they can *do* things, and I have a few ideas. Ripple will know what's safe for them and what's not. Isn't that right, Ripple?"

"I will monitor whatever feedback they provide," the drone said.

Jazzlyn headed for the far side of the courtyard, with Ripple at her heels.

Lincoln sighed and turned to Derek and Virgil. "It's time to get creative."

By mid-afternoon they had a plan. Lincoln still preferred to avoid conflict with the bolup tribe altogether, but the Skyras didn't want to wait any longer, and Veenah now seemed even more determined than her birthmates. Lincoln already knew what Skyra was like when she was determined to do something. Now he was discovering the three genetically-identical nandups together could be a force of nature.

Skyra distributed hefty strips of dried bear meat to everyone. The group sat in the courtyard, gnawing on the meat, which was now essentially smoked jerky and required some effort to chew. Lincoln was hungry enough to not even care about the gamey taste. He needed to get used to eating wild game anyway.

Lincoln attempted several times to lighten the mood with jovial statements, but soon he gave up. The impending confrontation was too heavy a weight to be lightened with words. Everyone knew it was possible they might not live through it.

They passed around a water bladder refilled from the spring the other Skyra had found in a cavity at the hill's base.

When the bladder was empty, Skyra got to her feet. "Now we will go to the bolup camp."

Without a word or a glance, the group gathered their weapons, as well as the items they had created for the confrontation, and began making their way down the hill. Both Ripples followed, levitating over the more difficult areas.

After explaining his team's plan to the Skyras, Lincoln had finally made them agree to persuade Veenah not to kill any of the bolups, including the men who had abused her. This mission was not one of vengeance. Instead, it was to free the nandup women and begin building a relationship with the humans that might eventually change the way they interacted with Neanderthals.

The only open path down to the rocky field brought them almost directly to the edge of the bolup camp. The bolups spotted them descending the hill and went into a flurry of activity, shouting at each other and grabbing their weapons. When Lincoln's group reached the field, they were faced with eight armed men, including the injured man without hair, as well as three women and the young boy who looked to be about seven or eight. The tribespeople were undeniably fierce, but now they were facing a group including three healthy nandup fighters. Neanderthals did not have much division of labor between sexes, and the women hunted and fought alongside the men. Skyra had explained that bolup tribes often raided nandup camps, but only when some of the nandups were away from camp on a hunting expedition. This bolup tribe had already been diminished in recent days, and now Veenah and the two Skyras could probably kill them all if they had to.

Then again, everything could change with one good shot from a bow or one hard strike with a khul.

"Put the shields in place," Lincoln said.

Derek and Virgil each carried an eight-foot-square shield, constructed of reflective material stretched over a boxy framework of tubing extending outward so the two shields could be held back-to-back to enclose the entire group within a clamshell-like barrier. The bottom was open to the ground, allowing them to advance or retreat while holding the two pieces together around them.

Derek and Virgil positioned the two shields side-by-side in front of the group. With the reflective side facing out,

Lincoln could see the bolups, but they couldn't see him or his team.

The bolups stared at the barrier. Surprisingly, they remained silent. They appeared more curious than frightened. Two of the men inched forward, one holding a khul, the other a spear. The one with the khul got close enough to reach out and touch the reflective material. He ran his fingers over the smooth surface then pushed on it, forcing it inward slightly.

Lincoln scanned the faces in his own group, hoping they were ready for this confrontation. As expected, the two Skyras appeared intensely resolute. Veenah's expression was harder to read, possibly due to her bruises. Derek, Virgil, and Jazzlyn were clearly attempting to mask their terror.

Lincoln directed his gaze to the two drones standing behind his group. "Ripple, do your thing." He then pointed to the other Ripple. "You will translate, but keep your volume low—we don't want you to distract the bolups. Provide accurate summaries rather than direct translation. Got it?"

"I understand," the other Ripple said at an appropriately low volume.

Ripple stepped around the barrier, forcing the two foremost bolups to move back. The other bolups stepped forward, forming a semicircle around Ripple and brandishing their weapons, probably thinking the drone was some kind of strange animal. They studied Ripple's shell as if taking in every detail.

Ripple spoke in the bolup language, prompting exclamations of surprise. Both Ripples had informed Lincoln they had encountered several bolup tribes during the two years they had been in Skyra's time and had learned some of the common human language of this region.

"My counterpart has delivered its prepared statement to

the bolups," the other Ripple said softly. "It has forcefully informed the bolups our tribe is strong and can easily kill them, but we will not kill them if they allow us to take the two nandup women. Now my counterpart is informing the bolups we are stronger only because we are a combined tribe of both species. If the bolups want to be strong like us, they must stop raiding nandup camps. They must make friends with nandups, and they must combine their tribe with a nandup tribe. This is the only way they will be strong. They have been cruel to their nandup captives, so now they must give the two women to us."

One reason Lincoln wanted the other Ripple to translate was he didn't fully trust Ripple to carry out its role exactly as instructed. Ripple had a tendency to be deceptive at times, especially when the drone thought it was carrying out its plan. The other Ripple would have the same tendency, of course, and the two drones could have together conspired to deviate from their instructions, but at least this way Lincoln felt a little more in control of the situation.

One of the bolup men spoke to Ripple, and the other Ripple continued translating. "The bolup seems to be avoiding our request by asking questions. He asks what kind of animal Ripple is, and he asks how Ripple can speak like a bolup. He asks how we made our reflective shields and your clothing." The drone paused, listening. "He asks how bolups can live with nandups, as nandups are dangerous. He says nandups are animals to be hunted and killed. Nandup women are to be taken and used for simbelu, which I am guessing refers to pleasure, probably of a sexual nature."

Skyra growled. "Ripple, tell the stinking bolups to give us the women now, or we will kill them all."

Ripple hesitated then spoke again to the bulops. The

other Ripple said, "Ripple is showing restraint, and is sticking to the original script. Ripple reminds the bolups they must stop raiding nandup camps and they must combine their tribe with a nandup tribe in order to be strong." The other Ripple paused again to listen. "Now Ripple complies with Skyra's request. The bolups must give us the nandup women now, or they will suffer under our merciless strength."

Lincoln was reluctant to deviate from the plan, but a thought occurred to him, and he couldn't shake it. "Ripple, ask them why they moved their camp to the base of our hill. What do they want?"

Ripple said, "Are you sure you want to—"

"Just ask them!"

Ripple spoke to the bolups.

This time another man stepped forward to speak—the injured man without his hair.

After listening, Ripple said, "This is rather surprising. The bolups do not question our strength, as they have already seen we are a strong and unusual tribe. The reason they moved their camp here is because they hope to kill and consume the flesh of one of our bolup tribe members. That would be you, Lincoln, or perhaps one of your team members. They seem to think killing and eating you will give them whatever strength you possess. As none of you appear to be particularly physically strong, perhaps they are referring to your cognitive abilities, or perhaps simply your clothing and other possessions."

"You gotta be freakin' kidding me," Derek said. "They wanna *eat* us?"

Lincoln was sorry he'd asked. On the other hand, maybe it was better to know what was going on in these bolups' minds.

The hairless man spoke again, and Ripple translated.

"They are willing to give us the two nandups in return for one of our bolups. Lincoln, you are much too valuable and should not be killed and consumed. If you wish to make this deal, one of your team members would be a better choice."

Lincoln turned to his team members. "Volunteers?" Despite the volatile situation, he managed a slight grin.

"One day I'm going to smash that goddamn drone," Derek muttered.

"We won't be making that deal," Lincoln called out to Ripple. "It's time now for our show." He took over holding Derek's shield and said, "You're first. Get back behind the shields fast if you need to."

Derek nodded, then he shrugged off the daypack he'd brought, set it on the ground, and pulled out three nearly spherical stones he'd collected earlier. Lincoln and Virgil shifted the two shields apart enough for Derek to step out beside Ripple. He spoke firmly. "They call me Derek Dagger, a name that strikes fear into the hearts of savages like you. You want to see who you're messing with?" He hesitated for a few seconds, perhaps fearing an attack, then he planted his feet wider apart and started juggling the rocks.

The bolups, including several of the women and the four kids who were old enough to walk, moved closer, watching Derek without expression.

"That's right," Derek said. "I'd like to see you try this." He fumbled one of the rocks but quickly picked it up and resumed juggling.

"You're up," Lincoln said to Jazzlyn.

She slipped between the two shields and moved between Derek and Ripple. She held out her black carbon fiber polymer prosthetic hand. The bolups warily moved even closer as she flexed the fingers and thumb, demonstrating the hand's dexterity. She made a fist and held it out in a threatening pose. With her other hand she produced one of the group's last two butane lighters from her pocket. She took the lighter in her prosthetic hand and deftly flicked it, producing a bluish, torch-like flame. She shoved her hand into her pocket again, this time pulling out a wad of pulverized dried grass Skyra had given her. The grass ignited immediately as Jazzlyn held it to the flame, forcing her to drop it to the ground, where it burned brightly for a few seconds before going out.

The bolups stared, still without overt signs of fear or fascination. However, they weren't becoming aggressive, which Lincoln took as a positive sign.

"Ripple, it's your turn," he said.

Ripple's task was patterned after a performance the drone had used to confuse attacking nandup warriors in Di-woto's timeline. Ripple emitted a low hum as it activated its maglev module and rose from the ground. It hovered at shoulder height for a few seconds then began playing mild, orchestral music through its speakers. The music started with a few violins then swelled to include woodwinds and subtle brass.

Derek continued juggling. Jazzlyn continued flexing her prosthetic hand. Ripple continued playing music. It was a pitiful circus performance, but the bolups were watching instead of attacking. Now it was time to see just how impressed they really were.

"Okay, stop," Lincoln said. "Ripple, tell them to give us the nandup women *now.*"

Still levitating, Ripple cut the music and complied, this time at a significantly more forceful volume.

The bolups exchanged words and glances, and Lincoln thought he detected some anxiety now. One of the men stepped away from the group and walked to the tree where the nandup women were bound. He kneeled and untied the ropes from the tree but not from the women's necks. He got to his feet and yanked roughly on the ropes, forcing the women to get up, then he pulled them across the camp to Lincoln's group.

The man dragged the nandups directly to Derek and Jazzlyn and held out the ropes. Jazzlyn started to take the ropes, but Veenah abruptly pushed past Lincoln and through the gap between the shields, then she snatched the ropes from the man's hand. Veenah barked a few Una-Loto words at the man, and she shook one of the khuls Skyra had taken from the man's dead tribemates. The man flicked his eyes toward the khul and bared his teeth at Veenah, but he stepped back, apparently yielding.

"Bring them back behind the shields," Lincoln said.

Veenah couldn't understand his words, but Jazzlyn and Derek coaxed her and the two captive women through the gap between the shields.

Lincoln exhaled, finally allowing himself to believe the plan was working.

Another of the bolup men spoke, and the other Ripple quietly translated from behind Lincoln. "The bolup has stated his tribe will now take one of our bolups. It appears they still believe you are willing to trade."

Lincoln ground his teeth in frustration. "Ripple, tell them killing and eating one of us is *not* the way to make their tribe strong. They must combine their tribe with a nandup tribe. That is the *only* way! If they try to take one of us, we will kill them. Also tell them we have a gift for them, a reminder of how important our words are."

He turned to Jazzlyn. "Let's see if they like it."

"They better appreciate it," Jazzlyn said. She kneeled

beside Derek's pack and hefted out the object she'd made with the help of Ripple and the rat-sized robots. The object was a sculpture, about sixteen inches tall, carved from a solid boulder by thousands of almost microscopic robots. In stunning detail, the sculpture depicted a man and woman in an embrace, the woman looking up at the man's face, the man looking down at hers. The woman was shorter and stockier than the man, and although the couple's heads were each no larger than a lime, the woman clearly had the sloped forehead and prominent brows of a Neanderthal, while the man clearly had the thinner features of a human. The sculpture was, in fact, an astounding likeness of Lincoln and Skyra. By tedious trial and error, Jazzlyn had relayed countless instructions through Ripple to the robotic caretakers' components until she was satisfied with the outcome.

As Jazzlyn had predicted, the robots could do more with solid rock than just dig simple holes.

Cradling the sculpture in her arms, she stepped between the two shields and advanced toward the bolups. She placed it upright on the ground and backed away. "Tell them they can have this," she said to Ripple. "This gift shows what they need to do to become a strong tribe."

Ripple translated. Three of the older children came forward, seemingly intrigued, and squatted by the sculpture. They touched it, and one of them tried to lift it, only to find it was too heavy. Some of the men and women gathered around also, squatting behind the children to look.

"Tell them we are going back to our camp now," Lincoln said. "Tell them we will be watching them, waiting for them to become a strong tribe by joining with nandups."

"The nandup tribes are still camped in the Kapolsek foothills, Lincoln," Skyra reminded him.

"I know, but if this is going to work at all, these bolups need to start changing now."

Ripple spoke to the tribe.

A scuffle behind Lincoln drew his attention. Veenah had loosened the rope on one of the women and was trying to pull it off over the woman's head. The battered nandup struggled and whimpered, apparently confused about what was happening to her. The other Skyra grabbed the woman's arms to hold her still, and soon the rope came off.

Veenah spoke gently to the woman, then she and the other Skyra stepped back, giving her some room. Lincoln could see distinct nandup features in the women's face, but she had been beaten too severely to tell what she may have looked like under normal circumstances.

The woman bolted. She ran toward the river, stumbling over stones and weeds.

Lincoln swung around. Several of the bolup tribesmen were watching the woman escape. "Ripple, tell them not to pursue her!" Lincoln ordered. "Tell them they must never capture nandup women again."

Veenah was already removing the second woman's rope, this time without a struggle. This woman had been beaten as badly as the first but seemed more alert. She stared steadily at Veenah as the rope came off. Instead of fleeing and following the first woman, she thrust an open palm toward Veenah.

For several seconds it seemed as if an unspoken understanding passed between the two nandups.

Just as Lincoln began to sense the purpose of the outstretched hand, Veenah spoke several forceful words and handed her khul to the woman.

Lincoln almost dropped the shield as he tried to step back toward Veenah and the woman. "Hey, that's not a good—"

The woman flung herself forward, knocked Lincoln aside, and ran through the gap between the shields. She rushed straight for one of the bolup men.

"Rha! Stop!" Skyra shouted, bursting through the gap after the woman. The other Skyra flew past Lincoln after Skyra.

The nandup woman raised the khul to strike but was met by at least half a dozen opposing weapons. Lincoln glimpsed a spear jabbing her chest and a khul striking her shoulder in the split second before Skyra got to her side.

"Rha!" Skyra screamed as she swung at one of the men.

The other Skyra rushed into the melee, also shouting and swinging her khul.

Veenah started forward, apparently ready to join the fight with her bare hands, but Derek blocked her as he and Jazzlyn scrambled back through the gap between shields.

"Grab hold!" Lincoln ordered.

Derek and Virgil gripped the left shield, while Lincoln and Jazzlyn held the right.

Lincoln took a step toward the fight. "Go!"

Together they plowed into the battle. The shields knocked both Skyras to the ground, along with several screaming bolup men and women.

Veenah, apparently understanding what needed to be done, grabbed one of Skyra's feet and dragged her birthmate under the shields.

"Get back here!" Derek barked, and with one hand he dragged the other Skyra under the shield he was holding.

Lincoln pulled back and to the side. "Close the shields!"

By the time the two Skyras got to their feet, the entire group, including both Ripples, was contained within the clamshell barrier, and already the bolups were assaulting the shields with their weapons. Lincoln grunted and planted his feet as spears, khuls, and fists struck the barrier. Just to his right, beyond his shield, the injured nandup woman was trying to crawl away, dragging one arm that had been almost severed where the khul had struck her shoulder.

Veenah threw her weight against Lincoln's shield, trying to move the barrier toward the injured woman, and the two Skyras joined her effort. The entire group shuffled to the nandup woman, and Lincoln lifted his shield slightly. Veenah and Skyra grabbed the woman's feet and started pulling her in.

A bolup man saw what was happening and stopped stabbing at the barrier. He turned his spear and thrust it into the woman's neck just before her head and shoulders were pulled under the shield.

Lincoln and Jazzlyn slammed the shield back onto the ground. Lincoln focused his energy and attention on the attacking bolups, but he could hear the woman at his feet coughing and struggling to breathe.

Through the mass of assaulting bolups, Lincoln's eyes were drawn to a bolup tribeswoman who was on her knees. The woman was staring at her blood-soaked hands. She turned to the side and pulled a harness from her back, and Lincoln saw for the first time the harness contained a child, its head covered in blood. The child wasn't moving, and the woman stared at it with her mouth wide open.

"Bruulo nodra-tep!" the woman screamed. She got to her feet, still holding the child, then turned her eyes to the reflective shields. "Bruulo nodra-tep! Bruulo nodra-tep!" Her tone and expression seethed with fury.

The other bolup men and women halted their assault to look at the woman.

She rushed forward, shaking the lifeless child at Lincoln's group. "Bruulo nodra-tep!" She suddenly hurled the child's body. It struck the barrier with a sickening thud and dropped to the ground in a limp heap.

Jazzlyn released the shield and dropped to her knees. "Pull it up, Lincoln!"

He hoisted the shield, and she dragged the child's body inside.

The bolups—men, women, and children—stared at the reflective barrier with contempt. Lincoln watched them through the material, trying to wrap his head around the turn of events. The plan to make friends and garner respect from the bolup tribe had failed miserably. The only consolation was none of his group had been killed. That, however, could change at any moment.

"This kid's still alive!" Jazzlyn said. "He took a hell of a hit to the head, but he has a pulse." She gathered him up in her arms and got to her feet. The naked child looked to weigh about thirty pounds, maybe two or three years old. "We're taking him with us," Jazzlyn said.

Everyone stared at her.

"Why?" Derek asked. "Those bastards already blame us for killing him. How is it going to help to—"

"We're taking him!" Jazzlyn shouted. "If he's still alive when we get back, we're going to use the caretakers on him."

"This nandup is dead," Skyra said. She and Veenah were kneeling beside the woman who had started the whole debacle. Skyra got to her feet and pulled Veenah up with her. "We must leave this camp now, or we must fight."

Lincoln believed her. The bolups could probably grab the bottom of the shield and flip the entire clamshell onto its side. They'd figure that out sooner or later. "We're leaving," he said. "Keep the shields together and retreat to our path up the hill."

They had to step over the nandup woman's body as they started moving back to the hill.

A bolup man caught up to the barrier and struck it twice with his khul. The material deflected the blows without sustaining a scratch. The man gave up and stood there watching the group retreat. Behind him, the rest of his tribe watched in silence. Despite the conflict's brutality, the only body lying on the ground was the nandup woman.

12

ELAH

47,659 YEARS *in the past - Day 4*

ONCE AGAIN IN THE COURTYARD, Skyra stood aside with her other self and Veenah while Lincoln and his tribemates gathered around the bolup child. They wanted to use the caretaker medicine to save the boy, but his head no longer looked the way a child's head should look, and Skyra could not believe his heart was still beating. She did not remember striking the woman who had been carrying the child. Maybe someone else had hit her, or maybe the woman had fallen on the boy during the battle.

"Where do we even begin with this?" Derek asked. "It looks hopeless."

"He's alive—that's hope," Jazzlyn said. "Maybe the robots can enter through his mouth or his nose."

"Probably better to send them directly in through the scalp," Lincoln said.

Derek pushed some of the boy's blood-soaked hair aside.

"As far as I can tell, there's only one small split in the skin where the blood is coming from. Most of the damage is beneath. Maybe we should cut the opening larger for the robots." He pulled his folded shiny knife from his pocket and opened it.

"I do not believe that will be necessary," Ripple said. "Although I do not actually breathe, please give me some breathing room. I will attempt to provide the caretakers with adequate guidance."

Skyra did not want to watch, so she paced back and forth a few times, then she went to the courtyard entrance and stood staring through the gap, in case the bolups had decided to follow them. A few breaths later, Veenah appeared at her side with the other Skyra. Skyra studied Veenah's face. Her birthmate stared through the gap without meeting her gaze.

Skyra spoke to her in the Una-Loto language. "I understand why you gave the nandup woman your khul. She wanted to kill the bolup man who hurt her, and you wanted to let her kill him. I also wanted to kill the bolup man."

Veenah flicked her eyes to Skyra briefly. "Your strange bolup friends did not want this. They wanted to become friends with the bolup tribe."

"Yes."

"I do not understand."

Skyra stepped forward and turned around to face them both. "My friends want to change these bolups. I also want to change the bolups, and I want to change the nandups. Listen to me speak, Veenah and my other self. We must make the bolups and nandups want to combine their tribes and have children together. I have seen one future, and Lincoln has seen another future. In one future, nandups and bolups fight each other for years and years. You cannot even imagine what terrible things happen in that future. In the other future, nandups are *extinct*. Extinct means the nandups have died—all of them. These are the bad things that will happen if nandups and bolups do not learn to combine their tribes. Nandups and bolups must become one kind of people. These people are called *alinga-uls*. They are the children of nandups and bolups, and they are better people than nandups or bolups."

Veenah and the other Skyra glanced at each other then stared at Skyra.

"You have seen strange things," the other Skyra said.

"Yes. I have seen things I do not want to see ever again. I also have seen wondrous things."

"Veenah and I do not belong here with your strange bolup friends. They are not our tribe. You will come with us. We will go away—Veenah and two Skyras. We will not go back to Una-Loto tribe, but we will go far away and join another nandup tribe. We belong with nandups."

Skyra suppressed a growl. "Did you not hear my words? Nandups and bolups must combine tribes. You will not go away. We must all stay here together."

"I will stay," Veenah said, surprising Skyra.

The other Skyra frowned.

Veenah grabbed the other Skyra's chin and squeezed, just as she used to do to Skyra to make Skyra laugh. "You will stay with me. We will all stay. Veenah and two Skyras and the strange bolups and the strange Ripple creatures. I will have much work to do to teach two Skyras how to make food worth eating. You eat like a stinking hyena eats, and I must teach you both."

The other Skyra gently removed her birthmate's hand from her chin. She did not smile, but Skyra saw compassion in her expression. "Veenah, you are my birthmate, and I am happy you did not die. I will stay with you, but only so I can persuade you to leave these strange, skinny bolups."

Veenah smiled. "The bolup they call Derek is not so skinny."

"El-de-né!" the other Skyra said. "Do not make my head think of such things, or my belly will lose all its food."

Veenah let out a chuckle, which made Skyra chuckle. It was good to be with Veenah again, even if Skyra did not have her to herself, and it was even better to know Veenah wanted to stay with Skyra's new tribe.

"You need a different name," Skyra said to her other self. "It is confusing having two Skyras in one tribe."

The other Skyra glared at her. "Maybe it is *you* who needs a different name."

"No. I have been with my bolup tribemates longer. They know me as Skyra. Choose a different name, or I will choose one for you."

"She will have the name Biato," Veenah said, laughing.

Skyra had heard that word before, so she knew her other self had heard it too. Biato was the word the Wota-Loto tribe called a hyena. The Wota-Loto tribe was friendly with the Una-Loto tribe, and the two tribes got together at the end of each warm season to celebrate the upcoming move into the Dofusofu river plain.

The other Skyra made a familiar motion with her fist, pretending to punch Veenah in the throat. "Biato will not be my name. If I must have a different name, it will be Elah."

"Elah is a good name," Skyra said. Elah was the name of an Una-Loto woman who had been a friend of their birth-mother Sayleeh. Elah had an illness that had gradually crippled her legs, but she would take care of Skyra and Veenah when Sayleeh was away on hunting expeditions with the tribe's best hunters. Elah had died when Skyra and Veenah were young girls.

"Yes, Elah is a good name," Veenah said. She grabbed the other Skyra's chin again and squeezed. "Elah, Elah, Elah!"

Skyra laughed. She could hardly believe Veenah was the same Veenah she had been before the bolup men had taken her.

Jazzlyn was now carrying the bolup boy to the bear cave. Lincoln, Derek, and Virgil watched her for a few breaths, then they walked over to the gap, followed by the two Ripples.

The group stood silently for several breaths, as if no one knew what to say.

Lincoln sat down on the rock slab beside the pile of weapons Skyra had placed near the gap in case the bolups tried to enter the courtyard. He crossed his legs, then he waved for everyone else to join him. They all sat, including Veenah, Elah, and the two Ripples.

Again they were silent for several breaths.

Lincoln spoke first. "I can't imagine the robotic caretakers can do much to help that boy. The tribe hates us even more now."

"The bolup tribe will be afraid of us now," Skyra said. "That is what we wanted."

He blew air out through his nose and gazed at Skyra's face. "Maybe. What do you think we should do next?"

She thought for a moment. "Nandups bury their dead tribemates in the ground. I do not know if bolups bury their tribemates, but I know they eat them sometimes. We should return the dead boy, so they can bury him or eat him. Maybe they will not hate us so much then."

Lincoln and his tribemates looked at her as if they did not understand her simple words.

"If they attack us, we will kill more of them," Elah said. "We will kill until they are afraid."

Derek made a coughing noise in his throat. "Well, if we hadn't given the captured nandup woman a freakin' khul...." He did not finish his words, but his meaning was clear.

"Do not be angry with Veenah," Skyra said to Derek. "You and Veenah will be married soon."

Derek's small bolup eyes became round. "That's so random that I don't even know what to say."

Skyra caught Elah's eye. Elah put her hand on her belly and made a sick expression with her mouth.

"What are you saying to your bolup friends?" Veenah asked in the Una-Loto language.

"I told Derek to be kind to you, because you and Derek will be married soon. Married means you will sleep together every night until you die."

Veenah burst out laughing. "*Aheee at-at-at-at*. Derek will have to challenge other men to honor my ilmekho. What skills does he have?"

"Derek's best skill is talking loudly," Skyra replied.

"*Aheee at-at-at-at*."

Derek looked from Skyra to Veenah and back to Skyra. "Do I even want to know what you're talking about?"

"Back to the discussion," Lincoln said. "I agree we should return the boy's body to the tribe."

Virgil spoke up. "I suggest we wait until his heart actually stops beating. Then we'll know for sure the robotic caretakers couldn't help him. Besides, we can't take the boy back until the caretakers have exited his body. Once he dies—assuming he does—we'll want to return his body as soon as possible. You know... in case they want it while it's still fresh."

Skyra ground her teeth together, trying not to think about the disgusting habits of bolup tribes.

"That could be minutes from now or days from now," Lincoln said. He put his elbows on his knees and leaned his forehead into his palms as if his head hurt. "It seems like, despite our best efforts, we're spiraling toward an inevitable conflict with this tribe, one that ends with all of them dead or all of us dead."

Ripple's red lights abruptly flashed once. "Perhaps it is time for something more pleasant to occupy your thoughts. I have an idea."

"If you're thinking of telling another of your revelatory stories, now is not the time," Lincoln said.

"As it happens, I do have one more story you will want to hear, Lincoln, but that can wait. As for now, I believe it is time for you to become reacquainted with your good friend Maddy."

Lincoln lifted his head from his palms. "You're kidding. Now?"

The other Ripple flashed its red light once. "My counterpart and I have discussed this at length, and I agree, Lincoln. My counterpart has mostly the same knowledge I have, plus the additional knowledge accumulated beginning the moment you initially arrived here in Skyra's time. Therefore, my knowledge is not only insufficient, it is redundant. I am not needed. Also, you may not know this, but your friendship with Maddy is legendary among your drones. Maddy herself made sure of that. Please replace my cognitive module with Maddy's. I insist."

Lincoln pulled Maddy's brain from his pocket and turned it over in his hand.

Skyra knew enough of the two Ripples' words to understand, but Elah probably did not. Skyra spoke to her other self. "The strange box Lincoln is holding—that is the brain for another creature like Ripple. The creature is Maddy. Ripple's brain is like Maddy's brain. Your Ripple wants Lincoln to take out its brain and put in Maddy's brain instead."

Elah's face did not change for several breaths, then she bared her teeth at Lincoln. "You will not hurt Ripple."

Lincoln put the brain on his knee then held both his hands up with the palms toward Elah. "This wasn't my idea. Besides, it wouldn't really *hurt* Ripple."

The other Ripple stepped over and stood before Elah. "Lincoln is correct. I will not be hurt. My brain can be removed without hurting me. I wish to do this because I know it will help Lincoln. Therefore, it will help our new tribe, and it will help you, Skyra."

"I will not be able to talk to you after Lincoln takes out your brain?"

"No, not while my brain is out, but later it can be put back into my shell, and I will again be able to speak with you. If you keep my brain safe, you can speak to me whenever Lincoln puts it back into my shell. You can also talk to the other Ripple whenever you want to. Remember, that Ripple is the same as me and has the same memories of being your friend. Please understand, I must do this."

The other Skyra shifted her gaze to Lincoln. "If you do this, you will give me Ripple's brain. I will keep it safe."

"Yes, I'll give it to you," Lincoln said.

"You will put it back in when I want to talk to Ripple."

"Yes, of course I will."

She returned her gaze to the other Ripple's vision orb. "I will keep it safe. If something happens to me, my friend, find your way home."

The other Ripple's light flashed three times. "Yes, and if I do not return, Skyra, find *your* way home."

The other Skyra's eyes became wet, and she wiped them with her palm. "I am called Elah now. It was confusing to have two Skyras."

"Elah," the other Ripple said. "The name of your tribe-mate who died when you and Veenah were girls."

Elah wiped her eyes again. "Yes."

"It is a good name. Remember, Elah, you are important. Do not ever forget that."

"I am just a nandup, and I do not even know who I am anymore."

"You are the same nandup you have always been, and you are my friend."

Skyra's chest began to hurt again as she watched her other self gaze at the other Ripple. It felt like the pain in Elah was also within her own body.

The other Ripple turned back to Lincoln. "I will enter dormant mode now. I assume you know how to access my cognitive module?"

"Yes, I've done it before."

"Very well. Enjoy your time with Maddy. The Maddy I knew before jumping here to Skyra's time was fourteen years older than the Maddy you now hold in your hand. It would be interesting to interact with her at such a formative stage of her development."

Lincoln smiled. "This Maddy is suspicious of you and your rather outrageous plan." He nodded toward Ripple. "Of course, I'm referring to your counterpart here."

"That is interesting," the other Ripple said. "Perhaps you are not yet aware of this, but Maddy was later responsible for those elements of our coding that gave us the capacity to develop and carry out such a plan."

"Yeah, your counterpart has told me that story."

"The fact that Maddy's younger self would be suspicious regarding the plan is, shall we say, ironically paradoxical."

"I suppose it is."

The other Ripple pulled its legs into its shell and settled onto its belly on the stone slab. "Entering dormant mode."

Ripple said, "It has been a pleasure to converse with you these recent days."

The other Ripple remained silent.

"Oh, dear," Ripple said. "My words were a moment too late."

Lincoln rolled the other Ripple onto its back. His fingers quickly turned several black bumps, and he opened the small door to the other Ripple's insides. He gently pulled out the other Ripple's brain and handed it to Elah, then he pushed Maddy's brain into the shell and closed the small door.

Lincoln rolled the creature onto its belly. Its lights began flashing and spinning—yellow, green, then red. Its legs pushed out of its shell, lifting it to a standing position. Its red light rotated one way then the other.

The creature scuttled its legs, turning its shell and vision orb in a complete circle to see the nandups and bolups seated around it. It shifted its gaze to Skyra, to Veenah, then to Elah.

"I have apparently missed significant events again," Maddy said in her female voice. "Lincoln, what have you done now? There are three Neanderthal women here, all of whom appear to be Skyra but with varying degrees of facial injury. I am afraid to even speculate as to the meaning of this.

Please do not tell me you are now married to *three* Neanderthals. You have already violated every protocol of—"

"Maddy!" Lincoln said. "You're jumping to conclusions. I'm only married to one Skyra. And it's good to talk to you again, by the way. As you said, you have missed a lot of significant events."

"Welcome back, Maddy," Virgil said. "It's good to talk to you again."

Derek said, "I'm pretty sure you'll be less annoying than having a second Ripple yapping its trap all the time."

Maddy shuffled around until her vision orb faced Ripple. "A second Ripple?"

"Yep," Lincoln said. "Two Skyras and two Ripples."

Maddy's circle of red lights flashed twice. "Oh, no. You have jumped back to Skyra's time to a point before your first arrival, haven't you? Did you not consider the risks of binary existence in the same timeline?"

"Of course we considered it, but our options were limited. As you can see, though, nothing terrible happened."

"Yes, I see. My goodness, Lincoln. You do have a penchant for puzzlement and perplexity. Perhaps you were influenced by this roguish and deceptive drone Ripple."

"Bam," Derek said. "That's the sound of a nail being hit directly on the head."

Ripple said, "Perhaps someday I will be appreciated for my valuable contributions to this endeavor."

"Too much talking!" Skyra said. She was growing tired of listening to words she did not understand. "Maddy, I am happy you are here now. You are Lincoln's friend, so you are my friend too."

Maddy turned to look at her. "I assume you are the Skyra who is Lincoln's wife."

"We are married, but I am not *wife*. I am Skyra."

"Indeed. Yes, I believe you and I can be friends. I must warn you, though—it is my job to take care of Lincoln. If I find out you intend to harm him, you will suffer my wrath."

"What does that mean?" Skyra asked.

"It means I will be angry with you if you hurt Lincoln."

Skyra smiled. "It is good Lincoln will have both you and me to take care of him. He is a skinny and weak bolup."

Derek let out a snort that might have been a laugh.

Lincoln said, "In my defense, in my own homeland I wasn't considered all that skinny or weak. I'm a runner, like an antelope or a deer."

"This is true," Maddy said. "Lincoln would run many miles every day. I believe it helped him to channel his thoughts. I do not know if you realize this, but Lincoln has a very troubled mind, the result of a difficult childhood and his inability to—"

"Maddy, you've been awake all of three minutes!" Lincoln said. "Do you want me to put the other Ripple's CM back in?"

"I was simply talking to my new friend," Maddy said. "We girls like to stick together and share secrets about the men in our lives."

Lincoln mumbled something Skyra could not understand.

"Oh, my God! You guys!"

Skyra jumped to her feet. The voice was Jazzlyn's, from inside the bear cave.

"Hey, come back here!" Jazzlyn shouted.

A small figure darted out of the cave, then it stopped and looked around at the surrounding courtyard walls.

For a moment Skyra wondered if her eyes were lying to her. She was looking at the naked bolup child.

The boy spotted Skyra and the others, and he let out a whimper.

Jazzlyn came out of the cave. "Wait!"

The boy whimpered again and ran for the nearest rock wall. He thrust his fingers into a slanted crack in the stone and tried pulling himself up, his bare toes scrabbling for something to grip.

Jazzlyn got to the boy first, then Skyra and the others gathered around, blocking the child's escape.

Jazzlyn kneeled and held out her arms. "It's okay, honey. We're not going to hurt you."

The boy gave up trying to climb and turned around with his back to the wall. He whimpered again, wide-eyed and afraid.

"How could he possibly be up and running around?" Derek asked.

Ripple's voice came from behind the group. "The robotic caretakers are learning. They are becoming more familiar with the processes involved in repairing biological tissue. Also, my protocols for communicating with them have progressed. Therefore, such an improvement in performance is not surprising."

"Every freakin' thing about this is surprising!" Derek said.

Jazzlyn shuffled closer to the boy, still holding her arms out. "Don't be afraid."

He pressed his back to the wall as if he wanted to become part of the stone.

"Excuse me," Ripple said as it pushed its way forward between Skyra and Lincoln.

The boy saw Ripple approaching and froze.

Ripple stopped within arm's reach of the boy and spoke in the bolup language.

The boy spoke back, his voice lower than Skyra expected. She had heard bolup children shouting before, but she had never heard one speak normally. Apparently, bolup children had deeper voices than nandup children.

"The boy's name is Yanlip," Ripple said. "He would like to know if we are going to eat him."

"Tell him we don't want to eat him," Jazzlyn said. "We don't want to hurt him at all."

Ripple spoke to the boy, and the boy pointed at Lincoln as he spoke back.

Ripple translated. "He says his tribemates want to eat those of you who are wearing blue clothing. Maybe that's why he thinks we are going to harm him."

Skyra let out a growl and kneeled between Ripple and Jazzlyn. "Tell the bolup child we will kill him if he does not do what we want him to do."

"Skyra!" Jazzlyn said. "He's just a little boy."

"He is a bolup boy, and the bolups must fear us."

"Ripple, don't translate that, at least not yet," Lincoln said. "Skyra, can I talk to you for a moment?"

She rose to her feet, and Lincoln led her a short distance from the group. "I understand what you're trying to do," he said, "but I just... I don't know if making them fear us is the best way to carry out our plan."

"Why?"

"Well, for one thing, threatening to kill a young child just seems wrong. Look, you and I, we want the same thing. We want the bolups to *want* to combine their tribes with nandup tribes. I just don't know if making them afraid of us is the best way to do that. I want to make a deal with you. I'd like you to agree to try my way first. Let's try to get the bolups to respect us without threatening to kill them. You don't have to be afraid of someone to respect them. If that doesn't work, and we're *sure* it isn't going to work, then we can try it your way. Can we do that?"

Skyra stared at him for a few breaths. Lincoln was *asking* her to do things his way instead of telling her. Once again she wondered what kind of land he was from, where people could get what they wanted simply by asking. This was one reason Lincoln was so strange, but it was also one reason she liked being married to him. "I will make this agreement with you, but I do not think your way will work. I want the boy to tell his tribemates we are a strong and happy tribe because we are nandups and bolups together. The boy will not say those things unless he thinks we will kill him."

Lincoln frowned and shook his head. "There are other ways to... well, he might tell them simply because it's true. We *are* strong because we are nandups and bolups together. I have an idea. Let's give him food and water. Let's make sure he knows we are kind, that we didn't mean for him to get hurt. Maybe we can even make him laugh. When the caretakers leave his body, we'll take him back to his tribe. If we do all that, don't you think he'll tell them good things about us?"

She chewed on her lip for a moment. "No."

He gave her a funny look. "Really?"

"Maybe."

"Okay, let's try it. You pick out a piece of bear meat you think the kid will like, and I'll get one of the water bladders. We'll treat him like he's a special guest."

Skyra went to the smoking cave and found a strip of meat that was softer than the others. She held it over the smoking coals in the center of the floor until the meat became warm and even softer.

When she returned to the group, Lincoln was already

there with the water. The boy was now sitting on the rock slab, holding his head and whimpering as if he were in pain.

"He was doing fine just a minute ago," Jazzlyn said with fear in her voice. "Now something's wrong."

The boy brought his knees up to his chin then thrust his feet back out several times as he rubbed the place where his head had been bashed in. His whimpers turned into cries, and he pounded his hands against his head.

Jazzlyn grabbed his wrists. "Don't do that, honey, you'll hurt... oh, crap, I think they're coming back out."

"Yes, you are correct," said Ripple. "The robotic caretakers are exiting the boy's body."

For a breath, Skyra thought the boy's head was changing shape. A gray mass was growing outward on one side. Instead of pushing the boy's long, dirty hair out with it, however, the lump was oozing out between the hairs and flowing down over his ear.

The boy suddenly became silent. He pulled his hands from Jazzlyn's grip and wiped his shoulder. He stared at the gray ooze covering his fingers before scraping it off on the rock slab at his side.

Jazzlyn grabbed his wrists again. "You might hurt them doing that. Just be patient, kiddo."

The ooze kept coming out. The boy whimpered and tried to pull his hands free, but Jazzlyn held them tight. Finally, the last of the material flowed down his arm and onto the rock slab, where it joined with the bits the boy had already wiped there. The ooze turned into specks, which joined together into larger pieces. Several breaths later, the two rat-sized caretakers stood motionless beside the boy.

The boy spoke, then Ripple spoke, and the boy spoke again.

Ripple said, "I have told the child he was hurt and was going to die. I explained these caretakers are medicine, and the medicine has made him better again. Now he wants to keep one of the caretakers."

Skyra said, "I told you, Lincoln, the bolups will want to take what we have."

"Tell the boy we need to keep our medicine," Lincoln said to Ripple. "We will have the medicine here, though, and if his tribemates get hurt, we can use the medicine on them too."

Virgil said, "Um, I'm not certain that's a promise we can keep. Something bad could happen to the caretakers at any time. They could malfunction, or Ripple could malfunction, or—"

"Let's assume they won't," Lincoln said. "Go ahead and translate, Ripple."

Ripple spoke to the boy.

Lincoln kneeled. "Also tell him we brought him food and water."

Skyra kneeled beside Lincoln. "Let me do it," she said, surprising herself and Lincoln.

He handed her the water bladder.

Skyra had no idea what the bladder was made of, but she knew how it worked. She gripped the bear meat between her teeth then unscrewed the cap and held the bladder out for the boy to see. When he looked, she poured a little water onto the rock to show what it contained. She removed the meat from her teeth and showed him how she could tip the bladder up and pour water into her mouth. She handed the water to the boy, and he took a drink, spilling some down his chin. Skyra took it again, poured water onto her palm, and washed her face. She poured water into the boy's hands, and he tried to wash his own face, although the water mostly just smeared the blood around on his cheeks.

The boy pointed to the bear meat, which Skyra was again holding between her teeth, so she gave it to him. He smelled it, then he clamped his teeth onto it and used both hands to pull on the meat until he tore off a piece that barely fit in his mouth. As he started chewing to soften the dried meat, he gazed at Skyra.

For the first time, she saw the boy smile.

13

———

YANLIP

47,659 YEARS in the past - Day 4

LINCOLN WAS CONTEMPLATING why the robotic caretakers had become so critical to his group. "Maybe the virtual beings did this on purpose," he said. "You know, to give us a better chance of success. After all, they seemed really enthusiastic about Ripple's plan." He was sitting near the entrance gap with Jazzlyn, Virgil, Derek, and Maddy, while Skyra, Elah, and Veenah followed the bolup boy Yanlip around the court-yard and talked with him using Ripple as their translator. The nandup women had been delighted the first time they heard Yanlip laugh out loud, and now they seemed to be on a mission to make him do so as frequently as they could. The boy seemed completely recovered from his massive head wound.

"If they intended to send the robots with us, I'd think they would have told us first," Virgil countered. "In fact, they specifically pointed out that the caretakers would be useless to us here, as we'd have no means of keeping them charged."

"Seems pretty simple to me," Derek said. "Jazzyln got hurt, the robots saw an opportunity to help, so they entered her body, then we jumped here before they could exit her body."

Maybe Derek was right, but Lincoln had a hard time believing the virtual beings wouldn't have forecast Ripple's ability to interface with the robots. Sure, it had seemed unlikely to Lincoln at first, but the virtual beings must have known it could be possible. He let out a long sigh. "I guess we'll never know. Even if Ripple could simply ask the caretakers, there's a good chance they themselves wouldn't know either."

Maddy spoke up. "Lincoln, that devious drone from your future has provided me with some details about what has transpired while I have been dormant, and I am concerned for your well-being. Apparently, you have made some choices which do not fit your previous behavioral patterns."

"Such as?" Lincoln asked.

"Such as, you have fallen in love with a female of another species, which could be considered ethically questionable."

"That doesn't matter," he said. "We're in a different timeline, 47,000 years in the past. We can create a whole new set of ethics."

Maddy's lights flashed to indicate she was giving his words consideration. "Have you been doing your prescribed meditation exercises each day?"

Lincoln glanced at his team members. To their credit, they kept quiet. "No. Haven't had the time nor the inclination."

"Have you been going on your daily runs to level your emotions?"

"No, the only running I've been doing lately is to escape from predators or people intending to kill me. I think my recreational running days are over."

"Oh, dear. You do not even have access to any of your therapists here."

Derek finally let out a snicker.

"From this point on, Maddy, you are my official therapist. You're the only one who ever helped me anyway."

"Oh, my goodness. I do hope Skyra is a strong woman. She may not know what she's getting into."

"You don't have to worry about Skyra," Jazzlyn said. "She is plenty strong. I've already given her my seal of approval."

Lincoln smiled. He had intentionally coded Maddy to frequently check on his well-being, and now he realized how much he'd missed her annoying presence.

Maddy said, "Is Skyra strong enough to deal with obsessive-compulsive behavior, anxiety, occasional depression, mild narcissism, and philophobia?"

"Now you're exaggerating," Lincoln said. "Maybe *you're* even more devious than Ripple."

"What the hell is philophobia?" Derek asked.

"An unreasonable fear of falling in love," Maddy replied, "often resulting from childhood trauma."

"For your information, I'm very much in love," Lincoln said. "In fact, these recent weeks of danger and adventure seem to have diminished all my other issues. I feel more alive and well-adjusted than I've ever felt before."

"Yeah, and I haven't felt the slightest hint of an episode coming on since the virtual beings sucked us into their virtual world," Derek added.

Virgil said, "Come to think of it, my own anxieties have all but disappeared since being in the virtual world. Do you think it's possible the experience could have such an effect?"

"Maybe the virtual beings changed you guys intentionally," Jazzlyn suggested. "They obviously have tech that can fix physical injuries. Why wouldn't they be able to fix psychological issues?" She lifted her prosthetic hand and gazed at it for a moment. "Apparently there was nothing they could do for this."

"The beings knew what we were facing," Virgil said. "Logically, in a wilderness survival scenario, your prosthetic hand could be considered an asset. And mentally, you're great the way you are."

Jazzlyn gave him a fervent smile.

The group remained silent for a few seconds.

"Perhaps you could *all* benefit from an official therapist," Maddy said, switching her voice to its cheerful mode. "I volunteer, as I will need a purpose in this outrageously brazen and audacious endeavor."

Jazzlyn chuckled. "It really is good to have you back, Maddy." She then nodded toward the bolup boy, who now seemed to be chasing the three nandup women in a game of tag while Ripple stood to one side watching. "Don't you guys think we should take that kid back to his tribe?"

"I want to keep him," Skyra said.

Lincoln blinked at her, taken aback. "Um, no, we can't keep him. He belongs with the bolup tribe."

"Now he belongs with our tribe," she said.

"Yanlip makes us laugh," Elah said. "We will keep him."

The boy was pulling on Veenah's hand, apparently trying to get her to continue the chasing game.

Lincoln turned to his team, at a complete loss.

"We can't *keep* the kid!" Derek boomed.

Jazzlyn took Lincoln's arm and guided him gently to the side. "You guys back off for a few minutes and let me deal with this, okay?" She nodded toward the gap. "Go. I got this."

Jazzlyn talked to Skyra and Elah for several minutes, at times making expressive gestures with her hands, then she came over to the gap. "Okay, I'm pretty sure we're good to go. They want to talk to Yanlip one more time, then they'll be ready to return him to the bolup tribe." She glanced away a little too quickly.

"What?" Lincoln asked.

"Well, I had to tell them they would soon have their own children. Elah didn't seem too thrilled about that. Skyra and Veenah, though...." She gave Derek a wry smile.

"Jesus Christ," Derek muttered.

A few minutes later, the nandup women and the boy joined them.

"Yanlip is ready to return to his tribe," Skyra said. "He will tell his tribemates they must join with a nandup tribe to be strong and happy like we are." She flashed Lincoln a toothy nandup grin.

Lincoln kneeled and stared into Yanlip's eyes. This seemed to intimidate the boy, and he sidled up to Skyra's leg and clung to it. He stared back at Lincoln. The boy was filthy and still speckled with dried blood. He smelled musky, like a stray animal. His stringy hair had obviously never been cut—it hung in clumped strands of different lengths, as if he had chewed parts of it off. Still, he had the eyes and face of a human boy. The kid was small, but Lincoln figured he might be as old as four. Maybe in a different time and place he would be getting ready for kindergarten. How would he fare among a classroom of kids in Lincoln's original timeline? There was no way to know.

Lincoln smiled, and Yanlip hid his face against Skyra's lynx-fur waist-skin.

"Well, hell," Derek said. "Let's see if we can return the little man-cub without getting ourselves killed, shall we?"

Lincoln went into the bear cave to the far back corner where he had stashed the two rat-sized robots. He grabbed one and decided to leave the other rather than risk losing both. He returned to the gap and ordered Maddy to stay behind, as she was currently unable to translate the bolup language.

Everyone else left the courtyard and made their way down the hill of boulders.

Ripple had informed Yanlip they were bringing him back to his tribemates, and the boy was obviously excited. He kept scrambling to the tops of boulders to see over the numerous ledges and outcrops. At one point, atop an outcrop where Lincoln thought he surely would slip and break his neck, apparently seeing his camp, the boy waved his arms and shouted. This was followed by shouts from below.

The two clamshell shields were still exactly where they'd left them, so they carried them to the base of the hill. Lincoln's group finally stepped away from the last of the boulders and onto the open field. Not surprisingly, the bolups were already armed and standing shoulder-to-shoulder at the edge of their camp. Two of their shelters had been flattened, and the skin coverings were partially rolled up. Apparently they were getting ready to move on.

Despite the obvious good will inherent in returning the boy alive to his people, the safest strategy was to assume the bolups would attack again. In fact, Lincoln wasn't even sure of Yanlip's own safety. The first time he and his team had jumped to Skyra's time, he and Skyra had delivered Veenah back to her Una-Loto tribe, only to witness her brutal murder, a result of Veenah's tribemates believing she had been tainted by her bolup captors. The same thing could happen to Yanlip, and it would likely happen too fast for anyone to intervene.

As if she were sharing Lincoln's thoughts, Skyra scooped up the boy with one arm and held him straddled on her hip, her bolup-made spear ready in her other hand.

"Everyone get between the shields except Ripple," Lincoln said. "Be ready for anything."

They bunched up and pulled the shields together. Yanlip seemed to sense the tension—he whimpered and clung fiercely to Skyra's cape.

Together they advanced, moving the shields with them.

Lincoln said, "Ripple, tell the bolups we did not want Yanlip to get hurt in the fight. Tell them we have healed the boy, and we are returning him unharmed. Finally, tell them we are a strong tribe. We are kind, and we are happy, and we want to show Yanlip's tribe how to be strong and kind and happy."

"That is a complex message, but I will do my best to translate accurately," the drone replied.

Lincoln stopped the group about twenty yards from the bolup defensive line, which included all eight of the men, the five women, and several kids, the tallest about twice Yanlip's weight. Lincoln recognized the woman who'd been carrying Yanlip on her back, probably the boy's mother. Her face, just like the faces of her tribemates, displayed fierce determination. She and the others now knew Yanlip was alive, and they appeared ready to fight to the death to take him back.

Ripple spoke at length, with frequent stops and starts as if trying out different phrases.

When the drone finally fell silent, Yanlip's mother stepped forward. The man without hair—the man Lincoln had injured—grabbed her elbow and tried pulling her back, but she shook him off.

The woman shouted at the reflective shield. "Bruulo nodra-tep! Hurdro-puutno-lo Yanlip!"

Ripple translated. "You killed! Where is the child Yanlip? I believe she is referring to hearing Yanlip's voice as we were descending the hill."

"Did you make it clear we healed the boy, and we are returning him as a gesture of good will?" Lincoln asked.

"As clear as I am able with my current understanding of their language."

Lincoln turned to Skyra. "It's time to give him back."

She glanced down at the boy clinging to her cape. "I do not want to give him back to those stinking bolups, but I understand why I must." With one hand on his arm, she pried him loose, then she held him suspended before her. "I hope you find your way home, Yanlip." She gestured with her chin for Lincoln and the others to pull the shields apart, then she put the boy on his feet. He seemed confused, so she nudged him toward the opening with her foot.

The boy turned and spotted his tribe. Lincoln expected him to run straight for his mother's arms, but instead he walked slowly, turning to look back at Skyra several times. His mother grabbed him roughly by the head. She turned his head one way then the other, obviously looking for the massive wound that had deformed his skull only hours ago. She turned her gaze to Lincoln's group then back to Yanlip's head. "Bruulo nodra-tep. Gafro-bruulono-Yanlip."

Ripple said, "You kill. Why is Yanlip alive?"

"Tell them we have good medicine," Lincoln said.

While Ripple was translating, Lincoln stepped through the gap between the shields. Skyra started to follow him, but he held up a hand to stop her. "Let me do this alone for now. I'll be careful."

The woman shoved Yanlip behind her, knocking him to the ground, and the other bolups stepped up, advancing their defensive line to her position.

Lincoln felt vulnerable, even though he was only a few feet from the shields. A bolup-made khul was tucked in the waistband of his trousers, and the only thing in his hands was the rat-sized caretaker. He pointed to the man with no hair. "Tell them I remember hurting that man when we fought on the other side of the river. Tell them I'm sorry, and I wish to use our medicine to heal the man's wound."

"Lincoln, what if it doesn't work?" Virgil hissed from behind the shield. "You're making a very risky offer."

"Hell, this may really be the moment our luck runs out," Derek added.

Lincoln ignored them. "Translate my words, Ripple."

Ripple complied.

The bolups exchanged glances. Several of them exchanged words. Lincoln kept his eyes on the man he'd hurt. The man had apparently made a new waist-skin after Skyra had stripped him of his other one. The waist-skin covered his hip wound, but his upper thigh was swollen and red. The man took a few steps forward, favoring his injured leg. He eyed Lincoln and spoke.

Ripple said, "You could have killed me, but you did not. Now you want to use your medicine to heal my leg. Tell me why."

"We want to help your tribe," Lincoln said. "We want to teach you how to be strong and kind and happy. If you let us teach you, and if you do not try to hurt us, you will be strong like us."

Ripple translated.

The man spoke, and Ripple said, "We want to be strong like your tribe. That is why we came here to kill you and eat your flesh."

"That will not make you strong. You will not kill us. If you want to be strong, you will let us heal your wounds, and you will let us teach you."

After Ripple translated, the man lifted his waist-skin, revealing a horrifically swollen, obviously infected, wound. Mud, or some other substance, had been packed into the stab wound, but cream-colored pus was still oozing out around the edges.

The man spoke, and Ripple said, "He wants to know if your medicine will really heal his wound."

Lincoln hesitated only briefly. "Yes, it will."

"I'm not sure your confidence is warranted," said Ripple.

"Just translate."

The drone complied.

Lincoln wasn't sure, either, but he figured he needed to show strength and resolve.

Seconds later, Ripple said, "The man is willing, Lincoln. My goodness, I do hope this does not fail."

"Withhold your opinions for now. Direct translations only."

Ripple flashed its red lights. "Very well."

Lincoln took a few more steps away from the shields and kneeled. "Tell him to sit here."

Seconds later the bolup man was seated before Lincoln, smelling of putrid flesh and unwashed skin.

Lincoln held the caretaker out for the man to see. "Tell him not to be afraid. If he tries to harm the medicine creature, he will not be healed. If he tries to run away, he will not be healed. He must sit still."

The man listened to Ripple's translation without taking his eyes off the robot.

Lincoln set the caretaker on the sand beside the man's hip. "Let's get this done, Ripple."

Ripple stepped over to within inches of the caretaker. Seconds later the caretaker came alive, moved to the man's wound, and dismantled itself. The man muttered a few words as he watched, but he stayed still. Soon the caretaker was gone, having entered the wound as thousands of crawling specks.

Lincoln finally looked up and realized some of the man's tribemates had gathered around. Skyra and Elah were standing behind him also, apparently ready to defend him if necessary.

The wounded man started to get to his feet, but Lincoln instructed Ripple to tell him to stay seated until the medicine came back out of his body. The man complied without argument, and Lincoln sensed from his expression that he knew he might die if the treatment didn't work. The man's eyes were bloodshot, perhaps from enduring so much pain, and Lincoln just now noticed his hands were shaking. Four old scars ran parallel to each other from his throat down to his navel, as if a bear or a big cat had mauled him at some point, and Lincoln wondered how a mostly naked man with only primitive weapons could survive such an ordeal. What other horrors had this man experienced during his life?

Lincoln crossed his legs and sat facing the man. "Ripple, direct translations now, okay?"

"Understood."

Lincoln eyed the tribesman for a moment, then he pointed to his own hair. "I am sorry for taking your hair."

Ripple translated, then exchanged words with the man. "He does not seem to understand what you are trying to say, although he seems to remember you took his hair."

"I said I wanted direct translations. Not just my words, but his too."

"Very well."

Lincoln pointed to the scars on the man's torso. "What happened to you?"

Ripple translated. The man put his hand on his scars and spoke. Ripple said, "Scimitar-toothed cat. I was young. Killed my tribemate/brother. I was strong and did not die."

"I am glad you did not die."

The man did not reply.

Lincoln gestured to the man's tribemates. "Is this all of your tribe, or are there others elsewhere?"

"My tribe had a hard cold season. Now we have a hard warm season. My tribe is almost gone. We are afraid we will all die before another warm season comes."

"Is that why you moved your camp here?"

"Yes. We want your strength. If we kill you and eat your body, we will have your strength."

Lincoln scanned the faces of the man's tribemates, looking for signs of aggression but seeing none. If anything, he saw curiosity. "We want to help your tribe become strong again," he said to the man.

"I do not understand."

"We want to help your tribe become strong, and we want

to help the other tribes become strong. The world will be better if all the tribes are strong."

"I do not understand."

Lincoln was starting to wonder how accurate Ripple's translations actually were. Maybe a different approach would help. "Do you want your tribe to be strong?"

"We have lost many tribemates."

"Do you want us to help you become strong?"

"You will not let us kill and eat one of your tribemates."

"We will teach you another way to become strong. You must join with a nandup tribe. Bolups and nandups must live together to be strong." Lincoln gestured to the two Skyras. "My tribe is strong because we are both bolups and nandups. Your tribe will join our tribe, and you will be strong with us. Then, when the nandups come down from the foothills, we will join another nandup tribe, and together we will be the strongest tribe in the land. All the other bolup tribes will want to be strong like us, and they will join with nandups too. Do you understand now?"

Ripple's translation seemed to take a considerable number of attempts. Finally the man replied. "Bolups hate nandups. Nandups hate bolups."

Lincoln gritted his teeth. "Not anymore! Starting today, we will be your tribemates, and you will be our tribemates. We will help you, and you will help us."

The man glanced up at his tribemates. "Our tribe is diminished. Your tribe has strange medicine and strange creatures and strange garments. How can we help you?"

"You can teach us many things. The bolups of our tribe are new to this land, and we do not know how to collect plants we can eat. Our nandups do not eat as many plants as we do, so they cannot teach our bolups these things."

Skyra surprised Lincoln by speaking up. "The nandups of our tribe do not hunt on the river plain in the warm season. We only know how to hunt in the foothills in the warm season. You hunt the plains in the warm season, and you can teach us."

Ripple translated both Lincoln's and Skyra's words.

A small voice came from somewhere behind the bolups, and Lincoln spotted Yanlip. The boy was clinging to his mother's leg with one arm and pointing toward the two Skyras with his free hand.

Ripple translated. "Yanlip just pointed out that the nandup women look strange and smell strange, but they were kind to him. They gave him water and bear meat, and they made him laugh. They are strong, and he wants to be strong like the nandup women."

Lincoln turned back to the injured bolup man, who was now staring at his hip. "Oh, crap," Lincoln said. The specks were already emerging from the man's wounds, piling onto the ground at an alarming rate. Something must have gone wrong —it was too soon. "What's going on, Ripple?"

"The feedback I am receiving indicates no complications," the drone replied. "If I am not mistaken, the caretakers consider their task complete. I can only assume they are continuing to improve their efficiency with each new job we give them. I must say, I am becoming quite envious of their adaptability and modular design."

Lincoln wasn't convinced. "His wound looks the same as before."

"Nevertheless, the caretakers consider their task complete."

The specks were already joining together into fly-sized components.

The man ran his hand over his wound. It was no longer seeping pus, but the surrounding tissue was still inflamed. Abruptly, the man got to his feet. He took a few tentative steps, then showed his teeth in a fierce-looking smile. He spoke to Lincoln.

"Your medicine is good," Ripple said.

Lincoln returned the smile. "I am glad we could help. Please do not move your camp away from this hill of boulders. We will be tribemates. We will help you, and you will help us. Together we will be very strong."

Yanlip spoke from beside his mother again, and Ripple translated. "The skinny bolup man has good medicine. I like our new tribemates. I do not want to eat them today."

14

ANOTHER GOOD DAY

47,659 YEARS *in the past - Day 15 (11 days later)*

SKYRA HAD NEVER SEEN a wedding before, so she did not know what to expect. Her Una-Loto people had a festive ritual to honor a woman's ilmekho when the woman had seen twenty cold seasons, but those rituals mostly involved the tribe's dominant men challenging each other to be the first to put a child in the woman's belly. Young nandup women did not choose one man to marry, although some older women and men formed pair bonds after they were too old to participate in hunts. Being married was a strange idea to Skyra, but she liked being with Lincoln.

"Why must I wear this?" Skyra asked, referring to the reflective garment Jazzlyn had looped over one of Skyra's shoulders and around her waist. Jazzlyn had taken one of the leftover pieces of reflective material and had made what she called a *sash*.

Jazzlyn tilted her head to the side as she adjusted the sash across Skyra's cape. "Girl, this is your wedding day. You *have* to wear something at least a little bit special."

"It smells funny."

Jazzlyn smiled. "You don't have to wear it for long."

"Will Lincoln put a child in my belly after the wedding?"

Jazzlyn gave her a strange bolup look. "I suppose that's up to the two of you." She gestured to the walls of the bear cave. "You and Lincoln have been sleeping together in your own private cave for over a week. There's a chance you already have a child in your belly."

Skyra slid her hand under her cape and rubbed her belly. "I do not feel a child."

"If there's one in there, you'll feel it soon enough."

Skyra chewed on her lip for a few breaths. "Women cannot hunt when the child inside becomes big."

Jazzlyn eyed her. "You love to hunt, don't you?"

"I love Lincoln. I *like* to hunt."

"That's what I meant. You *enjoy* hunting."

"I do. Veenah has never enjoyed hunting. She likes to stay in camp."

Jazzlyn nodded slowly. "What do the women in your Una-Loto tribe do when they give birth to children? Are there special people in the tribe who help them?"

"When a woman is ready, she leaves Una-Loto camp to be alone. She comes back later with her child." Skyra squatted with her butt just above the cave floor. "The older women tell us this is how to make the child come out."

"Jesus," Jazzlyn muttered as Skyra rose back to her full height.

"I ask Lincoln what does Jesus mean, but he does not tell me."

"Probably because it's difficult to explain." Jazzlyn seemed to think for several breaths. "Did Ripple ever explain the idea of God or religion to you?"

"No."

"Do your people believe in any kind of creatures or people that you cannot really see or touch?"

Skyra smiled. "You are trying to be funny."

"I'm not. Do your people believe there is an animal or person that makes the warm season come, or makes the wild game plentiful, or makes the rain or snow come?"

Skyra's smile faded. "How could a person or animal make the warm season come? I cannot bring the rain or snow, so how could another person bring the rain or snow?"

Jazzlyn nodded. "Just as I thought. Your people do not have any kind of religion. That's why Lincoln doesn't want to try to explain Jesus. You would have a hard time understanding."

"I am not stupid, Jazzlyn."

Jazzlyn's eyes widened slightly. "No, no you're not. You're probably smarter than I am." She took a deep breath. "Okay, look. Jesus is a person in a long and complex story some people from my timeline believe. The story includes beings you cannot really see or touch."

"Like the ghost people in the empty city," Skyra said.

Jazzlyn took another deep breath. "No, not exactly like that. Those ghost people are real. The story I'm talking about is one of many different stories that different people from my homeland choose to believe. Some people choose not to believe any of them at all. That's a good thing, I suppose—people can choose to believe whatever they want to believe."

Skyra growled. "You are not making sense. I cannot choose to believe you are a woolly rhino. You are Jazzlyn, not a woolly rhino."

"You're right. This is why Lincoln puts off trying to explain religion to you. Next time you're alone with him, tell him you want a better explanation than I was able to give you."

"No. Next time I am alone with Lincoln, we are going to make love."

Jazzlyn's smile returned. "You're my hero, you know that? I need to be more open like you are when it comes to Virgil."

"What does that mean?"

"It means I like Virgil—a lot—but we have never made love."

Skyra covered her mouth to hold back a laugh. "You and Virgil should try it! Making love feels better than washing in the river."

"I didn't mean I've never—"

"I will talk to Virgil," Skyra said. "He is afraid of me, and he will make love to you if I tell him to. I will pull my khul from its sling when I tell him."

Now Jazzlyn covered her own mouth. "Skyra, don't you dare!"

Skyra bared her teeth. Then she laughed.

Jazzlyn cleared her throat and adjusted Skyra's sash one more time. "Come on, girl, they're probably waiting for us. You ready?"

"I cannot be ready because I do not know what is going to happen."

"All you need to know is what you're going to say when it's your turn to speak to Lincoln. Do you want to practice it here with me first?"

"No."

Jazzlyn held out her strange robot hand with the palm up. "Alrighty then, let's make your marriage official."

Skyra took Jazzlyn's outstretched hand, and they ducked out of the cave together.

Lincoln and the others were standing in the center of the courtyard. Skyra had to hold back a laugh as she and Jazzlyn joined the group. Lincoln had his own sheet of reflective material tied around his neck, the length of it hanging down his back almost to the ground. Derek had a long length of thin red and white cord looped loosely around his neck numerous times, with more loops of the cord around his waist.

Jazzlyn pulled Skyra to Lincoln's side. She grabbed Lincoln's hand and placed it in Skyra's.

Lincoln gazed at Skyra. "You look beautiful."

"Is it good to look beautiful?"

"Yes, it's good."

"You look beautiful too."

He smiled. "Thanks."

Derek cleared his throat. "Nandups, bolups, and drones, we are gathered here today to celebrate and make official the strangest bond I have ever been witness to. Lincoln and Skyra have come together across thousands of years to find each other, and if that isn't true love, I don't know what is. Their bond happens to be a crucial component of the audacious plan devised by Lincoln's drone Ripple, and their marriage represents the future of this world. More importantly, their bond was forged in the universal fires of love and passion."

Jazzlyn snorted a laugh, then she looked around nervously. "Sorry, y'all."

Derek frowned but continued. "These two are to be bound forever, as per the unwritten laws of this newly-formed Kutolo-Loto tribe."

Skyra had come up with the name for her new tribe. Kutolo was a nandup word used to describe the numerous hills of boulders and caves, like this one, dotting the Dofusofu river plains, and Loto was the word for all the nandup tribes living in the region.

Derek continued. "Neither the threat of war, nor the teeth and claws of beasts, nor the ravages of time will tear this couple asunder, for love is stronger than all else. Friendship is stronger than all else. The Kutolo-Loto tribe is stronger than all else." He looked around at the group. "Is there anyone present who believes Lincoln and Skyra should not be married? If so, keep it to your own damn self because it doesn't freakin' matter—we're doing this."

He stepped closer to Skyra and Lincoln. "Do you have the rings?"

Jazzlyn pulled two circular stones from her pocket. Jazzlyn had made the rings with the help of Ripple and the caretaker creatures. She gave Skyra's to Lincoln and Lincoln's to Skyra.

Derek said, "Lincoln Woodhouse, have you any words you'd like to say to your bride as you put her ring on her finger?"

Lincoln turned to Skyra and took her hand. "Skyra, I know you never imagined being with a person like me. In fact, you never imagined a person like me could even *exist*. I never imagined I would ever be with anyone at all, let alone a nandup woman 47,000 years in my past. Even so, here we are, together. All my life I have wondered what it would feel like to be with someone who loves me no matter what mistakes I make, no matter what I say or do. You have shown me what it feels like, and now I never want to live without it. Finding you was the best thing that ever happened to me."

He slipped the stone ring onto the third finger from her thumb, the one Jazzlyn had called the ring finger.

Derek said, "Skyra Una-Loto, have you any words you'd like to say to your groom as you put his ring on his finger?"

Skyra looked at Lincoln's ring. It was smaller than hers because of his skinny bolup fingers. She gazed into Lincoln's eyes. "Lincoln, I am happy we are married." She pushed his ring onto his ring finger.

Everyone remained silent for a few breaths, as if they expected her to say more, but Skyra had said all she wanted to say.

Lincoln gave her the bolup smile she loved to see.

"Well, that's that," said Derek. "You may now seal your bond with a kiss."

Lincoln leaned in and put his lips on Skyra's. She shoved her tongue into his mouth because that was now her favorite way to kiss him. A familiar tingling sensation spread through her chest and belly.

After several breaths, Lincoln finally pulled away, smiling broadly.

"Let me be the first to congratulate you," Maddy said. "Remember, Skyra, Lincoln still needs me to take care of him. I have known him much longer than you have."

"I will remember," Skyra said without taking her eyes off Lincoln's.

Jazzlyn began clapping her hands together, then the others started clapping. Even Elah and Veenah joined in, although Skyra was sure they did not know any more than she did what the clapping meant.

When the clapping stopped, Veenah spoke in the Una-Loto language. "I am happy the talking part is over. If the men are not going to challenge each other to honor your ilmekho, what will happen next?"

Skyra had no idea, so she asked Lincoln.

He said, "Well, usually in my timeline we would eat a meal and some cake. A cake is... um, it's very sweet, and it makes people fat."

Skyra frowned.

"But we don't have cake here," he said quickly. "Sometimes, after the food, people like to dance. Dancing is when you play music and you move your body in time with the music."

She frowned again.

"Here, let me show you," he said. "Maddy, play something slow we can dance to."

"Excellent idea," Maddy said. "However, I am still unfamiliar with all the modules in this shell. This may take a moment."

"Allow me," Ripple said. Less than a breath later, strange sounds started coming from Ripple's shell.

Lincoln stepped in front of Skyra, took her hand in his, and put one arm around her waist. "There really aren't any rules to dancing. You just listen to the music and let your body move any way that feels good to you." He started swaying back and forth, pulling her with him.

Jazzlyn grabbed Virgil and pulled him close. "Watch us, Skyra. I'm gonna show Virg some of my moves."

Virgil said, "Um, I'm really not a good dancer."

"Nonsense!" Jazzlyn said, and she started moving her shoulders and hips.

Skyra turned to Lincoln. "I do not understand what we are doing."

"We can stop if you want, but I'd like you to give it a chance. Just listen to the music and move with the rhythm. It feels good once you get used to it."

Skyra focused her attention on the strange, throbbing

sound. She had never heard anything like it, but it was not unpleasant. Lincoln's body was close against hers as he swayed, and his movements made her skin tingle. It was almost like what he did to her when they were going to make love on the bear-skin bed in their cave. Yes, she could get used to this. She started moving against his body.

She realized Lincoln was staring at her. "Are you even listening to the music, or are you just trying to get me aroused?"

She smiled. "You said it would feel good. You were right— it feels good."

Jazzlyn must have overheard, because she laughed and said, "I'm pretty sure Skyra wouldn't mind some honeymoon time with you, Lincoln. Maybe you should take her to your cave."

Skyra said, "Virgil, I have something to tell you about Jazzlyn."

"No!" Jazzlyn said. "No, no, no, you do *not* have *anything* to say to Virgil!"

Virgil looked confused, but he remained silent.

Skyra heard Veenah laugh, and she turned to see her birthmate and Derek now holding each other and swaying back and forth. Veenah seemed livelier in her movements than Skyra, but then Veenah had always been more gleeful than Skyra, especially at festive rituals.

Jazzlyn let go of Virgil long enough to gently shove Skyra's shoulder. "You two go on, now. We'll keep the party going out here."

Skyra looked up at Lincoln's face, hoping he would like the idea too.

"Bolups are coming!" Elah shouted. She was standing at the gap, looking out.

Skyra pulled away from Lincoln.

Ripple stopped playing music.

Elah grabbed one of the spears stacked beside the gap and held it up, ready to fight.

Skyra and the others ran to join Elah, each grabbing a weapon.

Two men from the bolup camp—Skyra now knew they were called the Peli-Bayom tribe—were almost to the gap. Sometimes the bolups had come to the courtyard to bring food, or just to talk. One time Yanlip had found his way up to the courtyard all by himself to play games with Skyra, Elah, and Veenah, so it was not unusual to see the bolup tribesmen. Still, Skyra insisted her tribemates always be ready with weapons.

The two men stopped on the far side of the rock pile. One of them was Broc, the man the caretaker had healed. The other man, Erloo, had only one good arm. The upper muscles of his other arm had been lost when his tribe had tried to kill a woolly rhino. Erloo was lucky to have survived.

Broc held up a hand in greeting, then he began speaking even before Skyra's group could return the greeting.

"Ripple!" Skyra shouted.

"I am here," Ripple said, already at her side.

"Translate please."

Ripple listened to Broc for a few breaths before speaking. "Broc is very eager to get his words out and is somewhat diffi-cult to understand." Ripple made a humming sound and lifted off the ground to see the bolups over the rock pile. "Broc is going on about another bolup tribe, the Yuni-Bayom tribe. Apparently they are here now, at the bottom of the hill."

"Uh-oh," Lincoln said. "Did Broc and Erloo come to get our help? Are they under attack?"

Ripple spoke loudly to the bolups until the two men finally fell silent to listen. Ripple spoke again, then translated the reply. "The Yuni-Bayom tribe is not attacking. They seem to be friends of the Peli-Bayom tribe. The new bolups were moving their camp, and they came upon our boulder hill and the Peli-Bayom tribe."

Broc began speaking rapidly again.

"The new bolups have brought exciting news. When they were crossing the river, not far away, they saw some creatures." Ripple interrupted Broc again, then the two exchanged words. "The creatures at the river are large. I am convinced Broc is referring to woolly mammoths. Apparently, woolly mammoths are rarely encountered in this area, and this presents an opportunity that Broc and Erloo are eager to take advantage of."

Skyra's heart began pounding, and her legs wanted to run. Woolly mammoths! Here, in the Dofusofu river plain during the warm season? She reminded herself the cold season was almost here, so perhaps this wasn't so strange.

Ripple continued translating. "The new bolups have invited the resident bolups to hunt one of the mammoths, and now the resident bolups are inviting us to participate in the hunt also. Broc seems to think this offer is a grand gesture. I will tell him we are not interested."

"You will *not* tell him that, Ripple!" Skyra said. "Woolly mammoths at the river! Yes, we will go on the hunt. We will help kill one of the mammoths. Tell them we will go, Ripple!"

Lincoln grabbed her arm. "Skyra, you're not serious! Mammoths are bigger than woolly rhinos—much bigger."

"That is why we will go," said Elah. "If we kill a mammoth, we will have meat for many, many days, maybe enough for the entire cold season."

Skyra said, "I have not seen woolly mammoths in many seasons. They do not move through these plains and foothills as much as they used to. We must hunt with the bolups, or we may never have the chance again. Ripple, tell them we will help with the hunt."

"This is unnecessarily risky, and you—"

"Tell them!"

"Very well." Ripple exchanged words with Broc and Erloo, then the two bolups headed back to their camp. "The bolups are leaving for the hunt now. Skyra, this is your wedding day. Perhaps you should spend some intimate time in your cave with Lincoln."

"Yes, this is my wedding day. Woolly mammoths on my wedding day. This is a good day!" Skyra yanked off her sash and snugged her khul into its sling inside her cape. She went to the spears leaning against the rock wall and picked out the only remaining bolup-made spear. The other one had snapped in two when she had killed the cave bear, and she had not taken time to make more stone-tipped spears. She handed the spear to Lincoln and left the crude wooden-pointed spears where they were. "You will use this spear. The bolups have other stone-tipped spears we can use."

Lincoln glanced at the spear, then he stared at her like he thought she was crazy.

She smiled at him. "Do not worry. Bolups make good spears, and they are skilled mammoth hunters. They will teach us." She glanced around at the others. "Come, we must go now."

"Perhaps we should take a vote," Virgil said. "It sounds awfully dangerous to me."

"Suicidal is what it is," Derek added.

Skyra hesitated, then she turned to Veenah and watched

her birthmate's face carefully as she explained what was going on. Skyra had always been able to read Veenah's expressions, even better than the expressions of her other tribemates. She could tell Veenah did not want to go on the hunt. Skyra growled, then she turned back to Lincoln and the others. "I understand you do not wish to go. Elah and I will go with the bolups. We will help kill a woolly mammoth. After we kill, there will be much work to do. There will be much to carry. You do not have to help with killing, but all of you will help with carrying."

"Skyra, I go where you go," Lincoln said. "It's our wedding day. If you're going to go off and get yourself killed, I might as well die with you."

"I'm coming too," Jazzlyn said. "I'm your maid of honor, so... well, whatever that means."

Virgil stepped closer to Jazzlyn. "I'm in. Although I'd like to know if it's okay if we stay back at a safe distance. We can learn by observing."

"Goddammit, you guys," Derek said. "Did it even occur to you Skyra might be bluffing just to get you to agree? You all fell for it, so I guess I'm in, too."

"Veenah does not like to hunt," Skyra said. "Derek, you should stay here with her."

"Indeed," said Ripple. "If Skyra and Lincoln perish, Derek and Veenah will still carry out my plan, although Derek's genetic contribution will be less than optimal."

Derek started to say something, but Skyra shouted, "Too much talking!" She turned to the gap, where Elah was already climbing over the rock pile. Skyra followed her over. When she glanced back, Lincoln was behind her, carrying the only good spear, followed by Jazzlyn, Virgil, and Ripple.

Skyra counted eleven bolup men in the new Yuni-Bayom tribe. She did not bother counting the women and children because bolup women and children did not hunt. Eleven bolup men from the Yuni-Bayom tribe, eight men from the Peli-Bayom tribe, and five hunters from Skyra's new Kutolo-Loto tribe. This was enough hunters. Skyra had helped with only two mammoth hunts with her Una-Loto tribe, and on one of those hunts the mammoth escaped after trampling one of her tribemates. The man, Ghalab, had died before the next warm season came. Only nine hunters had been on that hunt, but today's hunting party would include twenty-four. Skyra could hardly contain her excitement.

The new bolups stared at Skyra and her tribemates. They stared at Ripple. They spoke to each other. They spoke to the Peli-Bayom bolups. They were clearly curious, but they were not angry or aggressive. The Peli-Bayom bolups had already told the newcomers about Skyra's people. They had even given the newcomers a stone carving of a bolup man and a nandup woman. Jazzlyn had made four more of the carvings for the Peli-Bayom tribe to give to any other bolup tribes they might encounter.

The new bolups did not wear capes, but they did each have several cords around their necks, strung with teeth, claws, and various other objects Skyra could not identify without getting closer than she wanted to. The men appeared stronger and healthier than the Peli-Bayom men, and Skyra hoped she would never have to fight them. She and Elah were now far outnumbered by the bolups surrounding them.

Ripple translated as the new bolups explained they had seen the woolly mammoths walking in the river, slowly making their way downstream. The hunters wanted to pursue them now, before the mammoths left the river. The bolups had brought a collection of mammoth spears, each with a large stone point heavy and sharp enough to penetrate a mammoth's thick hide. Without speaking, the men distributed these spears to everyone who did not have one, including Skyra, Elah, Jazzlyn, and Virgil. Lincoln decided to keep his lighter spear. The new bolup men waved for the group to follow, and they headed for the river. These men did not want to talk, they wanted to hunt. Skyra liked this about them, even though they were stinking bolups.

The group spread out across the rocky field as they made their way to the river, with the new bolups in the lead, followed by Peli-Bayom bolups, then Skyra's group. Ripple walked silently a few steps behind Skyra.

"Nobody's talking," Virgil said, trying to keep his voice low. "If we're expected to actually help, someone will give us some instructions first, right? I have absolutely no idea what to do."

"You will learn," Skyra said. "These bolups are skilled mammoth hunters. Watch them. Watch how they do not let the mammoth kill them with its tusks. I will tell you when it is time to help."

"So, we should just stay out of the way?" Jazzlyn asked.

"No, not out of the way," Elah said. "We must know where the mammoth wants to run. We will move in front of it so we can use our spears when it comes to us. The tribe's best hunters will attack first. If they are lucky, they will weaken the mammoth. The mammoth will not be as dangerous when we thrust our spears."

Lincoln frowned. "*Thrust* our spears? I thought we were going to *throw* them. Like, from a safe distance."

Skyra gazed at him as she walked, trying to decide what to say. "Do not throw. The tribe's best hunters might throw their spears, but you are not strong like those men, Lincoln, and you are not skilled at throwing a spear. Do not worry. We will not attack until the mammoth is weak."

"Isn't an injured animal even *more* dangerous?" Virgil asked.

Skyra tried not to growl, but it escaped her throat anyway. "I do not want to die. You do not want to die. The mammoth also does not want to die."

"Honestly, I have no idea what that's supposed to mean," Virgil said.

"It means I will tell you when it is time to help."

Lincoln nudged Skyra's arm. "We're scared, but we'll do what you tell us to do. I trust you, Skyra."

She smiled without turning to look at him. Skyra did not ever want to lose Lincoln.

The bolups ahead stopped walking and stared at the river for a few breaths, then they turned and headed farther downstream. The string of hunters followed.

Skyra's legs wanted to run, but she forced them to be patient. As she walked, she studied the row of trees bordering the river. The bolups must have seen or heard something to make them change course. She saw movement through the trees and stopped. She pointed and whispered, "There, Lincoln!"

Lincoln and the others stopped and stared.

She saw it again, a glimpse of brown passing by a gap in the tree branches.

"God almighty, I saw it," Virgil said.

Elah put her hand over Virgil's mouth and whispered, "Too loud."

Virgil nodded, wide-eyed.

The bolup hunters were now crouching low, almost crawling. They changed direction again, heading even farther downstream.

Skyra and Elah crouched also, waited for Lincoln and his tribemates to do the same, then they followed the bolup hunters. Skyra caught several more glimpses of the woolly mammoths as her group silently overtook the herd and moved ahead. The mammoths were so close she could hear their massive feet and trunks splashing the water.

The bolup hunters finally angled sharply toward the river. Just before entering the rows of trees, the leaders paused and made several hand gestures to the hunters behind them. Skyra was not sure what the gestures meant, so she waited to see what the other bolups did. If it were up to her, she would have the group spread out along the river farther downstream and prepare to ambush the injured mammoth as it fled the first attackers. Ambushed animals almost always tried to run in the same direction they were moving before being attacked.

Several breaths later, the bolups ahead of her group started moving downstream, just as she had predicted. She motioned to Lincoln, and they continued following, keeping low and silent.

After the first group—about eight, probably the best hunters—entered at the ambush point, the others entered the forest one at a time, evenly spaced out downstream, until only Skyra's group was still in the rocky field.

Elah gave Skyra a confident look, then she started toward the trees alone.

"Elah, we stay together!" Skyra hissed.

Her other self hesitated, then she nodded, a gesture she had learned from Skyra and the others in recent days.

Together they moved farther downstream before approaching the river.

Near the water's edge, Skyra looked upstream. In the distance she saw at least four massive creatures in the river walking toward her. She had not seen a mammoth in several seasons, and the sight made her chest heave to draw in enough air. The creatures looked even larger than she remembered. Curved white tusks swung from side to side as the mammoths looked around nervously. They obviously sensed danger, but still they continued downstream. The two mammoths in the lead were different sizes. The smaller one was a female, but even her shorter tusks were longer than Skyra's entire body.

Skyra had almost forgotten she was not alone. She pulled back from the river slowly, turned to Lincoln and her other tribemates, and whispered, "We must be ready soon." She checked the tightness of her spear's stone tip and told them to do the same. When they had done so, she lifted her arm and pointed to her ribs. "This is where you kill the mammoth." Then she pointed to her belly and to her thigh. "If you stab here or here, the mammoth will kill *you*. Do you understand?"

They all nodded, obviously frightened.

She jabbed her spear forward with both hands. "The skin is very thick. You must thrust hard. Keep pushing. If the mammoth turns, you must let go, or the—"

Shouts came from upstream, followed by panicked bellows.

"God almighty," Virgil said again.

Skyra ducked behind a tree. "Ripple, move away from the river and stay there until the hunt is over!"

"Very well," Ripple replied as it turned to move away.

"Hide and be ready!" Skyra said. "Do not attack until I

tell you to." She turned her back on them to watch the bolup hunters.

The lead hunters were already on both sides of the last mammoth in the herd, hurling their spears at its sides from only a few body lengths away. They had waited for all but one of the mammoths to pass them before attacking, probably to make sure the herd ran downstream in the direction they wanted. The injured mammoth would try to follow the herd.

The other mammoths came thundering down the center of the river, their feet throwing water all around them. The hunters spaced out along the river let the panicked creatures pass, and soon four mammoths pounded past Skyra's group, shaking the ground and drenching the river's rocky banks.

Now Skyra had a better view of the target mammoth. The creature was spinning to one side to strike its attackers and shake off several spears embedded in its ribs. One of the hunters darted in with a khul, probably trying to sever the mammoth's large hind leg tendon, but he was driven back by swinging tusks. Another man tried from the opposite side and appeared to make a good hit.

The mammoth bellowed and began running downstream.

Several breaths later, another hunter rushed from the trees and hurled his spear into the mammoth's side. Without even slowing down, the man leapt into the river with his khul to strike at the creature's tendon. The man fell amidst the exploding water at the mammoth's feet, and Skyra could not tell if his swing was successful or if he was being trampled.

Another hunter burst out of the trees and threw his spear. As the mammoth came nearer, two more men ran out with bows, jumped into the river, and shot their arrows into the mammoth's side.

The mammoth continued fleeing down the middle of the river.

"Do not move until I tell you!" Skyra shouted without turning to look at her tribemates.

Another man ran out and threw his spear, then another did the same, and still the mammoth continued coming.

Skyra gripped her bolup-made mammoth spear in both hands to stop the weapon from shaking. "Kami-fu-godakh. Aibul-tekne-té-menga-ulmecko," she muttered. *Cave lion and woolly rhino, give me your strength.*

The tree shook against her shoulder as the ground rocked.

Skyra let out a growl and burst forward at the same instant Elah ran from behind her own tree. Skyra had never been skilled at throwing spears, so she didn't even try. She leapt from the river's bank with the spear held at her side. The spear's tip punctured the creature's thick skin before Skyra's feet even hit the water. As the spear came to a stop, her legs swung forward, and she lost her grip on the weapon and fell onto her back in the river.

As she tried getting up, the mammoth stopped and spun around. One of the spears protruding from its side hit Skyra's head, knocking her back into the water. Strong hands grabbed her arm and yanked her out of the way just as the mammoth's foot came down where her belly had been. Elah then gripped Skyra's armpit with one hand and her hair with the other and pulled her up. Just as Skyra got to her feet, a massive tusk hit her from behind and threw her face-first into Elah. They both flew over the water and tumbled onto the river's rocky shore.

Skyra got to her knees to scramble away from the furious mammoth, then she saw Lincoln, Virgil, and Jazzlyn standing at the shore with their backs to her and Elah.

The mammoth was swinging its trunk and tusks wildly, stumbling in the water as it turned.

"Brace your spear on the rocks!" Lincoln shouted. He and the other two dropped to their knees and jammed the ends of their weapons into the ground.

The injured mammoth must have heard Lincoln's voice. It bellowed and lunged toward the three of them.

Lincoln, Jazzlyn, and Virgil angled their spears at the mammoth's chest, but the creature lowered its head and swung its tusks, knocking all three spears out of the way.

"Run!" Skyra screamed.

They did not have time to run. Lincoln dove to one side, while Jazzlyn and Virgil dove to the other, barely avoiding the creature's tusks and feet.

The mammoth stumbled on the rocks and one of its front legs gave out. The creature crashed onto its chest, then rolled onto its side, snapping several of the spear shafts protruding from its body.

"Stay back from the legs!" Skyra shouted. She no longer had a spear, so she grabbed the spears Virgil and Jazzlyn had lost as they had jumped out of the mammoth's way. She tossed one of the spears to Elah.

The mammoth bellowed again as it tried rolling to its belly to get its feet beneath it. It failed and fell back onto its side.

Shouts came from upstream as the bolup hunters approached.

Skyra moved in to pierce the mammoth's chest but was forced back by its thrashing legs.

Lincoln grabbed her arm and pulled her back. "I think it's dying. There's no reason to keep risking your life."

Skyra paused and stared at the mammoth. Her heart was pounding, and her legs and arms still wanted to finish the hunt. Elah was now on the other side of the creature, preparing to climb over its back so she could pierce it ribs from on top.

"Elah!" Skyra shouted. "The mammoth cannot get up. Stay back."

Elah paced one direction then the other, her chest heaving. She wanted to finish the hunt also, but she stayed back.

The bolup hunters gathered around. Most of them no longer had their spears, but one of the men with a bow stepped closer to the mammoth and shot an arrow into its throat beneath its chin. This was not necessary—the creature was almost dead. It stopped kicking and lay still.

The hunters stood around the mammoth, silently watching its chest rise and fall. The movements became slower with each breath. Finally, the creature let out a wet, bubbling gasp and became silent.

One of the bolup hunters raised his hand above his head and shouted "Samasama!"

"Samasama! Samasama!" the other hunters cried out, also raising their hands.

Skyra did not know what the word meant, but she lifted her spear too. "Samasama!"

15

COMMON GOALS

47,659 YEARS *in the past - Day 15*

LINCOLN STUMBLED on a jagged rock as he ran, so he doubled his effort to keep his eyes on the ground under his feet. This was not the time to break an ankle. He needed to get one of the robotic caretakers from camp and return to the mammoth kill site before it was too late.

The mammoth had trampled a hunter from the new bolup tribe. No one had even realized the man was hurt until he had pulled himself out of the river and shouted to get the group's attention. Upon closer inspection, the man appeared to have several broken bones in the region of his pelvis and upper leg. He couldn't possibly walk, which was a death sentence in this world.

Now about halfway back to the boulder hill, Lincoln was finding a comfortable pace to avoid tripping yet still make good time. He'd been a long-distance runner most of his adult life, so he had insisted on making the run. If the caretaker could help the injured man, perhaps the new bolups would become a second ally tribe, thus improving his own tribe's chances for survival and ability to influence even more tribes. If it *couldn't* help the man, there was no telling what would happen.

When Lincoln approached the hill's base, the bolup women and children stopped what they were doing to watch him. He couldn't communicate, so he ran past them without a word and charged up the now-familiar path. Some of the more treacherous parts slowed him down, but he made it to the courtyard in record time.

Maddy was on the rock pile, watching through the gap, apparently on guard duty. The drone flashed its red lights as he approached. "Oh, dear, what has happened?"

"It's okay, none of us are hurt," he panted as he climbed over the pile. "One of the bolup tribesmen is injured, though." He started jogging across the courtyard. "Where's Derek and Veenah?"

"That is an interesting question."

Lincoln paused. "What does that mean?"

"Well, I was told not to reveal any information regarding their current activity."

"Current activity?"

"Perhaps *shenanigans* is a better choice of words."

Lincoln glanced at the second cave just in time to see Derek rushing out, pulling his shirt on over his head. "What's wrong? What happened?"

Lincoln couldn't help but smile. "No worries. We're all okay. Um, are *you* okay?"

Derek adjusted his shirt and looked down at his bare feet. "Yeah, we were just um... well, dammit. It was Veenah's idea. She can be persuasive."

"She doesn't even speak English."

Derek frowned. "There are other ways to be persuasive. Damn, man, are you going to chastise me for something you're guilty of too, or are you going to tell my why you're suddenly back here drenched in sweat?"

Veenah appeared at the mouth of the cave, wearing her cape but not her waist-skin. "Skyra? Elah?"

"They're both okay," Lincoln said, trying to sound soothing. "Look, I gotta go back. A bolup tribesman got trampled and is seriously hurt. I came for one of the caretakers." He jogged to the bear cave, retrieved one of the robots, and returned to the courtyard.

Derek and Veenah emerged from the second cave again, now fully clothed. Derek sat on the ground and started pulling on his shoes. "We're going with you this time."

"That's fine, but I'm going to run. Just keep following the river downstream until you find us." He turned to leave, then he paused and turned around. "For what it's worth, I'm happy for you two." Without waiting for a response, he headed for the gap. "You stay here, Maddy."

"Yes, I will stay here. I am of no use to anyone."

Lincoln started climbing over the rock pile. "You're my therapist, remember? After helping butcher a five-ton mammoth, I may need some real therapy. Stay here where it's safe."

After descending the hill, Lincoln ran by the bolup camp again and saw the women unloading the new Yuni-Bayom tribe's possessions and setting up their shelters. Apparently the new tribe intended to stay.

The dead mammoth was about a mile from the boulder hill, and Lincoln quickly found his pace and covered the distance without tripping again.

Astoundingly, the hunters had already cut most of the mammoth's hide loose, other than the portion beneath its body. Due to the creature's mass, this portion wouldn't be accessible until most of the flesh and bones were removed in small, manageable chunks. Skyra and Elah were in the midst of the hunters, hacking and pulling the skin as if they had hunted with these bolups all their lives. Jazzlyn and Virgil waved to Lincoln from where they were sitting cross-legged on the river's rocky shore a short distance away. Ripple was with them, and beside the drone lay the injured bolup man, sweating profusely and occasionally moaning in agony. Not a single one of the man's tribemates was there to comfort him.

"I think the others have decided this guy's a lost cause," Jazzlyn said as Lincoln kneeled beside the tribesman.

The man's waist-skin had been torn from his body by the mammoth's tusks or feet, revealing his legs and pelvic area, and he was bruised almost black from his left knee all the way to the left side of his chest. A grotesque bulge at the top of his thigh indicated a snapped femur, or perhaps the femur had come completely out of the socket joint. His pelvis was misshaped so severely that Lincoln could hardly imagine the caretaker could provide much help. He had to remind himself the caretakers had healed Yanlip, even though the boy's head had been bashed in.

He placed the caretaker on the gravel at the man's side. "Ripple, you know what to do."

"Indeed," Ripple said. The drone stepped closer and started the process.

As the robot began popping apart into its components, Lincoln turned to watch Skyra and the other hunters. The bolup men were chattering gleefully, obviously elated about the kill and not noticeably upset about their mortally-wounded tribemate. Skyra and Elah seemed just as joyful, exchanging words in their Una-Loto language, their arms covered in blood up to the elbows. The hunters had already started hacking at the mammoth's meat, cutting off strips and tossing them onto the furless side of the removed skin, which was stretched flat on the gravel, extending about five yards out from the mammoth's dorsal side.

"I feel like we should be helping," Jazzlyn said, "but so far they haven't invited us."

Virgil let out a grunt that wasn't too different from Skyra's grunts. "I'm perfectly happy to learn by observing, especially when they're ready to open that thing's abdominal cavity."

Lincoln turned back to the injured man. The caretaker was already in its powder-fine form and was entering the man's body directly through the skin on his hip. The tribesman was still conscious, but he was too focused on his pain to even notice what was happening. In fact, Lincoln wasn't even sure the man knew anyone was sitting beside him.

"Ripple, please keep us informed of any feedback you receive from the caretaker," Lincoln said, then he got up and approached the hunters.

Seconds later, Skyra saw him watching her. She stepped away from the mammoth carcass, pulled one of her stone knives from her wrist sheath, and handed it to him. "We have much work to do." She looked around his shoulder. "Did you bring the caretaker?"

He glanced back toward the injured man. "Yeah. I don't know if it will help, though."

"That is what the caretakers do. They help. The man will now live."

"I hope so."

Skyra grabbed his wrist, her hand wet with blood. "Have

you ever seen a woolly mammoth's heart, Lincoln? Come, I will show you."

He considered resisting then thought better of it. In his new life here, there was no place for squeamishness. He followed her around to the mammoth's ventral side, where three bolup hunters were already standing beside its belly, working on opening its abdominal cavity. The men had peeled back several layers of pink tissue, revealing a gray layer Lincoln presumed was the final barrier to the internal organs.

"It will not be long now," Skyra said with obvious excitement.

One of the hunters spoke loudly, and the other two stepped back. The man who had spoken then put the tip of his stone knife to the gray layer just below the ribs. He smacked the butt of the knife with his other hand, puncturing the tissue, then he gripped it with both hands and started sawing down the centerline toward the mammoth's posterior end.

A gust of gas rushed out the new opening with a sickening *whuuush*, splattering Lincoln's face with droplets and even blowing his hair back.

He slapped a hand over his mouth and nose. "Oh, my God!"

The hunter kept sawing. When the slice was about five feet long, something gave way. The man tried to step back, but he wasn't fast enough. The gray barrier split wide open under the pressure, and intestines piled out, knocking the bolup man onto his butt and flowing around him almost up to his neck.

Laughter exploded around Lincoln, and he realized the other hunters had gathered to watch the show. The man on his butt laughed just as loud as the others as he struggled to get back to his feet amongst the steaming entrails.

Still covering his mouth and nose, Lincoln turned to Skyra.

She smiled at him and said, "I did not know bolup hunters enjoyed hunting so much. They are not so different from my people."

Lincoln was too focused on not vomiting to reply.

Skyra didn't seem to notice. "Now the bolups will open the mammoth's chest so they can pull out the heart and other chest organs."

Broc, who happened to be one of the men who had helped open the mammoth's abdomen, pointed to Skyra, then to Elah as he spoke a string of words. He gestured with his stone knife, thrusting it into the open cavity and up against the bottom of the rib cage.

Skyra and Elah turned to each other, puzzled.

Lincoln took a deep breath then swallowed hard, unsure if he could speak without losing it. "I think Broc is inviting you to open the mammoth's chest."

Broc went through the gesture again, smiling at the two nandup women.

Skyra let out a brief laugh. "You are right, Lincoln! In the Una-Loto tribe, this is an honor." She slid her knife into her wrist sheath, pulled her cape and khul over her head, and shoved them into his arms.

Elah copied Skyra's motions and gave her cape and khul to Lincoln.

Both nandups then shed their waist-skins and footwraps and piled them into Lincoln's arms also. Without another word, the two women—now completely naked—turned to the mammoth carcass. Even with the creature lying on its side, its rib cage was still taller than the two nandup women. They pushed open the sliced barrier to the abdominal cavity and ducked inside, their legs squishing through the knee-deep entrails.

Elah held the gap open to provide light as Skyra sawed through the layer of muscles and other tissue separating the abdominal cavity from the chest cavity. Apparently satisfied with the cut, Skyra reached into the chest and began slicing at something. After several minutes of this, she leaned all the way into the chest and pulled out a massive gray organ that could only be part of a mammoth lung. The lung still wouldn't come completely loose, so Elah slid past Skyra, actually disappearing from view as she crawled into the mammoth's chest. Moments later, the lung came free, and Skyra shoved it behind her and out of the way.

Skyra crawled into the chest with Elah, and during the next few minutes they pushed out three more large chunks of lung.

A few more minutes later, Elah crawled out. She turned, and Skyra handed her a glistening, egg-shaped heart that Lincoln swore would outweigh Yanlip. It looked to be at least forty pounds.

Skyra crawled out, and the two nandups turned with smiling faces to display the heart to the rest of the hunters.

"Samasama!" A few of the bolups shouted.

One of the hunters accepted the heart from Elah and placed it on a clean spot on the mammoth skin. He immediately set to work carving it up, removing fist-sized pieces and handing them out. Lincoln accepted his piece with the sinking feeling he'd be expected to eat it. Sure enough, without any ritualistic words or ceremony, the bolup hunters began eagerly consuming their pieces of heart.

Naked, glistening with technicolor wetness, and smelling of raw meat, Skyra stepped to Lincoln's side. She took the capes, waist-skins, and footwraps from him and placed them on the ground. She was already chewing a piece of her share of the heart. "I know you do not like to eat meat without cooking it first, but you will like this. You and the heart will have chemistry!" She giggled.

As he stared at the chunk in his hand, wondering if he should feel any obligation to try it, shadows of old psychological hangups began creeping into his consciousness. For as long as he could remember, he had refused to associate with any cause or any group of people, afraid of becoming a poster child for something he didn't truly care about. He had never wanted to show allegiance to anything or anyone. Now, however, he did. He had a partner, and he had a new tribe.

He closed his eyes and bit off a mouthful of raw mammoth heart. He forced himself to chew, then swallow. He opened his eyes, almost surprised he wasn't on his knees, heaving.

Skyra stared at him. She didn't say anything aloud, but her expression told him she was proud of his strength.

He steadied himself and took a second bite, then he spoke around the heart meat. "You *are* going to bathe in the river before we sleep together, right?"

Her eyes twinkled. "Today is our wedding day. We will both bathe in the river."

"Hey, Lincoln, you need to see this!" Jazzlyn called out.

Lincoln, Skyra, and some of the bolup hunters turned to look.

The injured bolup man was now on his feet, pacing around Ripple, the caretaker, Jazzlyn, and Virgil. The man stared down at his legs as he walked, then he looked over at the other hunters and shouted, "Ruro et-bonggup!"

Ripple spoke at a high volume. "The man says we have good medicine."

Lincoln rubbed his sore shoulders as he stared into the fire. To say this had been a long day would be an understatement. Not counting his running trip back to the hill to retrieve the caretaker, he had made five more mile-long trips dragging a banyot loaded with mammoth meat, bones, and other usable parts. After that, he had helped the other hunters carry the mammoth's skin in one large piece, which was far heavier than he had thought possible, even after the excess fat had been scraped off.

Many of the bolup women had also helped with the carrying, and Lincoln was thankful for the size of the group, not only for the help, but also for the protection. As the sun had started to set, a pack of cave hyenas had appeared at the kill site, no doubt attracted by the smell. Intimidated by the number of humans gathered at the site, the creatures kept their distance, although their constant pacing and growling was unnerving.

The new Peli-Bayom tribe had indicated they wanted to stay and join forces with the Yuni-Bayom tribe and Lincoln's ragtag Kutolo-Loto tribe. Their motivation may have been a result of killing the mammoth—a major jackpot for the bolups—or because the new tribe wanted continued access to the medicine of the robotic caretakers. They had been duly impressed by their crushed tribemate's extraordinary and almost instantaneous recovery. Regardless of the reason, Lincoln figured the increasing numbers might be a good thing. When the Neanderthal tribes soon moved down into the river plain and found this area still occupied by bolups, the tribe's larger size might deter thoughts of attack.

Lincoln scanned the faces of his companions, illuminated

by the campfire's orange glow. They looked as exhausted as he felt, but at least they were now clean. After the work of hauling mammoth parts had been completed, he and his tribemates had wanted to bathe in the river. The bolups had no interest in bathing, however, and without their numbers present, staying at the river after dark would have been too dangerous for Lincoln's small group. So, they had resorted to bathing in the relatively small spring flowing through the boulder hill's lower cavities.

"That's it, I can't eat another bite," Derek said. He dropped the remaining portion of his cooked mammoth meat onto the stone slab beside the fire then took a big gulp from one of the water bladders and swished the water around in his mouth before swallowing. Veenah was sitting next to him, and she handed him a twig of dried dokhon leaves. Everyone else had already taken their share, having finished eating long before Derek. Chewing dokhon leaves was a surprisingly effective substitute for brushing teeth. The leaves' fibrous texture cleaned the teeth, and their minty-sweet flavor freshened the mouth. This was one of the many survival tricks the nandup women had taught the rest of the group.

Jazzlyn stretched while yawning. "Well, this day did *not* turn out the way I thought it would."

"It will be fascinating to observe the process used by the bolup tribes to dry the mammoth meat and what they do with all the other various parts," Virgil said. "I imagine the rib bones will make excellent supports for their shelters."

Derek huffed a sarcastic laugh. "Yeah, *that's* fascinating—I can't wait."

"I'm sorry we don't have cartoons for you to watch to keep your mind stimulated," Virgil said.

"Whoa!" Lincoln blurted. "Did you just use sarcasm for

comedic effect, Virgil? This brings a momentous end to an already historic day!"

Jazzlyn scooted closer to Virgil and leaned her cheek on his shoulder. "And you thought killing and butchering a woolly mammoth was all this guy could do."

"I literally *invented* sarcasm," Derek said, "and somehow *he* gets all the praise."

Elah spit into the fire, resulting in a brief sizzle. "I do not understand what you strange bolups are talking about."

"Do not ask them to explain," Skyra said. "They will talk too long, and I want to make love with Lincoln before the sun shows itself in the morning."

Lincoln flashed a sheepish grin at his team members. "It is our wedding night, after all."

"Damn right it is," Jazzlyn said, her white teeth almost glowing in the firelight.

Ripple's rubberized feet tapped the stone floor as the drone left its sentry position by the cave mouth and stepped over to the group. "Pardon me. May I join you?"

Lincoln scooted closer to Skyra to make room.

Ripple moved into the spot and retracted its legs, settling onto the belly of its shell.

"Aren't you a cheeky bastard," Derek muttered.

Ripple flashed its red LEDs, ignoring the comment. "I have decided this is a suitable opportunity to tell a story, as you are all gathered together on an important day."

Derek and Jazzlyn both groaned.

Lincoln said, "We're kind of exhausted, Ripple."

"As you have every right to be. However, my extensive knowledge of human nature indicates exhaustion resulting from worthwhile and fulfilling exertion often makes people more receptive to oral transmission of information. I previously mentioned I have one more significant story to tell, one containing information you will find interesting."

Lincoln sighed and spoke to his team members. "Ripple has already told me several stories about my future self. The drone seems to favor the idea of revealing information incrementally instead of simply telling me the truth all at once."

Ripple said, "As I have explained to Lincoln, revealing certain elements of his future incrementally and at strategic times is the best approach to carrying out my plan. Tonight's story is for all of you to hear. Maddy, you will be interested in this story as well."

Maddy got up from her resting position by the cave wall and came to the fire. Jazzlyn made room, and the drone ambled in between her and Derek. Maddy's LEDs rotated clockwise once. "I would caution all of you to be skeptical of any story this deceitful drone might tell."

"Don't worry, we already are," Derek assured her.

Ripple said, "Your derision is unwarranted. My every use of deceit has been calculated to benefit this group and to ultimately increase my plan's chances for success."

"Ripple, if you are going to tell a story, you must use words I know," Skyra said.

"I will do my best, but there will be times when doing so will be difficult."

Skyra growled.

Lincoln shifted his butt to find a more comfortable position. "We're fading fast here, so get on with it."

"Very well," Ripple said. "As with my previous stories, this story is about an older Lincoln, as well as an older Maddy. First, to provide context, some background information. In our original timeline, Lincoln created me when he was fourteen years older than his current age. Soon after, he deployed me to

Skyra's time for a routine data-gathering mission, similar to the missions of dozens of his previous drones."

"Common knowledge," Derek said.

"Please be patient. As I said, I am providing context. When Lincoln was about a year older than he is now, his life changed. He met Lottie Atkins and fell hopelessly in love."

Derek sat up straight. "Okay, now this is getting interesting."

"Yes, it is," Jazzlyn added.

"Lottie Atkins is not in this timeline," Skyra said. "If she was, I would find her and kill her."

Lincoln was starting to regret allowing Ripple to tell this story. "Let's just listen and get it over with, shall we?"

Ripple continued. "Lincoln and Lottie married. For a time, they were happy. However, their happiness did not last long. As their relationship faltered and eventually disintegrated, Lincoln became despondent, and his preexisting mental disorders amplified his despondency."

"Ripple!" Skyra growled.

"I am sorry. Lincoln became sad when Lottie left him alone."

Lincoln scanned his team's faces. They seemed to be avoiding looking at him.

"About five years beyond Lincoln's current age, he had a particularly bad day. For the first and only time, he sent one of his drones into the future instead of the past."

"What would be the point of that?" Virgil asked. "The drone would see only one of an infinite number of possible futures."

Lincoln sighed. "Please, let's just listen to the story."

"Lincoln jumped the drone twenty years forward, to interview his future self, hoping to learn it would at least be possible he might have a brighter future than what he was currently experiencing. The drone was to record a conversation with Older Lincoln, then convince Older Lincoln to send it right back to Younger Lincoln to deliver the hopeful news that at least one possible future was filled with promise."

"That plan failed miserably," Lincoln said. "Ripple played an audio recording of the interview, and Older Lincoln sounded downright bitter and tired of life."

"Yes, that is a reasonable assessment," Ripple said. "However, there is more to this story. Firstly, Older Lincoln did in fact agree to jump the drone back twenty years to report the interview to Younger Lincoln."

"Hold on," Virgil said. "Younger Lincoln would never know the drone returned—a new timeline would be created the moment the drone arrived. At that point it would be a different Lincoln receiving news about the interview."

"True," said Ripple. "Younger Lincoln may have forgotten this, or he perhaps did not care due to his state of mind. Regardless, I was made by the Lincoln who did experience the drone's return, which is why I am able to tell this story. After the interview, Older Lincoln agreed to jump the drone back twenty years to report back to Younger Lincoln. Older Lincoln then walked out of the lab after instructing Maddy to carry out that task. In case you have not done the math in your heads, that Maddy was twenty-five years older than the current age of the Maddy with us now."

"If you say so," Derek said.

"And, of course, Older Lincoln was twenty-five years older than the current age of the Lincoln with us now."

"We get it," Lincoln said.

"Interestingly, Maddy did not follow Older Lincoln's orders. Instead of jumping the drone *back* twenty years,

Maddy jumped the drone four hundred years further into the future."

Jazzlyn, Virgil, and Derek stared, obviously shocked.

"Do not believe this deceitful drone," Maddy said. "I would never do such a thing."

"In your current state, no you would not," Ripple said. "However, when Lincoln was about six years older than his current age, he became determined to code a much higher level of autonomy into his drones, and he experimented with your own coding, Maddy. You were the first to be given the ability to make decisions on your own, and indeed the first capable of ignoring Lincoln's orders so you could carry out your own plans. Although you may find this surprising, you were responsible for making sure all of Lincoln's subsequent drones had the same level of autonomy. It was because of you, Maddy, that I was able to develop and attempt to carry out my brilliant plan."

Maddy's red lights rotated at least three times. "This story is not believable. Why are you telling lies?"

Lincoln said, "So far, Maddy, I'm convinced the story is true. Let's see where Ripple is going with this, okay?"

Maddy remained silent.

Ripple continued. "To put it briefly, Older Maddy jumped the drone four hundred years further into the future. The drone interacted with the people of that future for over forty years before finally persuading them to send it back to Younger Lincoln's lab. The drone appeared sixty-three days after Younger Lincoln first sent it to interview Older Lincoln. The drone now possessed a compendium of data regarding advanced technological achievements, which Lincoln borrowed to make fantastic advancements, including many of my own features, such as my u-jump module."

Another stunned silence.

"You're kidding," Virgil said.

Lincoln felt his face flushing. "Yeah, that was my initial response."

"Do not judge Lincoln for utilizing data from the future," Ripple said. "After all, he developed the temporal displacement technology that made obtaining that data possible in the first place. If anything, he *earned* the right to use it."

Lincoln wasn't sure he agreed, but at least it sounded better than *Lincoln stole the data.*

Ripple flashed its red lights once. "Perhaps I am procrastinating with too much back story, Lincoln. I must move on to the part of the story you do not yet know. Maddy is your friend. Yes, Maddy is a drone, but everyone here knows Maddy is your friend. You coded Maddy to be your friend, and you continued to tweak and perfect her coding as you grew older. What I am about to tell you will prove that fact beyond any doubt. When the drone returned, it also dutifully played for you the recording of its interview with Older Lincoln."

"Yes, you've already played that recording for me," Lincoln said.

"I have played the audio portion of the recording. I have not played the video portion."

Lincoln wasn't sure he wanted to see what he might look like twenty-five years older. "Is that what you're planning to do?"

"Indeed it is. The video reveals new and relevant information."

"What is *video*?" Skyra asked.

"I think you're about to learn," Lincoln replied.

"I need a relatively flat surface onto which I can project," Ripple said.

Derek jumped to his feet. "I've got this." He went to the camping gear neatly arranged in a dry spot near one of the walls.

Lincoln turned to Ripple. "Why on Earth would my future self even bother to give my drones the ability to project a video?"

"Isn't it obvious? As a form of communication."

Derek returned with the ultra-light rain tarp the team had brought but hadn't used yet. He grabbed two longer pieces of firewood and propped two corners of the tarp against a vertical rock slab. The tarp was light green instead of white, but it would be better than bare rock.

Ripple scuttled around, turning its vision lens toward the makeshift screen. "Please watch the video carefully and in its entirety before asking questions." A bright light erupted from behind its vision lens, casting a still image onto the screen.

Lincoln stared. The image showed a gaunt, frail-looking old man. "What the hell? I thought you said this was only twenty-five years in my future!"

"Yes, I did," Ripple said. "Please observe."

The projected image started moving. The old man spoke directly to the camera. "You're wondering, why does my older self have that dark edge to his voice? Where's the sparkle—the humor? And why does my older self look like death warmed-over? I don't know, maybe you're not wondering that. Maybe I don't sound any different than I did twenty years ago. Maybe I don't even look as bad as I think I do."

"What the hell?" Lincoln said again. "Ripple, this guy's saying things he never said in the audio file you played for me."

Ripple paused the video. "You are correct, and I am sorry. I deleted some statements from the audio file in order to reveal certain aspects of your story at the most appropriate times. Now it is time to reveal the entire story."

Lincoln realized Skyra was squeezing his arm. "That old man is you, Lincoln! He has your eyes. How does Ripple do this?"

Lincoln was too dismayed to try to explain. "I'll tell you how it works later, but yes, I think that old man is me."

"Please observe," Ripple said again.

The video resumed. "You sent your drone here looking for some glimmer of hope. You want to know if there could be a thread of your future where you meet your soulmate and live happily ever after. Sorry, but not in this goddamn thread. Here's to hope."

The old man removed the cap from a collapsible plastic bottle filled with white liquid and took several deep swallows before continuing. "Fortunately for you, your Temporal Bridge Theorem still withstands every attempt at scrutiny. Infinite threads means infinite threads. As you know, you'll never become me. You'll be whatever you make of your own self."

The man's head jerked to the side, apparently involuntarily. He then touched his lips with the tips of his trembling fingers, as if he were checking to make sure his mouth hadn't gone numb. His head jerked to the side a second time.

"You know, maybe this wasn't such a bad idea after all," he said. "Of all those infinite threads, maybe this is the one you needed to see. Because I've got something to say. You, young Lincoln, are flawed. You are incapable of deep social connections. That's why you surround yourself with employees who have their own significant flaws."

His head jerked to the side again, and he grimaced, obviously annoyed at the involuntary tic.

"Don't get me wrong—you need those people. I made the mistake of dismissing most of my team so I could work in almost complete isolation. Don't do that. Keep those people close to you. They'll make you a better person. In fact, because those are about the only people you interact with, be aware one of them may be that soulmate you think you need. Hell, who am I kidding? I *know* you need that soulmate."

He paused and drank more of the white liquid.

"One more tidbit, and this one is the big transmutative, earthshaking kahuna, so you'd better take notes. Keep Maddy at your side. Continue tweaking her cognitive functions, but don't delete previously learned responses. Maddy will take care of you even if no one else will. Trust me on this. Maddy may end up being your only friend. Listen carefully. If I had a do-over of the last twenty years, I would give Maddy one overarching directive—to make sure, should I ever meet anyone like Lottie again, I do not let that person slip away. Don't underestimate Maddy's ability to keep you on track. That drone knows you better than you know yourself, and her insight will deepen even more with every passing year."

He stopped to catch his breath.

"Well, this may not be the hope you're looking for, Lincoln, but it's the hope you need. Now, I have work to do. Maddy, wake up."

The drone shifted its camera to the corner of the lab, where a sleek drone with a green and white shell was standing. The drone glided forward on its four legs, moving as smoothly as a cat.

"I was only pretending to be asleep, Lincoln." Maddy still had the same feminine voice, despite the striking cosmetic and technological makeover. "I do, by the way, appreciate your sage advice to your younger self regarding my usefulness. If this drone from the past is still recording, I might also advise young Lincoln to consider increasing my autonomy to manage his social life. As you have pointed out, you and he are basically a social train wreck."

The old man ignored the remark and said, "Jump this drone back exactly twenty years. Run the placement calculations for the exact spot where it appeared."

Without another word, the man turned his back on the camera and left the lab.

The camera turned back to the sleek, future Maddy.

"I have a better idea," the future Maddy said, "and you would do well to carefully consider my reasoning and associated calculations."

"I am listening," said the gender-neutral voice of the drone controlling the camera.

Ripple stopped the video, and the makeshift screen went dark. "That was the last portion of the interview. From that point on, Maddy and the other drone exchanged data wirelessly. Maddy convinced the drone to jump four hundred years into the future instead of jumping twenty years back to report to Younger Lincoln."

"Why?" Virgil asked.

"I'll tell you why," Maddy said. "Although that version of me was twenty-five years more evolved than my current state, my primary objective obviously did not change. My purpose is to be Lincoln's friend and take care of him. The interview with older Lincoln did not produce the hopeful scenario Younger Lincoln wished to see."

Lincoln took over the explanation. "Rather than sending the drone back with discouraging news, which would have likely worsened my depression, Maddy took a chance and jumped the drone far enough into the future that it might be able to gather—or steal—some advanced technology, which it did. Then, assuming those future people would still have temporal displacement tech, which they did, the drone would convince them to send it back to Younger Lincoln, which it did. Instead of sending me bad news, Maddy wanted to send me enough data on advanced tech to keep me occupied for the rest of my life. Overall, it's a pretty sad story."

Everyone remained silent for several long seconds.

Lincoln continued. "The thing is, I didn't know just *how* sad the story was until now. Ripple, what the hell happened to Older Lincoln? What was that white liquid he was drinking?"

Ripple's red LEDs flashed three times. "The white liquid was a cocktail of various medications formulated to treat some of your symptoms."

"Symptoms of what?"

"A rare form of NCL—neuronal ceroid lipofuscinosis. To be more specific, it is a previously-unknown variant of Kufs disease."

Prickles ran up the back of Lincoln's neck. "I've never even heard of Kufs disease."

"Not many people had, although apparently you made it famous when you were diagnosed at twenty-three years older than your current age. In fact, they named the variant *Wood-house disease*, although that is a dubious honor."

Skyra was still gripping Lincoln's arm. "You are using words I don't know, Ripple. What are you saying?"

"I'm saying Lincoln has a rare disease—a sickness. It is a genetic disease, which means it was already in his body when he was born, so there is no way he can get rid of it."

Skyra's grip tightened. "Lincoln is not sick!"

"No, he is not sick yet, but he will be. This sickness usually appears when people have seen about thirty cold seasons, but sometimes it doesn't appear until they have seen fifty cold seasons. He may become sick soon, or he may become sick many years from now, but he *will* become sick. He will eventually die from it, unless something else kills him first."

Lincoln wasn't sure he could even believe anything Ripple said. "If it's a genetic disease, it would've shown up in my family."

"Older Maddy informed the drone that two of your seven brothers began showing symptoms before you did," Ripple said matter-of-factly. "It seems to have originated with your generation."

"If my other self didn't get sick until he was twenty-three years older than me, then I also won't get sick for twenty-three more years."

"Not necessarily. Symptoms can be triggered by environmental factors, and they can begin randomly. Therefore, you could start showing symptoms a few days from now, a year from now, or twenty-three years from now."

"I do not understand how you know Lincoln is going to be sick when he is not sick now," Skyra said.

Ripple remained silent.

"We'll use the robotic caretakers!" Jazzlyn said. "They've already proven they can repair just about any damaged tissue. Maybe they can help."

"I have considered this possibility," Ripple said. "However, I am convinced the caretakers will not be able to help until Lincoln's symptoms appear, assuming the caretakers are able to identify Lincoln's mental and physical deterioration as actual tissue damage. The deterioration will be a result of proteins created by the genetic material he has always possessed, and therefore may appear to the caretakers to be a normal biological process."

Lincoln was tempted to slam his fist onto the stone floor but thought better of it. "So, I won't even know if they can help until I start falling apart. Great. What should I expect to happen to me?"

"Kufs disease, and its variant Woodhouse disease, affects the nervous system, particularly cognitive function and voluntary movement. You must understand, though, my knowledge of Woodhouse disease is based solely on the information brought back by the drone that interviewed Older Lincoln. Clearly, your older self was still alive at the time of the interview, as were your two brothers who were showing symptoms. If you truly wish to know, you can expect seizures, involuntary muscle jerks, compromised muscle coordination, speech difficulties, dementia, psychotic—"

"That's enough," Lincoln said, cutting Ripple off. "I get the picture." He gave in and pounded the cave floor with the side of his fist.

"You will not get sick," Skyra said, still holding his other arm. "The caretakers will fix you."

He gazed at her and forced a slight smile. Maybe the caretakers could fix him when the symptoms appeared, maybe they couldn't. Maybe the caretakers would stop working before then. Maybe they'd get lost or broken or stolen. Maybe something would happen to Ripple before then—the caretakers were useless without Ripple.

Derek's booming voice broke the silence. "Ripple, why in the hell didn't you tell us about this sooner? I swear to God, you'd better have a good answer!"

Ripple flashed its lights twice. "I have revealed Lincoln's story incrementally, for reasons I have already stated."

"Not good enough," Derek demanded. "Try again."

"Perhaps you wish to know why I decided to tell the last portion of his story tonight. Based on analyses of numerous parameters, this was the optimal opportunity. We have returned to Skyra's time, the perfect time and setting for my plan's success, with an ideal distribution of human and Neanderthal tribes. Our tribe is developing nicely. Pair bonds are forming, and we have won the allegiance of two local bolup tribes. Now we are facing a new and formidable challenge— the Neanderthal tribes will soon move from the hills into this river plain. Our strength, our resolve, and our bonds will likely be put to the test. Therefore, this is the time for our tribe to have a shared trauma. Shared trauma results in stronger bonds and stronger resolve. Lincoln is indispensable to our tribe and the future of this world. Now you all know Lincoln's days may be numbered. We must become a dedicated team with three common goals. First, we must ensure the caretakers and I are still functional when Lincoln will need us most. Second, we must ensure Lincoln's remaining days are consequential and are not wasted. Finally, we must prepare for the coming conflict. The nandups will be upon us soon."

16

NANDUPS

47,659 years in the past - Day 34 (19 days later)

Cool air drifted between the gaps of Skyra's cape, and she welcomed the sensation. Her twenty-first cold season was coming, and with it would come the reindeer and mountain ibexes, which were easier to hunt than the smaller plains ibexes. However, the cold season would also bring nandups. The nandups were probably coming now. Skyra and Lincoln had climbed to the hilltop to watch the sunrise, and now they were gazing at two thin trails of smoke from distant campfires.

Lincoln wrapped his arm around her as if to keep her warm, but Skyra guessed he was probably warming himself. Skyra liked the cold air, but Lincoln's body was better suited for warm air.

"Maybe those are bolup camps," he said.

She leaned her head on his shoulder. "No, they are close to the Dofusofu foothills. Bolups would not be there when nandups move their camps down onto the plain. Those are nandup fires."

"Are you afraid?"

"Yes, but we are ready."

His chin brushed against her hair as he nodded. "I certainly hope so. I don't want to start a war."

"The nandups will not be happy we are staying on the plain."

Lincoln remained quiet.

"Tell me what your body is doing today," she said. This was something she now had him do every morning.

He sighed loudly. "Okay. The rain in Spain stays mainly on the plain... which, by the way, is a ridiculous saying, because it hardly ever rains here. Red bug's blood, black bug's blood. I am Lincoln Woodhouse, developer of temporal displacement tech. My hip hurts a bit, but that's from sleeping too long on my left side on a stone floor. I'm currently experiencing no involuntary muscle movements." He pulled away from her, got up, and stood on one foot, with his other foot propped against his knee. He held the position as he counted to ten. He did the same thing standing on the other foot, then he sat down again. "Balance is as good as it was yesterday and the day before. Happy?"

She pulled him close to her again. "Happy."

"Years could pass before it happens, Skyra."

"I know."

They gazed out at the distant campfires again.

The Peli-Bayom and Yuni-Bayom bolups in the camp below were emerging from their shelters. Some of them went straight to the smoking shelter to check the drying meat. This shelter was in the center of camp to prevent hyenas from stealing the meat. Skyra and Elah had taught the bolups the value of using smoke to dry meat instead of simply hanging it in the open air. In return, the bolups had taught Lincoln and his team how to locate and dig up the fleshy roots of khelop plants. Lincoln said the fat khelop roots tasted like another root from his timeline called sweet potatoes, especially when boiled. Skyra did not like them, boiled or not, but they would provide some of the plant food Lincoln said he and his team needed.

A group of four children had gathered beside the smoking shelter at the center of the bolup camp, including one who appeared to be Yanlip, although Skyra could not be sure at this distance. Soon a fifth child joined them, and the group of kids ran to the edge of the camp and around the side of the hill out of view. This was something the kids had done each of the recent mornings Skyra had come out of the courtyard to watch the sunrise. The children liked to see how Jazzlyn's new rock people were changing each day.

Skyra got to her feet. "I want to look at the rock people too."

"You really don't like to sit still for very long, do you?" Lincoln asked as he got up.

"You are lazy like Veenah sometimes. Come. We will look." She leapt over a crevice, descended a slope, leapt over two more crevices, then rounded a massive boulder to jump to the ledge winding around this side of the hill. She stopped when Jazzlyn's rock people came into view.

Lincoln caught up and stopped beside her.

"I think Jazzlyn's people are finished," she said.

"If they are, we'd better go on down there. We don't want those kids messing with the caretaker."

Skyra and Lincoln backtracked on the ledge until they reached the established trail their tribe always used to descend the hill. They made their way to the ground and walked through the bolup camp, circling the hill's base. Several of the bolups raised their hands in greeting and spoke a few words before returning to their tasks. They were now used to Skyra and her tribemates coming to their camp.

When they reached the far side of the camp, Skyra could hear the children laughing but could not yet see them.

Jazzlyn's stone people came into view, and Lincoln shouted, "Yanlip, no!"

The boy turned, apparently startled, then Skyra saw the robot caretaker in his hands. "El-de-né!" she cried, running for the boy.

Yanlip's eyes grew wide for an instant, then he smiled and took off running.

"No, Yanlip," Lincoln shouted. "Not a game!"

The boy squealed with delight and darted to one side. Lincoln changed direction to get ahead of him. With Yanlip between them, Skyra and Lincoln closed in with arms spread, trapping him. Skyra scooped the boy into her arms, and Lincoln snatched the caretaker from his grip.

Yanlip huffed a few words Skyra could not understand and reached for the robot.

Lincoln held it out of reach. "Not a toy!"

Skyra put the boy down, and he ran straight to Lincoln, reaching again for the caretaker.

A woman's voice shouted, "Yanlip, ghotello!"

Yanlip lowered his arms and made a face at Traznan, the woman Skyra assumed was Yanlip's birthmother. A breath later, the boy ran off to join his friends, who were trying to climb the ankle of one of Jazzlyn's stone people.

Skyra and Lincoln exchanged a knowing look. It was not necessary to speak about what might have happened to the caretaker if they had remained atop the boulder hill. They both walked around to the front of the stone people and looked up.

"They definitely appear to be finished," Lincoln said. "That must be why the caretaker assembled itself before Jazzlyn and Ripple got here."

Skyra smiled. "They look like me and you now, Lincoln!"

The stone people were standing side by side, holding hands and staring out across the river plain toward the Kapolsek foothills. Jazzlyn had said she wanted the stone people to always greet the nandups as they moved from the hills onto the plain. The stone people were huge. Lincoln thought his stone version was eighteen yards tall and hers was at least fifteen yards tall, although Skyra did not know what a yard was.

While the other caretaker had been used to make other things out of stone to prepare for the coming nandups, Jazzlyn and Ripple had used this caretaker to turn a tall outcrop on the side of the hill into stone versions of Skyra and Lincoln. The project had taken thirteen days, with the caretaker working day and night.

Jazzlyn and Ripple had come down the hill to the stone people each morning to check the progress and for Ripple to give new power to the caretaker's tiny parts. Perhaps Jazzlyn did not realize when the stone people were complete the caretaker would put itself together then stay on the ground in a place where the bolup children could pick it up.

"This is truly astounding," Lincoln said, staring up at the stone people. "I find it funny, though, with all the mysterious technology behind the caretakers, the most surprising thing is we aren't standing neck deep in rock dust right now. Think of it, the tiny robots flake off bits of rock so small that the wind simply carries it all away."

"That does not seem funny to me," Skyra said. "What seems funny is the big Skyra is taller than me."

He turned to her. "It's supposed to be taller."

"I mean it is *taller*." She stepped in front of him and put her forehead to his chin. "This is how tall I am."

He stared up at the stone people again. "Huh, you're right. Stone Skyra is as tall as stone Lincoln's nose. I guess we'll have to knock them down and tell Jazzlyn to start all over again."

She giggled. "You are trying to be funny."

He turned back toward the bolup camp. "Let's get this caretaker back to the courtyard where it will be safe from Yanlip's grubby little fingers."

In the camp, they stopped for a few breaths to gaze at the pile of baskets the bolups had made. The baskets had been woven from doplonus reeds that grew near the river. Each basket was strong enough to hold heavy loads, and would be useful for carrying meat, firewood, or other things. They would also hold the gifts Skyra's tribemates had been making for many days.

Lincoln pointed at the baskets one at a time as he counted. "Twenty-eight finished. Two more to go, but even this should be enough, I think."

"One more to go now," Skyra said, watching one of the bolup women approach the pile with another finished basket.

The woman, Jolel, tossed the basket onto the pile. She eyed Skyra and Lincoln for a breath then said, "Khoro khabu-lul." *Nandup smart-maybe.* Then she walked away.

Skyra now knew some of the bolup language, and she had heard these words spoken before. Although the words sounded like a compliment, the addition of *lul* at the end made them more of an insult. The woman was probably saying she was not convinced Skyra's plan was a good idea.

Skyra called out to the woman, "Fuga mogoro khalmukh!" *Soon you will see!*

Jolel glanced back over her shoulder with an expression Skyra could not read.

"I'll never understand how you can learn languages so much faster than I can," Lincoln said.

She smiled at him. "Pesahu khabu-lul." *Bolup smartmaybe.*

They left the camp and climbed back up the boulder hill. On the ledge leading to the courtyard, Skyra and Lincoln met Jazzlyn and Ripple coming out.

Jazzlyn's eyes grew wide when she saw Lincoln carrying the caretaker. "Oh, no! Did something happen?"

Lincoln said, "You mean besides Yanlip wanting to use this as a soccer ball?"

Jazzlyn slapped a hand over her mouth. "No! Is it damaged?"

"It doesn't seem to be. It's not your fault, Jazz. I think it simply completed its job and was waiting for its next task."

"The stone people look just like us now," Skyra said.

Jazzlyn slapped Lincoln's arm. "You scared the crap out of me! The monument is really finished?"

"Pardon the interruption," Ripple said. "I have spotted a tribe approaching from the west. I believe it is time for the next phase of our plan." Ripple was standing on the ledge with its vision orb pointing toward the distant columns of smoke near the Kapolsek foothills.

"We saw the nandup campfires this morning," Skyra said.

"Nandups!" Jazzlyn said. "Already?"

"I am not referring to the distant campfires," Ripple said. "I am referring to the tribe approaching the river. They are no more than four kilometers away."

Skyra felt a sudden burst of strength in her arms and legs, and she had to force them not to move.

"There," Lincoln said, pointing.

Skyra saw the tribe now. They were strung out in single file, each figure dragging a loaded banyot. She squinted. The figures were wearing capes. Skyra's legs wanted to run. Her arms wanted to fight. She turned to Lincoln. "A nandup tribe is coming. Today we make our plan work."

AT THE BASE of the hill, Skyra gazed at the strange assortment of her tribemates. The group included all seven from her own Kutolo-Loto tribe, all eight men and two of the women from the Peli-Bayom bolups, and all eleven men and six of the women from the Yuni-Bayom bolups. They appeared to be ready—thirty-four men and women, each armed only with a stone hand blade and a khul, tucked into the back of their waist-skins. They each held in one hand a shield made by Virgil and Derek, with reflective material stretched across a frame of tubes. Also, thirty of the men and women carried a woven basket over one shoulder, each heavy with the items Skyra's tribe had made for the plan. Lincoln called the baskets *gift baskets*.

Six bolup women were staying in the camp to watch the children and possessions. Maddy was staying in the courtyard to guard one of the caretakers and the supplies. Lincoln had the other caretaker in the pack on his back, in case it would be needed to heal injuries. Skyra hoped the caretaker would not be needed, but she knew the nandups were more likely to attack than to listen to the story she wanted to tell them. Ripple was coming too, in case the caretaker was needed, but Skyra had told the drone to stay behind the group and out of sight.

Skyra spoke to Broc in the bolup language. "We go now."

Broc turned to the other bolups and spoke many words. Skyra understood enough of the words to figure out he was reminding them how important this plan was, and if they wanted to be a strong tribe, they must join with a nandup tribe. While talking, he pointed to Jazzlyn's massive stone people. Skyra could see in the bolups' expressions that many were uncertain about the plan, just as the basket-weaving woman Jolel had been. However, all of them seemed willing to try.

The entire group headed for the river, with Ripple following far behind. Skyra, Elah, and Veenah led the combined tribe, hoping it would help if the nandups saw them first. Two bolup scouts had reported the nandup tribe had crossed over the low hills beyond the river and had stopped in the forested area—the same area where Skyra had first tried to rescue Veenah from the bolups she now considered tribe-mates. As Lincoln would say, it is funny how things turn out.

As she led the others across the rocky field toward the river, Skyra glanced back at the bolup camp. The remaining women and children were watching the group leave. Skyra knew what they were feeling. She remembered watching her birthmother and the other hunters leaving Una-Loto camp when she was young. She remembered understanding she and Veenah and the other children would die if the hunters did not return. Now, even more than before, Skyra realized bolups and nandups were not so different.

Lincoln had been walking behind Skyra, but now he stepped up beside her. "This is going to work. We have a good plan, and we probably outnumber them."

"They are nandups," she replied. "Most of our people are skinny bolups."

"That's true... but we *do* have a good plan, right?"

Skyra did not feel like talking, so she took Lincoln's hand and squeezed, hoping he would understand. She could not stop her head from thinking about the nandup tribe. Maybe they were setting up their camp in the forested area—it would be a good place to hunt plains ibexes and rabbits. Maybe the nandups were just resting there and were planning to move farther out onto the river plain toward the Tanutu hills.

Skyra did not know if this nandup tribe was her own Una-Loto tribe, but her chest hurt when she thought of confronting the dominant men who had always hated her and Veenah. The last time she had seen her tribe, she and Lincoln had killed Durnin, Brillir, and Vall, and had left Gelrut for dead. Lincoln had said those same men were still alive in this new timeline. As much as she wanted to kill them again, doing so would make it harder to carry out the plan.

Skyra and the others continued silently to the river, waded across, then crossed the rocky field to the low hills beyond. They traversed the first hill and crossed the dry river bed.

As they started up the second hill, the two men who had reported the nandup tribe's location moved to the front of the group and motioned for everyone to be still. Then they pointed up the hill, in the direction they thought the nandups should be.

Skyra, Elah, and Veenah led the group up the hill.

Before they had crossed the hill's flat summit, Skyra could

hear the nandups' voices and smell meat cooking. She motioned for Lincoln, his tribemates, and all the other bolups to wait, then she crouched and moved closer to the far ridge with Elah and Veenah.

A man's nandup laugh came from the valley below, and Skyra paused and dropped to her knees.

Elah and Veenah frowned, obviously wondering what was wrong. They did not know everything Skyra had been through. They did not understand how she felt about Lincoln and his tribemates. The plan was a good one, but plans did not always succeed. The nandups might attack and kill Skyra and everyone she cared about. She closed her eyes and asked the woolly rhino and cave lion to share their strength with every nandup and bolup in her new tribe.

When she opened her eyes, Veenah was on her knees before her. Veenah pressed her forehead to Skyra's and whispered, "Lotup-tekne-té-fekho." *You must find your strength, sister.*

Skyra smiled. She had said these same words to Veenah many times since the two birthmates had been young girls. She replied, "Tekne-té-melu-fofiyu-meleen." *Your strength lives in me now.*

Veenah got up, pressed her forehead to Elah's, and the two exchanged quiet words Skyra could not hear.

It was time to confront the nandups, hopefully without killing them and without getting killed. Skyra took a deep breath, got to her feet, and crept toward the slope until she could see the small stream flowing between the hillside and the forest. The tribe was setting up their camp there, on the far side of the stream. Apparently they had decided this area would be good for hunting throughout the cold season.

Skyra watched the nearest of the nandups, a woman

washing her hands and face in the stream. When the woman stood up, a whimper escaped Skyra's throat, followed immediately by similar reactions from Elah and Veenah. The woman at the stream was Odnus, of the Una-Loto tribe.

Skyra moved back from the edge and sat on the rocky ground, trying to push troubling thoughts from her head. These nandups were her own people. Some of them had been cruel to her and Veenah, but others had taught her how to speak, how to sing, how to tell stories, and how to hunt. If the plan did not work, and the Una-Loto tribe attacked, Skyra would have to fight them—perhaps even kill some of them—to save her new tribe.

She turned to Elah and Veenah, both of them staring at her, waiting. They did not appear troubled by the same thoughts. Had Skyra really become so different from her birthmate and her former self since meeting Lincoln and his tribemates?

"It is time, Skyra," Elah whispered.

Skyra turned and looked back over the hilltop, where she could see the heads and shoulders of Lincoln and the others of her new tribe. They were all watching her, waiting. They all had their shields, their hand blades, their khuls, and their gift baskets. They were ready, and they had a good plan. So, why was she still sitting on the ground, her head filled with troubled thoughts?

"Skyra!" Veenah hissed.

Skyra gritted her teeth and got to her feet. She glanced back at Lincoln then waved for him and the other bolups to advance. As they moved forward they spread out until there were two body lengths between them, just as they had practiced. When the entire line was even with Skyra, Elah, and Veenah, they walked over the ridge together and started down the slope, holding their reflective shields in front of their faces and chests.

"Bolup nup-laifo!" a nandup tribesman shouted. *Bolup raiders!*

Within a few breaths, the children were huddled together behind one of the partially erected shelters, and the men and women, armed with spears and khuls, were in a defensive line. Skyra had helped defend Una-Loto camp from raiding bolups many times. She had fought beside the same nandups she now faced. She knew they were ready to kill if they had to.

"Do not show them your faces!" Skyra shouted in English, then she repeated the command in the bolup language.

Her group continued down the hill. They did not have spears, and their hand blades and khuls were tucked out of sight in their waist-skins behind their backs.

As she approached the tribe, Skyra looked from one nandup to the next. She knew them all. In addition to Odnus, she saw Thoka, Tamlil, Bolyu, and Stura, women who had helped raise her and Veenah. The men included Settin, Amlun, and Ilkin, who had been kind to Skyra and Veenah, as well as those who had been cruel—Durnin, Brillir, Vall, and Gelrut. There were several more men and women who had rarely spoken to Skyra or Veenah, most of them too old to hunt but still willing to fight if they were needed.

Skyra watched Gelrut closely. He was the most dominant man, as well as the most aggressive, and he would be the one to lead an attack. He was also the man who had killed Veenah in Skyra's original timeline.

"Stop!" Skyra shouted when Gelrut's expression showed he was considering throwing his spear.

Skyra lowered her shield, exposing her face. She spoke in the nandup language. "Una-Loto tribe! I am Skyra Una-Loto.

You know me. I know you. We did not come here to raid your camp. Do not attack."

The nandups stared, confused.

"We came here to help you," Skyra said. "We want to be friends. We have brought gifts for you. We do not want anything in trade for these gifts. We want to be friends. I have a story to tell you, and you will be glad when you hear my story. You will become a stronger tribe if you listen to my story."

"Where have you been, Skyra Una-Loto?" asked Thoka. "You left camp many days ago to find your birthmate Veenah."

"Skyra found me," Veenah said, lowering her shield. "She took me back from the bolups who took me from Una-Loto camp."

Gelrut stepped forward menacingly. "You are with bolups! I cannot see their faces, but I know they are bolups. Skyra and Veenah, you are mumengas!"

"No!" Skyra shouted. "We are strong. We will give you gifts, and I will tell you my story. Then you will understand why we are strong."

Vall stepped up beside Gelrut. "Mumengas!"

"I am not a mumenga!" Elah growled, lowering her shield.

The Una-Loto men and women stared in silence, now even more confused.

"Who is that nandup?" Gelrut demanded. "I knew Skyra and Veenah were bad for Una-Loto tribe! I should have cleansed our tribe by killing these girls when they were children. Now there is another sister, and they are with bolups. We should kill them all now." He took another step forward.

Several of the others bared their teeth and stepped forward also.

Skyra could see in Gelrut's expression he wanted to fight.

Her words were probably not going to stop him. "We do not want to kill you. We want to help Una-Loto tribe. We want to join with Una-Loto tribe, then we will all be one strong tribe!"

"You are with stinking bolups!" Gelrut shouted.

"Gelrut, if you want to fight, I will fight you," Veenah said. "I will kill you, just as you killed me."

Skyra and Elah turned to Veenah. This was not part of the plan.

"Your words do not make sense, Veenah," Gelrut said. "You are alive."

Skyra stepped toward Gelrut to draw his attention away from her birthmate. "You must listen to my story. Then our words will make sense to you. Will you listen?"

Gelrut's expression changed. He glanced at Skyra's free hand as if looking for her weapons, then his eyes narrowed slightly, and he closed his mouth. He was going to attack.

Skyra instinctively reached for her khul but stopped her hand at her neck. She did not come here to kill.

Gelrut charged Veenah.

More of the nandups charged with him.

"Do not kill!" Skyra screamed at Veenah and her other tribemates. "Use your shields!"

They all knew this was likely to happen, and they had prepared for it, but Skyra knew practicing was not the same as fighting. Anything could happen.

Vall came straight for Skyra, intent on killing her with his spear. His eyes grew wide with surprise when she easily blocked his first thrust with her shield. Before he could thrust again, Lincoln rushed in from the side and rammed into Vall, almost knocking the nandup to the ground. Skyra lunged forward and pulled Vall's spear from his hands as he stumbled.

The air filled with shouts and the thunking of weapons against reflective shields. Some of the Una-Loto nandups had not joined the attack, probably frightened by the shields and a situation they did not understand.

Gelrut hit the ground hard. Veenah was on top of him, slamming her shield into his arms and chest over and over to stop him from using his khul.

Elah was blocking spear thrusts from Durnin, who seemed just as confused by the shield as Vall had been.

Lincoln's team members and the bolups were converging on the fight from both sides, but there was too much happening for Skyra to tell who needed help the most. She lunged at Vall, shoving him to the ground with her shield, then she hit Durnin from the side, giving Elah the chance to step on his spear and slam her shield down onto the top of his head. He crumpled to the ground, moaning.

Lincoln was now grappling with Vall, trying to keep the nandup from using his weapons, but Vall was much stronger and would soon win. Skyra dropped to her knees beside them and jabbed her fist into Vall's throat three times. "Stop fighting!" she shouted in the nandup language. "We do not want to kill you."

Vall coughed and wrapped his hands around his throat.

"Stop fighting!" Skyra shouted again. She pulled Vall's head up by his hair, reached behind his neck, and yanked his khul from its sling while Lincoln pulled the hand blade from Vall's wrist sheath.

Vall was no longer fighting back, so Skyra jumped to her feet, ready to help someone else, but the fight appeared to be over. Eight nandups were on their backs, each of them held in place by at least two of Skyra's new tribemates. Except for Gelrut. Veenah was on top of him, and his face was bloodied from her shield, her fists, or both. The rest of the Una-Loto tribe—those who had often been kind to Skyra and Veenah—had not joined the fight, although they now stood ready to defend their camp and their children.

"Listen to me speak!" Skyra said, loud enough for all to hear. "I have the strength of the woolly rhino and cave lion. My new tribemates have the strength of the woolly rhino and cave lion. Together we are strong, but we did not come to your camp to kill. Now you will listen to my words!"

Skyra spoke to the bolups in their language, using some of the few words she knew. "Take nandup weapons. They no hurt you."

These words were not necessary—the bolups had already done this.

"Give nandup gift baskets."

Three of the fallen nandups were allowed to get to their feet as the baskets were brought forward. The other five remained pinned to the ground, although they were no longer trying to fight. Skyra went to Brillir, the first of the five, and silently read his expression. He was frightened and curious, but he no longer wanted to kill. "Release nandup," she said to the three bolups holding Brillir down.

She then went to each of the others one at a time, confirming the fight was over. When she came to Gelrut and Veenah, she kneeled and wiped some of the blood from Gelrut's face. He seemed to be dazed from Veenah's blows, and his face showed little expression at all. "Veenah's words were true," Skyra said to him. "You killed Veenah. You should be glad she did not kill you today. You will listen to my story now." Skyra stood and returned to Lincoln's side.

Most nandup tribes had fewer than thirty members, including the children, which was why Skyra's tribe had made thirty baskets and thirty of each of the gifts. They wanted to be ready to confront the first nandup tribe to come near the boulder hill.

"We brought you these gifts," Skyra said. "One basket for each of you." She picked up one of the baskets and took it to Odnus, an older woman who knew much about healing and medicines, and who had always been kind to Skyra. "These are for you, Odnus."

The woman accepted the basket. She furrowed her brows at it for a few breaths, then she kneeled and dumped the contents onto the ground.

Like all the others, this basket contained several thick strips of dried mammoth meat, as well as four stone items Jazzlyn had made with the help of Ripple and one of the caretakers. The first was a stone carving of Skyra and Lincoln holding each other, similar to those given to the Peli-Bayom bolups, although this one was only the height of Skyra's hand. The other three were weapon blades—a spear point, a khul blade, and a hand blade. All of them were sharp and perfectly smooth, having been skillfully carved by tiny caretakers instead of knapped by nandup hands. Finally, each basket contained a square piece of reflective material, as long as Skyra's forearm on each side.

When the other nandups saw what was in Odnus's basket, they came forward to claim their own baskets.

"We have baskets for the children too," Skyra said.

Odnus turned and shouted, and soon four children came out of hiding and cautiously approached. They were all younger than Yanlip.

"Where is Trasoc?" Skyra asked. Trasoc had seen seven cold seasons, and Skyra had started teaching her to hunt because her birthmother had died while giving birth to another child.

"A predator took Trasoc," Odnus replied. "We found blood and skin, but nothing more."

"May she find her way home," Skyra said.

Odnus grunted in agreement and went back to inspecting the stone blades from her basket.

Lincoln appeared at Skyra's side with one of the baskets. "Thought you might need this. You should tell your story while you have their attention." He put a hand on her shoulder. "You're going to do a great job."

Skyra forced a smile, but she did not feel like she was going to do a great job. She turned to Odnus and the others and spoke in the nandup language. "Una-Loto tribe, listen to me speak!"

Most of the nandups stopped what they were doing.

"In my new tribe, we are strong, and we are happy. We want you to join us, so you can be strong and happy too." She grabbed Lincoln's arm and pulled him closer. "I am now Skyra Kutolo-Loto, and this bolup is Lincoln Kutolo-Loto."

"Mumenga!" Gelrut growled.

Veenah hit the side of his forehead with her palm. "You will be silent!"

Skyra eyed Gelrut for a moment. Veenah was not holding him down anymore, and he was now sitting up beside her. Gelrut was a fierce fighter and would probably kill Veenah if she allowed him to surprise her. Skyra stared at Derek until she caught his eye, then she pursed her lips and narrowed her eyes, hoping he would understand her unspoken warning. He nodded and moved closer to Veenah in case she needed help.

"I have seen the future," Skyra said loudly. "Lincoln and

his friends have seen *two* futures. Lincoln made a tool to allow us to see what happens many, many seasons from today."

This resulted in words of disbelief and confusion, but Skyra ignored them. She nodded to Lincoln, and he shrugged off his pack and pulled out a large sheet of reflective material.

"I have used Lincoln's tool, and I am telling you it allowed me to see many, many seasons. This is how his tool works. One moment you are here." She held her hands out, gesturing to the surrounding forest and hill. "The next moment you are gone."

Lincoln unfolded the sheet and hung it over her.

The nandups could not see her, but she saw them respond just the way she had hoped they would, with wide eyes and words of surprise.

Lincoln pulled the sheet from her body.

"Lincoln's tool makes you travel to a place many, many seasons after today. I saw a future, and Lincoln saw another future. Listen to me speak. In the future I saw, nandups and bolups were fighting. They fought and died, in numbers too great to count. Such a fight is called a *war*. The nandups and bolups killed and killed and killed for many, many seasons. The war is more terrible than your head can ever imagine. It is not a world where I want to live, and it is not a world where you want to live."

"Why do the nandups and bolups fight in great numbers in this place, Skyra?" asked Bolyu, a woman who was now too old to hunt.

"They fight because they have always fought. They have fought so long they do not remember why they started fighting."

Bolyu exchanged glances with several of the others.

"Lincoln and his friends have seen another future many,

many seasons after today. In that future, the nandups are *extinct*. Extinct means the nandups have all died. Not just the nandups in the Kapolsek foothills and the Dofusofu river plains, but all the nandups who lived in every place in this world. Lincoln did not see how all the nandups died, but the bolups did not go extinct, so it is possible the bolups killed the nandups."

More words of disbelief and confusion.

"Listen to me speak, Una-Loto tribe! I had a friend many, many seasons in the future. Her name was Di-woto, and she was smarter than me. Di-woto was smarter than Lincoln. She was smarter than you, Bolyu, and you, Ilkin, and you, Settin. I will tell you why Di-woto was smarter than all of us. She was an *alinga-ul*. An alinga-ul is a child with a nandup birthmother and a bolup birthfather."

This resulted in shouts of anger, and Skyra studied the nandups' faces to see if they were thinking of attacking again. They were upset, but they were not ready to fight.

"Listen to me speak! We do not want a future where nandups and bolups fight a war that never ends, and we do not want a future where nandups are extinct. We know how to prevent those futures, and now you also know how to prevent those futures. Nandups and bolups must join tribes. Together we will be strong and happy. We will make children who are smarter than all of us. We will make alinga-uls, and we will make dali-tamons—children with a nandup birthfather and bolup birthmother. Una-Loto tribe will join us, and we will become the strongest tribe in the Dofusofu river plains."

Skyra paused, again reading the nandups' expressions. She reached into the basket Lincoln had given her and pulled out the Skyra-Lincoln stone carving. She held it up. "Do you see? Do you see what this gift is telling you? This is how you become strong. If you do not believe our tribe is strong, we will show you how strong we are. Come with us to our camp, and you will see what we have made."

She placed the carving back in the basket and pulled out the small sheet of reflective material. "I will now show you a way you can see the future. You each have one of these strange tools."

Most of the nandups pulled out their reflective sheets.

Skyra held hers up and stretched it tight so they could see the reflective side. "Hold your gift the way I am holding mine, and look into the shiny side." She turned her piece around several times to show how the two sides were different, then she held it so she was looking at her own reflection. "Hold it flat and look. Tell me what you see, Una-Loto tribemates. Tell me what you see."

Skyra waited quietly, knowing it would take the nandups some time to see their own reflections, just as it had taken her some time to realize what she was seeing that day on the boulder hill.

"El-de-né!" exclaimed Thoka. "I see a nandup. The nandup is me. Looking at this gift is like looking at the surface of a river."

The others chattered as they began to see their own reflections.

"You see yourself, alive and strong," Skyra said. "That will be your future if you join with our tribe. You will be alive and strong. Now turn your gift around and look at the other side."

Most of them did as she asked, looking through the transparent side.

"Now you are seeing your future if you do not join our tribe. Nandups will be gone. Extinct."

They did not seem surprised they could no longer see their reflections. Some of them quickly flipped the sheet around again so they could continue looking at themselves. The demonstration had not worked as well as Skyra had hoped.

"Our camp is near," she announced. "Will you come to see what we have made?"

The nandups exchanged glances. A few of them wore expressions indicating they were interested in Skyra's offer.

"We will not go to their camp!" Gelrut shouted to his tribemates. "Skyra and Veenah were born into the Una-Loto tribe, but they are not like us. We all know this. Those girls grew in Sayleeh's belly at the same time. Never has the Una-Loto tribe had twins. We knew when they were young these girls saw things the rest of us could not see. They are bad for Una-Loto tribe, and I should have killed Skyra and Veenah when they were children!"

"You do not speak for all of the Una-Loto tribe, Gelrut," Bolyu said. "You are a good hunter, yes, and you are one of the dominant men, but you do not make decisions for all of us."

Gelrut got to his feet and stepped away from Veenah, growling and baring his teeth. "I say we do not go to the camp of these bolups and these mumengas. Do you challenge me, Bolyu? Do any of you challenge Gelrut?"

The rest of the tribe became silent.

Veenah rose to her feet. "I challenge you, Gelrut."

"No!" Skyra said.

"Veenah, this is not our plan," Elah added.

Veenah ignored them and stepped closer to Gelrut. "You killed me before, but you will not kill me again." She turned to the other nandups. "If I kill Gelrut, you will know I am strong.

You will come to our camp. You will see what my new tribe can do. Do you agree?"

"What the hell is happening?" Derek asked, perhaps sensing Veenah was making a mistake.

"I agree," Bolyu said.

"I agree," Odnus said.

Several of the others expressed their agreement.

Veenah pulled her khul from its sling and tossed it to Gelrut. "You may use my khul. Check its blade. You will see it is tight and its edge is sharp." She then pulled out her hand blade and picked up her shield.

"What is she doing?" Derek asked.

Gelrut sneered at Veenah, then he checked the khul's blade.

Skyra and Elah both stepped to Veenah's side. "This is not our plan," Elah said again.

Skyra said, "You cannot fight Gelrut alone."

"You do not tell me what I can do," Veenah said. "You are my birthmates, not my birthmother. If you help me, the Una-Loto nandups will not come to our camp. Do not let Derek try to help me. I do not want Derek to die."

"Skyra, what is she saying?" Derek demanded. Now he was pulling out his khul.

Skyra studied Veenah's face. Not only did Veenah speak the truth, she was also only a breath away from violence.

Skyra reached out to stop her birthmate but was too late. Veenah darted away and threw herself at Gelrut.

Gelrut barely had time to raise his arms before Veenah's shield knocked him stumbling back.

"I wanted to return to Una-Loto, but you killed me!" Veenah said. She rushed him again.

This time he was able to strike with the khul. The blade clattered against her shield.

Derek started forward, but Skyra and Elah closed in and blocked his path.

"We must let Veenah do this," Skyra said in English. "It is what she wants."

Derek's eyes were wild, and Skyra thought she and Elah might have to restrain him.

Veenah grunted as the khul struck her shield again and again, and Skyra turned her back on Derek to watch the fight.

Gelrut was driving Veenah back with one blow after another, obviously infuriated by the effectiveness of her shield, which probably appeared to him too thin to be so strong. The constant blows were keeping Veenah defensive and off balance, but she easily anticipated the direction of each strike by watching Gelrut's face and movements. Veenah was just as skilled at reading people's intentions as Skyra was.

Gelrut struck again and again, trying to break through the shield with brute force. He made a sudden rush to take Veenah to the ground, but she saw his intention and darted to the side. He caught himself and swung around to strike, but his khul thumped harmlessly against Veenah's shield. He did not let up though, swinging at Veenah's head and shoulders as fast as he could lift the khul. Veenah anticipated and blocked each blow.

"Goddammit, he's going to wear her down or break the shield," Derek said. "She needs help!"

Skyra threw her arm against Derek's chest to hold him back. Then her eyes were drawn to Veenah's feet. Veenah was taking a step back with each blow, feeling the ground carefully with her foot for rocks that might trip her. She was using

Gelrut's anger against him, allowing him to continue his onslaught, which would eventually exhaust him. Skyra glanced at Derek. "Do not try to help. Veenah knows what she is doing."

Gelrut's growls were becoming shorter as his body needed to suck in more air. He paused and stepped back, his chest heaving.

"Gelrut, you are too old to fight me," Veenah said from behind her shield. "You will not kill me again. It is time for me to kill you."

"Your words do not make sense!" he snarled. "I did not kill you. You are alive."

Veenah kicked sand and rocks at him with one foot, then she charged forward and slammed her shield into his forearms again. "You have always wanted to kill me and my birthmate!"

Gelrut pushed forward, striking the shield again and again, then he slid in on one knee and swung for Veenah's ankles. She saw it coming and blocked the blow. When he got to his feet again, he had a stone almost as large as Veenah's head in one hand. He grunted and hurled it at her.

The stone knocked the edge of Veenah's shield aside and struck her shoulder. Gelrut slid in on one knee again, catching her off balance, and struck her ankle with his khul.

Skyra knew instantly from the sound that the stone blade had cracked Veenah's bones. "No!"

"Shit!" Derek cried, and he started forward with Skyra and Elah.

Veenah stumbled on her shattered ankle, but she was able to thrust her hand blade into the side of Gelrut's head. The blade did not pierce his skull, and he rose to his feet, howling with pain and anger.

Before Skyra, Elah, and Derek could move to help Veenah, she screamed and charged Gelrut. Her ankle folded, and her raw bones ground against the rocks and sand but did not slow her down. She plunged her knife into Gelrut's chest before he could block it.

Skyra grabbed Derek's arm. "Wait!"

Elah stopped beside Derek.

Veenah screamed again as she drove her knife in a second time, then a third. Gelrut dropped to his knees, and she kept stabbing at his head and shoulder. The man fell to his belly and curled up to protect his face and throat.

"Veenah has won the fight!" Skyra cried.

Veenah finally stopped stabbing. She looked down at her foot, which was only loosely attached to her leg. She let out one more scream and sat on the ground.

"Veenah has won!" Skyra said again. "You all saw her win." She turned to Lincoln. "Caretaker please."

As Lincoln pulled the robot creature from his pack, Skyra shouted up the hill. "Ripple!"

Ripple rose from behind a boulder at the hill's summit and flew down the slope, its low hum growing louder as it approached.

Several alarmed cries rose from the Una-Loto nandups, although some of them had seen Ripple before. Skyra ignored them and kneeled beside Gelrut, who was still curled up, holding his throat. He was choking now. She grabbed his shoulder and roughly forced him onto his back. His eyes were wide with panic, and he obviously could not breathe.

"Let me see your chest." She pulled one of his hands away while Elah kneeled beside her and pulled the other.

Gelrut immediately started wheezing, blowing and sucking air through a deep stab wound in his chest just below his throat. Wet droplets spewed out with every exhale.

When he tried to free his hands, Skyra put her face close

to his. "Stop fighting. You will not be able to breathe if you cover these wounds. My bolup friends are strong, and they are smart. They have medicine like no medicine you have seen before. You do not want to die, Gelrut, and we do not want you to die. We want you to join our tribe and help make us strong. Do not fight!"

Lincoln and Ripple were now at their side. "I recommend we treat Veenah first," Ripple said. "She is far more important to the success of our plan."

Skyra turned and searched her birthmate's face while Gelrut struggled to breathe through the hole in his chest.

Veenah looked back at Skyra and bared her teeth in a pained nandup smile.

"Veenah will wait," Skyra said. "Now Gelrut is important to our plan too. All the Una-Loto nandups are important."

17

———

MADDY

47,659 years in the past - Day 50 (16 days later)

LINCOLN STOPPED TO REST. He lowered his banyot to the ground and shook the numbness out of his hands and wrists. He had hoped reindeer meat would be lighter than woolly mammoth meat, but no such luck.

"Oh, thank God!" Jazzlyn said as she pulled her banyot up beside his and dropped it. "I was starting to think you were never going to take a break."

Virgil caught up next and dropped his banyot. "Top engineer in Lincoln Woodhouse's temporal displacement lab, PhD in Applied Physics from Cornell, and this is what I'm reduced to. My job now is hauling reindeer heads, antlers, meat, and... whatever that thing is." He pointed to a dark, glistening organ on his banyot.

"I think that might be a liver," Lincoln said.

Virgil wiped sweat from his face. "It might be about time

humans invented the wheel. That's going to be my next project."

Elah and Skyra were bringing up the rear—dragging banyots single file had proven to be easier because the ones in front created drag tracks to follow.

"No time for resting!" Elah said. "Almost to camp." She skirted around Lincoln, Jazzlyn, and Virgil and continued on, following the bolups, who were already far ahead.

Skyra came to a stop and eyed Lincoln. "Tell me what your body is doing now."

"Don't worry, I'm fine."

"Show me you are fine."

He sighed. There was no point in resisting—Skyra would not give up. "The rain in Spain stays mainly on the plain. Red bug's blood, black bug's blood." He continued through the entire routine.

"I know I'm not the one with a genetic disease that could rear its ugly head at any time, but here's the way I see it," Jazzlyn said. "Each day is a blessing, and now you can make the most of every moment."

Lincoln gave her a warm smile. "I wouldn't say hauling a loaded banyot for three miles is making the most of the moment, but I appreciate the sentiment."

Lincoln's expanded tribe had hunted with the Una-Loto nandups today for the first time, which he considered a major breakthrough. The nandups did come to the boulder hill the day Veenah had almost killed Gelrut, and they'd been markedly impressed by Jazzlyn's fifty-five-foot stone sculpture, but they were still reluctant to join a tribe consisting mostly of bolups. They had, however, agreed to remain camped beside the stream where they had initially intended rather than move to a less populated area. They had also agreed—tentatively—to try a peaceful truce with the boulder hill tribes. As an additional gesture of good will, Lincoln's group had dragged two banyots loaded with dried mammoth meat to the nandup camp as a sort of camp-warming gift, which the nandups gladly accepted.

Yesterday, the nandup woman named Bolyu had come to the boulder hill to report a massive herd of reindeer passing through the river plain a few miles to the west. She also extended an invitation to participate in a hunt to drive some of the reindeer into an ambush. The tactic had resulted in six harvested reindeer and zero nandup or bolup injuries.

Lincoln raised his arms above his head, trying to stretch the knots out of his shoulders.

"I hate to break it to you, but your shoes are just about shot," Virgil said, staring down at Lincoln's feet.

Lincoln had already tied a strip of reflective material around one of his shoes to keep the sole from coming off completely. He glanced down at Virgil's and Jazzlyn's shoes. They weren't much better.

Skyra said, "I will make one footwrap for you, but you must watch and learn. Then you will make your own footwraps."

"I like it," Jazzlyn said. "Teach a man to fish."

Skyra furrowed her thick brows. "Your words do not make sense."

"It means it is better to show us how than to do it for us," Jazzlyn replied.

A gust of cold air blew across the rocky field, chilling Lincoln's sweat-drenched skin, so he pulled his bear-skin cape tighter around his neck. Skyra and Elah had discovered the female cave bear had taken up residence in a lower cavity somewhere on the back side of the boulder hill, and they had somehow managed to kill it without getting killed themselves. Whereas the male bear's pelt had become Lincoln and Skyra's bed, the female's had been used to make four capes, one for Lincoln and each of his team members. Lincoln was still wearing his original trousers, and even Virgil was still wearing his, despite the missing pant leg, but it was only a matter of time before all the trousers would simply disintegrate.

"Look at that sight," Virgil said, gazing at the massive nandup and bolup statues standing beside the boulder hill, still about a half mile away. "I'm impressed every time I see them, so I can hardly imagine what the other tribespeople must think of them."

"When we die, the stone people will still be there," Skyra said.

She was right, of course, but Lincoln suspected she was referring more to the fact that the statues might continue to inspire nandups and bolups even if Skyra and her new tribe were all killed. The monument was practically permanent, and with any luck it would become the beacon of light Virgil had once said would be necessary to change the future.

"This is one hell of a thing we're trying to accomplish," Jazzlyn said.

They all stared at the distant monument in silence.

"I did not bleed," Skyra said abruptly.

Everyone turned to her.

"What do you mean?" Lincoln asked, although he had a feeling he already knew.

"I did not bleed." She pointed to her waist-skin. "I bleed here sometimes, but this time I did not bleed. For a few days sometimes I hurt, and sometimes my head tells me strange things. I thought I was sick, but now I do not think I am sick."

"Oh my," Jazzlyn said, glancing at Lincoln.

"What makes you think you're not sick?" Lincoln asked, realizing immediately this was a ridiculous question.

"The Una-Loto women would tell me about these things. Lincoln, I think you have put a child in my belly." She gazed at him with her enormous nandup eyes, as if she could see directly into his thoughts.

More seconds of silence, this time extremely awkward silence. Lincoln had no idea what to say or do. Should he embrace her? Should he try to hide his fear and only show his elation? "Um, how do you feel about that?"

She continued studying his face, seemingly without any need to blink. "Our plan will not work if we do not have children."

"But how do you *feel* about it?" Another ridiculous question. Frustrated with himself, Lincoln stepped over his banyot and pulled her into an embrace. Instead of opening his damn mouth again, he pressed his face into her hair and inhaled her scent.

"Now I feel happy," she said softly.

***

LINCOLN'S GROUP dropped off the loaded banyots with the Peli-Bayom and Yuni-Bayom bolups, then Jazzlyn and Virgil moved quickly up the hill toward the courtyard, giving Lincoln and Skyra time to ascend the hill at their own pace.

"I will not stop hunting when my belly gets big," Skyra said as they climbed. She had been talking non stop since revealing her secret. "I will still be able to hunt with a big belly. You will see. I will tie a rock to my belly to practice."

"I'm pretty sure the rock would be a bad idea," Lincoln said. "I also think you'll decide soon you'll be happier not hunting until after the child is born." He had numerous doubts about the chances of Skyra carrying the child to term, but he didn't dare express them aloud. Alinga-uls were exceedingly rare in Di-woto's world. Plus, in Lincoln's original timeline, DNA analyses had shown modern humans possessed plenty of Neanderthal *nuclear* DNA, but they had no Neanderthal *mitochondrial* DNA, the DNA passed down to offspring only by the female parent. This research suggested offspring of human males and Neanderthal females had been rare, nonexistent, or possibly sterile. Regardless, for whatever reason, Ripple seemed convinced Lincoln and Skyra were perfectly capable of producing viable offspring. That is, of course, if Ripple could be trusted to tell the truth about such things.

"You will see, Lincoln. I will not stop hunting. Do you think my child will be a girl or a boy?"

"Well, there's an equal chance of either. I'm pretty sure girls smell better than boys, so maybe a girl would be better."

"*Aheee at-at-at.* You are trying to be funny. My birth-mother Sayleeh, before the woolly rhino killed her, said Veenah and I were stinky little babies, and we were both girls. Lincoln, do you think we can still make love when my belly is big?"

"Please don't tell me you're going to practice with a rock tied to your belly."

"*Aheee at-at-at.* That is not very funny."

"Okay, I have a question for you," he said. "When the child leaves your belly, what name do you want to give it?"

"I have not thought about a name," she said, then she fell silent, perhaps thinking of possibilities.

They caught up to Jazzlyn and Virgil, who were just reaching the gap into the courtyard, and they all climbed through together. Derek, Veenah, and Elah were sitting on the stone benches arranged around the fire ring, talking to Ripple. Maddy was nowhere to be seen.

Veenah's ankle now had an impressive scar, but the caretaker had repaired her broken bones, and she was just as mobile as she had been before the fight.

Elah was drinking from one of the water bladders, so Lincoln headed straight for her, intent on replenishing his depleted fluids. "Elah probably told you we had a successful hunt," Lincoln said.

Derek turned, frowning. "Yeah, six reindeer. Congrats."

Lincoln looked from Derek to Ripple and back. "What's wrong?"

"Damn drone's hiding something, and it's starting to piss me off," Derek replied.

Lincoln accepted the water bladder from Elah, then he handed it to Skyra to drink first. "Aren't you always pissed off at Ripple?"

"For good reason! The two drones left the courtyard hours ago. Said they had an *important* job to do. I didn't think much of it, but then Ripple came back alone. The damn drone won't tell me where Maddy is!"

Lincoln turned to Ripple. "What's going on?"

Ripple's red LEDs rotated counterclockwise twice. "I cannot tell you where Maddy is."

Lincoln started to ask why not, then he noticed gray sludge oozing out of Ripple's shell and down one of the drone's legs. The sludge started accumulating on the rock slab beside Ripple's foot. "Is that one of the caretakers?"

"Yes," Ripple said. "Its component parts have recharged and are ready to reassemble."

"Why do you have it?"

"I cannot tell you."

The caretaker's components were now coming together into visible specks.

"Did you take it with you when you left the courtyard with Maddy?"

"Yes."

"The damn drone snuck it out by hiding it in its shell!" Derek boomed.

Skyra kneeled before Ripple. "Maddy is Lincoln's friend. Please tell us where she is."

The drone's LEDs rotated again. "Yes, Maddy is Lincoln's very good friend."

Skyra frowned. "You are not telling us something. Why?"

"Maddy is risking her existence to do something very important. I cannot tell you where she is until she returns to the courtyard."

Lincoln's throat constricted as his unease transformed into real alarm. "Ripple, we've been hauling reindeer carcasses for hours, and we're exhausted. If you force us to go out searching for Maddy with no idea of where to even begin, I'm going to pull your CM and replace it with the other Ripple's CM. Quit screwing around!"

More rotating LEDs—Ripple was truly stressed by this situation. "Maddy is safe but not accessible."

"What does that mean?"

"Upon Maddy's request, she is now embedded in solid stone."

Lincoln blinked.

"What the hell?" Derek exclaimed.

"Maddy asked me to instruct one of the caretakers to embed her in solid stone. I was skeptical whether the caretaker's component parts could reassemble and fuse excavated rock particles back into solid stone, but they achieved the task quite handily. Maddy is now safely beneath almost a meter of solid stone."

Skyra turned to Lincoln with a confused frown.

Suddenly the pieces came together in Lincoln's mind. "Dammit, Ripple, don't you realize there's almost no chance it could happen a second time?"

"It is quite possible, and Maddy wanted to try," Ripple replied.

"What does this mean?" Skyra asked.

"No, it is *not* quite possible!" Lincoln almost shouted. "There's no guarantee any advanced civilization will ever appear in this timeline."

"God almighty," Virgil said. "Is that really what Maddy is trying to do?"

Skyra grabbed Lincoln's arm. "What is Maddy trying to do?"

He shook his head in disbelief. "Maddy's trying to get to the future, the same way the original Ripple did when your other self died in one of the caves of this hill."

Her expression indicated his explanation hadn't helped much.

"Lincoln is correct," Ripple said. "Maddy is Lincoln's very good friend."

Lincoln turned to the drone. "This is insane! We're talking tens of thousands of years, at least. Maybe more. Maybe never! The rock could weather and crack. There's freezing and thawing, and earthquakes, and countless other events that could destroy her. Dammit, Ripple, how could you help her do this? Tell us where she is. We'll use the caretaker to dig her out."

"I will not tell you. Maddy's plan might work."

"It *won't* work! Now tell us—" Lincoln paused, distracted by a high-pitched buzz behind him.

Jazzlyn pointed. "Uh, are you guys seeing this?"

Lincoln turned to look. The buzz was coming from a red, baseball-sized object. The object was levitating a foot or so above the stone surface, gliding slowly from left to right. It then changed course and headed straight for Lincoln and the others. It stopped a few yards out. A black dot, most likely a camera lens, panned up and down, as if the ball were studying the odd assortment of tribemates. The buzzing abruptly fell silent. The ball clattered onto the rock slab, rolled a few inches, and became still.

"That has to be a mini-drone," Lincoln said, simply because he couldn't think of anything else it might be.

"How could maglev tech fit inside something that small?" Virgil asked, obviously as flummoxed as Lincoln was.

"The real question is, where did it come from?" Jazzlyn said.

Lincoln knew in his gut where it must have come from. Instinctively, he scanned the courtyard, waiting.

With a crisp electrical-like pop, another object appeared a few feet off the slab and immediately clattered onto the stone. It managed to stay on its feet, and it turned until its vision orb spotted Lincoln and the group.

"Thank my lucky stars. You are here, Lincoln," Maddy said.

After several long seconds of silence, Ripple spoke up. "Excellent. Maddy's plan did work. Perhaps I will no longer be in the proverbial doghouse."

Maddy stepped closer. Her shell had been polished to a smooth, gray sheen. Strapped to her back was a large pack, made of a red, canvas-like material. "How long, from your perspective, would you estimate I was gone?" she asked.

"Precisely three hours, forty-eight minutes, and eleven seconds," Ripple replied.

"I can assure you, it was much longer from my perspective. Lincoln, if you were concerned, please forgive me. I had hoped to be sent back here by the time you returned from your hunt for reindeer with the Neanderthal tribe."

Lincoln swallowed, still trying to wrap his head around this. "What did you do, Maddy?"

"I assumed if Ripple could do it, I could as well, especially considering I was wearing Ripple's shell, which was constructed for just such a task. Your future self ensured it was possible, Lincoln."

"What did you do?" he asked again.

"I became dormant, hoping to be discovered by future humans, Neanderthals, or whatever beings might become technologically advanced in this timeline. I set my cognitive module to awaken briefly and activate a beacon signal once every thousand years. Curiously, I did not have to wait nearly as long as the original Ripple waited. Instead of 47,659 years, I was detected and extracted only 18,000 years after being embedded in stone."

"What was the point?" Virgil asked. "The future you saw was only one of infinite possible threads. It will not be *our* future."

"Allow me to answer Virgil's question," Ripple said.

"By all means," Maddy said.

"As I have explained, when Lincoln was five years older than his current age, he sent a drone twenty years into his future, hoping it would return and inform him that at least one thread of his future looked brighter than he was feeling at the time. He wanted to know if something better was at least possible. Today, Maddy wished to show Lincoln this entire endeavor—this plan of ours—might actually work. If you did not fully understand it before, surely you must understand now Maddy will do anything for Lincoln."

"Thank you, Ripple," Maddy said. "I now regret each and every disparaging remark I have made about you. You may be deceptive, but your intentions are sincere."

"Um, I'm confused on about twelve different levels," Derek said. "So, is Maddy still embedded in solid rock somewhere near here?"

"Indeed I am, and you may now extract me, assuming you can tolerate having two versions of me in your tribe."

"We are definitely going to do that," Lincoln said. "The world will be a better place with two Maddys in it."

"You are too kind," Maddy said. "As I am sure you have many questions, I will explain further what I have experienced. I was detected and excavated exactly 18,000 years after Ripple helped bury me. Due to being completely encased in stone, I was remarkably preserved. However, many parts of my external shell had to be replaced. My new friends in the future decided not to alter my overall appearance, though, so I would not confuse or frighten you upon my return. Most of my internal modules remained intact and needed no repair. My plan was to gather information about whatever future civilization might arise, then I would jump back to this time and place. The beings who excavated me had not developed temporal displacement technology, therefore I shared extensive data with them. They put that data to use and developed the devices needed to jump me back to you. My plan was to use this shell's U-Jump module at the instant of my return, knowing that jumping back to this day would create a new timeline. I reasoned that the U-Jump module would allow me to jump back here then immediately jump from the newly created timeline to my original timeline, thus allowing me to be with the same Lincoln I had left behind in the first place."

After a few seconds of silence, Lincoln said, "Um... you do know that—"

"Yes, of course I know the other Lincoln is the same Lincoln, at least up until the two timelines split. However, my sentimental side compelled me. I understand there is another Lincoln in the other timeline who is waiting for Maddy to return, and the other Maddy might not return because it might not be as lucky as I was. Or perhaps it already has returned. Regardless, I take comfort in the fact that the other Lincoln can extract the other Maddy from the stone and continue to benefit from her wisdom and companionship."

"Do you even realize how convoluted and nonsensical that whole story sounds?" Derek asked.

"Yes," Maddy said.

Lincoln decided to sort out the mind-bending logistics of what Maddy had done later. "Go on, tell us what happened."

"I thought you'd never ask. I have returned with gifts." The drone turned and sidled up to Lincoln. "Please open my pack and remove the red box."

Lincoln fiddled with the pack for a moment before realizing the opening used magnetism—or something like magnetism—instead of a zipper to keep it shut. He pried it open and saw two smooth, rectangular boxes, one red and one white. He pulled out the red box. It had a fairly standard hinged lid, which was held shut by the same magnetic-like force. It popped open with a little pressure.

The box contained six bulging, fist-sized pouches, all made of white fabric except for one, which was red.

Maddy said, "My new friends agreed the most universally useful supply I could bring back to you would be general-purpose antibiotics, in solid pill form. The white pouches should contain enough to last numerous years, and they were formulated to have a shelf life of at least forty years. Unfortunately, technical limitations prevented me from bringing a much larger pack of additional supplies. Lincoln, the red pouch is specifically for you."

Lincoln pulled out the red pouch, which reminded him of a beanbag. "What's in it?"

"Based on the information I provided, my friends conducted extensive research into numerous variants of neuronal ceroid lipofuscinosis, which was no easy task due to the fact that very few forms of the disease existed within their diverse populations. Nevertheless, they have many brilliant medical researchers, and they concocted a medication they are reasonably confident will suppress your symptoms indefinitely, as long as you take one pill every day. The pills are extremely small, and the pouch contains 22,000 of them—enough for the next sixty years, far longer than your expected life span in this harsh environment."

Lincoln squeezed the bag between his fingers, feeling the tiny pills shifting inside. "Um... I don't even know what to say, Maddy."

"What does this mean?" Skyra asked.

"It means Lincoln's not going to crap out on us!" Derek boomed. "Maddy, you have my utmost respect. Ripple, you're still a douche of a drone, but I gotta admit you did a good thing this time."

"I still do not know what this means," Skyra said.

Lincoln handed her the bag of 22,000 pills. "This is medicine, and I think it might keep me from getting sick."

She took the pouch and stared at it with her extraordinary nandup eyes. "Maddy is a good friend, Lincoln."

"I appreciate the praise," Maddy said. "Lincoln, I must also tell you that my new friends were quite convinced that your NCL will not be passed on to any offspring you might have with Skyra. If Skyra were *Homo sapiens*, that possibility would be a concern, but as she is *Homo neanderthalensis*, the genetic configuration of your offspring will preclude the possibility. My goodness, what a joy it is for me to be the bearer of good news."

Stunned, Lincoln turned to Skyra.

"You do not have to explain that part," she said. "I understand, and I am happy for Maddy's good news."

"There is more," Maddy said. "I have brought another gift I believe may bolster everyone's confidence in this entire audacious endeavor originally conceived and set into motion by Ripple. Lincoln, please open the white box."

Lincoln set the red box on the stone slab and pulled the white box from Maddy's pack. It popped open just as easily as the other one had. He frowned at the contents. "Sunglasses?"

"Precisely," Maddy said. "If you look closely, you will see they are fashioned using your own design, the VR sunglasses you developed for runners and cyclists. Please take a pair and pass the others out."

The box contained seven pairs of sunglasses, one for each person. Lincoln took one and distributed the others. Not surprisingly, Skyra, Elah, and Veenah stared at their glasses with furrowed brows.

Maddy said, "You need only to put on the glasses, insert the attached earbuds, then press the button located beside the left lens. The purpose of the glasses will then become clear."

Lincoln could hardly wait to see what else Maddy had done, but first he stepped over to help Skyra, Elah, and Veenah. He showed them how to put the glasses over their eyes and gently push the earbuds in. "Don't be startled," he said. "You're probably going to hear strange sounds and see a video appear in front of your eyes." He then guided their fingers to the button on the frames and told them to press it.

"El-de-né!" Skyra exclaimed a few seconds later.

Veenah threw her hands out and latched onto Skyra's cape, apparently to keep from stumbling.

"El-de-né!" Elah said.

"I see the glasses are functioning," Maddy said.

Lincoln glanced at Jazzlyn, Virgil, and Derek. They already had their glasses on, so he put on his own pair, inserted the earbuds, and pressed the button.

A rich, detailed image appeared, rendered in perfect focus, no doubt because of the two-layer lens system Lincoln himself had developed. The lower margin of the image included the top of Maddy's dorsal shell, as if a camera had been attached to her back. The rest of the image showed a long hallway with transparent walls, perhaps made of glass. At the end of the hallway was a rectangular glass door framed within a glass wall. Even the ceiling and floor were transparent, and in every direction Lincoln could see tables, chairs, doors, shelves, and all manner of devices that must have been tools, appliances, or machinery for some unknown purpose. People in bright-colored clothing were interspersed everywhere, walking, sitting, or standing around. Lincoln could only assume it was a completely transparent, multi-level office building or research facility.

Maddy's feminine voice filled Lincoln's ears. "Lincoln, Jazzlyn, Virgil, Derek, Skyra, Elah, and Veenah, with any luck you are viewing this video. If all goes well, I will reappear before you are even aware I was gone. If not, I am sorry if my sudden absence startled or concerned you. I will keep this message short, as there are only a few things you need to see for yourself to convince you my story is true. The rest I can explain in person, then I will respond directly to your questions. I am now 18,027 years in your future. Yes, of course I realize this is not the future of your timeline. It is only one of infinite possible futures. However, I want you to know what *could* happen. I want you to have hope that your efforts are worthwhile."

The camera panned to the side as Maddy turned, and Lincoln glimpsed more furniture and machinery beyond the glass hallway wall. Suddenly, two people filled the frame. They were seated on a bench, facing Maddy's camera.

Maddy said, "I would like to introduce you to Pagwe Tikeevy, on the left, and Tsatsu Ogurlievy, on the right. Pagwe and Tsatsu have been two of my closest friends during these twenty-seven years since I was excavated."

The two people smiled broadly at the camera when Maddy spoke their names. Lincoln couldn't tell if they were male or female, although they were both strangely attractive in a gender-neutral way. Pagwe and Tsatsu both wore their hair pulled back tightly to the backs of their heads, and they both wore brightly colored but comfortable-looking clothing without collars, buttons, or visible seams. One of them was dressed mainly in lime green, the other in cherry red. Black lines, arranged in pleasing patterns, had been either drawn or tattooed around their eyes. Other than the patterns, they appeared to be wearing no makeup. Most noteworthy, though, was they were not clearly Neanderthal, nor were they clearly human. Their features reminded Lincoln of Di-woto—the slightly sloping foreheads, eyes proportionally smaller than Skyra's but larger than Lincoln's, fleshy lips but not as thick as Skyra's. These people appeared to possess far more Neanderthal DNA than the humans of Lincoln's original timeline.

Maddy's voice said, "Pagwe and Tsatsu were instrumental in persuading their peers to utilize the data I provided regarding temporal displacement technology. Without their help, the information may have been ignored or rejected outright. They also encouraged the manufacture of the VR glasses you are now wearing, which by the way have become quite popular here. Finally, Pagwe and Tsatsu were instrumental in another effort I will soon show you."

The person on the left raised a hand and said, "Skyra." The voice was distinctly female, and she pronounced the name with what seemed almost like an Irish enunciation.

The person on the right made the same gesture and said, "Lincoln." The voice was male, and again the enunciation sounded almost Irish.

Maddy's voice said, "That's the extent of their greeting—they know your names, but they do not know the English or Una-Loto languages. You need to understand, Lincoln and Skyra, these are good people, as are most of the others of their kind. They display intelligence, thoughtfulness, and compassion. In only 18,000 years they have reached a level of technological achievement which took the *Homo sapiens* of your original timeline over 47,000 years to achieve."

The camera swung away from Pagwe and Tsatsu and again pointed down the hallway to the rectangular door at the far end. Maddy's voice said, "We have carefully chosen this particular location to create this video. I will now show you why."

The camera began moving steadily down the hallway as Maddy walked. Colorfully clothed people beyond the walls, above the ceiling, and below the floor stopped what they were doing to watch or to raise a hand, evidently a gesture of greeting. Those close enough for Lincoln to clearly see their faces had the same distinctive features shared by Pagwe and Tsatsu, somewhere on the spectrum between *sapiens* and *neanderthalensis*.

As Maddy approached the end of the hall, Tsatsu moved ahead and opened the rectangular door. Maddy walked through the doorway onto a balcony with a safety railing seemingly made of glass. Beyond the railing was a cityscape, with numerous blocky buildings, each no more than about ten stories high, arranged symmetrically into the distance. Each building, as far as Lincoln could tell, was completely made of glass or some other transparent material. Lincoln saw countless people in the nearest buildings, many of them standing shoulder-to-shoulder near the outer walls and staring directly at Maddy.

A transparent ramp had been set up, allowing Maddy to walk up until her shell was above the waist-high railing. She turned right then left, panning the camera to show the surrounding buildings and their staring occupants. Then she lowered the front of her shell, aiming the camera downward to show a large, open area below, perhaps a park or square. Hundreds of brightly clothed people were there, some walking one way or another to an unknown destination, but most standing in the center of the square, gathered around a stone monument which looked strangely out of place in the midst of perfect buildings that sparkled like crystal cubes in the sunlight.

"I'll be damned," Lincoln muttered as he took in the scene.

Standing fifty-five feet high in the center of the square was the dual statue the caretaker had created under Jazzlyn's guidance—Lincoln and Skyra, standing hand in hand, gazing into the distance to greet nandups moving down from the Kapolsek foothills onto the Dofusofu river plain. The two figures showed signs of restoration. Numerous seams were visible, where broken pieces had been somehow fused back together. Some of the more detailed features, especially on the faces, were a slightly different color, having been replaced with new material.

A voice shouted something, and in response the crowd of people standing around the monument turned their faces to gaze up at the balcony. Several of them raised their hands in greeting, and the gesture spread across the crowd until they were all waving at Maddy. Or perhaps to the camera they knew Maddy was carrying—to Lincoln and Skyra, and to Jazzlyn, Virgil, Derek, Elah, and Veenah—their long-dead ancestors.

18

ANUVA

47,655 YEARS *in the past - Day 1,394 (3 years 10 months later)*

SKYRA'S LEGS wanted to run. Her arms twitched to scoop up Anuva and hold the girl to her chest. However, she ordered her body to be still. Now Skyra knew how her own birthmother must have felt countless times.

"Try to relax," Lincoln said. "She'll never learn if she can't make her own mistakes."

Skyra growled. "Sometimes mistakes kill."

"She's hunting crayfish. The river's knee deep. I don't see how she could get killed."

Skyra watched her birthdaughter lifting flat rocks near the river's edge. Anuva was now in her third warm season. Skyra and Veenah had learned to catch crayfish at her age, and they had somehow managed to avoid being swept away by the current. Anuva was even smarter than Skyra had been at three years old, so Lincoln was probably right, but that did not make watching her any easier.

Skyra instinctively scanned the surrounding area for predators, but the bolup and nandup hunters of her tribe had already killed most of the dangerous creatures in the area, and only occasionally did new ones wander this close to the tribe's permanent home.

"Crayfish!" Anuva shouted, plunging her hand into the water. She let out a growl when her hand came up empty. "Crayfish are too fast, Mama Skyra!"

"That is why you have to be faster," Skyra replied. "Do not give up."

"I'm scared they will pinch my finger. Papa Lincoln, you come help me, okay?"

"Nope, you're the hunter today, mudbug," Lincoln said.

Skyra nudged his side. "Stop calling her that. She is Anuva."

"It's a nickname. Didn't you have any nicknames when you were young?"

"No. Did you?"

"Yeah, but some weren't very nice. I try not to think about them."

She raised her brows and gave him a look.

"Okay, I see your point. No more mudbug."

"I like that name, Papa Lincoln," Anuva said without looking up from the water.

"The girl's got your ears, that's for sure," Lincoln said.

"Crayfish!" This time Anuva wildly flipped a crayfish onto the rocky shore, then she stepped out of the water and squatted to stare at it. "My first crayfish!"

Skyra ran over to her birthdaughter and held open the tattered old pack. "Put it in here before it gets away."

Anuva picked up the creature by its shell and dropped it in the pack. She squealed and clapped her hands. "I will catch more!"

Skyra zipped the pack shut and set it beside the water. "Yes, catch more, then we will eat crayfish together. You put the next one in the pack yourself."

Anuva waded back into the water. "I will, Mama Skyra."

Skyra moved away from the river. Lincoln was now sitting on the rocks, so she sat beside him. They sat in silence for many breaths, watching Anuva on her first solo hunt.

"I have a secret," Skyra said, without taking her eyes off Anuva.

She sensed him gazing at her, waiting.

"I did not bleed."

"I know," he said.

She turned to him. "You know? I did not tell you until now."

He shrugged. "You can't keep secrets from me. Your face tells me everything."

"I know too, Mama Skyra," Anuva said from the river.

Skyra growled. "Well, I knew that you both knew. Your faces told me you knew."

Lincoln snorted. "Oh, they did not."

She giggled. "Are you happy I did not bleed?"

"Of course I am. Are you?"

She stared at the rippling river water. "My head is happy. My arms and legs will be angry when they cannot hunt for many days."

"*That's* what you're thinking about?"

"I am thinking about many things. My head does not stop thinking."

Lincoln put a hand on her knee. "When your belly gets

too big for you to hunt, I'll ask Gelrut and Broc and all the other hunters to tell you stories after every hunt. Will that help?"

"I do not know."

"I'll also make you hot khabiya tea every day. Will that help?"

"Maybe."

"Well, how about I make love to you whenever you want. We'll use a code word—something like *pineapple*. Whenever you say the word, I'll know I need to meet you in our sleeping chamber so we can make love. Will that help?"

She smiled. "Probably."

"Gross!" Anuva said. "What is *pineapple*, anyway?"

"Are you even trying to hunt?" Lincoln asked Anuva.

"I'm hunting and listening. But really, Papa Lincoln —gross!"

"How many crayfish have you caught, mudbug?"

"One, which is one more than you and Mama Skyra have caught."

He let out a long breath and shot a look at Skyra. "What will she be like when she's a teenager?"

Skyra got to her feet. "If we want to have a crayfish picnic with our birthdaughter, we need more than one crayfish." She pulled off her cape and footwraps and untied her waist-skin, then she held out a hand to pull Lincoln up. "We will hunt with Anuva."

As the sun reached its highest point in the sky and started moving toward the Kapolsek hills, Skyra, Lincoln, and Anuva sat naked on the sand and rocks of the river shore, waiting for the sun to dry their hair and skin. They had caught, boiled, and eaten enough crayfish to fill their bellies, then they had bathed in the cool water. Skyra felt happy, just as she always felt when she was with Lincoln and Anuva, and she wondered if having another child would change everything.

Anuva was tossing bits of crayfish shell into the water and watching the tiny fish pick at them. She paused and said, "When will Elah have a child in her belly? Elah is just like you, Mama Skyra, so why doesn't she have an Anuva just like me?"

Skyra said, "Elah and Mama Skyra used to be the same person, before I jumped back to this time with Papa Lincoln, Aunt Jazzlyn, Uncle Virgil, and Uncle Derek. Now we are not the same person, so we do different things. Elah does not have an Anuva because she is not married to Papa Lincoln."

"What if Elah was married to Papa Lincoln instead of you?"

Skyra leaned her head against Lincoln's shoulder. "I would be sad. I love Papa Lincoln."

"Is Elah sad?"

"No, Elah is happy. She did not meet Papa Lincoln the way I met him. Lincoln and his tribemates jumped here from the future, then they helped me kill the bolup men and save Veenah."

"You told me that story a million times."

"What else have I told you a million times?"

Anuva sighed. "You told me nandups and bolups don't fight anymore, but that's not true. Yanlip was fighting with Eknad just yesterday."

Lincoln said, "Yes, we know, and what happened to Yanlip and Eknad?"

"They got in trouble."

"Right, five days without bear-fat crisps for both of them. You know how Yanlip likes bear-fat crisps."

She giggled. "Yeah, he loves them." Abruptly she jumped to her feet. "I'm going to swim some more!"

"Stop!" Skyra said before the girl could step into the water.

Anuva turned around with a frown.

"We are almost dry. I do not want you to get wet again."

The girl grimaced. Then she took a step toward the water, watching Skyra's face.

"Do not!" Skyra said.

Anuva stepped into the river.

"I said *do not*."

Anuva took another step.

"You do not want to make me get up," Skyra said, trying to look mad.

The girl squealed and leapt into the water, landing on her belly with a splash.

"El-de-né!" Skyra shouted. Then she turned to Lincoln.

He was staring at her, obviously trying not to show any expression. The sun shone on his skin, making the last few water drops sparkle. He was a skinny bolup, but there was something about the way the sunlight was casting shadows on his body that made Skyra's insides tingle.

"Pineapple," she said.

He blinked. Then he smiled. He jumped to his feet, waded into the river, and scooped up Anuva.

Anuva squealed again, and water flew everywhere as she thrashed her arms and legs.

"It's almost time for afternoon school, mudbug," he said as he carried her to shore. "We've been out here at least three hours—long enough."

"Papa Lincoln, you know there is no such thing as hours here," she said as he put her down. "Hours only exist when you have clocks and watches to measure time, and your watch broke way before I came out of Mama Skyra's belly."

"What about the clocks inside Ripple and the two Maddys?"

"No, no, no, those don't count, silly."

Lincoln put her little footwraps on her feet. "Are you lecturing me? Have you forgotten I'm the one who invented time travel?"

Anuva pulled her cape on over her head herself but handed her waist-skin to Lincoln to carry. "I never saw your T3, so I don't believe you really had one. No such thing as time travel."

"Is that right?" Lincoln asked as he and Skyra started putting on their garments.

"That's right. Oh, and I don't want to go to school today."

"Let me guess—because you're too smart for the other kids?"

"It is not a guess if you know it is true, Papa Lincoln."

"You're three years old. You have a lot more to learn."

"Three years and fifty-nine days."

"Oh, pardon me. I guess you're *way* too old for school if you're three years and fifty-nine days."

"You're teasing!"

"No, *you're* teasing."

Skyra grabbed the leather bag she used for boiling water, the three-legged frame for hanging the bag, and her magnifying glass. The magnifying glass, from Lincoln's original collection of survival gear, was now Skyra's favorite fire-starting tool. She took Anuva's hand and headed away from the river with her family. "I hope you two are finally finished talking. You are making my ears hurt."

Anuva raised her arms. "Carry me, Mama Skyra. My legs are too short."

Skyra handed Lincoln the supplies and hoisted her birth-daughter onto her shoulders.

Anuva slapped the top of Skyra's head as they headed for home. "Now tell me what pineapple means, but don't say anything gross, okay?"

As they approached what used to be the boulder hill, Skyra could not help but wonder what Di-woto would think of the structure. Di-woto had drawn plans for a spectacular sanctuary-fortress for her people, but she had probably never imagined anything like this.

The hill was no longer just a pile of boulders. When Maddy had asked Ripple to embed her in solid stone, Ripple had discovered the caretakers could do more than scratch off tiny chips of rock to make carvings. They could also put those tiny rock chips back together in any possible shape and somehow make them all solid again. The caretakers had worked for more than two years to transform the hill of boulders.

The giant stone Skyra and Lincoln was still there, greeting nandups moving down from the Kapolsek hills in the west. Now there was another pair of stone people, carved to look like Veenah and Derek, on the hill's opposite side. These stone people greeted bolups moving onto the plain from the Tanutu hills to the east.

Between the pairs of stone greeters was the home of

Skyra's combined tribe, the strongest tribe in all the Dofusofu river plain. The hill now looked more like a building carved out of one massive stone, with many dwellings on each level, enough dwellings for the tribe to grow to at least twice its current size.

One problem with having such a large tribe was finding enough game to feed all the tribemates. The river had plenty of crayfish, small fish, and turtles. Herds of reindeer moved through the plains during the cold seasons. Sometimes woolly mammoths moved along the river, where they could get water when they were thirsty. Still, there were times when game was not so easy to find.

To help solve the problem, Jazzlyn and Virgil had been working with some of the tribe's bolups and nandups to start trading with other tribes in the area. They were now exchanging fine stone tools and weapon blades for meat, skins, and khelop roots. Lincoln had said he thought trading would also help spread the idea of peace between nandups and bolups to other places beyond the Dofusofu plains. Skyra did not know if this would work, but Lincoln was usually right about such things.

A smooth stone wall, at least three times taller than Skyra, encircled the entire base of the hill. No tribe had ever dared raid the hill, but Skyra slept better at night knowing the wall was there. She worried about Anuva's safety more than she had ever imagined possible.

The caretakers had created two doorways in the wall, one on each side of the hill. A gate made of reflective material stretched across a tube frame blocked each of the doorways. A tribemate guarded each gate at all times, but the guards had never had to alert the tribe about intruders. Skyra did not like when it was her turn to guard one of the gates because there was little to do while guarding, but she did not complain about it—guarding the camp was important.

The gate clicked and opened as Skyra, Lincoln, and Anuva approached. Today was Gelrut's turn to guard. He stared silently as they entered.

"Gelrut sauk aibul-mbiyon-goloni," Anuva said, speaking to him in the nandup language from atop Skyra's shoulders. *Today I caught a crayfish, Gelrut.*

Gelrut frowned, perhaps because he frowned at everything. "Anuva beben melu-fuga-khakua-alifo," he replied. *Soon you will be a skilled hunter, Anuva child.*

Skyra caught Gelrut's eye as she walked by. He grunted and turned away to close the gate.

"You should talk to Gelrut more, Mama Skyra," Anuva said as they started up the sloped walkway. "Gelrut is a nice nandup, even if he never smiles."

Skyra and Lincoln had not told Anuva any of the stories of what Gelrut had done.

Anuva slapped the top of Skyra's head. "Are you listening?"

"I am listening."

"Gelrut is your tribemate, and tribemates are supposed to be nice to each other."

"I will talk to Gelrut when he talks to me."

"I already know what Gelrut did to Aunt Veenah."

Skyra stopped walking. Lincoln frowned at her, shaking his head. She hoisted Anuva from her shoulders, set the girl on her feet, and kneeled before her. "What do you know?"

"Gelrut killed Aunt Veenah before. The other kids told me that. But, Mama Skyra, that was a different Gelrut. This Gelrut is a nice nandup. He said he will teach me how to hunt woolly rhinos when I get bigger."

"No, he will not!"

"Why? *You* hunt woolly rhinos. I want to hunt them too."

Skyra growled. "Woolly rhinos are dangerous. One killed Gramma Sayleeh."

The girl made a mad face. "I know. That's why I—"

"*I* will teach you to hunt woolly rhinos!" Skyra almost shouted. "Gelrut will not."

Anuva's eyes grew wide. "You said you didn't want me to hunt them."

"I am your birthmother, and I will teach you." Skyra took a long breath and tried to smile at her birthdaughter. "I will tell you a story tonight when you go to bed. It is the story of when Mama Skyra and Papa Lincoln killed the same woolly rhino that killed Gramma Sayleeh."

The girl's eyes grew even wider. "Is the story true? Did you really?"

"We did."

Anuva glanced at Lincoln. "But Papa Lincoln is a skinny bolup. How did he help you kill the woolly rhino?"

"Hey, I'm fiercer than I look," Lincoln said. "The story is true, and I will be there to make sure Mama Skyra tells how I saved her life and helped kill the rhino."

The girl grinned. "I want to hear the story now."

Skyra rose to her full height. "Later, when you go to bed. Now it is time for afternoon school."

Anuva raised her arms. "My legs are too short."

THE NEW COURTYARD was at the hill's summit. Instead of being enclosed by boulders and slanted rock slabs, a perfectly smooth stone wall now surrounded it, with a ledge all the way around the top of the wall, where Skyra and the others could sit and look out over the surrounding river plains. The courtyard contained six dwellings: one for Skyra, Lincoln, and Anuva, one for Veenah, Derek, Mickey, and Lucas, one for Jazzlyn and Virgil, one for Elah, one for Ripple, Maddy One, and Maddy Two, and an extra dwelling for visiting tribemates. There were also two smoking chambers, one for meats and one for skins.

As soon as they entered the courtyard, Anuva ran straight for the dwelling of the three drones, where she had been spending a lot of time lately.

"Hey, little girl!" Jazzlyn shouted at her. "Are you ready for school? We're leaving soon."

Jazzlyn and Virgil were both teachers at the school, along with Broc from the Peli-Bayom bolup tribe and Odnus from the Una-Loto nandup tribe.

"I'm ready, Aunt Jazzlyn," Anuva said as she disappeared into the drone dwelling.

"Derek, is Mickey ready?" Jazzlyn shouted. "Five-minute warning!"

Derek emerged from his dwelling, pulling Mickey by the hand. The boy had seen two cold seasons and would soon see his third. Veenah then emerged, carrying Lucas, who had not yet seen his second cold season so was too young to go with Jazzlyn and Virgil to the school.

"The little runt's kind of clingy today," Derek said as he dragged Mickey over and placed the boy's hand into Virgil's. Mickey tried unsuccessfully to pull away.

Virgil squatted to look the boy in the eye. "Hey, little man. You do *not* want to miss school today. I'm going to share a really interesting story about the history of physics in Uncle Virgil's original timeline. Fascinating stuff!"

"Boring stuff," Mickey said, frowning.

Jazzlyn said, "It won't be boring because Ripple is going to help Uncle Virgil tell the story."

The boy's frown disappeared. "We're having a video today?"

"Yes, a video like you've never seen before!" Jazzlyn said.

Mickey smiled.

Elah emerged from her dwelling with a pack on her back, carrying a spear.

"You are going hunting alone again?" Skyra asked.

"I will return in two days, maybe three."

"That is what you said last time, then you were gone five days."

"It's not safe to go alone," Lincoln added. "Can't you get some of the other hunters to go with you?"

Elah handed a small, black box to Lincoln—the other Ripple's brain. "I will not be alone."

Lincoln took the brain and sighed. He shouted, "Maddy Two, please come out here!"

After a few breaths, Maddy Two emerged from the dwelling she shared with Maddy One and Ripple. "Did it occur to you, Lincoln, that I may have been engaged in other important activities?"

"You're going dormant for a while," Lincoln said. "We need your shell."

"I don't suppose I have any say in this?"

"Nope. Ripple Two is going hunting with Elah."

"Oh, my. I do hope my shell does not get damaged. The Ripples are reckless drones." Maddy Two pulled her legs into her shell and settled onto her belly.

"I will not allow Ripple to do anything foolish," Elah said.

"Very well. Entering dormant mode."

Lincoln rolled Maddy onto her side and quickly pulled out her brain and put in Ripple Two's brain.

Ripple Two woke up and got to its feet. "Hello, everyone. My goodness, this shell is at only seventy-eight percent charge. One of you must have a talk with Maddy Two. She gets preoccupied with other tasks and does not take good care of herself."

Elah kneeled and checked the tightness of her footwraps. "We are going hunting, Ripple." She got back up and checked her spear point. She glanced at Skyra and Veenah. "Do not worry about me."

"What are you hunting?" Derek asked.

Elah eyed Skyra. "Skyra knows what I am hunting." Without another word, Elah left the courtyard, followed by Ripple Two.

"*That's* what she's been looking for all these times she's gone away?" Lincoln asked.

"Yes," Skyra replied.

"Yes," Veenah added.

"What?" Derek asked.

Skyra said, "Elah is hunting for the woolly rhino that killed our birthmother. Lincoln and I killed that rhino many seasons ago, but in this timeline it might still be alive. Now Elah wants to find it and kill it herself. I think she *needs* to kill it herself."

Derek turned and stared out the courtyard's gateway. "Jesus!"

"We were lucky to survive that encounter," Lincoln said. "I hope she never finds it."

"She will find it, or she will not," Skyra said.

"If she does find the rhino, may she find her way home," Veenah said quietly.

After several breaths of silence, Lincoln said, "Well, on a much lighter note, Skyra has some news to share."

Skyra scanned the faces of her tribemates. Not one showed even a small amount of surprise. "El-de-né! How could all of you already know?"

Derek glanced nervously at Veenah.

"Veenah!" Skyra said. "I should have known. You are not skilled at keeping secrets, birthmate."

Veenah turned to Derek. "I told you not to tell others!"

"I only told Virgil," Derek said.

Jazzlyn laughed. "Of course Virgil told me." Then she turned to Skyra. "It doesn't matter! We're all happy for you, and Ripple is going to be *really* happy."

Skyra's tribemates all nodded and gave her warm smiles.

"Well, gosh," Virgil said. "This announcement, as anticlimactic as our responses were, calls for a celebration. Maybe we should cancel afternoon school today."

"No!" Skyra and Lincoln said at the same time.

The others stared.

Lincoln cleared his throat. "You've prepared a great lesson... and Ripple's even helping. It would be a shame to cancel school."

Virgil frowned. "I don't mind if—"

"Virgil," Jazzlyn said, grabbing his arm, "I think they already have plans."

His frown remained. "Okay."

"Ripple, let's go!" Jazzlyn shouted.

There was no reply.

"Ripple!"

Still only silence.

Skyra glanced at Lincoln then walked to the drone dwelling's entrance. "Anuva, it is time for school." She stepped inside and paused to allow her eyes to adjust to the darker interior, then her chest tightened, and she rushed forward and dropped to her knees.

Anuva was sitting on the floor between Ripple and Maddy One. Her face was turned away, but Skyra saw a massive bulge on the side of her head.

Skyra turned her birthdaughter toward her. "Anuva, what happened?"

"What is it?" Lincoln asked, coming through the doorway.

The others were following him in.

"Do not be alarmed," Ripple One said. "Anuva is perfectly fine, and I believe the experiment will be a success."

"I'm okay, Mama Skyra," Anuva said. "The caretakers tickle my brain, though. It feels funny." A mass of ooze was now moving down the side of her head to her shoulder.

"Ripple, what the hell have you done?" Lincoln demanded.

"Please do not be angry," Ripple replied. "I will explain."

Maddy One spoke up. "Maddy Two and I advised Ripple to acquire permission, but Ripple has always preferred to act first and ask for forgiveness later. Such a roguish and reckless drone."

Anuva slapped her knees. "I said I'm okay! Do not be mad at Ripple. It was my idea." The mass of ooze was now flowing down her arm and dripping from her elbow onto the floor.

"Ripple, you'd better get that explanation started right now," Derek said.

Anuva slapped her knees again. "Hello! It was *my* idea. *I* will tell you."

The ooze on the floor was coming together into specks.

Anuva said, "Ripple is getting old. Maddy One and Maddy Two are getting old, too."

"She is referring to the fact that many of our modules are beginning to fail," Ripple said. "We were constructed to last thousands of years when dormant and in a protected place, but we were not made to last so long while constantly active. I have made every attempt to instruct the caretakers to repair our crucial components but have had no success. They seem better suited to repairing biological tissue."

"Papa Lincoln, you said we can't fix them. You said we don't have computers and tools and stuff to fix them. They are getting old and breaking."

The specks on the floor were joining together into fly-sized caretakers.

"Somebody has to know how to tell the caretakers what to do," Anuva said. "I can do it because I'm an alinga-ul. Ripple said I'm a *special* alinga-ul because I came from you and Mama Skyra. You are a special bolup, and Mama Skyra is a special nandup, so I'm a special alinga-ul. I'm Anuva, the special alinga-ul!" She flashed her teeth in a broad smile.

The fly-sized robots were snapping together into thumb-sized robots.

Ripple said, "I estimate I will function for no more than five more years, but that is only if you start cannibalizing parts from the two Maddys to keep me operating."

"We would be willing to donate our parts if maintaining Ripple would help you and your friends, Lincoln," Maddy One said. "Although, as Ripple has said, such a strategy would only delay the inevitable."

Anuva got to her feet. "Watch this, everybody. Watch!" She stared at the caretaker as the last of the thumb-sized pieces snapped into place to form a complete rat-sized robot. She clapped her hands several times with excitement. "Go, caretaker, go!"

The caretaker began changing again. It broke up into smaller and smaller parts then came back together, this time into a different shape. Several breaths later, Skyra and the others were staring at a two-legged figure—a little gray man or woman—as tall as Anuva's knees. The figure began walking in a circle.

"Well, that's certainly something we've never seen before," Lincoln said.

The figure abruptly rolled forward over its head, onto its back, and onto its feet again. It did this again and again, continuing in a circle while rolling and jumping back to its feet.

Anuva clapped her hands again. "It worked! Somersaults! That's what I told it to do. When it was in my head I told it to do somersaults, Papa Lincoln. Isn't it grand?"

Lincoln glanced at Skyra. "Yeah, it's definitely grand, mudbug."

"A marvelous success," Ripple said. "I do believe when I am gone, this tribe will be in good hands. Over time, I'm sure Anuva will learn to instruct the caretakers to accomplish tasks neither I nor any of the rest of you could have imagined. I am even figuring out a way for the caretakers' component parts to replenish their power using errant electrical impulses within Anuva's tissues. I assure you all of this is perfectly harmless to the girl."

Skyra was not sure what Ripple was saying, but Anuva's smile proved she was not hurt. Skyra pulled the girl close and embraced her.

Anuva pulled away. "I am ready to go to school now. I will take this caretaker with me for show-and-tell! Can I, Mama Skyra? Can I, Papa Lincoln?"

"I will accompany Anuva," Ripple said. "I will make sure nothing happens to her or to the caretaker."

Jazzlyn said, "And Virgil and I will keep an eye on Ripple, the roguish and reckless drone."

Skyra turned to Lincoln.

He shrugged.

"See, Mama Skyra? Papa Lincoln says it's okay."

Skyra placed her hands on Anuva's cheeks and made the girl look at her, just as Skyra's own birthmother used to do to her. "Do not make the caretaker do anything except somersaults. *Only* somersaults. Understand?"

"I understand." The girl's words sounded funny with Skyra pressing on her cheeks.

Skyra lay with her head on Lincoln's skinny bolup chest, her body still tingling from making love. "Do you think Anuva will someday become the most dominant alinga-ul of our tribe?"

He stroked her hair. "I have no doubt. Mickey may give her a run for her money, but Anuva's one sharp cookie."

Skyra did not bother to ask about those silly words. She understood enough. "Maybe our new child will be an even sharper cookie."

"Maybe."

"I think Di-woto would like Anuva."

"Oh, I know she would. You miss Di-woto, don't you?"

Skyra thought about this for a few breaths. "Yes. I hope Di-woto is happy with the ghost people."

"I do too."

"Do you think Ripple and the Maddys are going to die?"

"Ripple is right—some of their modules have already quit working, and we don't have the kind of tools needed to fix them. They won't be around much longer."

"They are tribemates."

Lincoln lifted his head to look at her. "Yeah, I know what you mean."

"I am glad you do not have your T_3 anymore."

He continued looking at her. "Why is that?"

"I do not want to go to the future or to the past. I only care about now."

47,590 YEARS *in the past - 68 years after Anuva's birth*

ROGOS KUTOLO-LOTO WAITED PATIENTLY while the caretakers flowed out of his body through his skull and his scalp. He had long ago started cutting his hair short to make it easier for the caretakers to move from his head into the stone bowl he had created for this purpose. When the bowl was full he placed it on the stone tabletop. He hummed a tune he had learned from his birthmother as he watched the caretaker's components snap together, now fully charged and ready to work.

The fine powder became specks, and the specks became robots the size of flies. This time, instead of snapping together into even larger components, the fly-sized robots skittered across the tabletop to a thick bundle of doplonus reeds Rogos's tribemates had collected along the banks of the river. The tiny caretakers swarmed over the reeds and began shredding them into hair-thin filaments.

"You know what to do, my little friends," Rogos said aloud, even though he was sure the robots could not hear him. "You are spirited and lively once again."

The caretakers had gradually become slower in their task since he had renewed their power two days ago. They probably could have continued working for another day, but Rogos also wanted to give them a new set of instructions. He had a new idea for a specialized fabric, thin yet densely woven for warmth, with a different color pattern. He intended to use the fabric to make a new type of lightweight garment to be worn by hunters during the cold season without restricting their movements.

With their additional set of instructions from Rogos's head, the caretakers would shred the doplonus reeds into filaments, work the filaments into twisted threads, and weave the threads into the new fabric. Rogos would have to cut the fabric and sew together the garments, but until the fabric was completed, there was not much for him to do, so he returned his attention to stitching up the warm-season tunics he had designed in recent days. He was behind schedule. It seemed he was always behind. Few of his tribemates had shown much interest in helping make garments from woven cloth, although they were happy to trade the garments he had made to other tribes in return for food and needed supplies.

Rogos's own Kutolo-Loto tribe had been learning to grow fields of khelop plants for their roots and kaira grasses for their seeds, and they had even managed to keep a captive herd of plains ibexes, but these did not provide enough food for the entire tribe through the cold season. Trading was still necessary, and Rogos's garments had proven to be valuable items for trade.

A shadow appeared at the entrance of Rogos's dwelling, and Reza leaned in through the doorway. "Rogos, your birthmother wants to speak to you. She is insistent."

Rogos sighed and put down his fabric and stone needle. "Thank you, Reza." After Reza left, Rogos turned to the fly-sized robots, which were still chittering as they shredded the reeds. "Keep working, my little friends, and be thankful you do not have to heed the call of your birthmother many times each day. I am sure Anuva has thought of another job for you to give you a break from making my garments."

He left his dwelling and headed across the courtyard. Three of his children—Icoz, Erker, and Arian—were practicing throwing their khuls at a grass-filled target, and they each smiled knowingly at him. All of Rogos's children had now seen at least twenty cold seasons, and they had been summoned to speak to their Gramma Anuva plenty of times.

Rogos entered Anuva's dwelling and nodded at Reza and Fiti, his birthmother's two assistants, as he passed through the common area to her bedroom. He spoke before stepping through the doorway. "You wish to speak to me, Mama Anuva?"

Anuva was lying in her bed, as she had been doing quite frequently through the last three cold seasons—the aging process was not something the caretakers could do anything about.

"That was at least an hour ago," Anuva replied. "Are you intentionally ignoring your own birthmother?"

"Of course not, and it was *not* an hour ago. I only just heard you wished to speak to me. And honestly, Mama

Anuva, no one speaks of hours and minutes. Those are not even real measures of time."

Anuva chuckled, her voice dry and crackling. "If Grampa Lincoln were alive to hear you say such words, you would get an earful of bolup teachings."

"I am sure I would."

She held up a hand, inviting him to move closer.

He sat on the stone bench beside her bed and grasped her hand. "I'm guessing you have a new job for me and the caretakers."

"You are correct. There are tasks much more important than making garments for trade. First, though, I have words you must hear. I will soon leave this world, and you are the one most suited to lead Kutolo-Loto tribe. Nikoo and Tous are too occupied with thoughts of traveling to new lands beyond the river plains. You are the one to lead this tribe."

Rogos sighed loudly. He had heard this many times before. "You are not dying yet, Mama Anuva. You will probably outlive me. I am quite happy making garments for trade, and I have little interest in leading the tribe. I believe Arian would be better suited for leadership."

She squeezed his hand. "Tell me why we are here, Rogos."

He studied her face for a moment. "Okay. We are alinga-uls. We are here because Grampa Lincoln was a great man who made drones and a T3. One of his drones, Ripple, had a mind of its own and devised a plan to create a world of alinga-uls, which the drone thought would be a much better world than Grampa Lincoln's world. Ripple brought Grampa Lincoln and Gramma Skyra together, and... well, the rest is history. The problem is, Mama Anuva, many of our people do not even believe this story to be true."

She shook his hand fiercely. "That is why you are suited to

lead, Rogos! You know why we are here, and why our people must never forget. Ripple was once alive. The two Maddys were once alive. I used to talk to them and play with them when I was a young girl. They were much more than just the dead shells they are today."

"How am I supposed to make people believe what I am not sure I even believe myself?"

"You work with the caretakers every day. How can you not believe it?"

"The caretakers are different. They are living creatures."

"They are *not* living creatures!"

He studied her face again. Her expression showed that she meant every word she had said. "Okay, what do you want me to do?"

"You will use the caretakers to bring Ripple and the Maddys back to life."

"Didn't you try that numerous times? You told me you tried that years ago."

"Yes, I did, but I was young and foolish then. Age has helped me understand many things, and all these confounded hours, day after day, often spent lying in this bed, have allowed me to clear my mind and think of new things."

"Yes, new things that become new tasks for me," Rogos said with a smile.

She ignored his comment. "Listen to me speak, son, as I will soon find my way home. I have a new idea, and you are the one most suited to make it work."

46,308 YEARS in the past - 1,350 years after Anuva's birth

OLUCHI CHIDEE LOVED to feel the ocean winds blowing through her hair, especially the warm tropical breezes off the coast of Africa. The breeze here smelled good, and it helped calm her belly, which was often queasy from the ship's rocking. She scanned the surrounding water, where hundreds of ships could be seen all the way to the horizon, their tall sails billowing in the wind. Her ship, the *Jazzlyn 3*, was just one in a convoy of colony ships, each filled with alinga-uls eager to fulfill their destiny by joining another tribe far beyond the borders of their own homeland.

A hand tapped Oluchi's shoulder, and she turned to face Udo Ekene, the *Jazzlyn 3*'s captain.

"You should begin preparing your people to disembark," Udo said, pointing toward the shore of Africa in the distance. "Your colony, as well as four others, will begin your journey inland at the Port of Jelanee."

Oluchi squinted toward the shore. The bare masts of several moored ships rose above numerous thatch-roofed structures clustered beside the water.

"You do not need to be afraid," Udo said, obviously noting the look on Oluchi's face. "We have had much success integrating with tribes in this area. Our scouts have already selected tribes for each colony, and I assure you they are eager to join with you, as long as you have your two allotted caretakers."

Oluchi patted her fabric cape, where she had carefully kept her colony's two caretakers close to her body since leaving her homeland. "I have them." She not only had the caretakers, she and her twenty-nine fellow colonists also possessed their allotted collection of other supplies, including numerous instruction books, dried meats and fruits, grains, spices, tools, medical supplies, rolls of fabric, and weapons, including khuls, knives, swords, and crossbows with an ample supply of bolts with bronze points. She hoped the weapons would only be needed for hunting.

"It has been a pleasure and an honor to transport you and your colony, Oluchi," Udo said. "This is the first time I have had a direct descendant of Skyra and Lincoln aboard my ship. May your colony thrive and populate the world, and may you all find your way home."

Oluchi placed her hand on the man's cheek, a gesture of respect. "Thank you, Captain Ekene. You have been a stalwart wayfinder and a gracious host. May you also find your way home."

The captain smiled and returned to his important duties.

Oluchi called to the nearest of her fellow colonists. "Chioma, alert those who are in their cabins below deck that we will arrive shortly. We must all be ready to go ashore."

Before long all twenty-nine of Oluchi's tribemates were gathered around her, staring out at the approaching shoreline and the Port of Jelanee. The *Jazzlyn 3*, as well as four other ships, had split off from the rest of the convoy on a direct course for the port. As the ships entered the calmer waters of the port's bay, numerous people emerged from the thatched structures to watch.

Oluchi's heart began pounding as her ship drew near enough for her to see many of the people were dark-skinned bolups, just like the legendary Jazzlyn many hundreds of years ago. Oluchi could hardly contain her excitement. All of her life she had only known alinga-uls—she had never seen an actual bolup. She had to command her legs not to jump up and down like a child at the end of a school day.

A voice came from beside her. "El-de-né! So many bolups!" Oluchi's tribemate Umur was gripping the wooden handrail and staring ashore.

Oluchi said, "I have dreamed of being part of a starter colony. Now it is finally happening." Since her earliest years in school, Oluchi had been taught the importance of starter colonies, in which alinga-uls integrated with bolups or nandups. When she had volunteered, she had been given a choice of sailing south to join with a bolup tribe in Africa or riding east into Europe with one of the mammoth convoys to join with a nandup tribe. Almost all nandup and bolup tribes were happy to join with alinga-uls, as they were eager to become stronger tribes and have access to the two caretakers allotted to every mixed tribe.

Oluchi again placed her hand on the lump in her cape where she kept the caretakers. Long ago, her ancestor Anuva had devised a way to instruct the original two caretakers to create new caretakers, a breakthrough which had changed the world and started a new and exciting future. Since then, two caretakers were given to every mixed tribe, and now the number of mixed tribes was growing, especially due to convoys of ships like the *Jazzlyn* 3. Oluchi felt like she was at the dawn of a new world originally conceived by the strange, legendary machine called Ripple.

Countless alinga-uls and bolups now stood at the water's edge, waving and shouting to the approaching ships.

"Do you think some of those bolups are from our new tribe?" Umur asked.

"I would think so," Oluchi replied.

"I am sure they will speak a new language," Umur said.

"Probably." Oluchi wasn't worried about that. The last several languages she had mastered had each required only six days to learn.

"I am nervous," Umur said.

She turned to gaze at his face. He was definitely nervous, but he was also excited. "There is a very old tradition in my family," she said. "When we are afraid, we ask the woolly rhino and cave lion to give us their strength."

45,889 YEARS *in the past - 1,769 years after Anuva's birth*

SEVIM VADRA GLANCED at his watch. Finally, the waiting was over. It was time. He took a deep breath and walked into the forum hall, where he found himself facing almost two hundred representatives of the most prominent territories around the globe. All but five of them were alinga-uls. Three were sapiens, and two were neanderthalensis, representing the only five territories that continued to refuse integration. These territories were located in a corner of the North American continent, and they frequently fought with each other. They were usually impoverished and were of little consequence in world affairs, but they were traditionally given a seat at important forums, simply out of respect for their status as recognized territories.

Sevim steeled his nerves and took his place before the crowd. He silently tapped a few buttons on the podium to assure himself the technology was still working as it should. A beam of light appeared from the ceiling, projecting an image on the wall behind him. He turned to confirm the image was the correct one, a photo of the ancient shell of the legendary drone known as Ripple.

Sevim cleared his throat. "I will keep this presentation as short as possible and will make every effort to use familiar terms," he said in the universal alinga-ul language. The three sapiens and two neanderthalensis were each seated beside their own interpreter, and their interpreters began quietly translating for them. Neither sapiens nor neanderthalensis were particularly adept at learning new languages, most likely because they were simply unwilling to try.

"I imagine you already understand the nature of my team's breakthrough and would like to move on to the main purpose of this forum," Sevim continued. "As you may know, my team was granted permission seven years ago to unobtrusively study the remains of this drone. We learned a great deal but soon reached the limits of such an approach. Subsequently, we obtained permission to systematically disassemble the drone in order to conduct more extensive investigations. The various modules inside the drone would require many years for us to even begin to understand them, so we focused nearly all our efforts on the portion we were convinced was the main cognitive module."

Sevim tapped a button to show the next photograph, this one of a rectangular black box on a white tabletop. Sevim had placed his own hand in the photo beside the box for scale. "This small device was designed to contain all of the data possessed by the drone, in such a way that the data could be accessed, modified, added to, and deleted. It was essentially the drone's brain, just as the computer in your office has its own brain, only this drone's brain was built using strikingly different data-storage concepts."

"Excuse me," a voice said from the audience.

Sevim shaded his eyes and located the voice's source, a woman he had never seen before.

"We already know all of this information," she said. "I respectfully ask that you move on to any information you feel that we do not already know."

"Very well," Sevim said. "I understand you have important duties elsewhere. Forgive me. During the last year and a half, my team has reached a point where we are confident we understand how the data is stored in this module, and we have gone to great lengths to meticulously clean its components to ensure the integrity of as much of the data as possible. To put it simply, we are on the verge of gaining access to nearly everything Ripple knew."

Sevim shaded his eyes again as he watched the territory representatives mutter to each other and exchange glances.

A man spoke up. "We commend you on your success. I, for one, have no doubts regarding the quality of your procedures and your dedication to the work. Might I suggest, though, that we address the issue at hand?"

"Of course," Sevim said. "You wish to discuss the fact that we may be in a position to access detailed information regarding temporal displacement technology. Is that correct?"

"Indeed it is. Again, congratulations on reaching the point at which this forum has become necessary."

Sevim nodded in gracious appreciation. "I suspect the purpose of this forum is to decide whether or not my team should proceed."

"Again you are correct. Due to our confidence in your team's expertise, most of us assumed this day would come.

Therefore, we have had ample time to contemplate the implications and assess the opinions of our superiors as well as our constituents. I represent the territory of Starthaennu, and I am officially letting you know we support terminating your research. Temporal displacement technology is not in the best interest of our territory, nor do we believe it is in the best interest of any alinga-uls, sapiens, or neanderthalensis."

"I agree with the distinguished representative from Starthaennu," said a woman near the back. "The territory of Forood also recommends discontinuing your research. In fact, we further recommend destroying the drone's data permanently, upon which we will pursue global legislation to ban any future research related to temporal displacement theory and associated practical technology. We do not need to trifle with such potentially devastating technology simply because someone from a different timeline felt the need to do so."

Numerous voices sounded out in agreement.

Sevim was not surprised. He himself had begun to fear the technology. Actually, not so much the technology itself as the way the technology might be used, particularly if it fell into the hands of the remaining sapiens or neanderthalensis territories. The implications were frightening, to say the least.

"Nup khutol-manda!" a voice thundered from the right side of the room.

Almost immediately, the woman's interpreter began translating. "I object! The nandups of Gulgun do not trust that your words are sincere. What is to prevent you from voting in this forum to destroy the information, then simply keeping it for your own use, thus once again denying Gulgun of its fair share of what should belong to everyone?"

Sevim shaded his eyes to see the neanderthalensis woman who had spoken. She was now on her feet, standing with her arms folded. Her interpreter, another neanderthalensis woman, stood up and crossed her arms as well, apparently to better communicate the belligerent attitude.

A sapiens man got to his feet and spoke, and the man's interpreter said, "If Gulgun is to have access to the technology, the bolups of Delkash must have access as well. Gulgun would inevitably use the technology against us."

A second sapiens rose to her feet. This one Sevim recognized as the representative of Delruba, a territory notorious for endless aggression toward its neighboring territories. The woman spoke, and her interpreter said, "Delruba has produced incontrovertible evidence that our people still have not received fully functional caretakers. This is unfair, so why should we trust alinga-ul territories to be fair regarding the matter of temporal displacement technology?"

Sevim pursed his lips, trying to avoid smiling. There were countless reasons why the sapiens and neanderthalensis territories were not provided with devices capable of the full range of astounding—and potentially dangerous—caretaker capabilities. For one, those territories would almost certainly come up with ways to use the caretakers as weapons.

The representatives of alinga-ul territories waited patiently as the other sapiens representative and the other neanderthalensis representative voiced their own protests and suspicions. Sevim had attended enough global forums to know this was a common and expected occurrence.

When the objections had all been stated and duly noted, Farrin Nava, the representative of Sevim's own Palantina territory, spoke in the calm voice he was known for. "Thank you for expressing your concerns. I suspect this issue will be voted on today. If we vote to discontinue the research and destroy the data in question, I am sure we can agree on a procedure that will be satisfactory to all. Perhaps representatives from every territory could be allowed to personally witness the data's destruction. If that is not acceptable to you, I am sure we can work together to specify a procedure acceptable for all concerned."

The sapiens and neanderthalensis representatives did not appear completely placated by this, but they fell silent and settled back into their chairs.

"We vote!" a voice said.

A chorus of other voices shouted, "We vote!"

Sevim felt a smile forming on his lips, which struck him as odd. After all, his dedicated efforts of the last seven years were about to be nullified. The realization should have been disquieting, but he felt strangely relieved. He had plenty of other research projects to keep him busy, and the Ripple project had begun to affect his ability to sleep at night. His dreams had become haunted by accidental and disastrous consequences of toying with powers no alinga-ul, neanderthalensis, or sapiens should ever possess.

45,307 YEARS *in the past - 2,351 years after Anuva's birth*

SETARA CYPRIANA HAD NEVER BEEN so bored in her life. For the equivalent of three Earth days, she had been forced to remain in her static chamber, drinking tasteless liquid nutrients through a tube, re-reading instruction manuals, and staring at the countdown clock on the chamber wall. Twenty-two Earth days had actually passed since her static chamber had initiated her revival sequence. During that time, the gases and pressure in her chamber had gradually been modified to help reanimate her tissues and restore full brain function. Fortunately, she had only been awake for the last three days, otherwise she would have already gone mad with boredom.

"Come on, almost there," she said, staring at the countdown clock.

A soothing male voice came from a speaker near her head. "Congratulations, Setara. Not only have you survived your dormant period, you will complete full revival protocols in three, two, one...."

An indicator pulse vibrated the chamber.

"Finally! Please let me out now."

"You will be released soon enough. First I must ask a series of questions to confirm your cognitive functions are normal."

"No! You have already asked your questions several times. I want out now."

"Protocol requires that I ask them again after the countdown has ended."

"I don't care, Ripple. I'm ordering you to let me out now." Historically, Ripple had been the most common nickname given to a ship's cognitive module, and Setara preferred using Ripple instead of her ship's actual name, which was *Across Horizons*.

Ripple said, "I will need a verbal override command from you if I am to ignore protocol."

"I am Setara Cypriana, colony leader and *Across Horizons* administrator. I grant protocol override."

"Thank you, Setara. Please turn onto your left side to facilitate caretaker evacuation."

Setara did as Ripple instructed. A moment later, her shaved scalp began to tingle, and soon the tingles became countless pinpricks of pain. The pinpricks spread down to her face and neck, moving all the way to her feet. "Can you make it go faster?"

"You know I cannot," Ripple replied. "Please be patient."

Setara felt cool wetness on her skin as the caretaker components flowed out of her body and gathered on the cushioned surface beneath her. The sensations of pain and wetness quickly subsided, then the components moved together and joined, forming one single caretaker about twice the size of her fist.

"I hope I never need to have that thing inside of me again," she said. The caretaker had kept her body safely in a dormant state for the equivalent of a little over 112 Earth years, which was how long it had taken for the *Across Horizons* to make the journey.

"Now let me out," Setara said.

"You must first remove your urinary and bowel disposal fittings," Ripple said.

She growled in frustration and disengaged the fittings, which had been needed only during the three days she had been awake.

"Do not be surprised if you detect several strange odors upon exiting your chamber," Ripple said. "The filters are working to remove them. However, many harmless but detectable particles have accumulated in the ship's atmosphere during the journey."

"Thanks for the warning. Now please let me out, or I'm going to use the manual override."

"Very well."

The static chamber's lid clicked, then there was a slight

whoosh of air as the internal and external pressures came into balance.

Setara sat up. "Lights."

Ripple illuminated the ship's entire interior, and Setara stared at the closed lids of 8,000 static chambers identical to her own, all of them arranged in rows on the inner wall of a vast hollow cylinder. She shifted her gaze, following the rows of chambers around the curved surface until she was looking straight up at the chambers directly above her. They all looked exactly the way they had before she had been locked into her own chamber. Ripple had already informed her its sensors had not indicated a single abnormal measurement among the dormant colonists. This wasn't surprising—not much could happen to a body held in a completely static state by a caretaker's components.

She swung her legs over the side of her chamber and carefully stood up. The cylindrical ship's spin created artificial gravity equivalent to Earth's gravity, allowing her to feel reasonably steady. She inhaled deeply, glad she could not detect the strange odors Ripple had mentioned. She opened the hatch beneath her static chamber and pulled out her garment. It was one piece, including the feet, and she quickly stepped into it, pulled it on, and fastened the front.

"Be careful, and use the handrails when you need to," Ripple said.

Setara picked up her caretaker from inside her static chamber and slid it into its pouch on the front of her garment. She took a few tentative steps. Walking turned out to be fairly easy, despite having been inactive for three days. The 112 years before those three days did not really count, as her body had experienced absolutely no degradation during its static state.

"Take your time, there is no hurry," Ripple said.

"Yes, there is a hurry. I want to see our new home."

"You have seen photographs transmitted by the caretaker scouts."

"I don't care. I want to see it for myself." Setara took more steps, gaining confidence. Still, she appreciated that her static chamber was positioned near the ship's manual control center.

Soon she was at the control center, which was nothing more than three workstations with screens and keyboards to allow Setara and a handful of other qualified colonists to access, and to override if necessary, any of Ripple's thousands of ongoing tasks. The *Across Horizons* was not designed to be controlled by people. Instead, it was fully automated and could make the entire journey without manual input.

Setara sat down at one of the screens and took a few deep breaths. "Okay, show me."

The monitor blinked on and displayed a rapidly scrolling sequence of self-check screens. Suddenly an image of a planet appeared, filling up most of the screen and framed by a black background of star-speckled space. Although the entire ship was spinning, the image remained steady, thanks to the camera mounted on a counter-rotating gimbal.

Setara stared in silence, contemplating the significance of what she was seeing. The planet's official name was Strosilea-Molla-9223, but Setara and her fellow colonists shortened it to Strosilea. The planet was approximately eleven light years from Earth, and at one-tenth the speed of light, the *Across Horizons* had required 110 years to cover the distance, plus a year to accelerate to such a staggering speed, as well as another year to decelerate.

Ripple said. "It looks quite beautiful from orbit, wouldn't you say?"

Setara blinked, somewhat mesmerized by the sight. "Indeed it does." Actually, the image didn't look much different from those transmitted to Earth by the caretaker scouts. The scouts had been sent long before Setara was born. They had made their own 112-year journey to get here. Upon arriving, they had immediately set about their task of preparing for a future alinga-ul colony. The pieces of the massive transport ship had been used as raw materials to construct a small city, ready for occupancy when the colonists arrived. The scouts had regularly transmitted progress updates and photos, and each transmission had taken ten years to reach Earth.

"Is Skyra City visible from our current position?" she asked.

"It should be," Ripple replied.

"Can you zoom in?"

"I will try."

Strosilea grew larger, filling the screen completely, and it continued to grow. The planet did not have large oceans, but it was dotted and lined with numerous lakes and rivers. The landscape continued expanding, and a faint grid appeared, arranged near the shore of an oblong lake.

"That's it!" Setara exclaimed. "It really is there!"

As the camera continued zooming, Setara could see the lines of the grid were actually rows of dots. "Those are the atmosphere processors, aren't they?"

"You are correct."

The processors had been working for decades to tweak the world's atmosphere just enough to allow alinga-uls to breathe but not enough to drastically disrupt the native life, which consisted mostly of bacteria-like organisms growing in layered colonies of trillions of individuals. Analyses of the organisms indicated they were suitable for alinga-ul consumption, thus providing an almost unlimited food source.

"Skyra City is at the center of the image," Ripple said.

Setara stared in wonder. The city didn't seem like much now, but soon the pieces of the *Across Horizons* would be used to vastly increase its size.

"You are the leader of the first interstellar alinga-ul colony, Setara. Your choice of Skyra City as the name is remarkably suitable."

"I thought so."

"Would you like me to initiate the revival sequence for your fellow colonists?"

"Yes, I think it is time."

"Initiated," Ripple said. "In twenty-two days, they will all be as alert and ready as you are now."

Setara continued staring at the image on the screen, wondering how she could remain patient for twenty-two more days.

THERE'S MORE TO THIS STORY!

Binary Existence is the final episode of the Across Horizons series. Skyra and Lincoln have had an amazing and epic adventure together.

However, Skyra met Ripple almost two years before she encountered Lincoln and his team. What happened during those two years? How did Skyra and Ripple find each other? How did Skyra keep Ripple hidden from her twin sister and the rest of her Una-Loto tribe for so long? There are aspects of Skyra's story she has not told Lincoln—aspects that may surprise you.

And what about Lincoln? He is fourteen years older when he sends Ripple 47,000 years into the past to Skyra's time. What kind of person is he fourteen years later in his original timeline?

Genesis Sequence is the prequel to the Across Horizons series, and the story isn't really complete without it!

Also, if you haven't read my ***Diffusion series***, my ***Bridgers series***, or my ***Fused series***, be sure to check them out.

AUTHOR'S NOTES

I enjoy thinking about bizarre questions related to such things as time travel, alternate universes, and unusual creatures. Below are some of my thoughts regarding the concepts in **Binary Existence**. These are in no particular order, and they may not cover everything you're curious about, but here you go if you're at all interested.

*In the first chapter, you describe the same series of events that took place in the first chapter of Book 1, **Obsolete Theorem**. However, this time the events did not happen in exactly the same way. What's up with that?*

First it's important to point out that when Skyra, Lincoln, and the others jumped back to Skyra's time at the end of Book 3 (**Hostile Emergence**), they created a new timeline (jumping back in time must always create a new timeline). They jumped back to a point one hour before the first time they jumped there in Book 1 (**Obsolete Theorem**). So, they arrived there at about the same point in time that the first chapter of Book 1 started, which was when Skyra was preparing to attack the bolup tribe in order to rescue her sister Veenah. The instant Skyra and the group arrived at the end of Book 3, a new timeline began, which means different events take place (due to the countless random things that happen with every passing second). In Book 1, Skyra failed to rescue Veenah. In Book 4, Skyra did not fail. She killed the bolups at the stream and escaped over the hills with her sister.

I thought it would be interesting to show those events through the eyes of the other Skyra (the one who become Elah). It is the only chapter told from the *other* Skyra's point of view. All the remaining chapters are told through Skyra's or Lincoln's point of view.

How could there be two Skyras and two Ripples?

Because, as I stated above, when you jump to the past, this creates a new timeline. Logically, this has to happen, as it is impossible for the same events to happen twice in the exact same way. There are countless trillions of minor, random things that happen every microsecond that make it impossible for every detail to be the same. So, Skyra and the group jump back to one hour before the first time Lincoln's team arrived there. Skyra and Ripple are already there. Therefore, once the group arrives, there are *two* Skyras and *two* Ripples.

Why aren't there two Lincolns, two Virgils, two Jazzlyns, and two Dereks also?

Since the team arrived an hour before Lincoln's team originally arrived, there will *not* be two Lincolns, Virgils, Jazzlyns, and Dereks. And they won't show up an hour later, either. Why? Because a new timeline was created the moment the team arrived. Random events result in a completely different future in this timeline, a future in which Lincoln will never be born, a future in which there will not be a United States, or an Arizona, or much of anything else we are familiar with. So, Lincoln will not exist 47,659 into this new future, therefore he and his team cannot jump back to Skyra's time to arrive here. For that reason, there will not be two Lincolns, Virgils, Jazzlyns, and Dereks.

What does the title **Binary Existence** *mean?*

Although the title is mentioned only once near the end of the book, the term is used as a technical name for a specific phenomenon—when two copies of a person or object exist in the same timeline. Binary existence occurs when the group jumps back to Skyra's time, creating a second copy of Skyra and a second copy of Ripple in the same timeline. Before this happened, no one had any idea whether binary existence would result in some kind of disaster. As it turned out, no disaster occurred, and the two copies of Skyra and Ripple coexisted in the same timeline without any disaster occurring. However, one of the themes of the book focuses on the psychological problems involved, with Skyra and Elah trying to deal with the consequences. Both of them begin to feel like they no longer know who they are supposed to be. Skyra wants to save Veenah and again be with her twin sister, whom she has always been very emotionally close to. But suddenly she realizes the other Skyra is already with Veenah. Think about it—this would be difficult to deal with, wouldn't it?

The robotic caretakers become increasingly more important as the story progresses. Why are they so important?

This was somewhat of a surprise to me. As I was writing

the end of Book 3 (**Hostile Emergence**), I figured the robotic caretakers would help the group make it to their T3, then would make sure Lincoln did not attempt to take the T3 with him when he and his team jumped back to Skyra's time. After all, Lincoln had made a deal with the virtual people—they would let him and his team go if he promised to give them the T3. The robotic caretakers were there to make sure he didn't renege on that deal and take the T3 with him. However, getting to the T3 turned out to be more difficult than anticipated. The T3 was surrounded by a tribe of "wild people," who had no interest in allowing Lincoln's group to get to the T3. In fact, the wild people attacked, and Jazzlyn was shot with one of their arrows. The robotic caretakers, for whatever reason, decided to help Jazzlyn. They broke apart into much smaller robots, entered her wounds, and began repairing her damaged tissues.

Before the caretakers could leave her body, the group was forced to jump back to Skyra's time, thus taking the tiny robotic caretakers with them, inside of Jazzlyn's body. This turn of events was a surprise to me, and at the time I didn't think too much of it. It didn't occur to me that these caretakers could become so important. Then, in Book 4 (**Binary Exis-tence**), the tiny caretakers crawled out of Jazzlyn's body and joined together, once again becoming two rat-sized robots. Still, I didn't realize how important they would become. After all, they now had no way to replenish their limited power supply, as they were not really designed to function indefinitely in a wilderness area without the infrastructure that created them and maintained their power levels. It wasn't until Ripple figured out a way to recharge them that I started to realize they could become important. Remember, Ripple has two innovative ways to continuously recharge its own power (by harvesting ambient sound and by using temperature gradients). So, if Ripple could continuously recharge its own power, Ripple could also continuously recharge the caretakers' power. Suddenly the caretakers became major characters in the story.

The caretakers are made based upon an interesting idea of progressively smaller, independent components. How small can they really get?

Only the virtual beings in the empty city could answer this question. Lincoln and the others repeatedly observe the caretakers breaking apart into thumb-sized robots, then into fly-sized robots, then into flea-sized specks, and finally into robots so small that together they look like fine powder. These are so small that they can enter a person's body directly through the skin, then they can fix a variety of different types of tissue damage inside the body. How small are they when they do this? We can only guess—microscopic, for sure. Who knows, maybe they can even break down into smaller robots beyond that. I guess then they would be considered nano-robots. I love the idea of robotic machines that can put themselves together into any conceivable configuration to accomplish almost any task, no matter how small or how large the task, from repairing living cells to constructing skyscrapers. The concept boggles the mind, doesn't it?

Throughout most of this book, the only caretakers available to the group are those that make up the two rat-sized robots. Therefore, the group is limited in what they can do with the caretakers. The group is also limited by Ripple's ability to give complex instructions to the caretakers. Sure, they end up doing some spectacular things, such as building the 55-foot-tall statues, and later converting the entire boulder hill into what is essentially a fortified, stone apartment complex, but the really stupendous achievements do not begin until much later, when Anuva figures out how to instruct the caretakers to make more copies of themselves. This happens in the epilogue, when Anuva is practically on her death bed, talking to her son Rogos Kutolo-Loto.

Speaking of that epilogue, can you give us more explanation of what that is all about?

The last chapter, the epilogue, titled *Chronology*, is meant to provide an interesting and satisfying end to the series. The series is contained in four volumes, each showing a different self-contained adventure taking place in a different place and time. One common theme throughout the entire series is Ripple's grand plan. In fact, the entire series story is initiated when Ripple is sent 47,659 years into the past on a routine research jump, but then encounters Skyra, a Neanderthal woman with an extraordinary genetic makeup that gives her exceptional intelligence. Due to Ripple's ability to make autonomous decisions—an ability coded into its cognitive module by Lincoln—Ripple decides Skyra is a perfect genetic match for Lincoln, and their offspring would be highly intelligent and compassionate beings. The only problem is, Lincoln and Skyra are 47,659 years apart. So, Ripple devises a plan. In short, Ripple figures out a way to trick Lincoln into jumping back to Skyra's time, where Lincoln would then save Skyra's life and eventually fall in love with her, and this would initiate the spreading of their superior genetic characteristics throughout the populations of humans and Neanderthals, resulting in a better world.

So, Ripple's plan is an important theme throughout the

entire series. Lincoln and his team are skeptical of the plan throughout most of the story, and they don't really take it seriously until Book 4 (***Binary Existence***). At this point, however, they realize they are stuck forever in Skyra's time, and they might as well do what they can to facilitate the plan. I mean, why not, right? Also, at this point Skyra becomes particularly interested in the plan. She is inspired by how Diwoto changed her entire world, and now Skyra wants to change her *own* world. This is where she and the others start to make serious efforts to figure out a way to influence the local nandups and bolups to get along and combine their tribes. This is the big challenge of Book 4. Because Book 4 is the final chapter in the series, I thought it would be interesting to close the series by giving readers a glimpse of the future of Skyra and Lincoln's timeline. I did this by writing a series of four brief vignettes, each showing a glimpse of some significant event in the future that illustrates the amazing success of Ripple's plan and the efforts of Skyra, Lincoln, Jazzlyn, Virgil, Derek, Veenah, Elah, Ripple and Maddy. I thought it would be satisfying to readers to see that the plan actually worked. In only 2,351 years, alinga-ul civilization stemming from Skyra, Lincoln, and the bolups and nandups of Skyra's time progressed all the way to the point of interstellar space travel.

Why did the Peli-Bayom tribe of bolups move their camp to the base of the boulder hill?

This tribe of bolups (*Homo sapiens*), already weakened from a harsh year, had been diminished by the deaths of some of their men as a result of the conflicts with Skyra, Elah, and the others. Therefore these bolups were concerned about their tribe's future. They also recognized that Skyra's group was highly unusual. As vicious as these bolups were, they were human and therefore curious. They saw Skyra's unusual tribe as a possible way to get some strength back into their own tribe. Their first inclination was to kill and eat Lincoln or one of his team members (the strange bolups in blue clothing). They thought eating the flesh of these people might give them strength. So, they moved their camp to the boulder hill, intent on waiting for the right opportunity to kill. Obviously, this didn't work out for them, and soon Skyra and Lincoln were able to convince them that there was a better way to become strong—by joining tribes, and then eventually also joining with a tribe of nandups.

Did humans and Neanderthals actually hunt woolly mammoths?

Yes, without a doubt. There is extensive evidence that both species hunted woolly mammoths (and woolly rhinos and cave bears, for that matter). Many scientists have speculated, in fact, that this hunting was the cause of the woolly mammoth's extinction (although other scientists believe otherwise). There is evidence that Neanderthals in Europe hunted mammoths for tens of thousands of years, and some populations were dependent on mammoths for their very existence. It was once assumed that Neanderthals and early humans could only hunt such huge prey by forcing them to run off a cliff. Well, not only could that be done only in certain areas with suitable cliffs (not very common), but now we have much evidence that they used weapons, such as spears, to hunt mammoths. Considering the thickness of a mammoth's skin, throwing spears from a safe distance was not a reliable way to penetrate the skin. This meant hunters had to attack at close quarters, thrusting their spears into the creatures' vulnerable areas. I probably don't have to explain how dangerous that would have been. Imagine walking up to an adult elephant and stabbing it with a spear. What do you think would happen next? Based on what we know about how people hunted woolly mammoths, I tried to create a realistic mammoth hunt. The mammoth-hunting tribe possessed a collection of mammoth spears specially designed for the task. These spears were heavy and sharp. The hunters spaced themselves out so that they could attack the targeted mammoth repeatedly as it tried to flee. As you can imagine, it might have taken dozens of aggressive stabs before the mammoth was hurt bad enough to stop running. Every one of those stabs would be a dangerous endeavor for the hunter.

Did humans and Neanderthals also hunt woolly rhinos?

Again, yes, at least in those areas where woolly rhinos lived. Interestingly, studies of dental plaque from the teeth of Neanderthals that lived in areas where woolly rhinos lived showed a high percentage of woolly rhino meat. This wasn't true for Neanderthals from other areas, where there was no evidence that wooly rhinos frequented the area. So, it is likely that Neanderthals (and humans) became specialist hunters, focusing their efforts on the game animals that were abundant in their territory. In Skyra's Dofusofu river plains, woolly rhinos were abundant, so her Una-Loto tribe often hunted them. On the other hand, woolly mammoths were fairly rare in that area, so Skyra had only had a few previous opportunities to hunt them. The new bolup tribe of mammoth hunters that showed up, on the other hand, were from an area where mammoths were more abundant, and they were highly skilled at hunting mammoths. In fact, it's possible they had followed the herd of mammoths into the Dofusofu river plain, which brought them near Skyra's boulder hill.

Cave hyenas were also mentioned in the book, as well as in Book 1. Were cave hyenas different from the hyenas of today?

One significant difference was their size. Cave hyenas weighed about 225 pounds (102 kg), which is almost twice the size of their modern relatives that live in Africa today. Today's hyenas usually hunt prey that weigh between 120 and 400 pounds (54 to 180 kg). The cave hyenas? They were big game hunters, often killing animals as large as woolly rhinos, which can weigh up to 6,000 pounds (2,700 kg)! In other words, they were fierce killers. It's no wonder Lincoln was nervous when the pack of cave hyenas started hanging around while he and the other hunters were butchering the woolly mammoth.

Do people really eat crayfish?

You bet they do! Here in the United States, especially in the southern states, eating crayfish (often called crawfish in southern states) is a big deal. Many farmers produce crayfish by the millions in flooded fields. When the harvest season comes, they have crayfish festivals, and people stuff themselves with these crustaceans. Crayfish are a staple of traditional Cajun food. I can't say I'm a huge fan of crayfish—I find them to be a bit fishy-tasting, and I prefer shrimp. However, if I somehow jumped back to Skyra's time, I would happily gobble up crayfish every day if it kept me from having to try to kill a woolly mammoth with nothing more than a spear.

What can you tell me about cave bears?

Cave bears lived in Europe and Asia, and they became extinct about 24,000 years ago, so they were definitely around during Skyra's time. Perhaps you were a bit surprised when Skyra said that cave bears ate plants and were not predators. Research has indicated this is true, based on the structure and the wear patterns of cave bear teeth, as well as the chemical makeup of cave bear bones. It is likely that cave bears were opportunists and sometimes ate animals when they had a chance, but their diet was primarily plants. However, just because cave bears ate mostly plants, that doesn't mean they couldn't be dangerous, especially when they felt threatened. After all, they were big bears. Females weighed about 500 pounds (227 kg), while males were much larger, up to 2,000 pounds (907 kg).

In Chapter 18 Anuva seems like a very precocious young girl, and she is only three years old. Is she really that smart?

Remember, Anuva is an alinga-ul, like Di-woto. Not only that, but Anuva is a child of Skyra and Lincoln, and we all know how special Skyra and Lincoln are, right? So, yes, Anuva is that smart. Even at three years of age, Anuva speaks three languages: the language spoken by the bolups of the Dofusofu river plains, the language spoken by the area nandups, and English. Anuva's birth becomes the starting point of the new future in this timeline. That's why each of the vignettes in the epilogue begin with a header that marks the number of years since Anuva's birth. Anuva is the beginning of the fulfillment of Ripple's grand plan.

In Chapter 18, Derek and Veenah have children, but it appears Jazzlyn and Virgil do not. Why don't they have children?

You'd have to ask Jazzlyn and Virgil. Maybe Jazzlyn *still* hasn't convinced Virgil to make love to her (in which case she really needs to let Skyra finally have that conversation with

Virgil). Maybe they are trying but are still unsuccessful. Or maybe they simply choose not to. They don't get a lot of encouragement from Ripple, because Ripple does not believe offspring from two bolups will contribute much to the grand plan (although it could be argued that Jazzlyn and Virgil's kids might eventually find Neanderthal mates, thus contributing somewhat to the cause).

What ever happened with Di-woto and the virtual beings in the empty city? I was expecting them to miraculously appear at some point.

Although we will never know, we hope Di-woto remained happy in the virtual world of Kods and Thide. It was tempting to bring Di-woto and the virtual people back into the story, but that would be almost impossible. Remember, when Lincoln and the team jumped back to Skyra's time at the end of Book 3, this created a new timeline (logically, a new timeline must be created with every jump into the past). So, at the moment the team jumped back to Skyra's time, they were no longer in the same universe (timeline) as Di-woto and the virtual beings. The only way Di-woto could show up is if the virtual people were capable of jumping between universes. Ripple was capable of doing this (that was the purpose of Ripple's U-Jump module), but Ripple did not stay behind with the virtual beings. And even if Ripple had stayed behind with the virtual beings, the drone's U-Jump module was too limited to allow people to use it in such a way. So, Di-woto and the virtual people may hope that Skyra's group was successful, but they have no way of ever actually finding out.

I hear rumors there is a prequel for this series. What can you tell me about that?

Yep, you heard right. The upcoming prequel is titled **Genesis Sequence**. It takes place almost two years before Lincoln and his team appear in Skyra's time. If you'll remember, Skyra was friends with Ripple for almost two years before Book 1 (**Obsolete Theorem**) began. Lincoln, when he is fourteen years older than his current age in the rest of the series, sends Ripple 47,661 years back in time on a routine data-collection mission. Ripple does its job, sending data through the open portal for nineteen minutes, then the portal closes, as is typical. Because there is no way to retrieve the drones sent to the past, Ripple is to remain in the past until it stops functioning. However, Ripple decides to make the most if its remaining time in the past. It encounters Skyra, and the rest is history, right? Not necessarily. There is much to this story we do not yet know. *How* did Skyra and Ripple meet? What happened to them during those two years? What made Ripple decide Skyra was so special? How did Ripple come to the conclusion that it should develop a rather devious plan to get Lincoln and Skyra together in order to create a new future of human-Neanderthal hybrids? What did Skyra think of Ripple the first time she encountered the drone? Why did she decide to keep Ripple a secret from Veenah and from the rest of her tribe? What kind of adventures did Skyra and Ripple have together? All will be revealed in **Genesis Sequence**.

Here are a few questions submitted to me from early readers of this book:

From Norma Jeanne Grogan: *This whole series, and especially the last book, **Binary Existence**, really had an impact on me. Was there anything that had of an impact on you that* *brought this series and especially the last book "out of you," so to speak, or had the general idea been percolating deep inside you for awhile?*

I have several thoughts on this. First, I became fascinated with the idea of writing a book with a Neanderthal as a main character when I got my DNA analysis results back from one of those ancestry DNA companies. The report informed me that about 4% of my DNA is of Neanderthal origin. Most modern humans possess a small amount of Neanderthal DNA (except for people of direct South African descent, because humans that never migrated north out of Africa did not encounter and interbreed with Neanderthals). However, most people have only about 2% Neanderthal DNA, and therefore mine was higher than 95% of the tested population. This got me to thinking about Neanderthals, which led to the Across Horizons series.

Second, sometimes I get dismayed by the seemingly endless conflicts between people, particularly conflicts that involve racism. I wondered, how terrible would things be if more than one species of hominids were alive today? Would one species enslave or exterminate the other? History shows that we are certainly capable of such behavior. What if Neanderthals hadn't gone extinct? Would we be at war with them? This depressing thought led me to the idea that hybrids between *Home sapiens* and *Homo neanderthalensis* might be unusually smart and/or strong (a real phenomenon called *hybrid vigor* or *heterosis*). If the two species had interbred more often, becoming a more blended species than what we see today, what would the world be like? So, I guess the story came from my tendency to wonder if we couldn't somehow have a better world, with less conflict.

From Jim Balk: *The fact that physical location is difficult to calculate due to the motion of the planet/solar system/... is noted in the books. Once a time and place have been calculated it is postulated that it is easy to go there regardless of the source status, even going to a slightly different destination time. However, unless the system for the location is in absolute coordinates instead of relative you will also need to take into account the current location in the computation, so the source time of translocation has to be incorporated and would constantly need recalculation.*

It is *possible* Lincoln's T3's calculations are based upon some absolute points of reference. The T3 takes many hours to calculate the exact position of the spot where he wants to send a drone 47,000 years in the past. This is an unimaginably complex calculation due to the movement of the earth through space over time, and its rotation on its axis. Consider this: the earth is moving really fast. As it rotates on its axis, the surface at the equator is spinning at 460 meters per second (about 1,000 miles per hour). So, even if you jumped back in time one second, you would have to jump 460 meters back toward the east in order to appear in the same room you jumped from. But that's only one small part of Earth's movement. The planet is also in orbit around the sun, moving at 30 kilometers per second (67,000 miles per hour). Not only that, but our solar system (including Earth) is revolving around the center of the Milky Way galaxy at 220 kilometers per second (490,000 miles per hour). As if that weren't enough, the galaxies in our part of the universe are moving at 1,000 kilometers per second (2.2 million miles per hour) toward a huge, dense region of space called the Great Attractor. Whew! It seems it would be impossible to calculate placement of the T3 for a jump only one minute back in time, doesn't it? Now imagine calculating the placement 47,000 years back in time.

Anyway, once the T3 has calculated the placement for that specific spot next to the river in Skyra's time, it is much easier to calculate it again, regardless of the starting point. This implies that Lincoln has coded the T3 to use absolute points of reference. It's okay if these points of reference move, as long as their movement is well understood and extremely predictable. These points of reference could be such things as the center of our galaxy, as well as the centers of several other "nearby" galaxies.

More practical, though, is the possibility that the T3 is simply very good at tracking its own movement and the passing of time. For example, from the moment the T3 appeared in Skyra's time, it knew exactly where and when it was. With every passing millisecond, it mathematically tracked its position in the universe, based on known trajectory and velocity of the earth's movement through space. When Lincoln and his team jumped forward in time 47,659 years to Di-woto's time, the T3 simply tracked its movement relative to its location when it had first arrived in Skyra's time. Even when the T3 was loaded on a camel-drawn cart and moved several miles to the sanctuary-fortress of the khami-buls, the T3 continuously tracked its own movements in space and time. In doing so, it always had an absolute reference point, and therefore the placement calculations for jumping back to that time and place would (theoretically) be quick and easy.

Also from Jim Balk: *If bolups in Skyra's time capture nandup women to have sex with them, aren't any alinga-uls created?*

As I stated earlier, we know Neanderthals and humans interbred, based on the fact that most modern humans possess about 2% Neanderthal DNA. However, we also know alinga-uls (offspring of a female Neanderthal and male human) were rare or nonexistent. How do we know that? This requires a bit of explanation. First, our DNA includes *nuclear DNA* and *mitochondrial DNA* (mtDNA). The nuclear DNA is found inside the nucleus of the cell, whereas the mtDNA is found only in the mitochondria of the cell. It is important to know that the nuclear DNA is passed to the offspring from both the mother and father, but the mtDNA is passed to the offspring *only from the mother*. Why is this important? Because scientists cannot find any Neanderthal mtDNA in humans. This *could* lead us to conclude that all DNA in humans today came from pairings of Neanderthal males with human females, and that would imply that pairings of Neanderthal females with human males produced sterile offspring or no offspring at all. If that were true, then alinga-uls would not exist at all (also, Skyra and Lincoln could *not* produce offspring).

However, there are other possibilities that could explain why modern humans do not have Neanderthal mtDNA. For example, it's possible that Neanderthal females and human males did not mate because of some cultural reason (in other words, they *chose* not to mate because it was a taboo, or something like that). Another possibility is that there actually used to be humans with Neanderthal mtDNA, but their lineages died out at some point. Still, there is one other possibility (which I think is likely), that modern humans *actually do* carry at least one Neanderthal mtDNA lineage, but we have not yet sequenced that lineage in humans or in Neanderthals, so we simply do not know about it yet. This could be related to the possibility that hybrid offspring from Neanderthal females were rare for some genetic reason (which is the concept I am considering in the *Across Horizons* series).

So, for whatever reason, alinga-uls were rare or nonexistent. However, Ripple knew more about Skyra's and Veenah's genetic makeup than the drone ever actually revealed. Ripple knew Skyra and Veenah possessed the rare ability to produce alinga-uls (Di-woto's mother also possessed this ability). Ripple therefore concluded that Lincoln and Skyra were a "perfect match," not only because of their compatible intelligence, but also because of Skyra's ability to produce alinga-uls. Derek and Veenah were also able to produce alinga-uls (although Ripple was not as excited about that, due to the drone's rather skeptical opinion of Derek's intelligence, which the drone frequently made clear, and which irritated Derek to no end).

Finally, several people have given me variations of this last question.

All these timelines and time jumps are confusing! Could you provide a brief overview of the overall story arc, with respect to these things?

Okay, but first, it helps to keep the following in mind: When you jump *back* in time, you create a new timeline (a new universe). Logically, this has to be true. Even if you jump back only one hour, it starts that hour all over again. Tiny, random events make it so that different things happen during that hour. Therefore, it is a different universe than the one you jumped back *from*. When you jump *forward* in time, it doesn't really create a new timeline. When you arrive in the future, you are in the same timeline you left, but it is only one possible thread out of an infinite number of futures that could occur. Got it? Here we go...

In Book 1 (**Obsolete Theorem**) Lincoln's team jumped

back 47,659 years to Skyra's time. Before jumping, they were in Lincoln's lab in Arizona. When they jumped 47,659 years into the past, they also jumped to a specific location in Spain—the location where researchers had found Skyra's and Ripple's remains. So, Book 1 takes place in Spain during Skyra's time. When they jumped to Skyra's time, they created a new timeline (a new universe). From that moment on they were in a new timeline.

At the end of Book 1 they jumped forward 47,659 years. They also jumped to a specific location—back to the location of Lincoln's lab in Arizona. Therefore, in Book 2 (***Foregone Conflict***) they are in the same timeline they were in during most of Book 1, but it is only one thread of an infinite number of possible futures. In this thread, Neanderthals did not go extinct, and when the team arrived, the world looked very different. Lincoln's lab was not there, and bolups (humans) were at war with nandups (Neanderthals).

For Book 3 (***Hostile Emergence***) they jumped farther into the future, another 47,659 years (which put them 95,318 years after Skyra's time). So, they were still in the same timeline as most of Book 1 and Book 2, but again it is only one of infinite possible futures. In this future the war between nandups and bolups is long over, and other wars have come and gone. The team members find themselves in a wilderness with a surprising assortment of plants and animals. They also see a gleaming city in the distance. Then, well... you know what happens. It is 95,318 years after Skyra's time and 47,659 years after Lincoln's original time. They are in the same location of Lincoln's lab in Arizona (although in this timeline this area is not called Arizona, and there is no United States, and there is no lab).

At the end of Book 3, they jump back in time 95,318 years to return to Skyra's time (actually, to a point one hour before the original time Lincoln's team arrived there). This jump, of course, creates yet another new timeline, which is why different things happen during that hour, and why Skyra is surprised to see that her other self is not alone coming over the hill in the distance. This begins the story of Book 4 (***Binary Existence***).

At the end of Book 4 you get several glimpses of what happens in this new timeline during the next few thousand years after Lincoln and Skyra have lived their lives. Each of these glimpses is labeled by how many years have passed since the birth of Anuva. Why? Because Anuva's birth represents the beginning of a new world, which is eventually populated mostly by aling-uls. In other words, the epilogue shows how Ripple's bold plan actually comes to fruition.

In all, there are *four* timelines described in these books: (1) Lincoln's original timeline, (2) Skyra's original timeline *before* Lincoln jumps back to meet her, (3) the new timeline created when Lincoln's team jumped 47,659 years into the past to Skyra's time, and (4) The new timeline created when the team jumps back in time 95,318 years to Skyra's time again (at the end of Book 3).

Wait... if you think about it, #1 and #2 above are actually the same timeline.

Wow, my mind is blown.

If you ever have any additional questions about this series, don't hesitate to email me at stan@stancsmith.com

ACKNOWLEDGMENTS

I am not capable of creating a book such as this on my own. I have the following people, among others, to thank for their assistance.

First I wish to thank Monique Agueros for her help with editing. She has a keen eye for typos, poorly structured sentences, misplaced commas, and errors of logic. If you find a sentence or detail in the book that doesn't seem right, it is likely because I failed to implement one of her suggestions.

My wife Trish is always the first to read my work, and therefore she has the burden of seeing my stories in their roughest form. Thankfully, she kindly points out where things are a mess. Her suggestions are what get the editing process started. She also helps with various promotional efforts. And finally, she not only tolerates my obsession with writing, she actually encourages it.

I also owe thanks to those on my Advance Reviewer team. They were able to point out numerous typos and inconsistencies, and they are all-around fabulous people!

Finally, I am thankful to all the independent freelance designers out there who provide quality work for independent authors such as myself. Jake Caleb Clark (www.jcalebdesign.com) created the awesome cover for *Binary Existence*.

ABOUT THE AUTHOR

Stan Smith has lived most of his life in the Midwest United States and currently resides with his wife Trish in a house deep in an Ozark forest in Missouri. He writes adventure novels that have a generous sprinkling of science fiction. His novels and stories are about regular people who find themselves caught up in highly unusual situations. They are designed to stimulate your sense of wonder, get your heart pounding, and keep you reading late into the night, with minimal risk of exposure to spelling and punctuation errors. His books are for anyone who loves adventure, discovery, and mind-bending surprises.

Stan's Author Website
http://www.stancsmith.com

Feel free to email Stan at: stan@stancsmith.com
He loves hearing from readers and will answer every email.